Best wishes.

David Maidment

The
Child
Madonna

David Maidment

Published by

**MELROSE
BOOKS**

An Imprint of Melrose Press Limited
St Thomas Place, Ely
Cambridgeshire
CB7 4GG, UK
www.melrosebooks.com

FIRST EDITION

Cover designed by Catherine McIntyre

ISBN 978-1-906561-29-1

Printed and bound in Great Britain by:
CPI Antony Rowe, Chippenham, Wiltshire

FSC
Mixed Sources
Product group from well-managed
forests and other controlled sources

Cert no. SGS-COC-2953
www.fsc.org
© 1996 Forest Stewardship Council

CONTENTS

DEDICATION

To the small streetgirl, perhaps six or seven years old, who accosted me on Churchgate Station, Bombay, many years ago and, exploited and coached by some unscrupulous adult, was whipping herself to provoke my sympathy and alms. She was the catalyst for the founding of the charity, 'Railway Children', which partners non-government organisations in ten countries of the world offering street children living in railway and bus stations protection, food, health care, counselling, education and above all, love and care.

All author's royalties from this novel will be
donated to the Railway Children
(www.railwaychildren.org.uk)
and the Consortium for Street Children
(www.streetchildren.org.uk).

PREAMBLE

I'M WATCHING AND WAITING. WAITING, oh so patiently, for the confusion to sort itself out a little. Each time I think I can perceive a glimmer of sense, a pattern developing, the anarchic mists roll in once more and the opportunity is lost. But I am infinitely patient. I can see the end as well as the beginning. I know the chance moment, that is no chance, will any moment now be glimpseable, provided, in that very moment, I do not nod or blink.

And yet within me some wiser or more cautious 'alter ego' bids me look the other way. It would be so much easier just to let my eyelids droop, to choose by default the supine road. I must gird my loins to superhuman effort, interface with so many destinies and then take responsibility for both the joys and pain. Success will demand risk, a response that causes adrenalin to surge when perhaps it would be more prudent at that moment just to balance in passive animation. The end I see is tinged with pain, let alone the beginning and the middle. Why should I cause suffering to you, the one I love, because you alone have the potential to deliver my plan? Will you count it a privilege or curse?

The deed is done now, irrevocably. Yet I could go back and rub it out and start afresh or delay another eon. "No man, setting his hand to the plough, looks back…" said someone whose instincts reflect my own. The utterance is made; I cannot call the words back to my lips unheard, renounce the promise made. You are bound in time that only I can abrogate. I'm sorry, chosen one, my heroine. You shall be lauded, crowned, even venerated, although not in your own time. In retrospect you might have preferred private nonentity, even had you glimpsed the future, for it is distorted in the mirror men set up to reflect their own grand designs, exploiting your vulnerability to their own ends, consciously or in self-deception.

I did not ask your permission early enough, even in your mother's womb. By the time I shall ask, because of what you already are, you will not refuse me and then you too will be unable to retreat. Onward to joy through pain you'll go, then back to pain, not once but many times. Few will regard your sleepless nights, your anguish. They only see the honour, the purity they venerate, a garlanded tradition, a milk white insipid vision; they do not see the blood and disgrace, the suspicion, the ruptured bigoted culture of which you and I were so nearly victim. And the inner gutsy strength that was so abnormal that I could only grasp that opportunity, for such tenacity and loyalty in one so young is a very rare gift. They extol you with the comforting assurance of hindsight of which you, poor you, never caught a glimmer.   Forgive me, my beloved. Once I had looked deeply into those huge brown eyes of yours and saw what you reflected there, we were committed, both of us. This is your story, then, as I saw it at the time and from far hence towards eternity. Don't let them hurt your soul: I shall protect your inner self from their curses and their flattery despite the outward scars that you will bear until your time has come. Don't forget that in all your, our, travail, I love you with all my strength and all my heart and all my being.

Chapter 1

On the Edge

We're watching and waiting. Messenger and spy. When is it? You, reader, need to fix a point in time. We can try to prolong the soft-edged ambiguity in sonorous sentences with grand phrases about the timelessness of cosmic symbols. But that sudden clarity of hindsight pinpoints a real moment in time between the old year and the new, which we erroneously now call 10 BC. And somewhere, down in that darkened village, framed by a black dense brooding hillside against the eerie soft moonlight, you, all innocent, are slumbering – dreamlessly, or is there a stirring even now flitting across your smooth brow?

Why now, you ask? Why at this particular causal moment in time? Why should eons of waiting ever be rewarded with mundane hard-nosed fact rather than mystical poetic expectancy that could be ascribed to the archetypal longing of the soul? Because we were instructed and obeyed, that's why. And when we did, dreams became reality that altered lives, for better or for worse. Not just in that time, but reverberations echo down the years. We – I and my creator – both have to live with this knowledge now and bear the consequences, ever repeating, ever fresh, ever the same.

So we gaze down below at squalid unsung Nazareth, you and I; and, as I said before, there is little that can be discerned. As our eyes grow accustomed to the darkness we may make out the jagged edges of a few rough-hewn walls or hutments, awkward gaps and angles that suggest a confusion of alleyways, a higgledy-piggledy cluster of dwellings clambering clumsily up the barren hillside as if on each other's shoulders. If we climb higher on our own hillside, massing on the opposite side of the valley, we could, with some imagination, perceive the signs of nearby Sepphoris, a city of some fifty thousand souls straddling the highway, which runs from the coastal plain into the heart of fertile Galilee, and further across the Jordan valley into the Decapolitan cities of Gadara and its sisters.

Our little backwater here – perhaps off the beaten track is a more apt epithet – with barely a thousand inhabitants eking out an existence just above the poverty line, owes its survival to that cosmopolitan city just five miles away; source of work and culture, tenuous link with the outside world so hated by the pious locals for its contaminating Gentile influence. Stress and tension seep through the daily mix of Jew and foreigner with all their cacophony of myriad beliefs culled from Judea, Samaria, Syria, Babylon, Persia and the Arabian Gulf. At the western terminus of that highway the Romans are just completing their new administrative centre at Caesarea: a further offence to our insulated villagers who, no doubt, will be taxed for the dubious privilege of contributing to its completion, at best an irrelevance to their lives.

So, far away down south in the capital, so the gossip goes – from those making their annual pilgrimages there – the glory of their nationhood, the Temple of Jahweh, is at last nearing its final construction phase. The bastion of the Jew against the usurping of their land? Not a bit of it. Herod's folly some call it, spoilt in its conception by the very identity of the conceiver. Oh well, they're a rum lot here. You'll never please some of them. Indeed, it's hard to imagine just what it is they want. If they could put it into words and you delivered exactly according to specification, they'd like as not throw it back in your face.

But we must not anticipate, you and I. Somewhere down there is the spark we're looking for, hostile environment though it be. And anyway, it's beginning to spit with rain, and despite the common misconception, it can seem remarkably bleak on a winter's night up here. Let me cease my brooding, go back into the village and find some shelter, where, as I prepare for sleep, I can ponder my mission in this seemingly god-forsaken spot.

It's best to wear the cloak of darkness for now, until I'm ready to act. To reveal myself too soon will cause needless suspicion and trouble and, as likely as not, abort the very purpose of this quest. A spy, they'll think, if not something worse; a fair-haired foreigner tainted with goddess-worship, come to seduce and pervert our young. I shall be lucky to escape with a running out of town pursued by a hail of rocks. So, drawing my cloak around me as I snuggle into the bales of straw in the corner of the barn at the edge of the village, I rehearse once more in my mind the train of events that has led me to carry out this assignment in this inhospitable community.

Creation comes from turmoil. To bring order, you must first have chaos. You may not like this truth, uncomfortable as it is; few create chaos deliberately in order to impose their order, but the fact remains. Unless there is darkness, raging night, light cannot be created. And, of course, the will to change.

The time and place of which I tell have the right ingredients. That is why I have been sent here to watch, extra attentively.

INTERLUDE 1

THE CAULDRON

SOME FIFTY YEARS AGO THE Romans thought they were bringing their brand of order into a turbulent local maelstrom of politics, incomprehensible to outsiders like themselves. Then unrest hit hard the heart of their own hearth, as civil wars gave way to murder and anarchy, spawning further upheavals as rivals strutted round the spinning stage. More murder and mayhem disposed of Antipater, and brought Herod and his elder brother to the fore until distant power struggles eradicated Pompey, then gave Antony as star to hitch your wagon to. The unseemly gallop to be first to pledge loyalty to the new conqueror – long live the Emperor and all that – was joined not only by Herod and his brother, but also by the Jewish leader Hyrcanus and his scheming nephew, Antigonus. This, therefore, solved nothing. Herod watched with increasing dismay from his northern outpost as Jerusalem fell to the young pretender, and with even more alarm as his brother was imprisoned and the elderly Hyrcanus carried captive to Babylon.

Poor Herod, at the nadir of his fortunes, decided that little could now be lost by throwing himself on the mercy of his Roman masters and, to his own astonishment, found the jackpot tumbling into his lap. Equipped with a Roman army of conquest, he returned, giving rout to his enemies, besieged Jerusalem and found himself King of Judea within three months. Now for his revenge. Or, perhaps you might argue, using the realpolitik of the age, the bringing of order to the chaos by executing his rivals and those factions that would have hampered proper administration of his kingdom.

Unfortunately, in the very implementation of his campaign of orderliness, he sowed the seeds that were to exacerbate his frustrations and rages at a later date. He dealt swiftly with Antigonus and then moved against the Jewish Sanhedrin, that overripe pompous talk-shop that found a dozen sanctimonious reasons for double-dealing whenever his back was turned. They would be sorry now that two years before, he, Herod, had been summoned like a common criminal to explain why he had had the temerity to rescue his much-harassed Galilean peasants from the marauding brigands masquerading under the flag of zealot patriots.

He rounded them up, the whole bloody lot of them, in one night of retribution, drove them into the stadium still sleepily protesting at the outrage, and had the Syrian troops slaughter every one after the most summary of secret hearings. Then, to drive his position home the harder, he confiscated their property, and with the proceeds bought himself a new Sanhedrin, stuffed with Pharisees of a more complaisant kind.

It was a pity that in the process he forgot to tell Hyrcanus' daughter (his own mother-in-law, Alexandra), not to mention his beloved wife, Mariamne, of the changing scene, as they had believed – until rumours confirmed otherwise – that Herod, with Rome's connivance, was setting darling nephew Aristobulus, Mariamne's young brother, on the Judean throne. And now, when his own accession was a *fait accompli*, they discovered that Herod himself had obtained from Octavian a short cut to the seat of power.

To the average Jew in our humble Nazareth, all these conspiracies and manoeuvrings would have meant nothing, even if they'd known of them, which most of course did not. But for one or two of the leaders in the village – -the rabbi and the elders of the local synagogue – -such issues were the very source of argument and prejudice, invective and scandal. And one family of influence and status in the village had been disturbed and marked quite traumatically in these affairs. It is the family I have come to watch.

THE COURTYARD

𝒩 EAR THE CENTRE OF THE *village, within a stone's throw of the plain white synagogue, is a larger than average one-storey house built around an enclosed courtyard. This property, together with a number of fields on the hillside opposite and a couple of terraced vineyards, belong to a native Pharisee of solid reputation, known to all as Heli – or more often, Eli. He has lived in the village since his youth, and his family have had roots here for many generations. A widower for over fifteen years now, since his wife died giving birth to a cripple child, long since buried also, Eli brought up his brood of son and four daughters under the respectful gaze of the village elders and gossips alike. A pillar of the local synagogue, he takes his turn to read and expound the scriptures, teach the children, and partake in the judgement of petty squabbles and disputes and the counselling of those seeking assistance in their affairs.*

The income from his farming interests makes him one of the wealthiest men in the village and certainly the largest local employer of casual labour in the harvest season. Eli's wealth, of course, has been well tapped to provide a tax source for the Romans, and like so many provincial Pharisees, he resents both the use to which the money has been put, and the inevitable contamination of the pure Jewish culture by alien elements that are destructive to his innate conservatism.

Alongside Eli's ordered residence off the main courtyard are the crowded couple of rooms belonging to his son, Clopas – a confident young man in his late twenties – and his 21-year-old wife, Miriam, and their three children, the eldest barely seven years of age. Whilst Eli retains contact with his married daughters, all living within a five-mile radius of Nazareth, his heart is firmly here in his son's home, cherishing in particular his two grandsons, James and Jude, whom he sees as the ultimate heirs of the family business.

The remaining parts of Eli's home are shared by another branch of his extended family, for whom Eli is both saviour and benefactor. Opposite his own rooms lives Salome, a widow of nearly sixty, sheltered here during the last twelve years following the catastrophes that have overtaken her. The first traumatic shattering of her life took place on that dreadful night when her revered husband, Joseph, Sadducee and leading member of the Sanhedrin, was manhandled from her embrace by Herod's mercenaries, never to be seen again, whilst she cradled her sons for fear that the soldiers would deprive her of them as well. Thrown out of her home the next day, as her husband's property was annexed, she sought refuge in her cousin's home in Ein–Karem, some ten miles out of central Jerusalem.

During her sojourn there, she watched in trepidation as her sons grew in maturity and political awareness and, part in reaction to her husband's fate, became sucked into the anti-Herod plots and conspiracies that were rumoured to be rife. Supporters of the Alexandrine strategy to bring Hyrcanus' grandson, Aristobulus, to the throne, they unwisely allowed their allegiance to be too evident. After a near-successful putsch when Herod was in Rome, the Queen and her mother were disgraced and Salome's two eldest boys were arrested in the subsequent royal panic.

Her youngest son, Joachim, only a baby when his father was murdered, had grown up a wild and rebellious lad much influenced by the other youthful hotheads in the city. The knowledge that his adult brothers were still incarcerated in Jerusalem inflamed and shaped his political and religious beliefs, which in turn put him at risk. In an effort to stabilise him and get him to give priority to other responsibilities, Salome had contracted to betroth him to her cousin's youngest daughter, who had just reached marriageable age. Astonished and thankful that her son had not been arrested, Salome had eventually fled with the youth and his little bride-to-be, Anna, together with the few possessions they could carry and flung herself on the mercy of her late husband's cousin, Eli, in Nazareth. This was sufficiently remote from court, she hoped, to escape Herod's vicious mopping-up operations against all suspected conspirators.

Eli had been very good to her, despite the fact that her husband had been a Sadducee, and too embroiled in Greek culture for the likes of a strict Jewish Pharisee. Without a qualm he had taken her and her embryo family in and given them a home and work within his interests. As they were virtually destitute, he had provided the young girl's bride price and paid for the wedding celebrations as, in effect, Joachim was being forced to set up home with his cousin immediately. Salome's cousins and their families and other more distant relatives from Bethphage and Bethlehem, beyond Jerusalem, joined Eli's local family and neighbours in the wedding feast, and the two young folk were given a room next to Salome off the courtyard next to the opening to the narrow street.

At first Joachim accepted his new lot and quickly made his young wife pregnant. Salome, by now grieving for her other sons, whom eventually Herod had had crucified by his Roman allies along with thirty or forty other men caught up in the so-called Alexandrine conspiracy, channelled her emotional energies towards the new baby, a girl, whom Joachim and Anna named Mariam. Even while Anna was still pregnant with his second child, however, Joachim was contacted by factions hiding in the hills in western Galilee and was persuaded to join forces in occasional harrying skirmishes with Herod's foreign soldiery. Whilst he was sympathetic to the nationalist fervour of the Zealot idealists, Eli was a cautious man with too much to lose, and had a strong sense of duty towards those for whom he had responsibility, so that he forbade Joachim to allow others to use his home as sanctuary, although he covertly financed the outlaw cell through the young man. Eli could count on the hostility of the village elders to the Herodian forces to keep his secret, and indeed profited from a network of information which gave him prior advice of troop movements and the periodic raids that Herod's soldiers carried out, searching for terrorists and their sympathisers.

Salome, then, has good reason for the anxious frown that perpetually sits on her visage, except when she is cooing over Anna's children, now four in number – the latest a darling little boy spawned during one of Joachim's infrequent clandestine visits home. The toddler, Benjamin, now weaned and nearing his fourth birthday, is idolised and spoilt by his sisters: seven year old Rebecca; Salome, who is eight; and the 'little mother' Mariam, the eldest, who is eleven. Anna is relieved to have produced a son – he has given her a position of increased value and status in Eli's household, where previously the only boys had been in Clopas' home. Anna had felt this keenly. She had always been aware of her obligation to Eli for giving her a home, her family work and sustenance, and then more charity as her husband ceased to provide for her on a regular basis. Anna, at twenty-five years of age, is worn with fatigue; her face tanned and hardened by the elements; her hands coarsened and cracked. She and her mother-in-law draw mutual comfort and strength from one another; accept, mostly with good grace, their peripheral and charitable status within the household; and yearn that life will be better for their children.

CHAPTER 2

FIRST MOVES

S O MUCH, THEN, HAS BEEN *easy to find out. It is common knowledge in the village. Even a suspicious stranger can glean this far without undue curiosity. I lie back on my bale of straw, mind whirling in my allotted task. The facts are easy. But how do I evaluate the inner life, even with my heightened sensitivity? Second-hand observations are no longer valid. I need to sense their hopes and fears; listen to the nuances; feel the words unsaid; see the reaction of tiny children, true diviners of character. I am nearing the end of my mission. Soon I shall have to reveal myself to the subjects of my scrutiny and risk creating a façade of false reaction — though if this happens it will identify a weakness in the plan revealed already to me. I need to make myself Eli's house guest. I have to ask and risk rebuff. But Eli has a strong sense of obligation: he is an upright man, with a reputation to defend. And he has the space.*

I hover near the corner of the rough street, where I can watch the comings and goings at Eli's house without actual intrusion. Children are swarming all around me, preoccupied with their play, taking no heed of me whatsoever except occasionally as a prop to hide behind or obstacle to clamber over. On the other hand, to the women of the village, I am an object of considerable interest, not to say outright curiosity — except that they dare not make a direct approach, but hurry past, eyes averted whilst whispering avidly to their neighbours. Most of the menfolk have long since left their homes for the fields, although sounds of a rhythmic hammering from a house in the next street indicate that the village carpenter is busy. Others have gathered down at the synagogue to while away the morning in debate, or teach the solemn ranks of boys I watched earlier making their deliberate individual ways, evading the shrieking tiny children grabbing at their tunics and the mocking voices of the girls calling after them. I saw Eli make his way towards the white-walled building — saw him from a distance, that is, for at that stage I was still observing from the barn at the edge of the village. I wanted time to judge my approach, to blend into the atmosphere, not to startle.

Two stray dogs begin to yap at the running children before the latter pause in mid-stride and pick up sticks and stones to throw at them. One of the younger boys runs screeching at them until the dogs turn tail and slink away whimpering. One of the village girls emerges from a doorway, leading a couple of goats which she coaxes towards a rough bank of dirty brown grass and tethers them there. Chickens peck absentmindedly around my feet, jerking haphazardly in the village rhythm. I can feel eyes staring at me from behind the doorways and windows of the secretive houses, wondering, guessing who I am. It is dry today although occasional gusts of wind blow from the eastern hills. I gather my cloak around my slender form and stare through my piercing blue eyes at the humdrum scene, disconcerting all who would stare me in the face.

Then I see a young girl returning with water from the well, trailing a bevy of younger children at her heels. I rouse myself and pay attention now. As she strolls towards me, challering to the children, hitching up her tunic with her spare hand, I concentrate all my powers of discernment on her wide-eyed high-cheekboned face, finely chiselled; watch her natural mirth pull her mouth into a smile that illuminates her gaze as she jokes with the little girl that is almost tripping her over.

I wait until she is approaching the corner where I am standing, then stretch and shake myself so that she becomes aware of my movement, flinching involuntarily in surprise. The younger children gape at me, open-mouthed, as I say, as softly and kindly as I can, "Young lady, I am a stranger here and have urgent business to undertake. I need lodgings. Can you tell me if your uncle would be prepared to give hospitality to one in need?"

She fixes me with her eyes, which widen perceptibly as she hears me correctly surmise her relationship with Eli, then, clasping one toddler to her side with one arm, and balancing her water pot more comfortably on her shoulder with the other, she politely replies, "Sir, wait here while I ask my mother."

I watch her dusty brown feet step nimbly over the uneven earth and her form slip inside the courtyard opposite, followed by her entourage of waifs. One more piece of the jigsaw is now in place – the first contact has been made; a request is given. A silence falls over the village while I wait.

Suddenly I notice the veiled face of a woman, nervous and hesitant, peering at me from the doorpost. She gestures me with a quick indecisive hand movement and as I walk toward her, she confirms that she has understood the message that I passed to her daughter. Suddenly sure of herself, she calls the girl, who comes scurrying from inside one of the dark low buildings in the far corner of the courtyard, and speaks to her in urgent tones. The girl gives me a quick glance, then dashes off lightly down the little street towards the synagogue.

"Wait for a moment, sir. My uncle will return in a minute and consider your request."

Then she is gone, leaving me standing facing the tiny yard, empty of everything except a few baskets and cooking utensils and the ubiquitous clucking chickens.

I wait. There is no risk. After all, I have prepared for ages for this moment.

Eli comes striding from the synagogue, his niece dancing and skipping beside him to keep pace. The tall, impressive Pharisee halts abruptly before me and appraises me briefly without acknowledging my attempts at eye control. He dismisses the girl with a flick of his wrist and she scampers off into the shelter of her own home.

"Sir," says the unsmiling but courteous head of this household, "I understand from Mariam that you have need of lodgings. Come inside while we discuss the matter further."

We enter the opening into the courtyard but halt before we reach his rooms. As I said, the yard is ostensibly empty. I feel eyes peering at me from within the low surrounding buildings: her eyes. She is already being ensnared by her own curiosity, her adventurousness. It is unfair of me to exploit this openness; I will disrupt. But I have made my opening move and the stage is now prepared. The drama must now be enacted.

"This is an unusual request, sir. What is your business here?"

"I am on a mission of some confidentiality and importance, Rabbi. I may not divulge to anyone the exact nature of my goal at this moment."

He does not look pleased at this answer.

"My home is not an inn. Why seek accommodation from me?"

"I wish to be in the centre of the village and in touch with the opinions of people of importance here. Your home was recommended to me as both meeting my requirement and being the most likely source of hospitality, given the space you have at your disposal and your reputation for generosity."

"I am flattered by your words and the opinions of my neighbours. But perhaps you presume too much. You are obviously a stranger here. Are you not also a foreigner? Your appearance seems alien to my eyes."

"I am not a Jew by birth, as you rightly perceive. But I am acquainted with your customs and in sympathy with your aspirations."

His eyes grow wary. He thinks I am a spy, perhaps for the Herodian party, even for the King himself, because he sees that I am no ordinary secret messenger. I can give him some reassurance.

"I see, sir, that you doubt my allegiance. I bear no commission for either King or Emperor. I intend no harm to any Jew. On this, you have my word."

He is torn. His ingrained sense of duty is struggling with his anxiety about my motives and his antipathy towards a foreigner, whom he still suspects of doubtful loyalty. He equates flaxen curls and bright blue eyes with other influences, shot through with Greek or Roman cultural abominations. I cannot with sincerity narrow myself to his strict and bigoted viewpoint, shaped as it is by the confines of this obscure village unaffected by the receptivity of ideas that Jews of Sepphoris or Jerusalem would now display.

I make a last effort.
"I am sorry, Rabbi, that I cannot put your mind to rest by taking you fully into my confidence

and disclosing my mission to you. It is one of honour to your household, please believe me. I would not risk rebuff, were it not so important."

Eli is in no hurry to bring things to conclusion. He is weighing my words most carefully, sifting them for inner meaning. But he is naturally cautious – a man moulded more by learning and upbringing than by imagination or intuition. He is going to refuse: I see the mask of polite rejection fall into place. His face grows blank, obscuring any doubts he may still hold.

"You push me hard, sir. And I do not wish to be discourteous. I will be honest with you and not seek excuse. If you will not trust me with details of your business, how should I believe your goodwill to us? I have a responsibility towards my fellow countrymen. I have to say, sir, that I feel no such obligation to gentiles, however innocent of guile they are. And despite what you say, or indeed because of it, I cannot take your request at face value. If you had some ulterior motive, some treachery in mind, you would not tell us so, but mask your purpose in honeyed words just as you do to me now. No, sir, I cannot grant your request. I have my family to protect. I do not know what influence, what disruption you would make on them. I will not risk it."

Can I say that he is wrong? Can I look him in the eyes, assuming he will not flinch from my gaze, and assure him I will not disturb and disrupt?

"Rabbi, I accept what you say. I will press my case no further. I must carry out my duties without your support; I see that. But I bear you no ill will for that, sir. I wish I could inform you of my purpose but to do that would break a sacred trust."

He nods in acknowledgement and indicates our discourse is over.

It is going to be harder than I thought, after all. I withdraw.

Chapter 3

Spying

MARIAM WATCHED THE STRANGER GO, with disappointment. She had guessed that this was going to happen. When she excitedly told him of the fair young man, Eli, after he had been interrupted in his discourse in the synagogue, was unenthusiastic and unreceptive to her chattering. Why did she want the stranger to stay? Well, he looked different and interesting. He would talk of different places and customs. There would be a new routine, perhaps a celebratory meal, to which they would be invited.

The other children were curious. They too had seen the young man, of course, but they did not hear or understand all that he was saying. Mariam had given them the gist, lending mystery and intrigue to his talk of sacred missions. Her mother had twice shooed her away from the doorway of their little room, scolded her for spying on the conversation taking place in the courtyard, then had abandoned discouraging Mariam's natural curiosity and had returned to her sewing.

For a moment or two Mariam whispered in a conspiratorial way to Rebecca, then seeing that Salome and Benjamin were engrossed in some mutual make-believe, the eleven-year-old sidled up to her mother and planted herself almost at her feet, her head lolling, half resting on her mother's lap. She glanced inquisitively at Anna to see if she was listening, and caught her eye.

"Why can't that young man stay with us? Uncle Eli's got plenty of room."

Anna stopped her sewing and looked exasperatedly at her highly-charged daughter.

"It's none of your business, my girl. Uncle Eli's got his reasons, I'm sure."

"He looked nice. It could have been interesting."

"Yes, I dare say, Mari. But you'd do a lot better minding your own affairs and leaving your uncle to deal with his."

"Oh, Mother! Really, tell me really why he couldn't stay here."

"I've no idea. And I don't intend to ask Eli either. And if you've any respect for your tender bottom, dear child, I strongly recommend that you don't ask him either.

Whatever the reason is, it has nothing to do with you whatsoever."

Mariam made to speak further, but Anna placed her fingers on the girl's half-open lips, and hushed her good-naturedly.

"You're too inquisitive for your own good, child. It's time you learned a little humility in life. One day you'll have a husband and you'll not find him too pleased with your incessant boldness. It's unbecoming in a young lady of your age."

Mariam pulled a face at her mother and was rewarded with a playful push that propelled her back towards her siblings.

"Take the children out and fetch the goats," Anna called after her, "and leave me in peace to get on with mending your sister's tunic."

They all trooped out of the shadowy room. Anna heard dwindling peals of laughter long after they had gone. She shook her head to herself and pulled at her lower lip, then shrugged once more, and concentrated on her stitches in the dim wintry reflected light.

She could well guess why Eli had sent the young man packing, despite his courteous mien and refined speech. Nowadays Eli trusted no-one, certainly not since he had become so embroiled in supporting Joachim and his friends. Nor was it unknown for Herod to send out spies into the villages in order to uncover the whereabouts of outlaws and their means of support and sustenance. Some four years previously Herod's troops had purged a neighbouring village, after spies had fed back rumours that brigands had found shelter there, and in the mayhem more than a dozen of the local men had been murdered or executed and much property destroyed or confiscated.

Eli was too canny to be caught this way. His lifestyle made him a clear target for suspicion, should Herod's friends look in his direction. He was a Galilean Pharisee, conservative, nationalistic in outlook, making no secret of his hatred for the occupying power and contempt for his own country's collaborators. He avoided their gentile pleasures, their so-called civilising customs imported from the fashionably decadent Greek mainland and its former dominions.

Even more cause for concern was the common knowledge of his generosity to Salome and her family fleeing in disgrace from Ein–Karem. How firm he had been in laying down the conditions of their sojourn here, how reluctant to encourage Joachim until the die was cast. Then, faced with the rebel's exclusion from the village, Eli had considered at length his duties and responsibilities, and taken the brave and risky course – despite his nature – because his sense of rightness and hope of justice under the Almighty outweighed his fear of persecution by the hated foreigners.

Of course he was right, thought Anna, who had much cause to feel grateful for the man's overwhelming sense of obligation. But to live in receipt of such martyred charity, always conscious of the peril your presence throws onto your benefactor – that was hard. And it didn't help to have your innocent foolhardy young daughter, who was not aware of half your history, continually reminding you by her ignorant questions of your subservient status.

Having restored Rebecca's best tunic, Anna turned to the pile of clothes neatly stacked alongside her bedding roll. With a sigh she picked up and shook out a patterned headpiece belonging to one of her neighbours. At least three of the garments waiting near the top of the mound had been promised to be ready for their owners that same day. She could well do without further interruption.

Meanwhile Eli was battling with his conscience. Oblivious to the greetings of those he passed, heedless of small children through whose innocuous pastimes he blundered, he tried to justify to himself his rejection of the fair-haired stranger. For, despite all his instinctive prejudices against foreigners and heathens, he had taken to this young man. He had hinted of important things beneficial to his family. What opportunities had he thrown away?

Ignoring the chanting schoolboys in the side room, now under Simon's supervision, he pushed past into Joel's quarters at the rear. There he found not only Joel himself, one of his fellow rabbis, but also Jethro the elder, both deep in debate. After a brief acknowledgement of his presence, the two Pharisees resumed their somewhat intense discussion, which Eli discovered was concerning possible steps that could be taken to mollify the impact of the latest tax impositions rather than interpretation of the scriptures, which was a more normal topic at this hour. Eli could well understand why. He, too, would normally be a trenchant participator in such complaint, as, of all locals, his contribution would be the greatest. Now, however, he wanted confirmation and support for his recent action and he waited impatiently on the edge of the conversation for a break sufficient to interject and change direction.

At last the topic ran its natural course.

"Have you noticed the stranger among us? Do you know who he is? Or anything about him?"

One of their womenfolk had remarked on the presence of the man, that was all. She had thought at first that he was a Sadducee. On the other hand, opined one of the men, when had a Sadducee last dared set foot in Nazareth? Surely they knew this was Pharisee territory.

"He kept referring to a secret mission. What could he have meant?"

Surely a spy would not have aroused suspicion so openly, with so weak a story? Yet why else be so secretive? There were no affairs of the village unknown to Eli or his fellow Pharisees, so could not they have helped the man? Perhaps the man should have been brought to the synagogue to explain himself to them as a group?

One of the lads was dispatched to scour the village and fetch him, but half an hour later the breathless boy, red in the face, stumbled back, reporting total failure. The man had left the village; no one at all had seen him since earlier that morning at Eli's house.

Strange. That suggested he was taking steps to cover his presence, or even deliberately hiding. Having failed to convince Eli of his story, he had gone to ground. Eli was quite right in refusing hospitality to the man. He was a spy. They would alert those who needed to be careful.

Then, having discussed Eli's concern, their conversation turned to the latest rumours emanating from Magdala of a man performing strange deeds there, whom his followers claimed to be the Messiah. Yes, yet another claim. It was becoming so commonplace that if ever the true Messiah were to announce himself, no one would have believed him. The Messianic currency was being debased. Eli felt reassured.

CHAPTER 4
THE WATCHED

A LITTLE SETBACK TO OUR PLANS. *But there is time, all the time in the world. And the countdown has begun. A tactical withdrawal for the moment; then to rebound with renewed vigour. I have seen the solution, though, and that is enough. I will bide my time. I know I can act the catalyst, the trigger at the moment when the execution of the plan will be conceived.*

Her face is in my mind's eye. Her faint expression of surprise when I called attention to my presence. The wide-eyed brimming look that trembled with barely concealed excitement, all against the rules. Those eyes! Great dark liquid depths mirroring my steely stare, yet allowing those whose gaze is bold and still to see beneath her surface, give insight to her soul. I saw more than enough to know we'd made a choice of quality. In the courtyard, peering searching eyes, bright with mischief, irreverent, conscience-pricking. Large, brown and bold, fearless and vulnerable like a cat. I know that, but does she realise it?

Then there is her movement: liquid and flowing like a mountain stream, clear and sparkling, spraying in all directions, glinting in the sun. Deft and lithe, she would make a stumble full of grace. Delicacy cannot be equated with lack of strength, however. Carrying tired infants, lifting heavy water pots onto her neat young shoulders, herding her uncle's flocks out in the winter rain and winds, all give her frame a skeleton of steel under the fragile surface glow. She stands apart in other ways. Most of the village children are all roundness – chubby arms and thighs, plump faces with curly black moppet hair arching over their rosy features. Life may be poor and hard, but outdoor ways encourage rude health. Mariam's dark locks hang loose and straight about her shoulders. Her bone structure is light and airy like her tripping gait. The little children do not see her as different though. To them she is older sister, minder, playmate; special only in the care she lavishes on them when they fall, or hurt.

She is special. She has a sharpness that counters any sense of oversweetness. She has an unforced wholeness bubbling from within, she is ungroomed, she does not conform to adult expectations, not yet anyway. Be prepared for surprises. You will not easily forecast her mood, predict her reactions. She might shock you. She is not necessarily sound of judgement, nor judicious in her taste. And she will not let you get away with easy statements, or a comfortable mode of life. You will have to be young at heart to keep up with her.

Look at her again, then. You may, without embarrassment. She is not aware of our scrutiny; in fact at this moment she is not even aware of our presence. Look down from the hillside; watch her languid progress down the rough track, hampered as she is by meandering toddlers, whom she has accumulated on her amble through the village streets. The sounds of shrill voices carry to our heights, clear but snatches only, offering no meaning but their merriment. Then the smallest infant, barely walking, trips and falls face down amid the protruding rocks and howls of anguish echo in the valley. Mari picks up the screaming baby and cuddles him on her knee, squatting on the tufted bank surrounded by the other children, Madonna–like. There is silence.

She tosses her head. She flashes a grin of gold, but it is secret; only the children will see it, or so she thinks.

Look at her again, serene – comforting the now sleeping child; wondering if she dare risk awakening him by moving onwards to the scrappy slope where her uncle's goats are tethered. You hadn't really thought, had you, how poor she is? That pale bleached tunic of indiscriminate colour is perhaps her only garment of that type. Her little shawl of blue pulled around her shoulders to ward off the whipping wind is luxury to her. Bare legs, bare head – she really hasn't very much.

But surely she is provided for in the house of the richest man in Nazareth? Well, yes, as a case of charity. Eli's wealth is relative, of course. No-one in Nazareth aspires to the opulence of the town dwellers. And Eli has his own family to feed, to clothe, to house; four daughters to have wed; synagogue expenses to be funded; tithes and taxes. And all Salome's family, including Joachim's Zealots living off the barren hillsides. Anna, too, is proud. She will not ask for more than she can justify by necessity.

Look at her then with realism. Search your conscience; are you embarrassed now? Do you feel guilty that she is picked out, plucked from her familiar surroundings to suffer as well as to shine? When you think of what we'll do to her before we're over, you'll see how vulnerable she is, down there protecting her flock with no one but us watching over her. And yet, and yet, we've seen that greed for life that surfaces irrepressibly through her pores. She is chosen, perhaps, because she would risk it, even if she knew.

Call her softly by name. Practise on this hillside, letting the wind tear the syllables away towards Tabor or Hermon. Mariam, Mariamne, Miriam, Mari, Mary. Rose of Sharon, Rose of Hebron, Rose of Nazareth, Rosemary. Five-petalled rose. Rose of the Temple. Chosen maiden. Maid Marion. Virgin. The dancing flower. The rite of Spring. Sacrifice. Mari! Mari! Are you listening? Do you hear our voices on the moaning wind? Stay, my love, a little while longer. Enjoy the last few months of innocent maidenhood!

CHAPTER 5

THE OMEN

It was spring. A late spring afternoon, with an arid warmth baking the bare rocks, so that the hillsides were already glowing brown in the sunlight. Moistness settled now only on the eastern higher slopes and in the fertile fields leading down to Genneseret. The season began early here and grew old quickly like its children. Already the harvests were ripening, workers were being recruited to supplement the family labours. No young fair-haired strangers here – just muscular youths over from the town, itinerant each new reaping, bringing their extended families with them, camping in the open under the minimum shelter of the stone walls.

Salome, Rebecca and Benjamin were on their hands and knees in the little courtyard, along with their cousins, James and Jude, seven and six years old respectively, and their little sister, 'baby' Mari, or 'Mo' as she was usually called, who was now trotting around sure footedly, messing up whatever the older children were trying to build. The heat of the day and the tiredness of the two youngest children was beginning to lead to ever-increasing quarrelling, raised voices, angry interjections; Mo was squeezed out of the inner circle and rejected, began to whine, then cry in protest. A call of admonition issued from the open doorway of one of the surrounding houses, tired, ineffectual, not anticipating any real response. Anna was too busy beginning her preparations for the evening meal.

Suddenly Rebecca happened to look up from whatever was taking her attention, and spotting a familiar figure in the distance through the open gateway, shouted to the others, "There's Mari coming, look!"

The effect of the announcement was instantaneous. All the children stopped their actions in mid-air, and looked as one towards the gate. One of the boys shouted to no-one in particular, "Race you!"

And they were up and away, all traces of fatigue and irritability vanishing at a stroke. The older boys and girls were running full-pelt down the track, the two toddlers trailing after them, wailing for the others to go slower, wait. Mari was walking slowly back to the village, with a couple of other girls of her own age; children of her neighbours, who – like herself – had spent all afternoon in the fields pulling weeds from the baked soil and carrying the limp discarded thorns and plantains to a bonfire in the corner by the wall. The three girls were ambling, chatting to one another, in no hurry to return to their homes, where they knew household chores would be awaiting them. They looked up when they heard the excited shrieks of the racing youngsters, and stopped while one child after another ran full tilt into Mari's waiting arms. The other girls were neglected as the children clamoured around their favourite, jumping up and down in impatience, each trying to shout louder than the others. Eventually the two youngest caught up and were swept into Mari's embrace. She had seen them coming and pushed the others aside so that they could get through to her.

"Play with us, Mari, come and play with us," chorused the seven- and eight-year-olds, whilst they pulled at her arms, whirling her in all directions.

Mari's two friends broke away from the hubbub and called out an ironic farewell as they left her in the lurch. Mari, meanwhile, allowed herself to be pulled and dragged towards their home, letting them do all the talking. She was bombarded with suggestions, pleas to organise a favourite game. She waited until she could get a word in edgeways, then, quietening them with a gesture of both hands, she said, "How do you know I feel like playing anything? I want to sit down first."

But they knew she didn't mean it. She rested a moment to brush off the dust from her feet and ankles; then she was with them, chasing and singing and dancing, holding the little ones spellbound, teaching the others some new trick or routine.

As she sat outside her house, squeezing and smoothing her aching limbs, her mother called out to her from deep inside her home, "Mari, is that you? Can you fetch some water for me quickly; I need some for the evening meal."

"There you are," said Mari to the surrounding children, "I've got to go at once. Find something to do till I get back, then we'll play a game."

They whined in disappointment.

"Mari, you promised," they said.

At least they had interpreted her silence as a promise.

"All right," she sighed, "I'll tell you what we'll do. We'll have a wedding procession down to the well. The boys can accompany me and beat the drums; you girls go and wait for me to come by and light your lamps and lead us to the feast."

She had hardly finished her suggestion before Rebecca and Salome were off, pulling Mo by the hand so hard that she nearly fell over in her effort to keep up with them.

"Benji, you be my groom and walk beside me. James and Jude can lead and bang the drums."

Mari picked up the two water pots and handed them to the boys, who'd found wooden ladles and were already practising striking any object within range.

"Like this," she said, upending the pot on her left forearm, so that the flat base was angled for striking.

And off they went, banging and singing stridently, often not in time or tune, with little Benjamin proudly clinging to his sister's arm, puffed up with manly pomp to have been chosen for this plum role.

When Mari, Benjamin and their drummers reached the last house in the village, they were ambushed by the laughing, clapping girls, who pranced out from behind the sand-coloured wall, waving their imaginary lamps wildly in the air. As the procession wended its way towards the well, a little lower down the hillside, the girls chanted and danced exuberantly round the bridal group, kicking up the dust into a cloud as they went. As they got near the well, they were suddenly besieged by a swarm of gnats and mosquitoes, and their waving arms, now joined by those of bride and groom, set about flailing in the air to greater purpose. The party broke up in disarray and ran the last few yards to the rim of the well, where two women were already in the process of drawing water. Shouts of greeting were exchanged, and the children crowded round the stone parapet, peering into the dark depths, whilst Mari waited her turn to draw.

Baby Mo had found something else to capture her interest. While the others peered over the edge, she was poking at a crevice in the stonework and watching, fascinated, as sand trickled out in a steady stream into her hand, through her fingers, and onto the ground at her feet. Something else was moving in the sand and the little girl scratched about avidly. James happened to glance at his sister, caught movement on her arm and, suddenly realising what it was, screamed in horror, "Mo, watch out! Scorpions!"

The children instinctively cried out in fear, alarmed by the boy's panic, whilst Mo was more confused than anything. Mariam whirled round and saw the scorpions on the toddler's arm and, lunging, she swept at the insects with her left hand. Two smaller scorpions were knocked to the ground but the larger insect was still crawling up the girl's arm towards the opening of her tunic sleeve. Mariam grabbed again at Mo's arm, snatched the scorpion in her palm, and tried to fling it to the ground. But at the first attempt she swatted the air in vain. It was only when she shook her hand wildly that it fell to the earth. And by then it was already too late.

For at that very moment Mariam shrieked in pain as she was stung. She was still gasping in shock as she rammed her injured hand instinctively under her right arm, hopping and jumping in agony. One of the women rushed round to her, holding her firmly in her own arms, and prised Mari's palm open.

"The scorpion's gone. Bring some water round here quickly," she shouted to a friend, and the two of them bathed the swelling flesh, while Mariam clutched at them with her other hand, grimacing, white with shock, her big brown eyes wet with tears that she was struggling to withhold for the younger children's sake. They were standing round in a cluster, bewildered, one or two crying in their fright.

Whilst one of the women sat Mari on the wall and sucked at her sting, spitting out the poison, the other girl – she was not much more – filled Mari's water pots herself, the stunned children watching in troubled silence. When the water pots were brimming, Mari was asked if she felt well enough to walk home, and the two older girls helped her lift one pot onto her right shoulder. Between them they took the other jar, leaving Mari free to clasp and unclasp her injured fist to relieve the throbbing pain. It was a slow and sobered company that staggered in mutual support back to the village centre.

As they entered the courtyard gate, Salome darted ahead to fetch her mother and Anna rushed out in concern, relieved the injured girl of her water pot, slipped an arm around her in support and stared at the swollen hand. She sat Mariam on the ground and fetched ointment, which she rubbed into the throbbing palm, then bound it tightly with a cloth bandage. By the time the practicalities were over, Mari was surrounded by the circle of children, who were all trying to tell Anna and Eli's daughter-in-law, Miriam, of the way Mari saved the little girl from the scorpion's sting. Both Miriam and Anna hugged the heroine in acknowledgement of the children's praise, then, as the little ones wandered off in search of new diversions, Mari slipped into her own home, cradled her head on her mother's shoulder and in the privacy of Anna's embrace, sobbed in delayed shock and weariness. Her mother laid her gently on the mattress in the corner of the room, soothed her and kissed her gently on the forehead.

"Try to rest, my dearest, and when the pain is more than you can bear, remember that your unselfishness has saved Mo from hurt she could not take. And remember, love, that we are all proud of you."

And Anna bent over Mari once more, traced the tear- and dust-streaked cheeks with her finger and kissed her glistening eyelids closed.

"May God ease your hurt in peaceful sleep," she prayed, so softly that her words were scarcely audible; but Mariam heard the gist and smiled ruefully, half to herself. Her mother noticed the familiar gesture and sighed with relief, ruffled her hair a little and returned to the neglected preparation of the evening meal.

A shadow flitted across the entrance of the home and there was a whispered conversation which she could not catch. A veiled figure went over to the tossing shape of Mariam on her bed and sank a little awkwardly to the floor, uncovering a weathered heavily-veined hand which alighted gently on the girl's shoulder. At first, its pressure was so soft that the half-conscious maiden did not realise its presence. Then, as she rolled in restlessness, she became aware of the old lady's watchful gesture.

She turned her head and opened her watery eyes to acknowledge the vaguely familiar face and smiled a brave unfelt smile.

"Granny," she mumbled to herself.

"Shush, Mari, don't disturb."

The old lady brushed her hand against the young girl's sweaty brow, wiped the moisture with her own fingers, left her palm resting on Mari's lovely hair pulled back tightly under its band, the long tresses fanning out in abandon across the mattress. Neither said anything for a long time. Mariam closed her eyes again, and lay still under her grandmother's soft embrace. Then, almost imperceptibly, the old lady began to sing a soft refrain. Mari heard snatches of the old familiar words, "…lead me beside still waters…"

Then again, and again, "…by the waters of Babylon we sat down and wept… it is hard to sing the Lord's song in a strange land…"

CHAPTER 6

THE VISITOR

*T*HE DAYS HAD LENGTHENED. THE first harvest was gathered. Eli's barns were thankfully full that year – they still remembered the dreadful droughts of a dozen years ago when porters had to be sent all the way to Egypt to purchase grain. The air was still heavily pregnant with heat which would normally have laid its drowsy hand on languid children exhausted from their day's labours. But tonight there was excitement despite the prickly heat. Rebecca and Salome were whispering non-stop to each other on adjacent mattresses, here on the open roof. Benjamin, confused, was wide awake between the two younger girls and Mari's bedroll, where she was still sitting cross-legged in her day tunic.

Mari was listening, strangely disturbed by the sounds she was hearing down below. The movement, the soft murmurs, the peculiar grunts and moans, the sudden raised sharp cry that made her pulse run fast. The other children were waiting with impatience. When would he come to greet them, hug them, tell them stories, which would both stimulate and frighten them? For they had all seen his dark shadow slip between the courtyard gateposts just as dusk was falling. They had heard his urgent footsteps, had heard Anna's shriek of recognition, concern, relief. Then silence, while they waited. Only Mariam knew why he was so long; sensed her mother's frustrations; felt both glad and bewildered at the frenzied sounds she tried to understand.

"Can I go downstairs?" whimpered Benji to his watchful sister.

"Yes, can we?" asked one of the two little girls unexpectedly, as the boy's request intruded upon their secret conversation.

"No, of course not," hissed Mari as loudly as she dared without letting her voice carry downstairs. Then, not being able to think of a satisfactory reason that would bear any weight, added non-committally, "I'm sure father will come up and see us when he's ready. He's come a long way."

For the moment Mari had stalled their curiosity and she found herself willing her parents to remember their presence above. She wondered if she ought to make some noise, drop something by the window that would convey her embarrassed concern for their privacy, but she was rescued by different sounds now: a steady masculine tread upon the outside stairway. She watched as the silhouette of her father gained substance in the blackness, dazzled initially by the sudden glow as he raised the oil lamp to his face. She started, as if she would rise to greet him, but he was already stepping briskly past her sitting form and gathering his son in his encircling right arm. The lad threw all his weight at his dad, and chortled into his beard, letting the wiry bristles rub and tickle his cheek and neck. Joachim, for it was he, placed the lamp gently on the roof floor, being careful to avoid spilling the burning liquid, and then offered the other arm to the two jumping girls, squeezing each around the waist in turn.

"My, how you've all grown," he exclaimed, "and, you, my bonny lad, you're getting a heavyweight, aren't you? I'll need both arms to hold you in a minute."

He ruffled the boy's hair, and stooped again to kiss each of the younger girls on the cheek. Then he turned to Mariam, who had risen to her feet behind him and was waiting hesitantly for his attention.

"And now, little mother, are you caring for my brood here? They seem in good hands, I hear."

He placed his large fist on her slender shoulder and bent to caress her brow. As he stooped, Mari was aware of his musty odour, felt the damp clammy touch of his cheek and glimpsed the glistening sweat upon his bare arm. She should have been ecstatic like the little ones, full of untrammelled joy at his return. But she was hurt that her own feelings were letting her down. She was nervous – waiting to say and do the right thing, rehearsing her actions and seeming uncomfortable. Perhaps she sensed his guilt, even his fear of presuming too much on her acceptance of him. In the urgency of his embrace and mutual desperation with which Anna and he had physically groped for each other, deep down he could not banish the unformed words of reproach that he knew must lie often on her lips when he was absent. And so from mother to child. How often had Anna in her loneliness spoken words of criticism, even betrayal, to her eldest daughter? It would not be strange, that in times of exasperation, in minor domestic crises, she should cease to bite her lip. Mariam would be her consort, her confidante. Behind those great dark pools of light, appraising him so inwardly, what thoughts were being conceived, dredged from the depths to confront his unready wit?

"Yes, Father. They are good and happy most of the time. And they are pleased to see you now."

"And you, aren't you pleased to see your dad?" he said firmly, hopefully, groping for the physical contact that would mask his trepidation at her awaited answer.

She buried herself in his chest, letting him hug and crush her until you might wonder whether the teardrops hanging in her eyes were not caused by physical hurt rather than the emotional crisis just passing.

Both withdrew with relief, ready to restore normality as they turned to deal with the eager questions of the others. You see, Mariam had not seen her father since the early autumn, when he and one of his band came together at nightfall to negotiate with Eli long into the early hours, and left at first light burdened with produce, Mariam accompanying them both for over a mile beyond the village well. Once he was a frequent visitor home, staying days at a time. There would be celebrations. The neighbours would make excuse to call. He was open, unafraid. Then there had been that dreadful sacking of Gethara. The villagers had become nervous, fearful at his presence. He knew from his scouts that travellers on the road were watched; strangers were earmarked. Herod's men knew too much for Joachim to take the risk. Then again, a year ago his band had trapped half a dozen of Herod's men, poor tools he knew but Herod's nonetheless, and although they'd been destroyed the other side of Hebron, he knew that vengeance would be poised if he left one telltale sign of source of sympathy or family tie. Mari knew what he did. But he told the other children he was working in another village – he did not dare to tell them the truth lest they innocently pass on some unguarded word in the wrong quarter.

The first questions were over. Benjamin climbed onto his father's back and clung round his neck. Rebecca took his hand as they clambered slowly down the stairway and into their room, where Anna was smoothing down the family bed. Joachim sat down, surrounded by his children, while Anna hastened to fetch bread and a jar of wine, which she placed at his feet. Then she picked up Rebecca and sat her on her own knees, thus making room to squeeze up to her husband. Only Mariam sat opposite, her long legs curled under her, barely covered by her short tunic skirt. She was listening – as were the others – as Joachim told stories to the children. Mariam found herself staring abstractly at the still life opposite her, grouped around the magnetic life force that was her father. In her tiredness, she saw her mother and younger siblings as shapes, silhouettes in the flickering lamplight thrown hugely on the far wall. But her eyes were watching her father, as if seeing him for the first time; she was being mesmerised by him. He was a powerful man, at the peak of his manhood, just thirty years of age. His thighs and arms were thick, heavily muscled, but flowing in a rhythm that rippled with a natural vitality. His clothes were rough and torn in places – no doubt Anna would see to that before he returned to the hills.

Later when the younger children were asleep he recounted his adventures of the last few months; a narrow escape from a Herodian search-and-destroy group systematically combing western Galilee; raiding parties on rich collaborators; sorties in disguise into Sepphoris to obtain provisions and spy on the enemy's plans and movements. He described with vigour, his voice emphatic, pounding his fists to make his point, how they had captured and ransomed a prominent Sadducee from Magdala city – a man destined for the Jerusalem Sanhedrin and therefore of considerable value. He could not hide his contempt for the man, not only because of his hated acceptance of all things Roman, but also for the abject panic that he showed in captivity.

Mari stared at his face. His dark curly hair and beard were dishevelled from recent physical exertion. The beads of sweat stood out on his brow, intensifying his eyes

– Mari's focus. And they were flashing as he talked, piercing in their intensity, wild and almost frightening, exuding an enthusiasm for his words, oblivious to the emotions being stirred up in his listeners. Mariam was observing her father at that moment almost as a stranger, unsure in her own mind of sharing his judgements and assumptions without a sense of distancing unease. She found her mind wandering, wondering with the fright of the poor Sadducee; imagining worried wife and children. When he described how he was nearly caught in the spring exercise of the troops based in Capernaum, she looked quickly at Anna and saw her nervous tremor. She imagined her mother distraught at the inevitable consequences of capture, looked at her father's limbs and saw them twisted in the agony of the two men she had seen crucified in Sepphoris when she was a little girl. But she was strangely objective, could not relate it to the reality of her own being, feelings and emotions, there, then, in that house in Nazareth. She found this upsetting.

It was only when it was time for Joachim to flee that she found a surge of real fear and panic deep within her. For a couple of hours she had dozed fitfully on the family bed, squashed alongside her brother and sisters, tangled in each other, while Joachim and Anna had talked quietly throughout the night. Sometimes she had picked up odd phrases, heard her own name mentioned, held her breath while she tried to catch some more. The next moment she had been struggling in a swamp, clutching at reeds to stop her drowning, confronted by snakes and serpents which she must strangle with her bare hands, but dare not, rigid with fear. Then she woke as she tried to turn over, and found her arm trapped underneath the body of Salome, who had rolled towards her, exhaling in her face.

Just before first light, there had been much movement. Mariam, eyes squinting in the dim light, saw that Joachim was preparing for departure. In that surge of dread and panic, Mari found that she was heaving herself out of bed, stumbling, clinging to his outer garment. Anna steadied the sleepy girl and said softly to her, "Mari, love, say goodbye to your father. He must be away before daybreak."

Mari saw the moisture in Anna's eyes, the tears now rolling down her cheeks, and choked back her own shock. She clutched at Anna's sleeve, then flung herself against her father's bulk, her eyes tightly shut, wanting to feel him holding her.

"Mariam, my lovely daughter, I have to go; you know that, don't you?" He dared not pause for reply. "I'll be back when I can. I'll try to make your birthday because I know how special this one will be for you. Just think, a daughter of mine will soon be of age; it seems scarcely credible. Take care of your mother for me. Help her with the children. I'm very proud of you. And now go back to bed, love. I want to say goodbye to your mother."

He kissed her and lowered her gently back onto the mattress, bent low and touched briefly each of the sleeping children and was gone, Anna slipping out of the room after him. And in the overpowering silence, Mariam slipped an arm around Salome and squeezed her so tightly that the little girl stirred in her sleep, opened her eyes in some alarm, stared briefly into Mari's face, smiled reassured, and fell asleep once more.

By daybreak it was as if Joachim had never been. Except of course in the dark psychological depths that no ordinary observer would perceive.

Chapter 7

The Vicarious Father

*I*T WAS ONLY TWO WEEKS before Mariam's twelfth birthday in the first month of autumn. The fields were baked and bare. The grapes and figs had long been gathered and work for the village's children was at a low ebb. Mariam had been in the fields with Eli's flocks, showing Salome and Rebecca how to tend the animals, what weeds were injurious to them, how to frighten off the stray dogs that occasionally sloped out from the village. James and Jude were with the other boys in the synagogue whilst Anna had had Benjamin at home with her.

By mid-afternoon it was ferociously hot, and an army of small children were charging around the dusty hillside and along the track by the well. A couple of older girls had been sitting on the well rim, chatting, until a group of boys, fresh out of school, came looking for them and they all walked back towards the village together, leaving Mariam alone with the motley crowd of toddlers and younger children. They had danced, played ball, celebrated a pretend wedding and buried at least two youngsters in mock solemnity and were now chasing a couple of stray dogs, throwing stones at them while the dogs kept yapping, snapping at their heels.

Mariam, her sleeveless tunic loose and unbelted, was lying on the dusty ground, leaning against the well, squinting into the sun, trying to keep an eye on all of the disparate groups. At her feet Mo, Benjamin and a couple of other toddlers were contentedly making mud pies with water that she had drawn for them. Salome and Rebecca, with two other girls of around their own age, were cupping the ball and lobbing it gently to one another, whilst chanting some childish rhyme in a game of ritual. She was more concerned, however, with the half-dozen lads who were tormenting the life out of two dogs, for she feared that if they were not careful, one of them would get bitten, and as well as the injury, she'd be in trouble for not supervising them properly. Deciding at length that she must intervene, she dragged herself up and sauntered over to the shouting boys, trying to make herself heard above the din and laughter.

Getting little response to her first entreaty, Mariam took James on one side and warned him of the dangers they were running. With his acquiescence, she gradually gained the ascendancy, making the boys calm down while she drew off the dogs and led them away from the well. She went some way over the hill, calling and cajoling the animals, until they darted off to scavenge in the village tip. Then she strode briskly back in case any of the little ones had come to any harm in her absence.

She was soon relieved to see that the toddlers were still huddled together in their created mudbath, and the girls were still happily occupied. The boys, however, were now clearly at a loose end and were becoming bored and fractious, and as she got closer she could hear raised voices of irritability. Two of the lads began to scuffle in the dust, wrestling energetically at first, then losing heart as they achieved a sort of stalemate. Mariam suggested games they might play. No response. Then she said she'd tell them a story, and they gathered in a circle on the ground at her feet, for Mari was a good storyteller. She told of Jacob and how he tricked his brother Esau. She made them laugh when she pretended to put on the animal skin and made them feel her 'hairy' arms and legs; they playfully tickled her on the sly. Then she told of Jacob's flight in fear, his dream when he saw the angel climbing the ladder to the heavens, and how he wrestled with the angel until daybreak. That happened, she finished, on the road through Samaria to Jerusalem at the place we still call Jacob's Well, near Sichem.

"What shall we do now?" they chorused when the story was at an end. They were looking eagerly at Mariam. The girl sighed, then said, "Why don't you act out the story? Go and find some sheep's wool where they rub themselves on the stone wall and pretend to be Jacob tricking his father."

"I'm going to be Jacob," exclaimed James, "you be the angel, ha, ha...!" and he pulled Jude roughly to him and they scuffled, eventually pulling each other down, kicking up the dust. At first it was good-natured wrestling such as angels do; but at some point in the struggle, as so often happens, one of the boys inadvertently trapped or pinched the other so that hurt was inflicted, and the first, presuming intent, retaliated until the fight was in earnest.

Mariam, preoccupied with finding activity for the others, did not notice the change come over the rolling boys until suddenly she heard a yelp of pain, and blood began to trickle from James' nose, dripping onto his tunic, which had ridden up round his hips. Spurred on by the indignity of being really hurt by his younger brother, James exerted himself and rolled on top of Jude and before Mariam could act to prevent what she saw was about to happen, he slammed his fist hard into Jude's face, hitting him in the mouth. The younger boy yelled first in shock, then in pain, as blood splattered as he coughed and spluttered. Mariam by now was pulling James off the injured boy and both began wailing as the awareness of their own injuries overtook their rage at each other.

Mariam found a dirty piece of cloth, which she gave to James to hold against his bleeding nose, while she attended to the still-sobbing younger boy. Getting Jude to cease long enough to examine his mouth was difficult, but finally she prised it open and saw immediately amid the mess that a tooth was hanging by the merest thread of flesh on his upper jaw. She tweaked it off and told the boy to spit out the blood.

Both boys had now calmed down a little and had fallen into a sulk, so Mariam decided to terminate the playing and get the children back to their houses. All followed as

Mari led the band into her own courtyard; and the boys' mother, Miriam, coming out to greet them – hearing their voices approaching – saw at once that both boys' tunics were spattered with blood.

"What on earth has happened?" asked Miriam of Mari. Then, when she realised that they were their own victims rather than being hurt by wild animals or other cause, she began to scold and berate them in rising voice. Hearing the harsh tones of disapproval brought first Anna, then Eli, to the doors of their houses. Miriam reproduced Mari's account for the benefit of both and Eli took charge. Asserting his role as head of the household – Clopas was away at the market in Sepphoris – Eli seated himself on the large smooth rock positioned outside his door, and called James over to him.

"Well, my boy, what have you to say for yourself? Who started this disgraceful fight?"

James looked at his toes and mumbled something that Eli could not hear.

"Speak up, boy, or I'll tan your hide until you tell me properly."

"I don't know, Grandpa. We were playing at being Jacob and the wrestling angel, and he hit me hard so I hit him back."

"I didn't hit him first," whined the younger boy. "I didn't mean to hurt him,; he just banged himself. Probably on a rock," he added hopefully.

"What were you doing scuffling on the ground in the first place?"

"Mari told James and me to pretend to be Jacob and the angel," volunteered Jude.

"Did she now! I'd have thought she'd have had more sense than to suggest you fight. Her job is to stop you."

Both boys stood glumly, head down, before their seated grandfather. They could guess what was coming next. Eli's reputation for firm discipline in his household was well known. He reached out towards James and, holding him by the forearm, said, "Over my knee, young James. You need to be taught more respect for one another. Miriam, fetch me my rod!"

Indeed, James well knew what to do, for he had in his seven years here on earth been across Eli's knees many times before. Eli pushed the lad's head down towards the dust and with the other hand, yanked the hem of his tunic up to his waist, then – with the surrounding children watching in a circle – bared James' buttocks ready for punishment. James wriggled while he was waiting for his mother to return, while Jude watched apprehensively, jigging from one foot to the other, well aware that his turn would be next. The cane was handed to Eli. At once he steadied the boy in the small of his back with his left hand and brought the rod swiftly down four times across the child's pale bottom. James howled and the little children stared, open-mouthed. But Eli was businesslike: he covered the boy, replacing his tunic and pulled him upright, leaving him to hobble shamefacedly to his mother, attempting to pull up his loincloth as he went.

"Now, Jude!" commanded Eli, and the six-year-old received his medicine in similar vein, though the little boy's shrieks were even more piercing than his brother's. He too stumbled, crying to his mother's arms for comfort.

Eli remained passively seated, the children staring at him in awe – not that they were strangers to the rod, because it was the means by which fathers controlled their offspring.

"Now, Mariam, come here!"

Mari glanced hesitantly at her mother, who avoided her eyes. Then she stepped forward from the circle and stood meekly before her uncle.

"You were in charge of these children. You are a lot older than the others and as such bear responsibility for their behaviour. Is there any good reason why I should not treat you as I have dealt with the boys?"

Mari blushed and stammered, "Sir, I was trying to keep them amused, but there were so many, I could not keep watch of all of them at once."

"Jude said that you told both of them to play-act the fight. Is that correct?"

"Well, I didn't say that exactly. I meant them to be characters in the Jacob story. I left them to choose what to do."

"You need teaching your responsibilities, young girl. I've cared for you for many years now and I expect a more adult attitude from someone who comes of age next month. Over my lap, Mariam!"

Mari hung back a moment, wrestling inside herself as if she wanted to say something more, to argue perhaps. A glance at her impassive mother did not help. Then she thought better of it, swallowed, and lowered herself over Eli's knees, both palms supporting her on the dirt below. Eli did not spare her modesty – he lifted her tunic and bared her flesh as he did with the little boys. He caned her swiftly, six stinging strokes bringing pink ridges to her smooth skin. She reacted stoically, grunting at each blow. She too was no stranger to this routine, for she was under Eli's discipline during the absences of her father, but she had never suffered such humiliation in front of other children before.

When he had finished, Mari struggled to her feet, letting her tunic fall over her throbbing flesh, trying to avoid the eyes of all around her. A sudden wild sobbing broke the tension – one of the little ones was upset and frightened to see her favourite punished so, for to her Mari was grown up and she had not seen a big girl whipped before.

Eli picked himself up, grunted non-committally towards the moist-eyed Mariam, gathered his robes about him and disappeared without a further word back inside his own house. Miriam, aware of the lingering phalanx of children, half of whom belonged elsewhere, exclaimed, "Go home, children, you've seen enough. All be more careful in future!"

And she went to Anna and said in a low voice that she did not intend to be overheard, certainly not by Mari, "I'm sorry about that, Anna. I did not mean my boys to get Mari punished. She is so good to them. I hope she will not resent it and refuse to look after them in future."

"You know Eli, Miriam. He deals with Mari harshly on many occasions. She has learned what to expect without resentment or rancour. But it is hard for her here, Miriam – sometimes she feels more like a slave than a daughter. And it is a bit much for us all to expect her to look after so many tiny children. She is only eleven, after all."

"I don't think he means to be specially harsh with her, Anna. Clopas often tells me that as a boy he was beaten to excess. He thinks Eli treats most severely those for whom he sets the highest standards and has ambitious plans."

"And what might those be for my daughter?" rejoined Anna quickly and with a hint of bitterness. "What can she expect here, except marriage to some village fellow who will buy her cheaply and fill her life with further toil?"

"Don't sell Eli short, Anna. You know he is generous to a fault where family duty is concerned. He will find a good husband for Mari. He'll see she's well provided for."

"I suppose so. I just hope he selects someone who can give her more support than my man."

Then Anna seemed ashamed of her little outburst and called over her shoulder as she slipped away, "Anyway, I must go to Mari, to comfort her as best I can."

Mariam was slumped on the mattress in the corner, face down, her hair hiding her face. Anna went over to her, squatted, brushed the tresses away and saw tears silently falling onto the damp cushion that was supporting her head.

"I'm sorry, love. There was no need for him to do that. Can I ease your hurt a little with some ointment?"

"No, Mother, please. Don't touch me. It's more comfortable just leaving it; I'll be all right in a minute. It's not the hurt from the rod itself: it was so humiliating to be punished in front of all the other children. They'll laugh at me next time and try to get me into trouble."

"Nonsense, child. Why ever do you think that? They adore you. The last thing they want is for you to be punished. Didn't you hear Mo scream when you were being caned? You see, next time you'll find that they'll obey you without question."

"Even the boys, Mother? They get carried away so easily and are so boisterous."

"Well, James and Jude have learned their lesson for a while. And I'll have a word with Hannah and Ruth over their boys if you like. Really the other girls of your age should give you more of a hand rather than always leaving things to you. It's just that the children like you best, you know. It's a compliment really."

"Thanks, Mum. I'll be alright. Let me just rest for a while; it's been a long day and I'm tired."

Anna kissed her child tenderly on her tear-stained cheek and smoothed her hair, then went off to check that the other children were not getting into further mischief. Mari, meanwhile, felt her hot pricking eyelids, her smarting bottom; readjusted her body in a gingerly fashion to avoid further friction between skin and cloth; and amid her confused thoughts, fell asleep, exhausted.

CHAPTER 8

COMING OF AGE

S HE WAS AWOKEN BY BEING bounced on. No, she was not still sore – luckily – from her beating: it was a few days later, at the beginning of the time of year we call September. At first her bleary vision focused on the pale blue dawn, stars fading in the early light. Then, as she tried to stir, she found she was pinned down by a weight astride her ribs and was peering into the laughing eyes of Rebecca. She was going to say something, but Becca clamped her palm across Mari's mouth so she was gagged. The little girl giggled and whispered hotly in her ear, "Happy birthday! Can I come in?"

Before waiting for an answer, Rebecca pulled the cord on Mari's night tunic and slipped her naked form inside tight up against Mari's warm body. Then she squirmed and wriggled until she had succeeded in loosening her older sister's flimsy garment sufficiently for her to pull it right across her own skinny form and nestled comfortably against Mari's flesh, entwined in her arms and legs. She liked doing this; it was their private joke which she had enjoyed ever since she could remember. Tangled together in their tent, Rebecca began breathing hot nonsense words in Mari's solar plexus, then started chortling and writhing around as Mari's fingers crept over the little body, finding her ticklish nodes, as Rebecca knew she would.

"Don't, don't, don't: we'll wake Salome up," she hoarsely croaked, but Mari let her fingers continue their playful probes, knowing that this was exactly what Becca wanted to happen.

Mari suddenly transformed her fingers into claws and grabbed Becca round her little waist, clamping her, digging into the flesh and growling in mock rage. Her victim shrieked in surprise and merriment and tried to scramble out of Mari's clutches, but was held powerless, drumming the backs of her heels against Mari's shins. As they collapsed in laughter, Mariam rolled Becca over from under her tunic. Then both were suddenly aware Salome was sitting up in bed next to them, yawning and glaring at them in pretended exasperation.

"Did you have to wake me up?" complained the eight-year-old.

The others answered by both pouncing together, grabbing a wrist apiece and pulling Salome onto Mari's mattress. A moment's free-for-all of flailing limbs, then all three sank exhausted on their backs, looking up at the fading reflection of the moon, listening to the sounds of hens and goats scavenging for food. In the near silence they tried to catch any sounds from downstairs which might indicate that their mother was tending to Benjamin, but they could hear no movement. Presumably the dawn light had not yet penetrated there to indicate that morning was stealing up on them. On the roof, however, it was now light enough to see silhouettes on the other houses. James and Jude were still huddled on their mattresses on their home next door and they could see Mariam's friend, Naomi, and her twin brothers still curled up on the roof below theirs on the other side of the narrow street. Beyond Eli's house they could see a man moving about, pulling on his outer garment. It would be Thaddeus getting ready to go to the market.

Mariam pulled her garment back together to cover her body and retied the girdle. As she adjusted it, sitting up to pull down the tunic where it had rucked up during the tussle with her sister, Salome said to her, "What does it feel like, being grown up?"

"It's no different of course, you silly. Anyway, I'm not officially of age until six months' time."

"I thought it was when you were twelve?"

"Well yes, in six months' time I shall still be twelve. So you're half right!"

"Can you get married then?"

"I could get married now if Father or Uncle had a husband for me. It's just when I'm adult I can help choose, or at least say if I don't like the person they choose for me. Bilpah is betrothed already," she added, referring to one of the girls she hung around with at the well and in the fields.

"Do you want to get married, Mari?" said a little voice in her ear. Rebecca had been listening only until then.

"Not really, Becca. I've not really thought about it, to be truthful."

"Why not, Mari?" rejoined Salome. "You could have lots of babies and we'd help you look after them. We'd be aunties!"

"Oh no," said Becca. "What if she gets married to someone from another village? She'd go away and live there and wouldn't play with us any more."

"Anyway, it's not going to happen yet so don't start worrying about it." Mariam put her hands behind her neck and cradled her head. "Becca, why don't you slip downstairs and see if Benji or Mum are awake yet?"

And as the girl jumped up to go, Mari called after her, "You'd better put your tunic back on; you'll be giving Ben ideas!"

Mari and Salome exchanged a grin. Becca didn't believe in clothes during the summer.

Mariam was reclining in the guest of honour's position between Uncle Eli and her mother, thinking about the fun she'd had with the children during the day. After the romp at dawn she'd helped her mother for a while, preparing the food for the evening's feast, then she'd been let off further chores and had taken the younger children into the fields with the animals. Some friends of her own age had joined later and there'd been singing, handclapping and dancing until they were all exhausted. Now here she was, guest of honour at the family party and she was feeling a little bored because the chatter of the children was going on at one end of the gathering. Mari could neither hear anything they were saying nor join in herself.

Uncle Eli, her host, seated to her left, was doing his best to involve her in his conversation, but he was surrounded by Clopas and a couple of his daughters and their husbands and whilst Mari was interested in the family talk, the conversation turned too often for her liking to business matters, or news of Herod's latest outrage, or even, for a full twenty minutes, to an argument over the interpretation of scripture in regard to a Jew's duties towards foreigners in their midst. Joshua of Nain, husband of Eli's youngest daughter Susannah, was an impish fellow and knew well how to rile Eli without laying himself open to a charge of insolence. By praising righteous foreigners and by a little judicious quoting from the prophet Isaiah, he engaged Eli in argument; for Eli was a Chasidian Pharisee, of the party and persuasion that held itself aloof from all foreign contact in the belief that it would contaminate the true religion. Soon hypothetical examples were flying thick and fast and Mariam ceased to try to follow what they were saying, turning to whisper to her mother. She was whispering because, even though she was chief guest, it was considered rude to start a rival conversation among the adults present. The children at the end, beyond, were, of course, excused this constraint of protocol.

What was Mariam whispering so urgently to her mother? One thing only was preying on her mind at the moment – and it had nothing to do with anticipating her birthday gifts, which soon would be presented to her. It had everything to do with the empty place set opposite her, waiting for the other chief guest. For, when he came to visit several months ago, Mariam's father had promised to join her birthday celebrations and she had believed him; and still did. The whispered question was, of course, "When is Father coming? Will he bring me a special gift?"

Anna tried to stall her answer. She had no idea how well-founded was Mariam's certainty that her father would appear. She vaguely remembered some reference: a passing remark she caught between the two of them, but she had not taken it seriously at the time. And she did not want Mariam disappointed on this, her special day; but she feared the worst.

"He promised me he'd come," whispered Mari urgently.

"I'm sure he meant it, then," said Anna, "only you know as well as I do the dangers that he runs when he comes home. If he is coming, it will probably be only after dark that he dares enter the village. And if he doesn't manage it, I'm sure it will not be through lack of trying," she added lamely in his defence.

The meal was finished. The children were beginning to show every sign of overtiredness: one of the babies was crying; James and Salome were quarrelling over some trifle. Anna had to quell the altercation before it intruded on the adult conversation. Eli spoke to Anna over Mariam's head, "We must now move to the presents; we cannot wait any longer."

"I agree with you. We have given him every chance."

Anna acknowledged Mariam's expression of alarm with a quick squeeze of the hand.

"We can't wait any longer, love. The youngest children must go to bed soon and they will be disappointed if they cannot give you their presents first."

"I know, Mother, of course they must."

And she pulled a little face, trying to hide the fact that tears of disappointment were welling. She suddenly forced a big shrug and a genuine smile as if she had come to terms with things. It was the sign for Eli to begin.

He paused for silence to fall, then made a pretty little speech full of careful compliments: references to her worth as contributor to the family wellbeing, her example to the children, the dutiful and pious wife that she would make some fortunate young man one day. At this point, if Eli were the sort of man to wink meaningfully, he would have done so. Knowing him, as everyone present did, the allusion to Mariam's marriageable status did not go unheeded, and others cast her teasing glances at which she blushed.

Then, from Eli's solemnity, the atmosphere lightened as the children were invited to bring Mariam their gifts. Mo and Benjamin were clutching between them a sprig of wild plants and berries they had gathered themselves; Rebecca proudly offered some little cakes her mother had helped her bake; Salome had made a lovely little picture of wild flowers pressed and stuck to a tiny square of linen – a wild lily and roses picked from the valley beyond the well. The children snuggled up on the grown-ups' laps when they had done their parts and the adults now brought their gifts, each making a little speech to Mari as they offered her their presents. Clopas and Miriam handed her a new pale blue tunic that Clopas had brought back from the market in Sepphoris; Miriam added her thanks for the care Mari bestowed on her own children to Clopas' words. Salome, Mari's grandmother, recovering from a bout of sickness that seemed to afflict her increasingly these last few months, referred proudly to her oldest grandchild and put a ring on Mari's finger: a family heirloom that she wished to pass on to the new generation. She enveloped Mari in an enormous hug, trying perhaps, instinctively, to make up for her own son's absence. Anna kissed her daughter and placed around her shoulders the beautiful embroidered shawl of royal blue that she had been secretly preparing for her eldest's coming of age for many months past.

Of all the speeches that night, Anna's words were the ones that remained etched in her mind in times that were to come: "Mariam, my dearest child, eldest daughter, now a young and beautiful woman, a very Rose of Israel; you have heard the words of praise from your other relatives. I am glad and proud to see from day to day what just cause you give them for their sentiments. Mari, often, at night, I have dreams for you which I would find hard to put into words. So often, my love, we are too busy with the day-to-day chores of life to stop and reflect on higher things. But I know you are a thoughtful girl. I ask you, therefore, to ponder on the fact that I have hopes for you that I cannot articulate. I believe God will show you the way one day when He is ready – be prepared when He comes and speaks to you, Mari."

The gathering had gone strangely quiet during Anna's little speech. Even the children sensed the hush and did not disturb it. Eli's eldest daughter, Michal, looked at her father's stony tight-lipped face and murmured to her husband so that only he could hear, "That was a little over the top. Do you think she is trying to enhance her status in the household by engaging Father's religious yearnings, to couple with her husband's nationalism with which Father has already been too lenient?"

Anna felt the latent hostility, the prickly silence, blushed and sat down in an embarrassed rush. Eli coughed somewhat conspicuously and chatter resumed, covering up the slight vacuum that had arisen. Mariam was sensitive to her mother's mood, knew how rarely she dared to express any views except on practical household matters and gave her an instinctive hug, and said to her alone, "Thanks, Mum. That means a lot to me."

Pondering later on Anna's words, she would have been hard-pressed to justify her statement. Perhaps she would think it will mean a lot. Perhaps she would search for meaning. Either way, she remembered Anna's speech, precisely.

"Now it is my turn to present you with your gift."

Eli reasserted his authority. He took from his flowing robes a decorated scroll of parchment, which he handed to Mariam.

"Read this, and mark it well, my niece. I have tried to find a text for you to match your name, beginning and ending with the letters forming Mariam. After I had identified several, Rabbi Simon and I spent many hours discussing their relevance to your life, trying to select the most apt. We prayed, we cast lots and eventually the signs indicated that, unusually, three sacred sayings from the Psalms and of the prophet Isaiah should together form your personal text. This is unusual, even for a boy. So read them well, Mariam; let the words of the Lord always be a lamp to guide your feet in the way of truth. And if these texts have been chosen to point a special path for you, the Lord God will give you signs if you care to look and listen."

Mari, astonished, received the scroll with some trepidation, and unrolled it before the company. Mari was privileged in that Eli had permitted her sometimes to join the boys after school and she had some literacy, unlike her mother. She first scanned it silently to herself, then, pressed by a chorus of inquisitive voices, she read slowly and in a quiet voice:

"From the Prophet Isaiah:
My devoted servant, with whom I am pleased, will bear the punishment of Many.

"From the twenty-seventh Psalm:
My father and mother may abandon me, but the Lord will take care of Me.

"From the hundred and fourth Psalm:
May he be pleased with my song, for my gladness comes from Him.

"For Mariam, daughter of Joachim, within the household of Eli, on her twelfth birthday."

Mariam, after reading these words, let the scroll roll up of its own accord and stared through tear-filled eyes at the empty space opposite her own. Anna too had blanched at the choice of texts, biting her lip, hurt, taking the message as a personal shaft aimed in her direction.

There was awkwardness round the table, for no-one had predicted the pertinence of the second text, too accurate for comfort. Even Eli, not a very sensitive man, was aware that pain was being caused, but he could not think how to make amends without exacerbating the barb, so he decided to add nothing further. Michal spoke in a low voice to her husband again, "I see I misjudged our father after all. Despite his serious mien, he too lets loose his mystical musings. Heaven knows what the poor girl makes of it all."

Shortly afterwards the guests dispersed; the children were put, protesting, to bed. The birthday girl was alone with her mother, watching over Benjamin, who was already dead to the world. Mari was still tense, fidgeting, and finding excuse to go to the door, looked for some trifle in the courtyard, keeping one eye on the gate and the street winding down the valley. Anna knew she was still hoping against hope that Joachim would fulfil his promise, but already she had given up: he would have been here by now, or sent a messenger. She let Mariam fuss around cleaning up the pots and pans to give her something to do to fill her mind. Then, when she could find no more occupation, Anna turned to Mari and stated quietly, "Mari, do not grieve. He is not coming now. Go to sleep, my child; do not keep restless vigilance. That is my role. If your father comes, I will come and wake you at once – I promise you."

She kissed her goodnight. And both women shared tears, which neither could prevent nor hide from the other. Neither knew what to say. They clung to one another for a long tongue-tied lapse of time. Then both realised that nothing needed to be said. There was already perfect communication. Mari climbed the steps outside the house in the warm still night air, and saw that both her sisters were fast asleep. She sat on her mattress, staring into the void for a long time, allowing her eyes to become accustomed to the darkness. Then her lips began to form a prayer, "Lord God, be with my father this night, wherever he may be. Protect him from his enemies. Comfort my mother too; I know she is upset. Help me to understand all the things that have been said tonight. My mind is in a whirl. Assist me, Lord God, with sleep, for it will be hard for me. Let it be according to what you want. Amen."

But an hour later Mari was still tossing and turning, hot and sweating despite her exposure to the night air. She could not stay on her bed any longer and crept down the stairs and went inside, tiptoeing up to her mother's still bulk, curled up on the mattress. Mari peered at her, trying to check if she was actually asleep. Anna, however, was as disturbed as her daughter, and soon sensed someone was standing over her. She turned and looked up at Mariam's dark silhouette, and made room for her on the mattress. She cradled the young girl silently in her arms: Mari needed the physical embrace. Both, worrying about the other, fell asleep.

CHAPTER 9

SHEPHERDESS

*T*HERE WAS NOT MUCH GRASS left now; it had withered in the baking sun, turned a dusty brown, scratchily barren. The few sheep and goats that Mariam took most days out onto the hillside had to be led much further afield to find some edible pasture. Indeed, the girl had been walking alone, in front of her flock for a full three-quarters of an hour, before she found, lower down the cleft that leads ultimately to the Tabor valley, rough tufts of grass that would give some succour to her animals.

"Now here we are, you daft old things," she said affectionately to the bleating stumbling beasts, "get your noses stuck in there while I lie down for a while."

She was off the barely visible track now, trudging over the uneven ground towards a solitary fig tree, which stood high to the side of the field, providing the only shade for miles around. From that vantage point she would be able to keep watch over her animals and see early the movement of anyone on the track, from either direction. She was not, however, expecting company. It was mid-morning. The full heat of the day would bear down on all living creatures shortly, deterring unnecessary movement. Mariam stretched out her tired limbs over the clumpy tussocks under the fig tree, lay back on the pillow her hands had formed under her head and stared bemused, vacantly, into the tracery of the grey leaves above her, catching glimpses of the blue sky. She shifted her haunches off the knobbly root of the tree, which she realised she had half uncovered as she brushed the earth to form a cradle for her body, and stretched out, letting her eyes go out of focus, the twittering sparrows becoming dark blurs shooting across her line of vision like falling stars.

For a long time she thought of nothing, just a lazy easy emptiness, letting go of tensions. The sounds were reassuring: birdsong and the nearby bleating of her charges. Somewhere nearby she could hear a grasshopper. Once or twice she eased herself up onto her elbows so that she could look down and check that all the sheep and goats were still around, that none had strayed away. The previous day Bilpah had said she'd come with her grandfather's goats, but Mari did not expect to see her. She knew Bilpah too well to expect her to come so far when she could probably find some fodder that the goats could be persuaded to eat much nearer home. Mari didn't mind being left on her own. Most of the time she was surrounded by children; in the home it was always crowded. Out here, she could think, could talk aloud, dream uninterrupted, wonder why.

Despite the shelter of the tree from direct sun, Mari was hot. At first she loosened the cord from her waist and let her tunic billow in the gentle breeze. Then, as no-one else was around, she pushed down the loincloth from her sweaty flesh, pulled it over her bare legs and rolled it into a small bundle to place under her head. She let the wind dry her clammy skin, and shut her eyes in trusting repose. She didn't quite go to sleep, however. From time to time she sat up, put her arms round her brown knees and screwed her eyes up to shield them from the brilliant light, checking her animals. Each time she was reassured. They had plenty enough to eat there without wandering off.

She lay back again and stared at the branches overhead. Despite the general movement of intermingled leaves and birds, Mari's eyes focused on one particular sparrow just overhead which was preening itself. Tough though the little bird must be to survive out here on the edge of the parched desert, Mari felt its vulnerability, imagined the dangers it had run so far in its little life. She knew full well that if it sought easy pickings of grain dropped in the village, a flurry of small boys, her own cousins among them, would harry it with pebbles slung from catapults. Turning over on her tummy, Mari squinted at blades of grass inches from her nose. Adjusting her depth of focus, she perceived the constant movement, ants and other tiny insects going about their secret business, imagined herself a giant of the olden days, randomly brooding over her power of life and death; subconsciously easing up her body from the red-brown earth for a few precious seconds as if to say, "Escape while you can, you poor helpless creatures. I shall not harm you!"

She lifted her right arm and, stretching out in front of her eyes, she brushed deliberately against fronds of dry grass, scattering the seeds still hanging by a thread. She smiled privately to herself, "See, God, I'm giving you a hand!"

Mari loved the solitude of this wild place, and talked to her maker here in intimate words she would never dare utter in the outer court of the synagogue, or even in her own home, in front of others. It was here she nursed her innermost thoughts: her pain at her father's absence; the unspoken hurt of stiff Eli's unthinking harshness towards her and her mother; the everyday worries she had for the children when one of them was ill, or put themselves at risk during their boisterous play. She shared the good things with him too. She wore her ring out here – smuggled it out of the home without her mother stopping her, just so that she could show it off to God. Well, of course he knew already. But she couldn't really talk to him about it in front of the others, could she?

Listen carefully with the breeze; you might just catch the girl's scarcely uttered words, formed only with her lips. "Make them grow," she seemed to be pleading, "come green and pretty, make my bed next year."

Look at her lying there. If you were to come across her suddenly, your heart would skip a beat; you'd fear that you'd found a young victim of a wild animal, or a brutal bandit, a ravished corpse. Dishevelled hair, limbs lying in abandon, brown and scratched, so still. Then a sudden sigh. Vulnerable she may be, but very trusting. If she were to hear you coming, she'd swivel round in fright; her first thought for her precious animals, not for her own safety.

Dream, my love, dream away this torrid morning. I'll watch your beasts. Don't fret. Imagine water: water to refresh your parched lips, water to wash your weary limbs, water glistening in the reflected sun. Water catching the light, sparkling between the tall overgrown reeds where your eyes are fixed, searching, searching for the dark nest camouflaged against the Nile mud. Yes, Mariam, Miriam, you are watching for the child, trembling lest you give away your secret. You watch the trail beside the sluggish water. Each time someone appears you slip behind a palm, pretending to gather leaves, but watching all the time, screwing up your nerves, willing your baby brother to be silent. Do not choose this moment to cry out, please, not now. If you fail in this self-allotted task all will be lost; Israel will still be in slavery. So dream on, young princess, to the rescue; do not be afraid when the challenge comes, but step forward boldly; you know someone who will help, just trust me.

Hold your breath a moment; she is stirring. She rolls onto her back, smoothes her tunic, flings out her limbs, abandoning herself once more to sleep. She hears the distant clapping of the celebration, music and singing; sees the flickering lights dancing in the dusk. The bridegroom is veiled in the dimness of the room, protected by his friends, who will not let her through to see. "Who is he? Who is he?" she pleads. Is he the prince of David's line? Why is he here in this dirty little hovel? And where is the bride? Who is she? Do I know her? Why am I not invited, yet am here in the centre of the swirling joyful crowd? What does it mean?

Yes, Mariam, you are the bride; the young prince will claim you soon, sweep you off to Jerusalem, make you the mother of the King. Seize his veil, see, turn him, unravel him, and you will see his face, know these things are true, become dazzled with the light of destiny. Don't fall, love; you're twisting too fast – you'll be dizzy. Careful, you're falling, watch out…

Mari sat up suddenly as if in a panic, realised that she had been dreaming, and stood up, brushing the dried grass from her skirt and legs. She shaded her eyes and peered to the horizon in both directions. No-one. She counted her flock. She breathed a sigh of relief. None was missing.

Vague snatches of the dream came back to her, disturbing her peace of mind. She had not thought of marriage as a reality before – it had always been something that she assumed one day would happen to her as a matter of course but was distant, unconnected to her life of here and now. Yet her uncle had mentioned it at her birthday feast. Did that mean that he already had someone in mind for her? Was he negotiating even at this moment? Would he act in these next few months before she reached the formal day of consent, so that she would have no say at all? Bilpah seemed so self-assured about her betrothal – she talked all the time of her cousin, Jonas, who lived in the city and would take her off there, turning her back on village life for ever, in less than four months' time. Was Bilpah as ready as she seemed? Was she hiding her nervousness in the spate of gossip and chatter over wedding preparations? She knew her cousin though. Supposing Eli was negotiating a husband for herself whom she had never met? Could she follow a total stranger into a distant place like her ancestor, Ruth? Or suppose he betrothed her against her will, so that she was powerless to resist, like Bathsheba? At least, she mused, her orders were from royalty: she produced children in the Messianic line. Eli was more likely to betroth her to some rigid solemn old Pharisee or the sly and inhibited son of one of his friends in the synagogue. And Mari clutched at the dusty earth, letting it and the dry seeds run through her fingers.

"Lord God," she breathed, "let me keep my freedom for a while longer yet. I do not want to be shut up in my home, however kind and considerate any husband might be!"

She looked down at her slender arms and stared at her palms and delicate fingers. Then she wriggled her bare toes and touched lightly, as if in disbelief, the soft tissue of her thighs. She shuddered, suddenly feeling small and vulnerable, this tiny frame at the mercy of the universe.

She began to quote scripture cherished in her memory. Whatever she might think of Eli, she was grateful for one thing. He let her go with the boys, when she was younger, to learn to read and write. She had recited texts; knew her nation's history and hopes; had made friends with Joel, the youngest of the rabbis, who had a daughter not far off her own age, whom he also encouraged to read. Often, when the boys had finished their lessons for the day, Joel would beckon the two girls into his room and take one of the precious scrolls from its resting place, letting them roam at random through its bleached parchment. Lately, amid giggles from Hannah, Joel was persuaded by his daughter to show them scrolls of ancient poetry and the two girls had pored together over the love songs that they discovered there. To Hannah it was only a slightly risqué game, letting her try out words and phrases that would normally have brought nothing but rebuke.

To Mariam, though, the words of the poems conjured up a different world – a beauty that filled her tongue, lit up her inner eye. As Hannah scanned the text, skim-reading down the long parchment, Mari recited, consigning to memory the most beautiful or enigmatic phrases that she found. One day she would try to entice from her memory such words to sing to God, here under the fig tree; in the meantime she hummed to herself couplets and single phrases tripping bell-like off her tongue.

And there she sat, cross-legged and unencumbered, under the shady tree, rocking to the rhythm of her pure young voice:

> "Daughters of Jerusalem, I am dark but beautiful,
> Dark as the desert tents of Kedar
> But beautiful as the curtains in Solomon's palaces."

And she threw her arms, waving them in the air, as she continued:

"My sweetheart, my bride, is a secret garden,
A walled garden, a private spring;
There the plants flourish.
I am only a wild flower in Sharon,
A lily in a mountain valley."

She broke her reverie. Looking up into the branches, she spotted a clump of wild figs, already offered as a second harvest, and swung herself up the smooth grey bark, gripping the overhanging branch to steady herself as she lunged at the drooping fruit. She staved off hunger for a while, then jumped agilely to the earth and picked up her loincloth where she had abandoned it, slipping it over her hopping ankles while she scanned the far side of the field, counting her flock. In a burst of repressed energy she tripped down the slope between the rough hassocks of grass, singing breathlessly as she went:

"The mountains skipped like goats;
The hills jumped about like lambs.
Tremble, earth, at the Lord's coming,
At the presence of the God of Jacob,
Who changes rocks into pools of water
And solid cliffs into flowing springs.

Alleleujah!"

She flung herself with a cry of merriment round the neck of one of her goats. While the nearest sheep scattered at her impetuosity, the old goat allowed the affectionate attention. Mari chattered to the animals very volubly, at which they began to regroup around her, drawn by her magnetism. Then, checking that the sun had begun to move from its position directly overhead, she told the flock to follow her; she skipped lightly down the valley path, the sheep waddling at the rear. Beyond the next ridge on the left, the path would descend to a remote and fertile valley, where the little stream that formed a tributary to the Tabor River, which itself flowed into the Jordan twenty winding miles away, would serve a rich refreshing pasture, quenching the thirst of both girl and animals.

She stopped suddenly at the head of her flock and laid her hand on the neck of the leading goat. As the vista had opened up and the valley sides had retreated to reveal the tumbling stream, more rock and stones than water at this time of the year, she glimpsed the small circle of black tents clustered on the bank. Mariam was hesitant. How would she be greeted? Would there be Arab nomads there who would try to take advantage of a young Jewish girl and her flock? While she was pondering what to do, she spied a couple of naked tots chasing among the tents. She lost her fear and continued leading her animals down to the water.

As she drew near, other faces peered at her from the tent flaps. A toothless old woman, eyes and mouth only visible between her black scarves and shroud; more eyes, more teeth glinting in the sunlight, stared at her. Only the children approached directly: the two she had seen, then a couple more, who emerged from the tents and stood in front of her, open-mouthed. They were dirty, flies buzzing near their eyes, the two older children wearing just tattered filthy shifts. Mari was sorry for them, smiled at them.

At this the children and the old woman burst into a cacophony of pleading, arms outstretched, in a language or accent Mari could not understand. She stood helplessly before this onslaught, shrugging her shoulders, trying to convey her lack of comprehension, though it was clear they were begging. Mari opened her palms to show she had nothing to give. Then the woman started pointing to the animals and Mari began to get worried. She dared not lose one of her uncle's flock. Suddenly she had an idea. She went up to one of the goats and mimed milking it and drinking the milk, indicating with her hands that she wanted to give it to them.

They understood. A battered old skin was produced from the depths of one of the tents, and handed to Mariam. She got one of the children to hold it for her, and began to milk the nearest goat until its udder was empty. She handed the warm milk over to the woman, who was probably the children's mother, then turned and led her flock down to the stream while the nomads followed, watching her every move, stopping as she stopped, moving on as she moved. When the animals had had their fill, Mari started to walk back up the bank, hoping that the strangers would not follow her.

At first she looked straight ahead, not daring to look behind her. Then, feeling foolish, she glanced surreptitiously, and saw with relief that the two women and children were stock still, watching her go. She waved. They waved back. Mari turned the corner and began the uphill climb. She was alone once more; indeed she saw no-one else at all, until nearly an hour later she came to the well on the outskirts of the village.

Mari led the animals into the courtyard and was greeted by shouts from Salome and Rebecca, followed by the appearance of both Miriam and Anna at the doors of their houses. They both brought earthenware pots, for it was milking time. Then Miriam noticed the flat udder of one of the goats.

"Mari, why is Jezebel already milked?"

Mariam explained what had happened at the stream. Both Anna and Eli's daughter-in-law looked put out at Mari's words.

"Did they threaten violence to you, Mari?"

"No, I was a bit nervous, but it was mainly because I didn't understand them."

"Then why did you let them have the precious milk? You had no obligation to them."

"But they were poor, Miriam. The children looked starving. They asked me for help, so I thought we could spare one goat's milk."

"But, Mari, they were outcasts, Arabs. We don't give to them. Your uncle will be cross if he finds out."

"Surely, Miriam, scripture tells us to be kind to those that are worse off than ourselves. Doesn't it say, 'He raises the poor from the dust; he lifts the needy from their misery.'?"

"Perhaps it does, perhaps it doesn't, Mari. If I were you, I shouldn't try arguing scripture with your uncle if he challenges you. Don't give away things that don't belong to you. I won't say anything more this time, but be careful, child. Now give a hand with the milking."

Anna said nothing during this exchange, but occupied herself with rounding up the flock and securing the courtyard door. She now looked at Mari without any betrayal of her own views. Mariam shrugged her shoulders good-naturedly and talked to the children as she began milking, letting Rebecca have a turn, moulding her little fingers between her own, squeezing them in the required rhythm. Only much later did Anna beckon Mari inside and hand her a crust of bread to assuage her hunger until the evening meal. As the sheep were penned into the corner for the night, Miriam, standing just behind Mari, suddenly squeezed her shoulder.

"Perhaps you're right, Mari, perhaps you are. I don't know."

Interlude 3

"Dance, dance, girl of Shulam,
Let us watch you as you dance.
Why do you want to watch me
As I dance between rows of onlookers?"

ou thought I had gone away. Eli, Anna, Miriam, all the rest, have long since forgotten me. Come on, admit it, you'd thought I'd gone as well; repulsed by Eli, my back nervously watched by the womenfolk. You should have known better; I told you I was biding my time. I watched the scurrying round the well when the scorpion stung. I saw her father slipping from shadow to shadow, entering the house at nightfall. I was the angel struggling with Jacob. I inspired Anna's little birthday speech. I was an Arab gypsy child. I heard a maiden praying under a fig tree. You saw me, under that fig tree, didn't you, even though Mari was unaware of our presence?

I think she suspects I'm here. She alone knows something's afoot. She knows I'm watching. "Why me?" she says.

"Tell me, my love,
Where will you lead your flock to graze?
Where will they rest from the noonday sun?"

You'll soon be of age, my girl. Is Eli plotting to find you a husband? Where will your precious freedom go then? In the meantime, your children follow you, full of heroine-worship; everywhere you lead, they follow. Will you leave your siblings, to found your own dynasty?

Through the cool damp winter, they cling to you for fear you'll leave them. Stories of Moses, stories of David, stories of the Promised One; mistress of storytellers, keep them spellbound round the cooking fire.

To you, reader, March 8th, 8 BC. To you, Mari, twelve years, six months, one day. Adult under the law. The stakes are raised. You have the power of veto. You are accountable; no child's excuse will stave off retribution if you transgress. It's a world of rough justice in a Galilean village. Can you cope? Who dares to be different here?

I'm still watching them, prepared to spring the trap. I've stalked you nearly long enough. Shall I stay my hand a while, or now take aim?

> *"The winter is over; the rains have stopped;*
> *In the countryside the flowers are in bloom.*
> *This is the time for singing;*
> *The song of doves is heard in the fields."*

Let's just wait a little time longer; let you sing a last song, carefree for the moment. Your swansong.

Chapter 10

Festival

$\mathcal{A}$T THE BEGINNING OF EVERY spring there was a festival and fair in Nain, about eight or nine miles south of Nazareth and a similar distance from the Samarian border. Whilst the prime reason was agricultural, with a major auction and sale of young livestock, especially lambs brought in from the local hills ready for the Passover market, most people flocked in from surrounding villages to enjoy the two-day celebrations with many entertainments, dancing, drinking and gossiping with old friends.

One of Eli's daughters, Susannah, lived in the village, so the whole family from Nazareth spent the two days there, crowding out the little house and courtyard, the children herded together somewhat precariously on the roof. Indeed, a couple of years ago, Michal's eldest boy fell off the house during some childish horseplay and broke a leg. The lad, now eleven years of age, still moved clumsily with a limp, for his broken leg had set some inch shorter than the healthy one.

The Nain Fair was one of the highlights of the villagers' year, followed within weeks by the Passover celebrations, so the children had been excited for days in anticipation and had pressed Mari to repeat time and time again the sights and incidents of previous years' gatherings. And, of course, as well as the festive activities, it was one of the few occasions in the year when all the children lived together with their cousins. There was never much sleep to be had on the Fair night, even assuming that half the menfolk of the town were not carousing, half-drunk, at the tops of their voices.

The Nazareth caravan set off at daybreak. Eli, Clopas, Miriam and Anna, with their children, joined three other extended families making their way southwards. Only Salome was left at home, Mariam's grandmother – she said she was too old to enjoy such fairs any more. Someone had to look after the livestock and it might as well be her. At first they took the Samaritan route to Jerusalem out of Nazareth, and after just over an hour's walk, with some of the smaller children already asking to be carried, they began to merge with other groups, joining them from the track on the right, which came from the village of Mizra. At this point they reached another junction in the road, with a rough track on the left taking the parties towards Nain, whilst the main pathway wound on due south through Afula into Samaria. They had been climbing out of the main Tabor valley for some time now, and, with the sun beginning to convey a shimmering heat dispersing early morning dew, some groups with elderly relatives or young children sat at the wayside and handed round skins of cool water and wine.

Wild flowers were growing in profusion along the banks beside the track, and the youngest children gathered them in handfuls and tipped them into Mari's lap, limp and bruised, for her to thread flower chains for them to hang around their necks. Bilpah's family had not come with them this year – she was being allowed to visit her cousin, Jonas, to make more wedding preparations – so Mari was the oldest child in this particular caravan from Nazareth and therefore she had no relief from looking after all the little ones. Miriam had taken advantage of the stop to suckle Mo; within weeks she should be relieved from that chore as the girl was weaned.

When the children were threatening to waste any energy conserved by the stop by dashing impatiently around the seated adults, Eli and Clopas urged their family onwards, so that they could get to Joshua and Susannah's house before the hottest part of the day. For a while the path followed the ridge of a hill, and they had long views over the rolling bare mountains, culminating in the bulk of Mount Tabor, not far short of two thousand feet high, just to their east. Then the path dropped gently down the southern flank of the hill and they could see Nain nestling in the glowing sun, a couple of miles away.

As they neared the village, following streams of travellers pouring into the Fair, James suddenly shouted to his father, "Look, there's an execution ahead. Can I run ahead and look?"

"You're right, lad. It looks like a couple of crucifixions. Just like the Romans to make an example and put them up for show when the village will be crowded out."

The boy made as if to run ahead.

"Wait, James, I didn't give you permission to chase on ahead. You're a bloodthirsty little brat, aren't you?" he added, tousling his son's dark curls affectionately.

"I don't want to see," wailed Rebecca.

"Nor me," added Salome.

Eli took Anna on one side and said out of the children's hearing, "Why don't you take Benjamin, Mo and the other two girls on a detour off the main path and into the village below Joshua's house? You'll have the crosses in your view, of course, but the children will avoid being too distressed by a close sight of the victims."

Mariam made as if to go with her mother.

"Mariam, you stay with the rest of us. We'll need you to help me with the carrying and sorting out of our baggage when we arrive. Anyway, you're old enough to face the facts. You can't go through life turning your back on the ugly."

"Why will they have been condemned to death?"

"They're probably bandits captured by Herod's soldiers and dragged before the Romans. They usually execute them in the cities, but if they're local or believed to have local support, the Romans'll have them sent here just to coincide with the festival, so that it has a deterrent effect."

Eli's words did nothing to reduce Mariam's misgivings. As they drew nearer, she was on tenterhooks, having to steel herself to walk slowly, calmly, with the others, although she was aching to rush on and convince herself that her worst nightmare had not come to pass. He was not a bandit, she said to herself; he did not come from here. No-one had told us. It couldn't be him. Yet still a nagging voice raised doubts. The Romans, nor for that matter Herod's men, who should have known better, did not distinguish between a bandit and a nationalist outlaw. A Zealot was a terrorist, murderer, to them; such a death would be his fate if caught.

They drew near to the outskirts of the village where the two crosses had been erected. A small crowd, mainly of fellow travellers arriving in Nain, congregated around the foot of the gallows, reading the sentences and identities of the villains. A few ribald remarks and shouts were aimed at the twisted and scarred near-corpses, who seemed only semiconscious. James and Jude stared in awe at the dreadful sight, silenced. Clopas returned from reading the inscriptions, and said to Eli, "As you thought. Zealots from beyond Sepphoris, but operating out of this district, and supported by villagers here."

Eli was tight-lipped and ashen. Mari, standing near him, saw him purse his lips and heard him mutter with venom, "You swine. Herod's dirty work again."

The others moved on quickly, but Mariam stood transfixed, looking up at the distorted grimace of one of the condemned men. She realised with a shock that the pain-disfigured face was making appear old a man who, on closer dispassionate scrutiny, could not have been more than a youth of around twenty years of age, if that. Not that Mari was able to see objectively, for pity was bringing tears to her eyes. If the youth were to have opened his eyes for a moment, amidst the jeering muttering crowds, he would have picked out the young girl whose expression seemed to be trying to convey some message of fellow-suffering to him. Glancing at the other, older, bandit, she saw that he seemed totally oblivious to the crowd, deeply unconscious, so she jerked herself back to her own reality, found that she was now alone amidst the crowd, and hurried after the rest of her party, pushing, twisting her way through the blocking throng. When she caught up with them, she did not attempt to join in the general conversation, but dropped into step behind them, silent and thoughtful.

The reunion of Eli's family lifted everyone's spirits and the children ran riot for a while until the adults had completed their greetings and sorted out the various eating and sleeping arrangements. Anna turned up with the youngest children, and in the afternoon all set forth for the Fair. Eli, Clopas and his sons-in-law made for the livestock and produce market, while their womenfolk detached themselves to explore the stalls in the bazaar filled with rich garments, embroidery, carpets and lacework.

The children, meanwhile, had been allowed to wander off to watch the various entertainments as long as they kept together as a group. Needless to say, Mariam, as the oldest, was in charge, though her limping cousin was only a few months younger. On the whole it was not too difficult to control the youngsters, as they became absorbed with the storytellers, actors and jugglers. The main difficulty was ensuring all moved on together, as someone always wanted to watch 'just another minute'.

The children were standing in the crowd around a juggling act and had been for some time now. They were gradually worming their way forward as other children left to rejoin their parents, until they found themselves positions where even the youngest could see without hindrance. This was the highlight of the Fair as far as Anna's girls were concerned. Two rabbis in their flowing robes were taking it in turns to juggle lighted torches, each attempting to outdo the other, as they increased to four, five, six swirling flames in mid-air. They continued for a while, flailing like burning dervishes, then one rabbi, to the open-mouthed wonder of his young audience, took on eight torches at once and succeeded in twirling them all successfully. This was the climax of his act. The children shouted for more and he obliged once, then, to their disappointment, extinguished the flames. Both men bowed with a flourish, brandishing their blackened torches, then disappeared into a tent, leaving the children chattering excitedly, wondering whether to stay in hope of a further display, or move on in search of fresh excitement. James, Jude and Rebecca were talking animatedly while Mari gathered them together and counted her brood.

"I've never seen eight before. I thought he was going to set himself alight."

"That's part of the act. He wants you to think that to make it more thrilling."

"Someone said he goes all round the country, even to Jerusalem, and that he's the best juggler there's ever been!"

James, meanwhile, had found three sticks and was attempting to juggle them himself, but only succeeded in dropping them after a couple of spins. When he finally did get into a rhythm, Rebecca snatched at one and brought his incipient bragging to an abrupt halt, as he chased her in mock anger and she hid behind Mari, clutching at her tunic, squealing as she ran.

As they joined the edge of another crowd, mainly children again, peering to see what was happening, they noticed a small group of Roman soldiers lounging amiably at the back, watching proceedings with faint smiles of tolerance, allowing young boys to examine their weaponry with impunity. James, Jude and Simeon were off to join them, so Mari and the others followed too, Mari noticing that one or two of the older girls were hanging round the soldiers, laughing and talking with them.

One of the soldiers called out to Mari in her own tongue, "Hey, pretty girl, are you the mother of all this lot?"

Mari smiled at him and pulled a face of mock indignation. "Of course not. They're my sisters and brother and cousins. Though they expect me to act as their mother a lot of the time!"

"I'm sure you'd make a pretty good mother. Like this one here!"

He pointed to one of the older girls chatting to another soldier, a girl of about fifteen years of age who had many ornaments and decorations on her colourful garment, and whose eyes and lips were heavily made up. Despite her age and apparent affluence, however, she was not dressed as a married woman and Mari was puzzled at the soldier's remark.

"She's not a mother, is she?"

"Whether she is or not, she certainly acts like one!"

"What do you mean?"

"Hey, Rachel," shouted the soldier to the girl, "come here and tell this innocent what you do for a living."

The girl looked up, saw Mariam and the younger children, and sauntered over, preening herself, grinning broadly at the soldier.

"You wouldn't want to spoil her innocence, would you, you crude soldier boy! Why," she said, poking him playfully in the ribs, "I believe you might, if you get half a chance!" Turning to the bewildered Mariam, she exclaimed, "I've seen you before. Are you from Nazareth?"

"Yes, I live with Eli, the Pharisee."

"You'd better not be seen talking to me, then, kid."

"Why not?"

"Let's just say, I help the priests at the temple. Or used to. I'm finished now and I'm betrothed to a man in Nazareth."

"The Temple in Jerusalem?" asked Mari in awe. "I didn't know they let women serve there."

"No, not quite that temple, darling," Rachel replied. "I – hey, kid, I think you'd better scarper; it looks like your folks are coming!"

Back at Joshua's house, a chastened Mariam asked her mother, when she thought no-one else could overhear, "Why, Mother, why was Uncle Eli so cross with us? We were only talking to the other girls with the soldiers."

"Mari, for an intelligent girl you can be very naïve sometimes. Don't you know why those soldiers are here?"

"No, Mother," said Mari, screwing up her face in puzzlement.

"They've been here to crucify those two Zealots you saw on the way into the village. They'd kill your father like that if they got half a chance. Now do you understand why we were upset with you?"

"Well, yes, I suppose I do."

"And, furthermore, don't you know what those girls with them do?"

"No."

"Oh, Mari, I wish you could keep your innocence. My child, they sell their bodies to anyone who will have them, like those soldiers, for an hour or two. They're evil, Mari. You must have nothing to do with them."

"One said she was betrothed to a Nazareth man."

"That'll be Rachel: she's betrothed to a Samaritan tax collector who lives opposite Josiah the potter. She's as bad as he is. The whole village shuns them, Mari. Don't be taken in by her. Her past is lurid; rumour is that she's been giving herself to men for years in a Samaritan pagan temple as a whore. No decent Jew would touch her, or even be seen with her. Please, Mari, have nothing to do with the girl. She'll bring you nothing but trouble."

Mariam fell silent. She looked as though she understood. Her mother, anxious to be off the subject, as though even talking about it was unclean, spoke rapidly of other matters. Mari heard, but she was not really listening.

CHAPTER 11

RACHEL'S STORY

A FEW DAYS LATER MARI AND the children were playing round the well. The boys had been frightening the younger children by pretending to carry out executions, until Mari had stopped them, then they had played at funerals. After a couple of mock ceremonies at which the boys had shrieked and wailed with such dramatic overacting that they had finished doubled in laughter until they were powerless to continue, Mari had insisted that they play something more cheerful.

So they had moved on to the younger children's favourite and had gone through a wedding ceremony, from the betrothal party right through to the pledges, the unveiling and the feast at the bridegroom's house. They were now dancing with gusto, totally oblivious to their surroundings, when Mari suddenly became aware of another presence.

Standing watching them, an empty water pot poised on her shoulder, was Rachel, the girl they had met in Nain. She looked very different here: none of the flashy adornments she was wearing at the Fair, but the smile playing on her lips was the same. Mariam realised in this instant that the girl had come to the well at this time only because she was an outcast. At the normal hour of fetching water, the other village women would have shunned her and spat at her. Despite her mother's warnings, Mari felt sorry for the girl and smiled at her, although she didn't say anything.

Taking the smile, perhaps, as an invitation, the girl walked through the children's cavortings and lowered the bucket into the well. As she hauled the water up, she called to the children over her shoulder, "What are you all playing at?"

"Weddings," chorused half a dozen little voices.

"What comes next?"

"We've nearly finished. We've had the wedding feast!"

"Oh...! From what I've watched, I think you've missed the best bit."

"What do you mean?" asked James, puzzled.

"Well, you silly, what do the married pair do together after the wedding feast?"

"They live together in the same house."

"Yes?"

"And they have children and cook and work and so on."

"But what do they do on their wedding night?"

Mariam had become uneasy at the girl's drift, and was trying to think of how to extricate the children without embarrassment. One of the boys sniggered, "They get in a huddle and try to make a baby."

"Clever boy!" mocked the girl with heavy sarcasm. "And how do you think they do that?"

No-one said anything.

"Come on, Mari, you're in charge of this game; show them properly. You're only half playing at it."

"Ach, she's no good," Rachel confided to James. "I'd better be the bride; you be the bridegroom."

And in the same moment, in front of a circle of open-mouthed and curious youngsters, she set down the bucket of water on the ground beside her empty water pot, lifted up her tunic in one movement and squatted on the smooth rock beside the well, baring her thighs.

"Come here, James," she called to the somewhat bemused boy.

"No, James, leave her alone," cried Mari in belated alarm, realising at last what Rachel intended. "Don't do what she says; it's wrong."

But James had already half committed himself by stepping forward to the girl, and she had simultaneously spread-eagled herself on the rock, naked from the waist down, and grabbed below James' tunic, holding him by his loincloth. The boy wriggled in uncertainty, frightened by his cousin's shouts, staring in fascination and horror at the dark thicket of pubic hair on display before him. The girl had managed to yank James' undergarment to his knees, before Mariam intervened, seizing the girl's wrist with sufficient firmness to allow James to recover his balance and stumble away, pulling up his loincloth in a frenzied movement.

Rachel grabbed Mari with her free hand and grinned wickedly right into her face, without the slightest hint of shame or any attempt to cover herself.

"Okay, okay. Don't get so rattled. I was only teasing. You know as well as I do that he couldn't do anything!"

Mari, held in the girl's vicelike grip, could only shout out to the children, as she was bent across Rachel's body, "James, get the others home. I'll follow later."

At first he and the others were reluctant to go. They hovered, curious, perturbed, waiting for one of them to move.

"Go on, all of you. Uncle Eli'll tan the hide off all of us if he finds out. Go on, now!"

This speech had more effect. They were all in fear of Eli's rod, and their respect for Mariam overcame their natural instinct to obey the older girl. Only when the last child had sauntered, reluctantly, back towards the village, and was rounding the corner out of sight, did Rachel relax her grip and sit up, allowing her tunic to fall down over her hips.

"Poor Mari, you'll get a shock when you get married."

"I know what happens. It was wrong to tease the younger children like that."

"Oh, Mari, you are so serious. Relax and have some fun."

Mari did not know what to say for the moment.

"You shouldn't have to look after all those children all the time. They'll make an old woman of you. Old Eli'll marry you off soon and then you'll be a drudge for all your days. Have a fling, girl. Laugh and dance and flirt with the boys like others of your age." She tried to pull Mari down on top of her, but the younger girl struggled free and made as if to run away.

"Mari, Mari, don't go. I'm sorry, I didn't mean to hurt you!"

Mari hesitated at the pleading in the voice and turned to look at Rachel.

"Please, Mari, no-one talks to me. It's lonely here. Stay and chat."

Mariam was torn once more between her family's warnings and the obvious need of the girl. She thought a moment and then, deliberately, sat on the well parapet. Rachel relaxed and sat up, clasping her knees to her chest.

"When will you be married to Althaeus, Rachel?"

"I don't know. It doesn't really matter because I'm already living with him."

"Oh." Mari paused, thinking. "Doesn't that cause problems with your neighbours?"

"So what? They already shun me anyway. At least Althaeus talks to me."

"My family says I shouldn't be with you because of what you used to be. What do they mean?"

"That's a long story, kid. Do you really want to hear?"

Mari hesitated, conscience-stricken.

"Yes, I think I'd like to understand."

"I was a temple virgin at Astarte's Grove, near Sichem. Then an acolyte."

Mari looked puzzled.

"A priestess. A prostitute. Now do you understand?"

A long pause. "How?"

And then, "Why?"

"We were always a poor family. Then my father died and we had nothing. Mother struggled for a few weeks, but there were six of us and we were all hungry. I was the youngest and prettiest girl, so one day Mother took me to the chief priestess of Astarte on the outskirts of the city and sold me to the temple. I was six years old."

Mariam gestured towards Rachel, concern flickering across her face.

"How could your mother do that to you?"

"Necessity, Mariam, sheer necessity! What else could she do? None of my brothers were old enough to earn more than the odd coin from errands run. In any case I soon learned to survive. Of course, for a few days I was miserable, but they fed me well, and there were lots of other girls for company, so after a while I began to feel fortunate."

Rachel lifted herself onto the rim of the wall beside Mariam and brushed her tunic down over her lap.

"At first I was given duties about the temple – cleaning, polishing lamps, lighting torches. But I was allowed to roam freely, mix with the older girls and see what they did. So I accepted the duties of the temple girls as quite normal. When one of the special festivals was celebrated, I was excited too – I saw all the rich strangers coming to us, giving us large sums of money for the goddess; I saw the girls giggling and dancing and kissing and making love, and longed to be like them. The girls used to pet me and show me what the men did, and when I was eleven, the chief priestess took me in hand to instruct me in my duties for when I would be a full acolyte. It did not seem strange; after all, this is what I'd been seeing for over four years. I couldn't wait to start."

Rachel sighed loudly and readjusted her skirt.

"At the first big festival after I'd come of age, they sold my virginity to a rich merchant from Jerusalem. It was a big ceremony. I was garlanded and sat upon the goddess' lap and offerings were poured out on the ground in front of me. I was given a large goblet of wine to drink. Then, my head spinning, I was led into the betasselled tent, and before I knew what had happened, was stripped and impaled under the heavy stranger. Afterwards I was in shock, but I became used to it, and, of course, in time I knew no other way, could live only for that satisfaction. As I grew older, I was allowed to go outside the temple to bring back offerings to the priestess. Then, when I was fourteen, I was replaced and told to leave the temple. For a while I frequented the markets with another girl from the temple. Then I met Althaeus and he offered me a home here in Nazareth."

Rachel dried up and sat fiddling with the hem of her tunic, waiting for Mariam to say something. The afternoon sun seemed hotter than ever. The empty track to the village shimmered. Gnats and mosquitoes hovered over the water.

"Uncle Eli has never said anything about a goddess. Nor has anyone at the synagogue."

"Of course not; it's a different religion. Lots of people in Samaria worship the goddess. It's the old way. All round here are pious Jews. They all curse and shun us in public, but you should see them flocking around at festival time, pretending to come from Jerusalem or Tiberius."

"Are the festivals the same as ours?"

"Good grief, girl, no. They worship the goddess to make the fields fertile. And their animals and wives! They know that only us women can create new life. That is why they plant their seed in us – at least, that is their excuse! We worship all new life. All things that die come round in a new cycle of life. Virgins become priestesses, the mothers. We hold the power – that is what the priestess used to say to us."

"Do you really believe that?"

"I don't know what to believe any more. I don't think I care. I just want enough to eat, a bit of comfort and a man."

"Now you live here in Nazareth, haven't you heard about our god, how he cares for us and looks after us? Can't you ask him for help?"

"Believe in your Jewish god? How could I, child? Look after me? That's a joke! All I ever get from you Jews is abuse. Huh! Your average Jew couldn't love his own wife, let alone a Samaritan whore like me!"

"Rachel, that's not fair! Lots of Jewish families love and care for each other. Perhaps they aren't very good at caring for Gentiles."

"There's only one thing Jews want from Samaritan girls like me and that's to get between my legs."

"That's not true, Rachel, really it isn't."

"Oh no? Let me tell you this, my girl, even that precious father of yours with his cronies are no better than the others. I know where to find them, and they don't turn me away!"

Mariam turned white at the mention of her father and tensed, clenching her fist, and turning to look Rachel full in the face, said defiantly, "Rachel, that can't be true. He loves my mother and would not be unfaithful to her. What's more, it's against everything he's fighting for."

"You poor benighted fool! Don't you know anything about a man's needs? How often does he make love with your mother? Once, twice a year? Let me tell you this, Mari: I service him far more than she does!"

Mariam clasped her hands over her ears at the end of this outburst and, flushed, shouted out in a strangled voice, "No, Rachel, no, no, no! You're lying. You're trying to hurt me. It can't be true. Please God, don't let it be true!"

And Mari was running, as if in a panic, tears flowing, along the empty track, stumbling, banging her bare toes against the rocks, but she did not notice the pain, not that pain.

And half an hour later the tears were still flowing.

Mari was in the arms of her mother, blurting out what Rachel had told her, pleading to be told otherwise. And Anna, clutching her daughter to her bosom, nearly crushing her in her anguish, did not know what to say, how to console, repeating over and over, "Do not believe her, Mari. The girl is evil. She is a liar. Do not believe her."

Meanwhile at the well Rachel, too, was crying. Lonely miserable tears. She had thrown it all away again. Why did she have to say that to Mariam, just when the girl seemed friendly? And the girl sobbed, slumped across the well, knowing neither how to appeal to the goddess nor to the Jewish god.

Chapter 12

The Volunteer

THREE DAYS LATER MARI'S GRANDMOTHER, Salome, who had been unwell for some weeks, suddenly deteriorated and was dead within twenty-four hours.

The shocked household made the traditional preparations and the body was quickly laid to rest. Mari, first and beloved granddaughter, was touched at first hand, for the first time, by death.

After the funeral, when the family had gathered together, Eli held counsel with his son and sons-in-law. How was Joachim to be informed of his mother's death? Joshua undertook to discover his hiding place from sources in his home village. A messenger had to be found: someone who would arouse no suspicions, and slip unobtrusively through the rolling countryside.

Mariam overheard the conversation and became excited.

"I could go," she interrupted their masculine deliberations. "I could go, really I could. No-one would notice me. I'm often walking in the hills. No-one would take any notice of me. Please let me go!"

Eli was cross and rebuked her for listening to their conversation. He was about to propel her from the room, when Clopas stayed him.

"Just a minute, Father. Listen to what she is saying. I think it makes some sense. What she says is right."

There was debate, then argument, raised voices. Mariam was banished but Anna joined in and pleaded for her daughter's offer to be rejected. It was dangerous. There were wild animals. She was so vulnerable.

Mariam should go. She was old enough. The decision was final.

Mariam was fetched and told.

"I will go gladly," she said.

For days, while news was awaited, Mari was impatient. Her mother's worries were met by eager pleadings, foolhardy reassurances.

"God will be with me, Mother, just you see!"

Then news filtered back; Joachim was on Arbel, using the rock caves on the northern flank below the summit and overlooking the lake of Genneseret. A messenger would be expected.

CHAPTER 13

THE MESSENGER

*A*LONE, BUT NOT ALONE. CHILD, but not a child. Mari had been walking for a couple of hours and was now resting beside the sheep track beyond the adolescent stream. In the warmth of the spring sun, she had flung her blue shawl across the grass and was sprawled there beside her basket. She bit into a bunch of figs and lifted the waterskin carefully to her lips, making sure that she spilt none of the precious liquid. She peered beneath the cloth that separated the food prepared for her journey from what she was taking to her father: the ingredients for the Passover meal, brought together faithfully by her mother, barely enough to taste for each of Joachim's band but symbolic, crucial tokens. Keep them covered, she had been told. On no account reveal their presence; if challenged, they form your sustenance.

She ate and drank and lay back on the rough hillside, her limbs spread-eagled; staring at the pale hazy blue sky overhead, drowsy. The rough walk and food should have made her doze. But her mind was too active, too excited, and after a while she pushed herself up by the elbows, drew up her knees and stared unseeing into the distant empty vista.

She had been painstakingly briefed. Clopas and Eli had taken her through the route, time and time again, until she knew exactly what to expect. Each track, each tree, each stream, each rolling hill was an anticipated friend. Mari was not nervous of the journey. Her steps were eager, confident, strong.

She had been coached in what to say if challenged. To fetch her master's flocks; what nearby village to claim as home; whom she might meet and how to recognise potential danger; whom to greet and whom to flee.

She had been reminded how to fend for herself, to seek water when lost, to scare off scavenging beasts, what tracks to notice, what noises to be alert for.

Despite her outward languid movements, however, she was nervous and keyed up. Hers was not an easy mission. The first message weighed heavily on her. It was a burden to herself, for the death of her grandmother was as painful as it was unexpected. To Salome she was always special – those little intimacies, the extra squeeze or wink, the kind word whispered out of earshot of the others. Death was all around her in the village, of course, but it had not touched Mari so closely before. She had cried. On her mother's shoulder, mingling her own tears. On her own mattress in the corner when she thought no-one could catch her out. When talking to Rebecca, trying hard to be cheerful for her sake, then feeling the tears coming unwanted, blurring her vision. But now she had a grown-up task to undertake. She must break to a son the death of his mother. She hadn't thought of it in those terms, but she had been practising to herself how she would break the news, and still she wasn't sure. The problem nagged.

Was this what was whirling round her mind as she stared at the blue unfocused infinity? It was an undercurrent, maybe, ready to surface if her churning emotions could be calmed. She was going to see her father again. For nearly a year she had yearned to be in his arms; for six months his unfulfilled promise had sapped her confidence. She had tried to excuse and rationalise, imagining him to be in hiding perhaps in the mountains way beyond Genneseret, not a night's journey away in Arbel or Tabor. And she couldn't keep Rachel's taunts at bay. Could she, dare she ask him? She longed to hear him laugh with her, at her, mocking her credulity. But she feared his anger at her insolence; or even worse, embarrassed tentative attempts at reassurance that in her mind would but confirm the worst. Her twitching feet wanted to be clambering up the valley of Arbel. The rest of her was unready, finding doubts in each desperate opening gambit. She was praying. Seeking to mask her vulnerability.

Don't hide your eyes; the crunch is coming. We need to be sure that she can handle it. So watch; and long for her to survive. Indeed, if we stand up on the skyline, masked by the blinding sunlight streaming from behind us, we can just spot the minuscule form of Mari picking her precarious way into the dry gorge of Arbel. Be careful. Do not disturb a rock with your foot: you'll send it tumbling down the hillside, betraying your presence. That is a distinctly peculiar path for a young shepherd girl to take: it leads upwards above the cleft, across the scree and up to the labyrinth of tiny caves worn out of the sandstone just below the summit crags. Watch how carefully she treads, alert and dainty, checking her bearings, halting momentarily each time the narrow pathway forks or threatens to disappear in the rock-strewn barren hillside. We peer to see where she is going. No other soul disturbs the scene laid out before us, nor is there any beast, neither wild nor domestic. If she is expected, no-one has shown their hand.

It was breathless work scrambling up the hard uneven surface, baked by the relentless sun reflecting its hot rays in the dust. The winter winds had lost their power; only now at daybreak and in the evening did the powdered dirt stir in flurries. She was tired; her bare legs were aching, the hot stones burned her soles, stubbed against her toenails, breaking them. She sat on a lone rock, outpost of the next steep little climb, put her covered basket down beside her, and lifted her right foot onto her other thigh, massaging it ruefully. The last onset of nerves was now befalling her; she was putting off the final fateful moment when she would find them. And then, with a pang of dread, she wondered if it would be anticlimax, would no-one be here at all, the information false. What should she do then?

She stood perplexed among the strewn rocks before the pitted cliff face. The lake unfurled itself before her. She was astounded – she had never seen so much water before. The far horizon shimmered. Overhead, great black birds circled, wheeling on warm currents, drifting and hovering. She began to feel frightened, terrified of this desolate spot, overpowered. It had no intimacy that she could share; it excluded her. She felt shut out, ignored.

But she had been noticed. In the deep shadows contrasting with the glare on the sandstone cliff, there was a subtle movement. The figure stepped from dark to light, and paused. Mari turned her head, catching a glimpse of hope, then in one flurry, dropped her basket and sprinted across the jagged stones, flinging herself into the arms of the man who was moving swiftly to meet her, shouting, "Papa, Papa," laughing and crying at the same time. They clung to each other for a long time, then the man disengaged the girl, kissed her on the forehead and sent her back to retrieve the basket she had thrown down so unceremoniously in her rush to greet him. When she picked it up, the man looked over her shoulder and nodded approvingly as she showed him the basket's contents. Then, arms encircling each other, they picked their way over the larger rock debris that had fallen at the mouth of one of the cliff caves, into the darkness within, where flickering shadows revealed nightmarish huge silhouettes thrown against the cave wall.

"It's Mariam," the man called out to his friends within. "She's made it on her own, and brought the Passover meal with her, bless her!"

Men stumbled from the back of the cave out into the brightness of the entrance arch, and squinted at the slender brown girl now standing shyly before them. They saw her bright dark eyes moist with tears, a dirty smudge up her high cheekbone, dark flowing shoulder-length hair, held back from her forehead with a band of dingy cloth. They stared at her scratched and bruised thighs and calves, and the congealed blood around her toes. These stocky sun-hardened men, in various disarray of dress, caught unawares so to speak, were nonplussed how to cope with this slim wraith of womanhood before them; at least they were inhibited by the knowledge that she was their leader's daughter.

Grunts and heavy clumsy pressure from calloused hands acknowledged the child, and Joachim said, as if on behalf of them all, "You are very lucky to catch us, Mariam; it is only that we got word from Nain that a messenger was coming to us that caused us to postpone our intended plan to cross over into Gadara on the other side of the Jordan. We have to avoid Herod's patrols, which he sends out each year to screen the pilgrim caravans on their way to Jerusalem for the Festival, and they're said to be in these hills at this very moment."

Joachim sat on a ledge at the side of the cave and pulled Mari onto his lap.

"Show us what you've brought, Mari!"

And she uncovered the basket and placed the Passover food prepared by Anna onto the rock beside her father.

"How was your journey? Did you have any problems?"

Mari shook her head. A voice from the group discordantly said loudly, "Why did your family send an inexperienced girl like this? She could have led Herod's men straight to us."

"She's here, and she hasn't, so shut up, Jonas! The girl's tired and probably hungry, so find her some of that rabbit you caught. Have you got any water left?"

Mari nodded and pulled the waterskin from her basket.

"Good girl. Water is our worst problem here. We daren't go down to the lake. Tiberius is headquarters of the Romans here and they swarm regularly around the villages on the lakeside and to the city of Magdala also. We have to go many miles before we can find a safe spring. Thinking we were going to be away, we haven't replenished supplies and are running very low. Take a good swig, girl, but leave some for your return journey."

Then, suddenly, as if thinking of it for the first time, Joachim asked Mari urgently, "How are all the family: your mother and the girls and especially young Benjamin? And my mother and Eli's family, of course?"

Mari hesitated.

"They are well, Father, especially the children."

She was going to say something else, then she stumbled over her words. Joachim was immediately alerted; he picked up the signals that something was wrong.

She had hardly whispered to him, "Can we have a talk away from the others?" before she had been scooped up and led to the edge of the cave.

"What's the matter, Mari? Is someone ill?"

She looked at her father's worried face and buried her head in his chest.

"It's Grandma," she sobbed. "She's died and we buried her last week." She felt her father's arms tighten around her narrow waist, almost roughly so that he seemed to be crushing her. He said nothing at first, then in a sort of choking voice, he forced from his lips, "You mean my mother is dead, child? Salome, your grandmother?"

The girl nodded against his chest, crying out loud at his words.

"Oh Mariam, Mariam, my lovely daughter, why could I not be there? What sort of life is this for anyone?" And the man let his tears fall, touched by the vulnerability and grief of his daughter as much as by his own sense of loss, which had hardly registered yet.

He rocked her gently on his knee for a long time, so long, in fact, that one of the other members of the gang came to see if everything was all right. The word was passed round. The boss was upset. Leave him alone. Another time they might have encouraged him to get his daughter to dance for them, have some fun, show off her lithe good looks and be recipient of bawdy banter. As night fell, and the chill penetrated their flimsy clothing, someone stirred the embers into life and found more debris to pile on. The flickering flames illuminated in the shadows the contorted bulk of Joachim, huddled with his eldest girl, arms tightly around each other for mutual comfort.

Even as she lay there in his arms, Mariam wanted to frame another question. She felt awkward, nervous, oddly dirty and soiled, and became restless as a substitute for what she really needed to ask.

"What is it, lamb?" whispered Joachim in the ear of the tossing girl. "There's nothing more you have to tell me, is there?"

Mari lay there on the hard earth, in the crook of his arm, staring at the black ceiling of the cavern. She was summoning her nerve, screwing herself up to be able to express the words she would be unable to retract, once spoken.

"No," she muttered miserably, "I was just thinking about Granny. Dad, when are you going to be able to come home and live with us?"

"Don't ask such hard questions, pet. You know that both Herod and the Romans have put a price on my head. Perhaps one day the political situation will change. Perhaps the Messiah will arise and rid us of these foreign usurpers."

Mari lay tense in his arms. Joachim felt he had not yet said all she required of him.

"I'm going to have to rely on you, my lamb, for a good while yet. Look after the little ones for me. Comfort your mother. And if you should come across a good candidate for Messiah, encourage him to act quickly before I get too old," he added in a feeble attempt to cheer Mari up. "You're a brave girl, I know. Your mother told me what you do to support her last time I was home. You're of age now, child. I should be doing my duty, finding a grand husband for you instead of hiding away in this desolate place. You'll have to rely on Eli, I'm afraid. He is your next nearest relative. He's done much for you already. Trust him and his judgement and you'll be fine, just you see!"

"Father?"

"Yes, child?"

She felt his powerful arms tightening round her shivering form and nestled back, seeking the comfort of his embrace.

"Nothing, Dad. I'd better try to sleep."

"Yes, lamb. You've got a long walk home again tomorrow." He kissed her on the forehead and held her while she snuggled against him, blotting out the sight and sound of the other Zealots moving noisily around the cave.

Mariam was awake early, even before the first signs of dawn, but was aware that there was already movement amongst the men. Her father was no longer next to her and she sat up in some alarm, seeking her bearings. Suddenly a dark shape bent over her.

"It's all right, Mari, it's only me. Don't be alarmed."

He bent low enough to whisper to her.

"I've put a bit more food in your basket for your journey. I've also brought this." And he showed her something in his hands, which Mariam could not make out in the darkness. "Come over here to the fire. Look, girl, give this to your mother. Tell her to put it on one side in case anything ever happens to me."

Mari caught sight of the glint of coins in the fire – gold and silver – lying on a cloth in her father's hands.

"So much money, Father? Where did all that come from?"

"Don't you worry yourself about that, Mari. It won't be missed, I assure you. Make sure you give it to your mother, and not Uncle Eli – he may be too particular about gentile gold! You'd better not put it in your basket or you'll be robbed on your way home. I've got a cloth bag for it. Let me have your loincloth a moment. I'll stitch it inside so that it'll be well hidden."

Mari watched her father sewing clumsily in the light of the fire while she squatted, feeling the warmth of the flames on her bare thighs. Instinctively she put herself back against the wall of the cavern, with her father between herself and the other men. She felt very nervous of them, despite the fact that they were her father's friends and he risked his life with and for them. She was torn by the urge to be away from this eerie and dreadful cave, and her reluctance to sever herself from her father. Something inside her was reminding her that their parting, as always, could be for the last time. Only before she never fully appreciated what that could mean.

As she pulled the laden loincloth back up her legs and adjusted the cord of her tunic to hold the hard little bag securely against her waist, she realised she was unable to say anything to her father about Rachel's taunts. The time for that was last night in his arms; this morning was needed for practical things. She did not wish to risk his anger when she was bidding him farewell, perhaps for ever.

In the first light of dawn she was ready at the mouth of the cave. Five pairs of eyes were trained on her. Mari was very conscious of their gaze. They were making her feel very uncomfortable although she could not identify why. She was saved by her father, who hugged her, almost crushing her in the intensity of his embrace.

"Be careful, Mari. Try to avoid meeting anyone until you get back to Nazareth. Don't tell anyone where you've been – yes," he said, acknowledging her attempt to say something, "yes, I know what Eli and the others have told you to say. I hope you don't have to use it, but if you do, stick to that story: our lives could depend upon it. Farewell, my lamb. Thank your mother for the Passover food. Tell her that I will try to come to her when I can, but for the moment we are moving on, beyond the Jordan River."

A last wave. The others were already scrutinizing her from the darkness of the cave. Only Joachim stood visible a moment longer, then he too turned and darted back into the blackness. She suddenly felt terribly alone and frightened.

In the half-light she stumbled over the rocks in her path, descending all the time, sometimes slipping as the loose gravel shifted under her feet. She went carefully though, reining in her fear lest she bring attention to herself in this empty landscape. A red sun behind her was bathing the rocks in a ghostly glow, the outline of the hill was now silhouetted harshly against the pale blue sky, and she was still descending into the shadow of the valley.

Look down there! I could swear I saw movement.

We watch again. All seems grey down in the gorge, where the rays of the sun fail to penetrate. But there is movement. There... on the narrow track descending the flanks of Arbel. Let us continue parallel on the brooding mountain, slightly behind, and head steadily westwards. Who is out here at this hour of the morning amid the rocky wasteland?

There is no need to pin our quarry to earth immediately. We can observe and corner at our leisure. From this height, a frantic descent would be both hazardous and obvious, causing a tiresome search amidst the caves and boulders on the valley floor. As the gorge opens out into a wider valley, and the rays of the rising sun bathe everywhere in a brightening hue, we can see that the moving figure is a young girl, on her own – a shepherdess without her sheep, a defenceless lamb at the mercy of prowling wolves.

Mariam had just emerged from the shadows out into the sunshine and had loosened her shawl for the first time to feel the gentle warmth. She shuddered, as if tossing off the darkness behind her, and began to relax, no longer needing to watch every step she took. The path in front of her stretched, empty, to the horizon. The rolling hills on either side, although still barren, seemed friendlier, leading as she knew toward Kana village. She turned, to take a last glance at the more awesome view behind her, and stood rooted to the spot in shock. For scarcely more than a couple of hundred yards away, advancing rapidly towards her, were eight horsemen: soldiers, on the same path as herself.

At first she told herself that perhaps they were merely using the same track and she stood aside on the rough grass, in the hope that they would pass. But they were calling to her now. She could only wait for them; she had nowhere to flee. Soon she was surrounded. They were dressed in the uniforms of Herod's soldiers, but they were not Jews. She could see from their faces and hear from their conversation that they were Arabs, probably from Syria in the north. The girl stood stock still, petrified, as all but one man jumped to the ground and formed a circle around her. She tightened her grip on the basket and waited for someone to speak to her.

One of the soldiers stepped forward and seized the basket from her hands, giving it to another to examine, and roughly, in an accent she had difficulty in understanding, demanded of her, "What is your name and where are you going?"

"Mariam, sir." Then she hesitated. "To Kana." She would skirt Kana if she veered to the north, on her way to Nazareth. It was nearer and therefore more credible for her cover story than her home village.

"What are you doing on your own out here in the wilderness?"

"Looking for my uncle's flocks, sir."

"Do you think we are fools? We saw you coming down the track at the top of the gorge below Mount Arbel. Surely you didn't expect to find your animals up in that barren spot?"

Mariam swallowed hard with nervousness and struggled to find an answer.

"I thought I might be able to see further up there," came a hopeful tremulous reply.

"What's in your basket?"

"Just food for my journey."

The soldier looked over his shoulder to his colleague, who took the girl's basket. The latter nodded in confirmation. Mariam was relieved that she had not put Joachim's money there.

"Search the girl to see if her story stands up!"

The leader of the band made as if to lay his hands on the girl, but she wriggled out of his clutches in alarm, only to be grabbed from behind by one of the other soldiers in the circle. For a moment he held the squirming girl, grinning at her pathetic, useless efforts to free herself from his huge groping hands. Then he suddenly realised that he could feel something hard under the girl's clothing near her waist and he called out to the patrol captain, "The girl's got something hidden under her clothing!"

"Then strip her!"

A second soldier stepped forward and grasped the struggling girl by her wrist, twisting it painfully behind her back. As she shouted in surprise, the captain threw off her shawl and snatched at the cord tied loosely round her waist, unravelling it and whipping it off in one movement.

Mariam shrank from the man, clasping her free hand to her skirt, holding it tightly pressed against her thigh, calling out, "No, no, please sir, let me go in peace. Let me go home!"

Her pleading was ignored. Her other wrist was grabbed and yanked behind her. Her tunic was seized by the hem and pulled up over her head despite her flailing imprisoned arms, and thrown down at her feet. The two soldiers then tore her loincloth from her with the brutal sound of ripping cloth and she was pinioned, stark naked, by her wrists, although she was pummelling her captors with her heels, having no effect whatsoever.

Mariam began to shriek in fright and was told in obscene terms to desist. Then when she continued crying, she was slapped hard about her childish breasts, followed by a resounding blow to the cheek, which silenced her. As she watched helplessly, pink imprints of the blows forming upon her face and chest, the captain was ripping off the cloth purse from the torn undergarment and spilling out the contents into his open palm. He whistled in disbelief.

"Well, what treasure have we here, girlie? Don't tell me you've been selling some of that precious flock of yours!" He paused and glared at the cowering girl.

"Who gave this to you?"

"Answer me quickly!"

Still she said nothing, trying to look as though she did not understand him.

"Tell me who gave you this money or I'll give you to these dogs!"

She shook her head, weeping bitterly.

"Are you a virgin?"

Mari nodded her head.

"Well, you won't be much longer unless you answer my question truthfully. For the last time, who gave you this money?"

Mariam tried again, vainly, to free herself from her captors, and pleaded with the captain not to harm her. But she did not meet his demand. The soldier lost patience with her, grabbed her by the shoulder and flung her to the ground, so that she fell spread-eagled on her back. He pinioned her with his foot and looked expectantly at his sweaty troops.

"Who's going to be the first then?"

One of the grinning onlookers was just about to take up the challenge, when the remaining rider spurred his horse and cantered over to the group, towering over the squalid scene. The Roman soldier, garrisoned in Judea as one of Herod's military advisors, snapped his whip on the ground.

"Enough of this sport. Raping the girl will achieve no useful end, and will only provide further just cause for the populace to hate you and heap further complaints on Herod."

The Arab soldiers fell back a couple of paces, leaving Mariam lying vulnerable and scared in the dirt.

"Don't be so dumb! It's obvious what has occurred. The girl has paid a visit to bandits on Mount Arbel – we all watched her on its foothills. We already suspect that Zealots use caves near the summit. The money is part of the proceeds of their thieving and banditry." He suddenly fixed the prone girl with a penetrating look from high above her. "Isn't it?!"

The girl looked bemused at the silhouette above her peering down from his horse, but remained silent in confusion.

"See, she does not deny it! It is pointless to question her further; we know all we need to know. Go back quickly into Nain and pick up reinforcements, including scouts cognisant of the Arbel cave system, and root out the Zealot band before they can move on. Give me the purse!"

"What about your movements? When shall we meet up with you again?"

"I'll take the girl to her home, before she gets raped or murdered by some other cut-throat mob like you. I might pick up some useful intelligence at the same time. And I'll meet you in Nain to receive report of your successful operations. Now get moving before I decide to report you to the Jewish authorities."

The soldiers, sullen and slouching, deprived of their fun, seething at the arrogance of the foreign officer, obeyed slowly and with reluctance. The Roman remained on horseback, fixing them with his unsmiling stare until they had galloped off, then he dismounted, dropping down to the ground beside the trembling naked girl. He stared at her from close quarters as she covered herself with her hands as best she could – embarrassment replacing fear – made as if to touch her, then thought better of it and squatted next to her.

"You'd better get up, girl, and slip your tunic back on before I change my mind and rape you myself." Although he said this smiling, Mariam did not trust him and scurried up, brushing the dirt and dust from her buttocks, and picked up her inside-out tunic, struggling to restore it to a wearable garment. At length, under the silent gaze of her rescuer, she succeeded and pulled it over her head with difficulty, retrieving her waist-cord and shawl from the pathway, where they had been thrown. Her loincloth had been torn to shreds beyond repair, and after poking the remnants of the cloth hopelessly, she turned to look at the soldier.

"Thank you, sir. You saved my honour and perhaps my life. My family will be very grateful."

"I'm not so sure about that, my girl. Let's see, shall we? Put your foot into my spur here, that's it, and climb up here with me. I'll see you home safely."

Mariam found herself hauled into the saddle in front of the soldier, and pinioned in position against his coarse uniform, between his solid arms. She was stretched wide across the broad saddle, experiencing the warm leather on her bare flesh and could now feel his strong hand clasping her tightly just below her breasts. Her clothing suddenly seemed very flimsy and she was disturbed by his proximity, his strength, his very breathing, which was being transmitted tangibly to her own body. As they began to canter Mariam felt insecure and tried to shift her position to get a better grip. The man behind her, sensing her perilous hold, dropped a strong hand on her left thigh and pulled it down, trying to get her to clasp the horse's flanks with her knees. As she did so, her tunic rode up, pulled tight across her hips and she felt the breeze lifting her skirt. She felt helplessly and totally vulnerable.

She shut her eyes and, holding on for dear life, prayed under her breath with great urgency, "Lord God, protect me," again and again in rhythm with the bouncing horse. After a mile or so, the soldier said to the girl, "Try to relax and lean back against me. You'll find it a more secure position. You're too tense at the moment. Let go and trust me. I won't let you fall."

Mariam shut her eyes and tried to obey the Roman. Despite her exposed position, she began to let herself adjust to the movement of the horse and let her body go limp. She knew she had sought her God's protection and consciously sought to make this leap of trust; she was struggling to let her mind control her body.

For a while she fastened her thoughts, behind her closed eyes, to the thudding beat of the cantering horse's hooves, whilst she let herself be cocooned within the arms of her strange rescuer. Then she was aware that they would shortly be crossing the Magdala–Samaria highway before entering the village of Kana, and her tensions mounted again as she realised the dangers inherent in the lie she had told the soldiers. At first, realising the increasing probability of being observed, Mariam tried to retrieve her modesty by pulling vainly at the hem of her tunic, and the soldier behind her, realising the fear behind her precarious movements, said gently to her, "We can slow down a bit now. We are nearly in your village. Lift your leg over here so that you are riding sidesaddle, and put an arm around my waist, you'll feel a bit more comfortable like that."

Mariam gratefully clambered into his arms and wondered what she would do now. She ought, she felt, to say something soon before they were riding into the village itself, but she didn't want to disturb her increasing trust in this Roman officer.

"Sir, I know you're in a hurry to meet up with your soldiers again. Drop me here and I can walk home easily."

"There is no need, girl. Another few minutes will make no difference to me, and I want to be assured by your parents that you have no complaint against us and to warn them not to let you undertake such dangerous lone journeys again."

Mariam became a little panicky.

"Sir, I really wouldn't bother. My parents will probably be in the fields and my home will be empty."

"Well, I'll deliver you to your neighbours, then."

She hesitated, and in desperation, whispered unconvincingly, "They might not be at home either."

The man halted the horse. He twisted the girl so that she was forced to look up into his face. He perceived her confusion and, for a moment, allowed no respite. Then, his hand under her chin, tilting her face to look into his own, he seemed to lose his temper with her. "Little liar, you thought you'd trick the Roman army, did you?!" He yanked her head back so far that she was cowering away from him, nearly prostrate. "Now tell me where you do come from, before I do you some mischief! And if it's the opposite direction to which we've come, I'll flay your hide until you'll wish I'd left you to the antics of those Syrian mercenaries."

"Sir, please, you're hurting my back. I'm falling."

"No, you're not, girl, I'm still holding you. And I want an answer first."

"I wasn't really lying, sir. Kana is on the way to my home. I live in Nazareth."

"You'd better not be lying this time! Say it again!"

"I live in Nazareth, sir."

The soldier, in angry silence, swung the maiden across the horse's back, pushing her thighs apart and holding her roughly round her waist. Then he turned the horse onto the roadway towards the west, and set off at a gallop. Mariam, petrified, abandoned all thought of modesty, and just concentrated on staying on the horse. From time to time they passed little knots of pilgrims making their belated way towards Jerusalem for the Passover, but before they could turn and stare at the exotic sight of the Roman soldier at full speed appearing to be abducting a near-naked Jewish girl, they were gone, out of sight.

As they approached Nazareth, the Roman allowed the horse to slacken its pace, and Mariam plucked up courage to ask if she could ride sidesaddle into her village. The man did not answer her. When she attempted to wriggle her way into that position, she felt his arm pinioning her thigh, preventing her. She felt his anger at being duped and whispered contritely, "I'm sorry, sir, I was so frightened. I just said the first place that came into my head."

The soldier still said nothing.

"And I'm very grateful, really I am. Without you I would have been raped and disgraced in the eyes of my people."

The soldier still said nothing, but acknowledged the thanks with a little squeeze of her waist. He did not let her change position though.

They were entering the village now, and the soldier had slowed his horse to a sedate walk. People stared at them, then ran back into their houses, and others emerged, pointing at Mariam and her guardian. The Roman seemed to be contriving maximum publicity to their entry. Mari was flushed and embarrassed at such public exposure, and tried to hide back in his arms, but felt herself pushed forward, humiliated in the eyes of her neighbours and acquaintances.

"Where is your father's house?" were the first words the Roman had addressed to Mariam since the Kana crossroads, and she guided him to Eli's home, explaining that she, her mother and the other children lived under his protection.

The courtyard gate was open. Miriam, Anna and the children were there; all came running to the gate when they heard the excitement and saw the horse coming up the narrow street. They stared at Mari, open-mouthed in shock. Then Miriam recovered first and dashed into Eli's house, calling for him urgently. Anna attempted to gather her daughter in her arms, but was repulsed by the soldier brusquely, who demanded,

"I want the head of the household. I will only release this girl into his custody."

Anna shrank back in dismay, asking plaintively, "What has happened, Mari? What has happened to you?"

Mari sensed from her captor that she was to remain silent.

The little group waited in tension in the stifling oppressive courtyard, the only movements coming from the scavenging chickens, and the angry tossing of the horse's head, irritated by the flies. The stillness was suddenly broken by Eli, sweeping into the arena from his doorway, still adjusting his white robes, whilst Miriam scurried behind him. Eli glared up at the mounted Roman officer, took in the sight of the exposed and frightened girl in his grasp, and demanded indignantly, "Let that girl down, sir! And what atrocity have you inflicted on her?"

The Roman waited for Eli's pomp to be deflated, then calmly said, "I have come to restore this young girl to her family. Are you Eli, head of this household?"

"Yes, I am."

"My patrol found her wandering in the hills below Mount Arbel. Can you explain why she would be so far from home?"

"She was looking after my flocks there."

"What, do you graze your sheep so far from home, and in the barren gorge of Arbel itself?"

"She should not have been there. What were you doing, girl? Had you lost one of my lambs, or had you a tryst with some lusting shepherd boy? If there's any evidence of the latter, I'll whip your hide until you scream for mercy."

"I think neither, Jew. We took from her a purse with a considerable sum of money in it. It is my belief that you sent her to make contact with Zealots."

"That is nonsense, officer. If that is what she told you, the girl has lied. She must have found the money or had some assignation of which we know nothing."

"I find that difficult to believe. However, it doesn't really matter. I have despatched my platoon to search the mountains and wipe out or capture any bandits or Zealots found hiding there. Their bodies will be returned to you, either on a bier or on the gallows. Any further sign of trouble, or support, from you, and the whole village will be severely punished. Is that clear?"

Eli, blanching, nodded in acknowledgement and said nothing.

"Now I suggest you take this girl back into your home before anything worse befalls her. Despite all appearances she has not been harmed. On the contrary, my intervention prevented her multiple rape." And he lifted Mariam by her waist with both arms and slid her down the flanks of the horse, rucking up her tunic as she dropped. Anna rushed forward to pull down her daughter's shift and enveloped her in her arms, hurrying her unceremoniously into her own room. The Roman soldier, without a further word, swung his steed around and galloped out of the courtyard in a cloud of dust, causing one of the smaller children looking on to scream in fright. Miriam gathered the remaining children and shut them inside her own home, at least for a while, until Anna and Mari had recovered a little from their shock.

And Eli stood, isolated, amid his animals, abandoned.

At first he seemed bemused by the whole affair. Then he took himself in hand and rapped sharply on Anna's door. After a few moments, during which Eli drummed impatiently on the hard earth with his cane, the door opened and Anna's face peered at her cousin. She looked quizzically at him. She had obviously just been crying.

Taken a little aback at Anna's tears, Eli hesitated for a moment, then remembering his purpose, ordered, "As soon as you've calmed the child down sufficiently to get an intelligible account out of her, bring her over into my rooms. We must find out the damage done as fast as possible. And don't let her be long. You mollycoddle the girl."

Without waiting for Anna's answer, he turned on his heels, assuming her compliance, and the door closed behind him with a loudness that might have been intentional, or might just have been due to Anna's trembling lack of control.

Half an hour later, the same door creaked open and Anna, shielding her daughter under her cloak, walked her swiftly across the courtyard and tapped quietly on Eli's door. They heard his voice bellowing at them from within, and slipped inside, out of view.

Eli was seated at a table on which he had several loose scrolls. He looked up and left both women standing. Ignoring Anna, he directed his gaze at the girl, who was peering nervously at him from beneath her mother's garment. For a long time he looked at her in total silence, until she thought he was waiting for her to say something. Mari was just about to clear her throat and make a first statement, when Eli cut across her, "Well, Mariam, this is a fine mess you've got us all into!"

Mari looked at him very uncomfortably. She did not know if he was finished yet.

"Before we go any further, you'd better tell me, slowly, leaving nothing out, exactly what has happened since you left this house yesterday. Don't hurry, don't skip over anything: it may be important."

Mariam, slowly, quietly at first, then with increasing confidence, told her story. Eli made her go over the explanation of the money that Joachim hid in her loincloth three times, and muttered under his breath at the folly of Anna's husband. Mariam told of her detention and near rape and of the role the Roman soldier played.

She was too eloquent here in the soldier's defence. Pushed by Eli, who was trying to get her to admit evidence that she was either technically raped, or at least indecently assaulted by the soldiers; now that he was no longer a threat to her, Mari described the Roman's chivalrous treatment of her.

Eli became exasperated. He did not believe any virtue resided in a gentile, let alone one of the occupying army's officers, and twisted all she said to demonstrate that she had been tricked into admitting damaging statements that would condemn not only her father and his group, but also Eli, his family and others in the village.

"The Romans are scoundrels, the lot of them: no morals, no respect. Look at the way they've treated our culture everywhere: in Sepphoris, in Jerusalem, in that abomination on the lakeside at Tiberius. Stadia, sports, gambling, nudity, immorality. Respect for you, indeed! Did he touch you?"

"Well, of course he did, Uncle. He had to pick me up and hold me on his horse. If he hadn't have touched me, I'd have fallen off."

"And he saw you naked?"

"Yes. The soldiers stripped me. He helped me up and fetched my tunic so that I could put it back on."

"And you rode right in front of him, with virtually nothing on, and he handled you all the time?"

"Uncle, it wasn't like that. What else could he do?"

"Quiet, girl; it's unseemly to argue so. To be handled in such ways by gentiles is contrary to all our practice. You are unclean, girl. When you get back to your own room you will take off and destroy all the clothes that those gentile soldiers contaminated. Your mother will rip them to shreds and bury them, and you'll be confined to your home for three days until you've been purified."

Anna interjected, agitated. "But Eli, those clothes are all the girl has. As it is, I have to find her a new loincloth, quickly. There is no way I can make her another tunic or shawl so soon, even if I had the cloth."

"Then you'd better wash them thoroughly instead. Three times to make sure they're undefiled. The girl will have to remain inside her room anyway, so it doesn't matter that she'll have nothing to wear."

Mari and Anna thought he was going to dismiss them. But Eli hadn't finished yet.

"Now, about the more serious aspect of the affair. Those soldiers will be back. The whole village will be in jeopardy, just because of the foolishness of your husband and the incompetence and laxity of your daughter. I will not have so many innocent people put under such threats. If the soldiers do return, wreaking vengeance, you and Mariam will sacrifice yourselves, saying that you and you alone were in contact with and supporting your rebellious husband and that you sent your daughter to avoid other members of the family finding out. There are scriptural precedents for such voluntary surrender, to serve a higher law: notably Lot's proffering of his daughters to protect his guests. And they were innocent of any provocation! If the troops find and kill your husband, perhaps the village will be spared. If they fail, they'll take it out on all of us. If I were in your shoes, I don't know for what my prayers would be."

"Eli, there is really no need to scare the girl like this. Wait and see what happens; if my husband escapes, how can we help them further? We have no idea what their plans are."

"I'm just warning you so it comes as no surprise to you, that's all. And do not, girl, think that this is the end of the matter. Before deciding what further action to take concerning your failure and your behaviour with the soldiers, especially the Roman captain, I wish to await the outcome. When you are purified, we shall consider further what penance you need to pay. Now go, and don't let me see you in public until the time I have stipulated!"

Back in her own home, Mari broke down in torrents of tears.

"It's so unfair, Mother; I couldn't do anything about it, could I? What should I have done differently? And he's accusing me of putting Father at risk; I'm scared of that. What will happen, Mum? What will happen to all of us?"

"Shush, my love. I do not blame you, though we may suffer from this visit. I know Eli is harsh towards us, but despite his words, when it comes down to it, he has always supported us. And I think he's angry because the Roman was kind to you. It would have fitted his prejudices better if they had all raped you: then he would have had pity and been shifting heaven and earth to avenge you, and see you decently married to stave off disgrace. Now, love, we'd better do what he said. Take this dirty old tunic off and I'll do the first wash immediately. I'll find you something to eat, then you can wrap yourself up in that old blanket and try to sleep on my mattress, while I get the children back from Miriam and give them their evening meal. And try not to tell them too much about your ordeal, Mari. They won't understand; it'll only upset them unnecessarily."

"Of course not, Mother. But after the meal they can come and cuddle me and tell me a story for a change."

Mari was exhausted. Despite her request, despite the noise of cooking and housework, despite clamorous calls and the bustle of small children, Mari slept, burying herself deep beneath the dirty old blanket that Anna had thrown over the naked girl. The children were put to bed, disappointed that their sister was asleep, and that they couldn't share her adventure. Anna climbed in beside Mari, and threw a protective arm around her daughter. She stirred a little, and then her breathing came easily once more. Only the lamps flickered on the wall, overshadowing a surface peacefulness.

In the middle of the night Mari suddenly sat up in terror, flinging the blanket from herself. She cried out, involuntarily, and the disturbed Anna sat up too, and shook the girl awake, saying, "Mari, Mari, it's all right. It's only me, your mother. You're at home, in bed. What were you dreaming of, girl?"

Mariam blinked hard at the older woman, seeming not to be aware yet of her surroundings, then said thickly, "There was this angel, and when I went up to him, I thought he had no face; then I saw that it was black, but he had no eyes, only sockets. He took a sword from his side and dipped it in a pool of liquid, then made me lick the tip of the blade and it was horrible, bitter and foul, then I saw that the blade was red with blood, it was dripping from my mouth..."

"Mari, my child, it was only a dream. Don't disturb yourself so much. Calm down. Shush..."

"But, Mother, what does it mean? Why was it so awful?"

"You've had an unpleasant experience, Mari; it is still disturbing you when you are asleep. Don't worry; it isn't real. Go to sleep again." And she laid the drowsy girl back on the mattress and watched her until she was breathing quietly and rhythmically, before she too relaxed.

Mari's facial muscles began to twitch, and her limbs became agitated once more. But her mother had gone back to sleep, and no mortal noticed. Mari was flying now, her robe replaced by flapping wings. She was looking down, way down. She could see a pool of still, black water. Now she was riding bareback on a charging horse snorting fire, bucking and bouncing so hard that she had to fling herself round its neck, hanging on to its mane to save herself from falling. They entered the water, throwing spray wildly in all directions. It splashed cold against her bare skin. Then she saw it was not water but flecks of blood; she was riding a huge sword, which was cutting her. The blood was flowing. She could not staunch it. She was fainting, she was going to swoon, she was becoming dizzy. She could hear someone calling to her far away, "Mari, Mari..." She woke, her mother's arms clamped tightly around her.

"Mari, Mari, my child, do not struggle so. I have got you. Do not be afraid!"

CHAPTER 14

THE DELIVERY

*T*HERE WAS A COMMOTION IN the street. At the hour of the morning when it was customary for flocks of sheep or other domestic beasts to be led out into the fields, the scale and type of noise was unusual. There were animals involved, but they sounded heavier and there was a human hubbub. Almost simultaneously all doors onto the courtyard opened; Eli, Clopas and Anna peering out in curiosity and some alarm. Anna was looking tired from her disturbed night.

The procession, or whatever it was, had entered the next street and soon horses could be already heard and soldiers glimpsed from the rooftops. Eli reacted at once with Clopas.

"Barricade the gate, Clopas, and I'll tell your family to hide as best they can. Anna, quickly, bring Benjamin and your two youngest girls over to Miriam; let her look after them. If it's what I think it is, it's best that only you and Mariam can be found in your house."

But even while bewildered children were being hauled, protesting, across the courtyard and bundled into the other house, there was a thunderous knocking on the gatepost, so loud that it echoed through the village. Eli sent Clopas to protect his own family, and then, taking his time, pulled back the wooden bolts, allowing the gate to swing open. He stood squarely in the gap, obstructing entry, and found himself looking directly into the cold eyes of the Roman captain of yesterday.

"I promised you that I'd be back. I have a delivery for you."

The captain turned and barked an order to the Syrian troops accompanying him, and a packhorse was drawn forward, level with Eli's court. Three men lined up and, one by one, manhandled heavy loads wrapped and tied in cloth from across the horse's back, each soldier swinging the load over his own shoulder. They marched past Eli, brushing him aside, and dropped their loads unceremoniously in the middle of the courtyard. Then they turned about and marched back through the gate.

"On this occasion the village can think itself lucky that I have ordered no further action. Any further complaint and I shall despatch a raiding party to the town, to execute an exemplary number of males and bind women and children into slavery, for shipment to Rome. That goes for other villages in the neighbourhood. I trust I can rely on you to ensure that this warning is passed on."

Eli had said absolutely nothing. Firstly, he could not think what to say. Secondly, he had been given no opportunity to say anything. And finally, even a man of Eli's insensitivity could feel when it was expedient to offer no argument or complaint. Mechanically he bolted the door after the departing visitors, thus depriving curious onlookers who had followed the soldiers of the climax of the drama. Then he turned to face the bundles in the open. Clopas was emerging from the shadows, but it was Anna who dominated the scene. On her knees, tearing at the knots in the cloth, she was beside herself. So frenzied was she, that she was making it almost impossible to unravel the cords, and before Eli could stop her, she was tearing at the cloth with superhuman strength. She ripped the material, then seized it in both hands and tore it apart until an arm flopped out, causing Anna to scream in horror. A further tearing sound and she pulled back the whole shroud, revealing the battered and blood-bespattered body of a weather-hardened man dressed in a torn and filthy tunic. Eli looked over Anna's shoulder and peered down at the bearded face in puzzlement. He did not know the corpse. He had not the remotest idea who he was. He looked at Anna. She shook her head, trembling uncontrollably.

Clopas joined them, glanced at the dead man they had uncovered and shook his head as well. Eli held Anna back while Clopas moved to the second bundle and began painstakingly and methodically to untie the restraining ropes. Anna was groaning and keening, and from the narrow window in her house, the wide and frightened eyes of Mariam could be glimpsed, staring from the blanket that enshrouded her. At length Clopas was able to part the cloth and at once he jerked back with a grunt of shock.

"Eli, come quickly!"

He left Anna, still kneeling beside the first body, and, with just one glance, recognised the distorted face of Joachim. The hair and beard were matted with blood; the limbs were stiff and cold. He was dead, long dead. Eli turned and tried to stop Anna approaching, but he was too late and with a heart-rending howl of rage and anguish she threw herself on her husband's body and bruised her head on his breast, sobbing so loudly that there was little need to tell neighbours what had happened.

Clopas and Eli were still trying to pull Anna upright, when Eli, hearing the door move behind him, suddenly cried out, "Stop the child coming, Clopas. Miriam, she must not come out!"

It was too late. She had shed the blanket in her haste and in three bounds she had flung her naked slender frame onto her father's body, joining her voice of pain to that of her mother. Shocked, Clopas gathered Anna's shawl and tried to drape it over the shaking child, then Eli bent and gathered up the blanket and flung it over Mariam, lifting her bodily into his arms. The girl struggled and kicked inside the cover, but

Eli carried the protesting child and dumped her inside the doorway, slamming it shut behind him, and fastening the outside latch. The girl thumped in vain on the door, and then she appeared at the window, in floods of tears, pleading to be let out.

"Clopas, get Miriam to go to Mari and restrain her. You stay with the younger children while I discover the identity of the third body."

And to the background of wailing women, Eli quickly unwrapped the third corpse and looked baffled at the unknown face.

Gradually, a parody of order was restored. Help from neighbours was forthcoming once Eli opened their private grief to onlookers, and the bodies of the two unknown Zealots were carried down to the synagogue for holding in one of the antechambers, while messengers were despatched to Nain, Mirza and villages to the north to pass on the news and seek identity of the dead.

When Anna was prised away from her lifeless husband, his body was carried to what used to be his mother's room until her recent death. Miriam helped the grieving Anna back into her own home, and reunited her with her desolate daughter, who was lying face down on the mattress, naked, abandoned, crying pitifully, totally oblivious to all movement around her.

It was a long day. More messengers flew to and fro. Eli's families were summoned for the morrow. Neighbouring women attended the body, cleaning it up and washing it to make it presentable for the funeral preparations. Eli was purifying himself after his enforced handling of Mari, whom he had declared unclean, and he sent word to Anna to do likewise. Miriam fetched Anna to break the news to Salome, Rebecca and little Benjamin, although the death of his father meant almost nothing to him as he could only just remember seeing him a couple of times in his life.

"Don't hurry back," said Miriam in a whisper. "Stay as long as the children need you. I'll watch over Mariam here, Eli has engaged plenty of help to prepare for the funeral guests, and he'll not need me."

Miriam looked at the huddled girl lying beneath the blanket in the corner of the room. She would have liked, instinctively, to lift the hem, touch her, comfort her, hug her; but her father-in-law had warned her that Mari was defiled and could not be touched for three days. She moved over to the mattress and reclined down beside it, propping herself up with the palm of her right hand.

"Mari," she said softly, "Mari, it is me. I've come to be with you while your mother spends time with the other children."

Mariam opened her eyes and sat up, letting the blanket slip to her waist, and held out her slender arms, waiting to be hugged.

"Mari, I'm sorry, I cannot touch you until you have been purified. They won't let me," she added in feeble excuse.

"Oh, I didn't realise. Does that mean that even Mother mustn't touch me?"

"Yes, I'm afraid it does. Nor must she touch any of your garments."

"She's got to touch my clothes, because Uncle Eli told her to wash them. And she didn't try to stop me touching her."

"I shouldn't tell anyone else. What your mother does is her own affair. It seems very hard to me, just because the foreign soldiers abused you. Did they hurt you?"

"Not really. I was more frightened of what they were going to do. And the Roman captain stopped them in time."

There was a long painful pause. Mari's eyes filled with tears, which began to trickle down her cheeks. She wiped the back of her hand across her face and rubbed her reddened lids and puffy flesh.

"It's all my fault, isn't it? If I hadn't gone to Mount Arbel, Father would not be dead! I should have been more careful, looked around and hidden in the gorge, but I just didn't think. It seemed so early and so quiet and I was anxious to be home. The path was so stony. I had to watch where I was walking. I didn't think of looking up…"

Her voice trailed off into choking sobs. Miriam looked round guiltily and seeing no-one watching, slipped an arm round the bare shoulders of the girl and squeezed her in sympathy.

"Don't blame yourself, Mari. They shouldn't have sent you on such a risky business."

"I do blame myself though. The worst is looking into Mother's eyes, seeing her crying. I can't bear it. I loved my father but I didn't see him very often; the worst was being afraid of what might happen. Now they can't do anything more. I will get through it. But every time I look at Mum I want to burst into tears because of what I've done to her. She won't say she blames me, but when I see her watching me, I can't help but wonder what she's really thinking."

"Your mother is a kind woman, Mari; she'll bear you no grudge. It's not in her nature. And she knows in her heart of hearts that it was not your fault. You know, I think she feels as guilty as you."

"Why, Miriam?"

"Because she let you go. She knew the risks you were running, but because the men felt it best and decided so, she went along with it. She feels she should have been stronger, spoken up more."

"But I pleaded to go."

"Yes. That didn't make it any easier for her."

There was another long pregnant silence. Miriam withdrew her arm and brushed it as if to remove physical dust and dirt.

"What is happening now, Miriam?"

"What, now, at this minute?"

"No, I mean Father's funeral and so on."

"Eli's sent for everyone to come tomorrow. There are women in Salome's house laying out your father's body, cleaning and dressing him. Most of the family will come in the morning and stay on after the funeral, having the evening meal together and not going home until the next day."

"Will they let me go to the funeral?"

"I really don't know, Mari. Perhaps as a special case Uncle Eli will arrange for you to be purified in time. Wouldn't it be better for you if you left it to the others? You'll only be upset."

"I want to be there."

"You'll have to wait and see. Would you like me to ask Eli for you?"

"Would you, Miriam? I don't want to be left here on my own."

"By the way, Mari, haven't you anything to put on? I know your mother has gone to wash your tunic, but surely you've something else?"

"No, I haven't actually."

"Poor you! If you like, you can wear an old tunic of mine. It'll be a bit big for you, but it's better than nothing."

"Are you sure, Miriam? Won't giving it to me make it defiled as well?"

"It doesn't matter. I don't need it at the moment. Tell your mother to wash it when you've finished with it."

"Thanks, Miriam. I do feel very self-conscious like this and I've been trying to avoid the children, so as not to have to explain things to them." She paused a moment, suddenly thinking of something else. "Oh, I suppose I won't be allowed to touch the children."

"That's all right. It doesn't matter for children under twelve. There'd be real problems if it did matter, because all women are unclean at certain times of the month, as you must know."

"Yes, I suppose so. I didn't know if this was different."

"I don't see why, Mari. Ah, your mother's coming back. I'll look out that old tunic and bring it over in a minute. Bye for now. See you."

Mari stayed sitting up, looking at her mother expectantly. Anna looked so worn that Mariam felt the pain clutching at her stomach.

"Mum, are they all right? Are they upset?"

"Oh, Mari, of course they are. But I don't think they've really taken in what has happened. Your father has not seen much of them since they've been old enough to know and remember him."

"When are they coming home?"

"Soon, Mari, when we've sorted ourselves out a bit. I'll have to see if I can find something to make up for you to wear."

"That's cared for. Miriam has promised me an old tunic of hers."

"That's kind of her," said Anna with relief, for she was really too exhausted and depressed to feel capable of anything practical. Anna sat on the mattress beside Mari and suddenly gave her an enormous hug.

"Mum, are you allowed to touch me at the moment?"

"Oh, Mari, how could I think of letting that silly rule affect us at the moment? I need you, love, just as much as you need me. Let me worry about dealing with Uncle Eli. Try not to let on though, eh?" Anna attempted a wan smile.

"Mother?"

"Yes, my child?"

"Do you blame me for what has happened?"

"Mari, I..."   Anna could go no further, but her voice cracked and she was crying, throwing her arms around Mari's neck and sobbing on her daughter's shoulder. When at length she pulled herself together, she added, "I'm sorry, Mari. I must think more of you and less about myself. How could I blame you, love? You did your best. It was as much my fault, Joachim's fault, even Uncle Eli's and Clopas' fault for sending you. Above all else, it is the fault of all those armies and priests and politicians who have created this misery through war and greed."

"Father talked about the Messiah, who will come and rescue us from all our problems. Do you really think that God will help us soon?"

"I don't know, Mari. How could I know? I thought that God would protect Joachim, but he didn't. More and more rumours seem to spring up these days that a Messiah has been found, then all is anticlimax; the claimant turns out to be a fraud or the Romans arrest and execute him."

"When I was frightened and thought I was going to be raped, I prayed to God and asked him to protect me; then the Roman soldier intervened. At the time it seemed like a miracle. Only Uncle Eli says God cannot use a gentile soldier and that I am being foolish."

Anna looked distant, and said something soothing and non-committal.

"I'm sorry, Mother. I did not mean to be so selfish and be pleased for my own protection. I should have prayed harder for God to protect Father, only I didn't think..."

And the two women were once more entwined, seeking mutual comfort for their heavy tears.

The night had come and gone. The children were brought back by Miriam, who, true to her word, left the old tunic behind for Mari. Salome and Rebecca were sombre, solemn, treating Mari with reserve and bewilderment, as if she was seriously ill. Only Benjamin was his normal self, and wanted a few minutes tumbling with Mari, which she forced herself to grant. During the sleepless night, there was much to-ing and fro-ing. When the women had finished preparing the corpse, they left noisily. A steady stream of neighbours called on Eli and a number of men remained in the courtyard, talking earnestly in animated voices, the intonation but not the meaning of which carried to Mari's ears, causing her to strain to interpret, in nervous curiosity, but to no avail. Strangers arrived in the middle of the night and took away the other two dead men. Then, when the movement died down, Mariam found that her tension and overactive brain did not allow her exhausted body any rest. She tossed and turned, awoke after a fitful doze and heard her mother sobbing in the darkness. The two of them spent some time together in mutual support and finally, around four in the morning, slipped off into a light slumber, only to be awoken within a couple of hours by the arrival of the first travellers, from Afula in the south.

As the sun arose, the bustle in the courtyard became frenetic, and wave after wave of visitors and relatives poured in from neighbouring towns and villages. Anna, veil pulled low in mourning, greeted her kinsfolk as was her duty and all the time Mari watched at a distance through the window slit, whilst busying herself with the needs of her younger sisters and brother. Occasionally one of the closer relatives would ask to see the children. Then Anna came for the little ones and took them out into the blinding sunlight, leaving Mariam alone in the darkness.

She had asked again if she might attend the funeral. But the uncompromising answer was received: she should remain indoors and out of sight, busying herself caring for the children, so that Anna might be available to carry out her duties without hindrance.

In the late morning the crowd began to congregate in the courtyard: a small group of musicians and other women whom Mari recognised as the wailers from her grandmother's funeral. A sudden cacophony of noise filled the village and the small children all ran to the open door, while Mari peered, invisible, through the tiny window aperture. Slowly and with great pomp, the bier was being carried from its resting place, positioned at the head of the procession, followed by Mari's mother, then Uncle Eli, Clopas and Eli's sons-in-law.

Mari stood transfixed, ignoring the crowd of mourners, staring at her father's body wrapped in clean shining linen, his hands and feet bound. She saw his face, unnatural. His eyes were pressed closed, his bearded chin was masked by a cloth tied round his jaw, his lips were tight and bloodless. And she watched grimly as he was obscured by blurred forms in the mist before her eyes, unseeing until the last form shuffled out of the gate, leaving it gaping so she could see the procession swaying noisily down the narrow street towards the synagogue and burial area beyond. All the village seemed to have gone. Only a few dogs still barked, a donkey brayed, a few toddlers played in the gutter. Mari felt bereft and tears began again to course down her face.

As peace descended on the arc of her vision, she prayed aloud, "Lord God, have mercy on me. Forgive me for any way I may have sinned in your sight. And help my father's dream come true. Amen."

She felt the children nestling round her. Rebecca and Benjamin were each clasping a thigh and rubbing themselves against the warmth of her body for their comfort. Salome alone seemed to notice Mari's tears.

"Mari, I love you. Don't ever leave us, will you!"

CHAPTER 15

THE CONSEQUENCES

*A*FTER THE FUNERAL MANY OF the mourners dispersed but Eli's own family gathered for a meal that women from the village had prepared for them. At the end all the women returned to their homes or lodgings to put their children to bed, and prepare themselves, while the men stayed behind to discuss a number of issues that Eli wanted to settle with his kinsmen. Only Anna was required to remain, as their talk would concern her state of widowhood and responsibility for her future, as well as for Mariam and her siblings. Anna returned briefly to ask Mari to settle the children and not to wait up herself, as it was clear that her long day at Mount Arbel, her grief and sleepless night had now taken a heavy toll.

Mari was vaguely aware of Anna's return. It seemed well into the middle of the night, but she no more than opened half an eye as her mother slipped past her, and promptly turned over and fell immediately into a deep sleep.

The next morning Mari woke up to find that the household had already been humming for some time. Rebecca, Salome and Benjamin had dressed and were off to join Miriam's three for breakfast, and play under their aunt's supervision. Anna was sitting on the end of the mattress, gently shaking Mari by the shoulder and saying, "Mari, Mari, wake up, love, there are things I have to tell you before it is too late. Mari, can you hear me? Are you awake yet?"

The girl shook herself from her heavy sleep, rubbed her eyes, and smiled at Anna's concerned face. Then she propped herself up on one elbow and waited for what her mother had to say.

"Mari, listen carefully. I've got a number of important things to say and I must know you've understood."

"It's all right, Mother, I am awake. Is anything the matter?"

"Last night, after the funeral meal, Uncle Eli, Clopas, Jonas, Simon, Zacharias and Joshua, with two of the rabbis from the synagogue, talked for a long time about our future. You know, of course, that many years ago I had to flee from my mother's home in Ein–Karem, near Jerusalem, when Salome, your grandmother, moved up here with Joachim your father, and I was but recently married to him. Uncle Eli took us in and gave us all a refuge for the sake of Grandma. He promised us then that we would always have a home here. Now that your father's dead, I was worried whether Uncle Eli would feel any further obligation to us, but we have no worries on that score. Eli says I may stay on here in this house with my family; he will assume full responsibility for us all and will act as head of the house to take all decisions now that Joachim is gone. In fact, that will not be much different, as Joachim was so seldom here to consult."

"That is good, Mother. At least we'll have no worries about a home. It had not occurred to me that Father's death could have led to us losing our house as well."

"Yes, child, that is good. But I have some other news as well that concerns you. I'm not sure if you will be so pleased."

Mariam sat up straighter and looked more alert. She said nothing but waited for her mother to continue. Anna was clearly struggling to put her thoughts into words. She continued slowly, choosing her words very carefully.

"Uncle Eli thinks it is time you were married – "

Mari made as if to interrupt.

"Hold on, my child, let me finish before you say anything, and listen carefully. He believes that you have many qualities, not least the obvious way you have with animals and children, but he thinks you are becoming too independent, too wayward, and he fears that if someone does not take you in hand soon, you will cause real problems for yourself and us, even worse than have just happened – shush, don't protest – those are his words, not mine. He knows that he encouraged you to read and write and learn the scriptures just like a boy, and now he worries that you do not know your role in life; he thinks you need the discipline of a husband who will command you."

"But Mother, I'm still only twelve."

"I know, love, but you're of age now, and many of your friends are already betrothed or their fathers are negotiating an engagement."

"Is he thinking of anyone in particular already, or is he just saying that he will start looking?" she asked nervously.

"He spoke at length to the others last night and asked their advice. There is a name that was suggested. Apparently one of your father's band managed to escape from the soldiers and has taken refuge in Nain. They think that he needs to find a home and settle down and they are suggesting your name to him as a wife."

"Is he one of the Zealots I met with Father on Mount Arbel?"

"I gather so, my child. He is the one called Isaac from Capernaum in northern Genneseret in Galilee."

"Oh."

Anna waited for further reaction. "You don't seem very enthusiastic."

"I didn't like any of Father's friends very much. They seemed so rough and dirty and I felt uncomfortable with them. I can't really say why. If Dad hadn't been there, I think I would have been frightened of them."

"Do you remember this Isaac in particular?"

"Not very well. I think he was one of the younger men, but very big and burly. Does it mean he would still be a Zealot and be a wanted man living in the hills nearly all the time like Father?"

"I'm not very happy about that, love. It's no life for a young girl like you; even I had a few years of marriage before your father took to the hills for most of the time. I think, though, he wants to try to settle down and avoid bringing himself to the notice of the soldiers."

"What say do I have in it, Mother?"

"You are of age, my daughter. You cannot be married without your consent. Uncle Eli and the others know that, although they expect you to do as you are told, especially in view of the charity that they are showing towards me and the children."

"Are you saying that they will throw us out of our home if I don't marry this man?"

"No, no, child, nothing as crude as that. If you will not marry this man, they will try to persuade you, but you have the final word and I will support you, whatever they say."

Mari leant forward and hugged her mother.

"Thanks, Mum, that makes me feel much better. What is to happen next?"

"Some time today Uncle Eli will formally ask you for your consent to marriage. It is up to you to ask to meet Isaac first and consider the proposal before giving your consent. You may need to stand up to Uncle Eli's blustering, but I think I understand you well enough to know you're well capable of that. I just ask you not to turn the man down out of hand: that would make Eli very angry with you, and he's already not very pleased, as you well know."

"All right, Mother, I'll take your advice. But you know that I'm not very keen. How will you get along here without me to help with the children? And what about them? Salome was saying only yesterday that she never wanted me to go away."

Mari then had a sudden afterthought.

"Mother, you said that this man came from Capernaum. Would I have to go and live with him all that distance away from you?"

"I'm not sure. That's one of the things the men are still considering. They think it may be too dangerous for him there as he could be known to the authorities. It might be safer for him to have a room with Joshua and Susanna in Nain. You would be in closer touch with us there."

"So I have to wait for Uncle Eli to send for me this morning when he will talk to me about getting betrothed?"

"Yes, Mari. That's part of what he will want to talk to you about."

"What? There's some more?"

"I'm afraid so, Mari. I don't really know how to tell you this. They have decided you are to be punished for placing yourself in moral danger with gentiles and putting the Zealots and whole village at risk."

"That's unfair! What should I have done?"

"I know, child, that's what I told them myself, but I'm afraid they accused me of being too soft with you. You know your uncle, how much he hates to be indebted in any way to a foreigner, and the visit of the Roman captain cut him to the quick. And everyone is nervous now that the soldiers will still come back to the village and trick us, despite what the Roman said. They don't trust him at all."

"What are they going to do to me?"

Anna paused and swallowed, unable to look her daughter in the eye.

"You're to be taken to the market place at sundown and submit to a caning from the priest."

"You mean a public caning with everyone looking?"

"I'm afraid so, Mari."

"Oh, Mother, it will be humiliating: everyone will be there from the village. Will Joshua and Jonas and the others still be here, or will they have gone home?"

"I think they'll be there, Mariam: they were part of the discussion."

Mari buried her face in her mother's breast and shook silently.

"I don't think I can bear it, Mum, not the shame. I know as a child I've had lots of spankings and canings here in the family, but so has everyone else. It's different in public. Rhoda told me it was awful when she was caned for stealing some fodder for her animals instead of driving them out to graze for themselves."

"Child, you will have to be brave and take it with dignity, knowing that you have not committed any sin that would earn such a punishment from the Lord God. And, my girl, it could have been a lot worse!"

"Worse? How could it have been worse?"

"Mari, you are technically an adult, admittedly only just. And an adult punishment is normally a whipping carried out in the outer courtyard of the synagogue – a full thirty-nine stripes. They wanted you flogged, Mariam, but I pleaded for you, and they relented. Even Uncle Eli, I think, admitted that that would have been too harsh for you."

Mariam had gone pale at her mother's words, and was realising with shock that she was in the process of putting her carefree childhood romps behind her. Her life was changing so fast that she was reeling with the pace. Her ignorance was being blasted away and she was frantically trying to make sense of the new realities.

The girl, still sitting upright in bed, shivered suddenly, despite the morning warmth. Anna, looking at her with compassion, said as gently as she could, "The time is marching on, Mari. I think you should get up and prepare yourself. I will excuse you going to fetch the water this morning; Miriam will ask Salome to go for you. By the way, Miriam brought over this old tunic of hers for you to wear. It will be a bit long and baggy, but it will give you something to cover yourself with when Eli calls for you. I shall finish washing your own tunic this morning, and you will be allowed to put it back on after the caning, because you will then have been purified."

"When will you have made me a new loincloth?"

"I'm sorry, Mari, I just haven't had the time in the last couple of days. It's about time you were able to do that. I'll ask Eli if I can purchase some suitable cloth this afternoon, and I'll show you how to make it. It's something we can do together while you're recuperating from your caning."

Mariam gave her mother a withering look at this reference as she stepped up from the mattress and pulled Miriam's shift over her naked body.

"I'm sorry, I didn't mean to keep reminding you. What will you have to eat now?"

"I really don't feel like anything. Telling me about the marriage plans and the punishment has made me too nervous to be hungry."

"You must have something. You'll feel faint otherwise. You don't want people to think you can't take it."

"Leave me alone for a while, Mum. I want to say my prayers."

Anna slipped outside into the courtyard and started to milk the goats, leaving her daughter alone in the little room. Mari was not used to saying her prayers here – she preferred the open air when she was caring for her flocks – but she felt at this moment a pressing need to say something to God.

"Lord God, listen to your servant Mariam. I hardly know what to say to you this morning: my mind is in so much of a whirl. I am frightened by the things Mother has told me. Help me to be a brave girl and bear the punishment without disgracing myself or my family. And help me to make the right decision about getting married, and to be strong enough to speak my mind. Look after Dad, take him to heaven to live with you, and comfort Mum, Salome, Rebecca, Benjamin and me."

When Anna came back carrying the pail of warm milk, she poured some out into an earthenware basin and handed the girl a ladle, saying, "Make some butter, Mari: we shall still need plenty to make up for what everyone has been eating in the last two days. And here," she said, pouring out some more milk into a cup, "drink this if you will not eat!"

Mariam put the cup to her lips, pulled a bit of a face, took a quick draught and swallowed awkwardly as though she was having difficulty in keeping it down. Then, unfinished, she laid it to one side and started stirring the milk in a distracted way, while her mother kept up a flow of talk of this and that, designed to prevent Mari dwelling on what had already been said. She grunted in acknowledgement from time to time, then suddenly interrupted, "Mother, you needn't try to talk to me all the time. I need to think."

"Sorry, love. I think I am as nervous as you are. When someone you love is worried or in trouble you feel it more than if it was yourself."

"I didn't mean to be rude. It's just that so much is happening, I need to sort it out in my mind a bit."

"Don't worry, love. You do what you feel is best. I'll go outside for a bit and see how the children are getting on over at Miriam's."

"Mum, I suddenly thought, they won't make Salome and Rebecca watch me being punished, will they?"

"No, don't you concern yourself about that; I'll ask Miriam to stay with the children, so that I can be with you."

"Thank you."

Alone, Mari continued to stir, her mind elsewhere. She gave no clue to her thoughts; her face was masked, her eyes were dull in the sunless room. And as she thought, she felt somehow that she was not alone. She felt stronger. She took a long deep breath. She breathed slowly, out and in, calming her fluttering stomach. She looked over her shoulder as if she sensed someone present. But there was no-one there?

She was daydreaming away when she heard the door open and a shaft of light fell across her lap.

"Mari, Uncle Eli is in the yard; he is ready for you."

Mari started, then shook herself and stood up, looking at her mother, and gulped.

"Listen carefully to what he says, and be polite; try not to argue too much with him. And accept his authority, child. It is for the best."

"I'll try, Mother, really I will."

"Good luck and God bless you, Mari."

Anna stooped and kissed her daughter on the forehead as she reached the door.

Mari stepped out into the bright sunshine and squinted around. In the corner, shaded to some extent by the wall of his own home, stood Eli, with Jonas and Clopas. Eli beckoned Mari across and then put up a hand, restraining her before she could touch any of them. She remembered she was still ritually unclean.

"Mariam, your mother has told you what we need to speak to you about?"

"Yes, Uncle."

"Then listen carefully, child; these things are of great importance."

Mari nodded. The other two men watched her without saying anything.

"You know of course that I've responsibility for you now that your father's dead."

"Yes."

"I've told your mother that I will support her and her family as long as it is necessary."

"Thank you, sir."

"It is no more than my duty, child, one that a Pharisee would be ashamed to neglect. Now, standing in place of your father, I have the responsibility of finding a husband for you. You are midway into your thirteenth year, just past the age of your maturity, and many young girls are already married by then. I believe you need a husband. It is not good for you to be roaming the hills and streets as freely as you do. Salome and Rebecca are of an age when they can take on your duties of caring for the flocks and helping in the fields, as well as working with your mother about the house. Do you agree with me?"

"Sir, it is not for me to say. If you feel that I should be married I must listen to your advice. I am happy still in the fields and looking after Miriam's children as well as my brother and sisters."

"I'm glad you are prepared to accept my advice. I discussed the question of a husband for you with Clopas and my sons-in-law last night and we are resolved to betroth you to a close friend of your father, Isaac of Capernaum. Do you know the man?"

"I believe I met him briefly when I was with my father on Mount Arbel."

"We have sent word to him to offer you in marriage. Do you give your consent?"

"Sir, I should like to meet him and discuss it with him, before I consider your proposal properly."

Her answer stunned the men – at least Eli and Jonas looked shocked. Clopas hid his views, whatever they were.

"Did I hear you right, girl?"

Mari, in a somewhat small voice, stuck to her guns.

"Sir, I ask that I might meet Isaac before I give my consent."

"Do you not trust your kinsfolk to have your best interests at heart?"

"Yes, of course I do."

"Well then, why the hesitation?"

"I would like to meet this Isaac, Uncle, when he is not living rough and on the run from the soldiers. Will he be able to live with me, or will he be hiding in the hills all the time?"

"Your cousin Susannah and her husband Joshua have kindly offered you both a room in their house in Nain. What more could you ask?"

"I am grateful to them, Uncle. But I would still like to talk it over with Isaac first. I am very young and he seemed a lot older and very large to me. I was a bit frightened of him."

"He is a fine man, Mariam, worthy of your father. He has fought alongside your father for many years, well trusted. He honours our nation, comes from a family of Pharisees, and abhors the gentile. He may be a little rough in his ways, but that comes from spending so many years living off the land. So let's hear no more of this nonsense about seeing him first. You saw him on Mount Arbel. Let me send your consent to him."

"Please, Uncle, don't rush me. It is a big step for me to take. I want to make sure it is right for me."

"What has got into you, girl?" exclaimed Eli in mounting anger, whilst the other two men were muttering between themselves. "It is not for you to decide these things. It is my responsibility, and your duty is to be submissive and accept what I arrange for you without all this quibbling."

"I thought I had the right to be consulted, Uncle?"

"And you are being consulted, girl! And I expected you to have been pleased with what we had fixed. After all the problems of the last few days, to put it mildly, I would have thought you'd have been bending over backwards to be co-operative. Are you telling me formally, child, that you will not give your consent to this match?"

"No, Uncle. But I am asking you to let me postpone my decision until I've met Isaac and we have talked together."

"And that is your final word?"

"Yes, sir."

Eli was clearly very frustrated and upset, and withdrew to discuss the matter with Jonas and Clopas. Mariam strained to hear what they were saying, but most was lost, except for an important phrase from Clopas' lips, "She is within her rights...". Eventually Eli turned back to the trembling Mari, who was feeling chilled and goose-pimply despite the increasing heat of the day.

"We can't make you go against your wishes, because you are of age, and the law demands your consent. I am not pleased, however. You are flaunting your independence and strong will, which is what I feel should be curbed by marriage to a strong husband. I shouldn't be at all surprised if your mother hasn't put you up to this. She has too much influence over you."

"No, Uncle, my mother has left it entirely up to me. She has not tried to advise me against Isaac. And she has said that she will support me, whatever I decide."

"So it is your will which prevails, is it, little girl? You ignore the views of your elders and betters – those appointed to look after your interests. I don't know why I bother."

"Please don't say that, sir. I am very grateful for all you have done for us. But please be merciful to me on this. I have prayed to the Lord God to show me what is right and I don't feel I have an answer yet."

"So you would use God's name against me now, would you? Be careful, young lady, you are coming within inches of blasphemy! If you insist on exercising your right as an adult, I could use that same argument in a moment on the other matter about which I have to inform you."

"What do you mean?" asked Mari with misgivings, suddenly in her mind making the connection Eli intended her to make. "No, you can't mean…"

"Indeed I do," said Eli with grim satisfaction, which he was unable to avoid showing in his face. "We spent a long time last night debating the penalty for your misbehaviour and had concluded that as you have reached your majority, you were liable to the full rigours of adult law and should therefore be subject to a whipping like any other adult condemned in this town. Your mother pleaded on your behalf, especially that your immature body would not be able to bear the full onslaught of thirty-nine lashes. I told her that that was your misfortune; if you had not behaved irresponsibly, you would not have had to suffer the consequences. Then your mother herself begged to be allowed to suffer the punishment in your place, so, after further discussion, we decided to be merciful to you and treat you as a child instead. And now you insist on making us treat you as an adult!"

"Did you say my mother offered to take my place and be whipped instead of me?"

"Yes, that is precisely what I said, child. You have your mother to thank for your reduced sentence."

"Oh."

"However, Mariam, despite your provocation now, I have to tell you that you are to receive a public caning in the market place at sundown tonight. You put your father and his colleagues at risk, you put the whole village at risk, you consorted with gentiles and allowed them to bring you home, and all this was highly irresponsible. You and your family have already been punished by the death of your father. However, so that you truly learn the lesson of your wildness and the errors it can lead to, you must be made a public example. I ask you, Mariam, do you submit to this sentence that I am communicating to you?"

Mariam looked at his stern face and decided that no good would come from further argument or excuse. She hung her head.

"Yes, sir."

"I'm glad to see some humility in you at last. Listen to me carefully then. You are to return to your home now, wash yourself and wear only the shift that you have on now. When the light is beginning to fade, I shall knock on your door and your mother will accompany you in procession to the market place, where you will be instructed what to do. Do you understand?"

"Yes, sir."

"After you have received twelve lashes of the rod, you may put on your own clothing once more, as your purification will be complete, and enter into the normal life of the village without restriction."

"Yes, sir."

Eli relaxed his face a little, staring at the frightened girl in front of him.

"I'm sorry, my child, that it has come to this. I have always had high hopes for you, but you have bitterly disappointed me. Do not now further disgrace your family by taking this punishment badly. Try to control yourself throughout, do as you are instructed, and do not break down or try to run away during the caning. These things sometimes happen. At least show that you have some dignity."

"I will try, sir."

"Right, girl, go and prepare yourself."

Mariam turned and tried to walk more calmly than she felt across the dusty yard, then nearly threw herself through her own door into the arms of her mother, who had been watching anxiously through the narrow window.

"How did it go, girl?"

"As you said it would. Why did you tell him that you'd take my place, Mum? You couldn't do that!"

"Oh, did he tell you that, Mari? I asked him not to say anything. I would gladly stand in for you, love, if I could. I am going to find this afternoon as difficult as you are. It sounds silly, I know, but when you see someone you love suffering, it hurts you too!"

"Oh, Mum, I love you!"

"Mari, my child, no mother could have a daughter who makes her so proud. Just remember that when others criticise and blame you. This nightmare will soon be over, love. This week has been dreadful for both of us. Let us hang on together and thank the Lord that we have each other."

Meanwhile Clopas was scurrying after Eli, clutching his sleeve, and saying angrily, "Have you already made up your mind? You said last night that such a punishment was still under consideration, that we'd talk further with the synagogue rabbis today. Have you already gone to them this morning and made the arrangements despite what we agreed?"

"You'd better come in and not shout so much lest Anna and Mariam hear you. Jonas, you too, if you are having second thoughts."

"I didn't think you were serious last night. I thought you wanted to shake the girl up a bit, just make her think about the potential consequences of her actions. The marriage is one thing, but a public beating? What sin has she committed? She hasn't killed or stolen or behaved immorally of her own volition. She was a victim, not the perpetrator of wrong."

"Not you too, Clopas? You're as bad as her mother and your wife. Can't you see she'll be the ruin of us: she's wild, she's out of control, she doesn't know the meaning of obedience. If we don't act now to curb her, she'll finish up bringing the wrath of the Romans down upon us, or go to her own execution first. Surely you can see that she is no longer the innocent child. She has dangerous dreams. Look at the way she answered back to us. She does not know her place."

"But you've encouraged her over the years. Why did you support her education with the boys? Why did you give her that scroll on her twelfth birthday? Now you regret what you've done?"

"I thought she could make a good marriage, she was intelligent, I thought I could shape her. I suppose you think it's my fault that she abuses those gifts."

"How does she abuse them? She cares for your grandchildren, she looks after your flocks, she is the first to be called on whenever there is drudgery to be done. Why should she not dream a little?"

"Jonas, you've said nothing. What do you think? Do you think I'm being unjust?"

"Well, we did say last night that she should be punished. We even thought the adult whipping should be considered, although the girl's mother talked us out of that."

Clopas interrupted Jonas. "If you must punish her in some way, why the public caning? Do you want to show up your own family? Do you want to heap ridicule on yourself by showing for all to see that you can't control your own niece?"

"Clopas, I am a Pharisee with some position in this town. How do you think it would look if I am seen to be lenient with my own kinsfolk? I could be accused of favouritism and people would lose trust in my integrity."

"Well, how would people know that you think Mari deserves a beating? Would it be public knowledge that you showed a little mercy for once? She has not been publicly tried of a criminal offence. Probably few others would think she deserves such a thing."

"All the town saw the way she was brought in by that Roman officer, flaunting herself shamelessly and then having the nerve to defend him in front of our neighbours. And everyone knows she brought the soldiers here and caused the death of the Zealots. There are many angry and fearful people here. We can't be seen to do nothing."

"I think you're out of order, Father. I'm ashamed that you can think of treating Mari like that. It's just not justice."

"And what is your view, Jonas? You didn't really help much last time you spoke."

"Well, perhaps you could carry out her punishment behind the family walls this time – that is, provided you haven't already given notice on the public board at the synagogue."

Clopas rounded on his father again. "You haven't, Father, surely not already before checking with us?"

Eli was discomforted because that's just what he had done earlier that morning. He had consulted with the rabbis with whom the discussion had taken place the night before and confirmed their provisional decision. One of the rabbis had been surprised and had challenged Eli, but the other had congratulated Eli on his strength in resisting familial pressure and said he would carry out the caning himself to avoid embarrassing Eli further. Eli was now reluctant to admit this, but Clopas realised from his hesitation that Eli had already notified the decision.

"That means it's already public knowledge. Now you've made it harder to retract the decision without it seeming just what you wanted to avoid."

"So we should stick to our decision, should we not? Otherwise we'll look fools who've been weakened by women's pleading and enrage those who were appalled at the soldiers' threats and actions."

"Father, you can't allow this brutal and humiliating punishment to go ahead just to spare your pride. For goodness sake, call it off, and quickly, before any more people read about it."

"It'll be all over town by now. It only takes a couple in this place to read something and within an hour it is common knowledge."

"I don't think people want to see Mari punished. I think the majority are sorry for her and think she was ill-used. If you like, I'll check out a few neighbours and townsfolk and see what they think."

"If you must. But be discreet. Just get a feel of people's reaction, don't make it seem as though we're asking their opinion and could be swayed by that. Go then and let us both know the general consensus. It doesn't matter what time we call it off, if we do, since, as you say, the town gossips will already be hard at work."

Clopas walked down to the market and the impending punishment was on everyone's lips. He did not have to ask anyone – he was grabbed by any who know him, who asked incredulously if it was true. Surely not, unless there's some guilty secret that has not been made public. People seemed to be appalled that such a sentence should be passed on an angel like Mari, everyone's favourite. Some even questioned Eli's sanity. Others were curious, perhaps just to see the disgrace of the rabbi's own niece.

It was not that uncommon to see miscreants brought to the market place or synagogue for whipping or stoning, and squalling children being spanked by their fathers on the doorsteps of their houses was an everyday occurrence. You would not have seen this in Jerusalem, of course: that was a much more refined city, where such public justice was frowned upon, except under Roman law. But here, well it was a backwater and justice was rough and quick and administered largely by the rabbis, whose word went unquestioned, although they soon picked up the vibes of the villagers over what behaviour was unacceptable and warranted such retribution.

The only discordant voice was that of the outcast, Rachel, who had already heard the rumour from Bilpah, whom she had met earlier that morning at the well. Rachel was glad that such a well-respected and liked girl was due to get such a thrashing and she was determined to observe it all, even if she would have to watch from afar, lest she receive the crowd's jeers and taunts herself. That would teach the sheltered little paragon. She was not the only one whom the crowds would shun. There would be the two of them – perhaps she'd talk to her now, no longer be afraid to be seen with her.

She was going to say something to Clopas, but then thought better of it. He'd only badmouth her. Best to say nothing and enjoy someone else getting it for once.

Clopas did not need to stay long in the town. The opinion was overwhelming. He hurried back and found Eli, now with both Jonas and Joshua and other male members of the family who had not yet returned to their homes. He was as diplomatic as he could be without undermining Eli in front of his kinsmen, but his message was clear. By exposing Mariam to such a public ordeal he would lose sympathy and respect. He must surely cancel the public notice at once and inform the synagogue authorities.

The men chewed over the options at length but the clear consensus was that Eli must retract. Only Joshua, Jonas and Clopas were implicated in the deliberations with Anna during the night over the family's future, but the other relatives concurred with the advice Clopas was now giving. To save his father further embarrassment, Clopas volunteered to advise the two rabbis at the synagogue of their decision, leaving Eli to debate with his sons-in-law and cousins what should happen in its place. Eli could not afford to step back any further. He had advised Anna and the girl of the punishment. He could not lose face by cancelling it totally. Without Clopas to argue on the girl's behalf, Eli convinced the others that the girl deserved chastisement and was given the backing he needed to decide to carry it out himself, but in the privacy of the family homestead.

The afternoon was long and stifling and full of tension.

As the sun began to lose its strength and sink toward the reddening hills, Rachel made her furtive way towards the village market clearing and was surprised to find few people there. She had expected a big turnout for such an infamous occasion. She latched on to a group of gossiping women, at a safe distance of course, and soon overheard the dominant topic of conversation. The public caning had been cancelled. Rachel felt a pang of disappointment. Then she heard them say that the girl was still to get a whipping but that the rabbi would execute it in the privacy of the Pharisee's home. Apparently Eli had let it be known that the girl was not to escape punishment completely. What should she do? She began to drift back to her own house but meandered via the walls of Eli's courtyard out of curiosity. She was not alone – a few other stragglers appeared to be occupying themselves doing nothing in particular. A couple of times someone looked as though they were going to come over and tell her to clear off and she shrank into the shadows, but still lingered.

Eventually she was rewarded. She heard a gaggle of voices. She dared not look through the cracks in the wooden gate. Silence. Then she heard the crack of the cane. Again and again and again. She had come to gloat, but as she heard the punishment unfurling and nothing more but strangled gasps from the victim, her sympathies changed. She began to feel sorry for the girl and hatred for the self-righteous clergy who ruled this village. The lashes reverberated around the still evening and Rachel grimly thought that this was too much. The bastards, she thought to herself, and, "One up to you," she muttered under her breath, "you're made of tougher metal than I thought."

There was a more general movement and the gates opened and a number of men walked slowly from the courtyard. Instead of slinking away, Rachel's anger had made her foolhardy. Throwing caution and decorum to the winds, she yelled at the top of her voice, "Well done, kid, don't let them grind you down. Come and see me sometime; I'll tell you a thing or two about priests and rabbis!"

Jonas, who had come to close the gate, chased Rachel, shouting after her, "Whore and Jezebel, don't you come near our home. Go back to the gutter, where you belong!"

The girl laughed brazenly at him, then gave him the slip, running up a side alleyway until she was lost in a maze of back streets, and Jonas returned red-faced and out of breath. He went up to Anna's house and shouted inside, "Don't take any notice of her: she's in league with the devil. Don't let anyone ever catch you with her."

Anna took the tearful Mari in her arms and said more quietly, "That is good advice, my child. She will only cause trouble; no decent Jew will be seen with her. You have other, better, friends here."

At midnight, when Anna had done her best to soothe and comfort her tortured child, singing softly as she used to sing lullabies when she was a baby, she said to Mari, "Mari, are you ready to hear some better news?"

"Yes, Mother."

"Uncle Eli's had a message back from Isaac in Capernaum. He's turned down your uncle's offer of betrothal to you. He won't have you because he thinks you betrayed him and the others. Are you pleased?"

Mari, her eyes still shut, let a smile spill across her red and blotchy face.

"Are you sure, Mother? He doesn't really want me?"

"Yes, quite sure, my love. Eli's furious; he's so angry, he couldn't bring himself to tell me. Clopas had to pass the message on."

Mariam began to laugh. Her body shook under her mother's fingers, transmitting her hysteria to Anna, so that she too began to rock in strained merriment. They laughed until once more the tears flowed.

"Oh, Mother, stop it, stop it. I mustn't laugh so much – it hurts so. Oh Mum, stop laughing. Oh…"

Chapter 16
Still Watching

I AM STANDING ON THE SKYLINE again. You would think after her previous experience that Mariam would be careful always to scrutinize the horizon, but she has not seen me. Perhaps I am invisible to her. Perhaps the sun is dazzling, shielding me directly from her sight. Never mind, it suits my purpose admirably. The last thing I want to do is frighten her away. For it is time I had a talk with her; I have important weighty things to provoke her imagination.

She has come to her favourite grazing ground with her small, devoted flock. She is a free spirit again; well, perhaps the spring in her step is anchored by knowledge and pain that dents her innocence, but she is not oppressed by constraining restrictions placed upon her. As she climbs the hillside towards me and her lone fig tree, you can see how much she's grown, taller and a little fuller than the first time I watched her down in the valley.

When she is satisfied that her sheep and goats are well provided for, she can relax. I see her ease herself onto the hard earth, a little stiffly to be sure. And as she draws her knees up to her thinking stance, a nasty yellowing bruise is visible on the back of her thighs. Well, I know about that. She has proved to my satisfaction that she is tough enough to take any consequences of the risk I might impose on her. And yet, my conscience begins to prick again. While she has, to my complete satisfaction, shown all the qualities necessary for her destiny, yet she is more vulnerable than ever. And I will act as catalyst for greater risks and pain. Dare I go through with it? Should I not show some pity, let her find peace and comfort in a quieter life? But I am under instruction. Have I the authority to hold back? Where would I find such a girl again to undertake this sacred task? Will it always be so for the chosen?

Be patient! Watch for a while. Let her sing and pray in peace. Do not interrupt! Wait till she is ready to listen. She listens well, that girl.

"Mari, Mari!"

She starts in fright; she has not realised that anyone is there.

"Don't be afraid, Mariam. I intend you no harm."

"I am sorry, sir. I did not see you there in the shadow of the tree."

"I have been watching you for a long time, Mari. I know your love and concern for others; I know your pain and grief, your fear of rejection by some of your family. But do not change – you are right as you are, Mari. Do not belittle yourself. It is praiseworthy that you do not hold others responsible for your tribulations, but you must not blame yourself."

"Who are you? What do you know about me, sir?"

"You wonder why your father died, why there is so much hatred and killing, why your mother has to suffer so, whether if you had been more submissive, it would have been easier for all of you."

"Of course. How could I wonder otherwise?"

"Then you wonder about your father's words; he wanted you to bring hope to him; news of the promised Messiah, to free your country from its slavery."

"How do you know that?"

"His last words seem prophetic to you, don't they? They assume an importance because nothing now can overtake them. The thought has crossed your mind that God is testing you to see if you are worthy."

Mari blushes with embarrassment, tries to protest.

"Do not shy away from the truth, Mari; it is your childish honesty and openness that commends you so. Study the scriptures further, Mariam; after all, your Uncle Eli gave you the opportunity. Read from the prophet Isaiah. You will learn that suffering and hardship are a necessary sacrifice to free the nation from its slavery to evil and misery. Prepare yourself. One day you may be called to serve the Lord God himself. After all, your family is of King David's lineage."

"What do you mean, sir?"

"Think about these things, Mari. Be aware of your power, of the presence of God with you. Ask him to guide you. You will need him. His constant reassurance. Now I must go. I'll talk to you again. Don't tell the others yet, not even your mother; they would not understand. The seed needs a little nurturing first. Farewell, Mari; don't be afraid!"

Mariam suddenly sat up and stared towards the sun, trying to shield her eyes. She couldn't see anything, just blinding light. Even when she turned away, her vision was impaired by the brilliance of the sun still etched upon her eyes, upon the inside of her eyelids.

She looked around and counted her flock, and with a panic, saw one of them was missing. She jumped up and despite her soreness, raced down the hillside. She would be in trouble for sleeping when she should have been attentive. Perhaps a wolf or stray dog had driven off the lamb. She had heard no bleating in her dreams. Then she saw that her eyes had been mistaken. The lamb was there, hidden for the moment by the protective flank of the ewe. Even as she watched amid waves of relief, she saw the old ewe shake as the lamb attempted to suckle, throwing itself with abandon at its source of succour. She sat down, trembling, in the grass beside her sheep; trembling all over. The ewe came up to her and nuzzled her knees, then pushed her arm. She let it rub against her and scratched the top of its head.

"You gave me quite a fright! But I should have known that you'd look after your lamb, shouldn't I, silly old me!"

In the heat of the afternoon she led her flock to the riverbank to drink. This time she was alone in the shimmering landscape, and as her animals browsed at the water's edge and quenched their thirst, Mariam waded into the middle of the stream until her knees were covered. Then she plunged her arms down into the cool liquid, so that the front of her tunic was saturated by the bubbling water, and playfully cuffed the surface so that spray flew in all directions, creating mini-rainbows in the shafts of sunlight. Her animals did not mind her antics. They stoically concentrated on taking their fill, whilst the fine spray cascaded over them.

She stirred the water with her foot, created great gulping suction motions around her calves and yelped as she stubbed a toe against a sharp boulder on the stream bed. At the edge of the eddying water, she paused a moment to stamp her footprints in the mud, and watched it oozing up between her toes; then she was off chasing clouds of butterflies along the lush green bank. She made wild slashes in the air and giggled hopelessly, then suddenly perceived a fluttering insect within her range and to her immense surprise, cupped her palms around it, trapping it between her fingers.

She peered, entranced, feeling the tickling wingbeats; enlarged the area so that it would not damage its scales. She watched with total concentration as the fragile blue creature basked in her hand, then, given its freedom, extended its probes to suck the moisture from her skin instead of flying away. She seemed to be talking to it, caressing it with her voice, until in leisurely fashion it fluttered briefly in front of her eyes, before soaring into the air to dip and entangle with its kaleidoscopic sisters.

When she reached the well, she waved excitedly to a little group of figures playing in the path. Salome, her sister, had brought the large water pot, and Rebecca had both Benjamin and Mo tugging at her belt in some mysterious rite. They laughed and talked a bit, then Rebecca said, quite suddenly, "That funny girl, Rachel, was here not long ago. She asked where you were."

"Why, what did she want?"

"She wouldn't really say. She asked if you were better and when you were coming home."

"She didn't frighten you or tease you, did she?"

"No, she seemed to want to talk. But Mummy said we're not meant to be with her, so we ran away and picked flowers."

"Did she follow you?"

"No, she just drew her water and went back home. She seemed to be a bit sad. Is it true we mustn't talk to her?"

"I don't know, Rebecca. Everyone seems to say not, but it seems very cruel. I know, don't talk to her if you're alone, but if I'm here it's all right; I'll see she doesn't do anything silly or hurt you."

"What will Uncle Eli do if he finds out?"

"Perhaps it would be better if he didn't find out, eh, sister?"

"All right. I'll not tell. You won't, will you Salome?"

"Not if you don't, Becca."

"Anyway, isn't it time you were getting home with the water? Mum will be wanting it soon for the evening meal. Here, let me take the pot. You lead the animals." She paused as the two toddlers started running round her in circles.

"Ouch, that hurt! Becca, try and keep them from pulling against me, I'm still sore and I can't take it when they yank me like that. By the way, where are the boys? Why are they doing lessons at this hour?"

"Uncle Eli had something to show them in the synagogue, he said, before we all start harvesting tomorrow."

"Let's hurry home then. There'll be lots to do tonight to prepare everything for the fields in the morning."

The end of childhood?

Chapter 17

The Suitor

O NE EVENING A FEW WEEKS later, when Mariam was helping Anna with some sewing, after the youngest children had clambered up onto the roof to bed, Anna suddenly put down the needle and thread and said, "Mari, it's time we had another talk. How are you getting on with Uncle Eli now?"

"Why, Mother, has he complained to you about me?"

"No, child, don't be so sensitive! I wondered if you felt any change in his attitude towards you since he chastised you."

"Not to speak of. He doesn't seem to want to talk to me much, he just tells me what he wants done. He even sometimes seems to be trying to avoid me."

"I think he is now ashamed of what he did. He feels guilty when he sees you. He's told me how surprised he was at how you took your punishment. He was impressed."

"No, he's never said anything like that to me."

"Has he ever talked to you about Isaac's refusal to betroth you?"

"No. Not a word."

"I suspected as much. He was most embarrassed after pressing you so hard, that Isaac turned him down without any discussion. I'm afraid your uncle finds it hard to admit when he is wrong. Anyway, the other day he confirmed to me again that all negotiations with Isaac have ceased."

"Good."

"He hasn't changed his mind, however, about the need to find you a husband. He has been very active in these last couple of months, although I think he has had one or two disappointments."

"Aren't I a very good catch, Mum?"

"Don't be silly, dear. Some young man will be very lucky to have you. It's just, well... a number of candidates are a little unwilling to align themselves with our family because of its known links with Zealots and the possible suspicion in which we are held by Herod's people. And your uncle is a bit fussy and rejects anyone who does not cleave to his particular brand of Pharisee dogma. A couple of possibles have failed that test."

"Is there another suggestion being made?"

"Possibly, Mari."

Mariam, alert now, put down her needlework and pulled herself up, kneeling, beside her mother.

"Come on, Mother, what do you mean: possibly?"

"Don't get too excited, girl, there's nothing definite, nothing decided this time without your voice. Eli won't risk that rebuff again." Anna smiled a rueful smile at Mari. "Some people round here have learned that presumption of your consent can be a little premature!"

"Who, Mother, who?"

"Well, first your uncle tested me with the name of Rabbi Jethro's son, Issachar, but you know of course that the lad is simple. I think Eli feels under obligation to Jethro, who has asked him to find a wife for his only son. I feel sorry for the boy but I told Eli he couldn't sacrifice you like that just to help out his friend."

"Perhaps God wants someone to look after Issachar. So many of the other boys and girls are cruel to him."

"Mari, sometimes you're just perverse. Are you telling me seriously that you would have considered him?"

"I don't know, Mum. I hadn't even thought of him before. It's not his fault that he's simple in the head. And he's very gentle and I can make him laugh."

"Well, whatever you think is immaterial. When your uncle thought about it, he realised that the match was impossible. The boy couldn't keep you and the likelihood is that he would pass on his defects to your children; indeed, he may not even be able to have children – he's probably impotent. His father is distraught at the possible discontinuity of his line. And lastly, and this influenced Eli no end, he couldn't possibly exert any authority over you. He saw you doing as you liked with him and neglecting your role as wife and mother."

"So I'm not to be betrothed to Issachar."

"No, Mari."

"Come on, Mother, I can see from your eyes that there is something in the wind. You're keeping me in suspense deliberately."

"Well, it's only a suggestion, Mari, no more."

"Who?"

"Have you heard me speak of my distant cousin, Joseph, from Bethlehem near Jerusalem?"

"I've heard the name, but I don't remember much about him."

"You've never met, of course. When I lived in Ein–Karem with my mother and her sister, Aunt Elizabeth, your grandmother and father came to live with us following the confiscation of their property and the arrest of your father's older brothers by Herod's soldiers. Elizabeth's husband, Zechariah, had, I remember, a nephew a year or two younger than me, whom I remember coming to stay for a short while when his father was caught up in the troubles. In the end his father was arrested and their property confiscated also, but after some years of imprisonment, he was released. I have never seen the family again, but Elizabeth tells me that both his parents died shortly after my own mother, a few years ago, and Joseph has had to struggle on his own with a small piece of property they'd managed to acquire back in Bethlehem. Because of his lack of close relatives and his poverty, he has never been able to marry. Elizabeth, who has kept in touch with him, says that he has managed to build up a small carpentry business, although he struggles still, and he is a thoroughly pleasant and orthodox Jew, although obviously older than would normally be considered in marriage negotiations."

"You think this Joseph would be a suitable husband for me?"

"I suggested his name to Eli, love. He is of our own ancestry, and by repute he is a kind man. Eli is prepared to pursue the matter further, even consider providing the man's bride price to help him if he has insufficient wealth of his own. What do you think?"

"Do you believe I'm ready to be married yet, Mother?"

"You are a very capable young woman, Mari; all the practical things that a wife must do are already well within your competence. You love children and would, I'm sure, be a marvellous mother. I know you value your freedom, and might be frustrated by the restrictions that being married would place on you, but your uncle is determined to have you married and I am keen that we have some influence, rather than being forced ultimately to accept his sole choice."

"I know you have my interests at heart, so I'm happy to be guided by you. Is it possible to meet Joseph before consenting or have I to agree to a betrothal right away?"

"I told you, Mari, nothing is yet fixed. Uncle Eli is waiting for the word from me that you are ready to consider Joseph, then he will send word to him and invite him to Nazareth to see for himself that he is a suitable match for you. At the same time, you will be permitted to meet him."

Word was sent via Elizabeth and Zechariah to Joseph, and about four weeks later, in the height of summer, a message was received that Joseph was making his way north, accepting Eli's invitation. Mariam grew increasingly apprehensive, spending more and more time in the fields, despite the heat, savouring her independence and talking with God with animated urgency, pleading with him to know if the proposed marriage was to be her calling. The words of the stranger beneath the fig tree filled her with confusion. What had he been hinting at, about a Messiah, and did she have a role in what he said? She took every opportunity to pester the rabbis in the synagogue after they had finished teaching the boys and smaller children, asking for the scrolls of the prophet Isaiah, to the extent that they grew curious about her obsession.

She explained her interest to Eli's satisfaction, as stemming from her late father's plea to her to search for news of a national saviour. There were, of course, many rumours of claims which were much discussed by the rabbis, but none of them seemed to materialise; Herod or his lackeys always seemed well informed and quickly suppressed any challenge before it could be mounted. And other claims died when the subjects of the rumours behaved in ways unfitting to the prophecies, or were shown up as blatant charlatans. So Mariam sought to understand the character of the Messiah, as revealed by Isaiah, and found more problems and inconsistencies in that she could not square the vision there with the orthodox hopes expressed during the synagogue rituals and preaching, which she attended with her mother, pressed eagerly against the trellis of the Women's Court.

And what of the stranger who had prompted her? Who was he? He seemed, so far as she could remember, to be the same fair-haired man who the previous year had sought lodging in her uncle's house. But she could not be sure. When she had seen him under the fig tree she realised that he had always been between her and the sun, so that she saw his silhouette only as she squinted at him, his outline delineated by the golden glow. Would he come again, speak to her under the fig tree? She had been many times since, half in anticipation, but always in vain. She was beginning to think it really had been a dream. She could not ask about him or for him. Her uncle would have been horrified that any stranger could have accosted and talked to her on her own. She would have been confined to domestic duties about the house – for her own protection, of course.

And yet several times she felt aware of the man's presence, as if she were being watched. She thought she saw figures on the horizon and when she peered more closely she saw nothing, or a twisted bush that looked like a man when seen from a certain angle. In the town she glimpsed a stranger's back in the crowd, but when she caught up she saw a familiar face, or perhaps it had just been a trick of the light? Why did this fair-haired stranger excite her so, and the impending visit of her possible future husband fill her merely with apprehension? Did she believe that this stranger was her intended and that to marry another would destroy the calling that she felt was somehow being offered to her?

After the evening visit to the well to draw water for the night's needs, Mariam and her two sisters entered the courtyard and realised immediately that something unusual was happening. Children were playing hide-and-seek round the clutter there and as well as Miriam and her own mother, a number of neighbours were clustered, gossiping in a huddle. The conclave opened up sufficiently to allow Mari to worm her way in, and they all turned to her to break the news simultaneously:

"Joseph of Bethlehem is here."

"Your future husband's come."

"Joseph is in Eli's house."

"A man's come to negotiate for you, Mari."

They watched for her reaction, with curiosity. Mariam's stomach lurched, her mouth ran dry and she had to take deep breaths. She looked to her mother for help. Anna slapped a hand on Mari's shoulder and squeezed it in affection.

"What's he like, Mother?"

"You'll know soon enough, child. I'm sure Uncle Eli will invite you to meet him later this evening."

"What does he look like?"

"His face looked friendly, Mari, he has nice eyes, a short dark beard and curly hair. He's not very tall, probably no more than I am. What else do you want to know?"

"How old does he look?"

"Well, I know he's a year or two younger than me, so that means he's about twenty-five. Although his face is a little weather-beaten and careworn from his times of struggle, his frame is more that of a youth than a full-grown man. In fact, for a carpenter he looks remarkably compact and slim."

"How did he come?"

"On foot, Mari. He's been on the road for four days now and seems pretty weary."

"When did he get here?"

"Only a few minutes ago. James washed his feet and he went straight in to your uncle. I think they're having a meal together first."

"Oh!"

"So you'll just have to be patient, Mariam, and wait till they're ready for you."

The women gradually dispersed to prepare their families' meals and Mariam was kept busy by her mother in chores about the house. After their own meal together, Anna took Mari to one side and began to brush her long dark hair, freeing it from its band while she shook out the dust and tangles of the day.

"Put on your shawl and the ring your grandmother gave you, Mari. You want to look your best for Joseph when Eli sends for you. There, let me have a good look at you!"

She held Mari at arms' length and appraised her admiringly. The girl had blossomed since we first met her. She was nearly thirteen now. She was a good two inches taller, though still only up to her mother's shoulder. Her limbs were brown and strong, though still slim as befitted an active girl, and her girlish breasts were beginning to swell through the plain cloth of her shift. However, it was her face which held the attention. Her nervous smile was infectious, her bone structure delicate. But above all, her lovely dark eyes drew your gaze.

"Mariam, you're beautiful. He will not be able to resist you!"

The girl blushed at her mother's compliment and carefully gathered her hair back into its band, pulling it from off her forehead, a few dainty wisps only escaping the clasp. Unlike many of her friends, she had, apart from her ring, no jewellery to adorn her neck or brow, but her beauty did not need enhancing. She was natural, and best so.

"He will want to meet me tonight, won't he, Mother?"

"I'm sure he will, my love, but be patient. Uncle Eli will have many things to discuss over their meal."

The sun had set and the lamps had been lit. Clopas had been supping with his father and Joseph for some time now, and at their request he had now slipped out across the moonlit yard and was tapping at Anna's door.

"Anna, bring Mariam now to meet Joseph."

"Is all well, Clopas? Does he please Eli?"

"Don't worry on that score, Anna. Just pray that this time Mariam is willing."

"I'll fetch her now. She has been ready and waiting for your word."

Anna stepped inside her door and reappeared immediately with Mari, who was nervously adjusting her shawl. Anna spoke reassuringly to her daughter.

"Come, Mariam, I'm sure you'll like him. There is certainly no reason to fear him!"

Eli and Joseph were standing, waiting to receive them.

"This is Joseph, your kinsman from Bethlehem. This, Joseph, is my niece and adopted daughter, Mariam. You may greet one another!"

Both acknowledged the other, silently, tongue-tied, staring with shy curiosity. Eventually Joseph summoned up, "Mariam, I have heard much about you from your uncle to your credit. I am honoured to meet you and hope we shall get to know one another better."

"Sir, I am at your service when it pleases you."

Mariam searched his face frankly, seeking to hold his eyes. He flinched under her gaze, turned to look at Clopas, then when he thought her attention would have been drawn elsewhere, he turned back to her and found her stare still on him. The man coloured slightly, fidgeted with his robe, and searched for something else to say to break the tension.

"Your uncle has given permission for us to spend some time together in the morning, with Clopas here to be your chaperone."

"Sir, I will be pleased to talk with you then."

The group stood silently, waiting for each other to speak. Eli, aware of his responsibility to break the ice, said, "Anna, I understand that you and Joseph met each other as children at Zechariah's home. Do you recognise each other from those days?"

Both adults referred to began to speak at once, then withdrew.

"Anna, please, after you!"

"I was just going to say that I know more of Joseph through hearsay from my aunt than I remember from those far-off days. After all, it was only for a few weeks, and a couple of years' age difference is a lot to a girl of twelve."

"I trust you have heard nothing to my disadvantage from Elizabeth," said Joseph hopefully.

"On the contrary, Joseph, she has been most complimentary."

The verbal fencing had run its course. Eli had more serious business that he wished to transact with Joseph. Mariam wanted the freedom to talk to him without the formality of an inquisition. Both the parties were relieved when the introductions were concluded, and Eli offered Joseph the vacant room, formerly belonging to Salome, for the next day's use.

Back in their own room Anna was a little worried at Mari's possible reaction to the shy carpenter. She waited with bated breath for her daughter's expressed reaction.

"Well?"

"He seems a sensitive man."

"Oh?" She was partially relieved. "How did you surmise that from such a brief meeting?"

"I just felt it, Mum. He knew I was nervous and so was he."

"You should find it easier tomorrow, love. You'll have more time and you won't have all of us judging every word you say."

"Having just Clopas there will help. He is easy to talk to. I don't mean that I wouldn't welcome you there, Mother, but I think you are as anxious as I am."

"You're right, Mari. As usual. Go and get some rest and let him see the best side of you in the morning."

Three people slept badly on that sultry night. A mixture of discomfort and overactive imagination delivered a heavy blow to adequate rest. As a result, drowsiness only came in the hour before it was time to wake; morning nerves were quelled by sluggish systems.

"Do something, child. Fetch the water if you will not eat properly! And Salome, you take the goats and sheep out to graze today. Mariam has more important things she has to do."

As a result, when Joseph was ready, Mariam had to run, flushed and sticky, back to her home, then, without careful preparation, was chased over to the room where Clopas and Joseph were waiting for her. Her obvious recent activity helped Joseph ask her naturally about her household duties and her skills, and Clopas endorsed her homemaking abilities when he felt the girl was being too modest.

"Are you hungry, Mariam, or have you had your breakfast?"

"I didn't eat much, sir: I slept too late because I was so agitated during the night."

"I hope that was not because I made a bad impression on you yesterday."

"No, it was just because it's all so important, and I could not stop my mind churning over."

"Me too."

"Oh, I thought that you, being so much more experienced than me, would be much less bothered."

"On the contrary, Mariam, just because I have more experience means that I am more fearful of making a mistake. Anyway, if you have had little to eat, let us both eat some bread; I think, Clopas, there are some figs and some milk, still warm."

Mari watched in astonishment as Clopas bade her remain seated and fetched the food as if he were the servant.

"You eat, Mariam, while you listen to what I have to say. Your uncle said much to me last night and I am overwhelmed at his proposed generosity. As you know, I have a trade, but little capital behind me. I will make no bones about it, Mariam, I am not a rich man and I would not try to hide that fact from you. I can offer your uncle little in the way of bride price for you to either compensate him for the loss of your service, or to pass on to you as a bridal gift. But he has waived all that, Mariam; he wants nothing for himself and he will see that you are adequately provided for at your wedding, if you give your approval."

Joseph reached across and broke a piece of bread from the loaf in front of Mariam. He paused, digested a little, then continued his discourse.

"Furthermore, Mariam, your uncle is in a position to help me greatly in my trade. I am finding it difficult in Bethlehem: I am so near to Jerusalem, where there are many craftsmen, and I have no family who will give me their business. Eli has contacts in Sepphoris, where so much building work is now in train, though," he added hastily, "I understand your uncle disapproves of much of it! However, in the short term he has offered to set me up with some contracts there, whilst in the longer term he suggests I settle here in Nazareth and serve the local community. The exciting thing, Mariam, is that he has offered me this room here as the base for my activity, and if you will consent to be my bride, this would be your home too."

Mariam looked at Clopas with a questioning eye, whilst allowing a smile to play around her lips.

"Is that true, Clopas? Would he really do that for us?"

"Yes, Mari. I was present when Eli made the offer to Joseph. It's not all disinterested, of course. He doesn't want to lose your skills with the children and the livestock. And," he said, pulling her leg a little, "he can keep a closer eye on you here in Nazareth than in Bethlehem. I don't think he trusts Joseph to master you properly: he feels your charms will cause him to be too pliant with you!"

"You see, Mariam," interjected Joseph, "I've really little reason to stay in Bethlehem. I have property there, but it is very poor and small, on the far outskirts of the town. I would find most of my work in Jerusalem itself, so you would be left for long periods on your own, with no kinsfolk nearer than Elizabeth and Zechariah in Ein–Karem. Here you would have your family all around you, when you have children," – Mari bent her head and blushed – "you'd have help from Miriam and your own mother. What do you say to that?"

"It sounds a happy arrangement, Joseph, that would please me dearly. I presume his offers to you only apply if we agree to marry?"

"Well, yes, I'd taken that for granted."

"You won't agree to marry me just to get Uncle's help, will you?"

"Mariam, you are a blunt girl! As you put it like that, I'll answer you; no, I will not marry you just to receive Eli's offers. But I'm sure I shall find you a suitable partner if all that everyone's said about you is true."

"I wonder what they have told you about me."

"Nothing to do you discredit, Mariam."

"That's what worries me. I don't want you to agree to marry me and then find out things about me that have been kept from you."

"Mariam," began Clopas, "there really isn't any need –"

"Joseph," interrupted Mariam, to his evident astonishment, "have they told you all about my father and the Zealots and how Uncle Eli has been supporting us here since we left Ein–Karem?"

"Well, yes, he explained that," said Joseph a little defensively. "I understand that your father has recently been killed by Herod's men. I really am sorry for you; I believe he was a true patriot."

"Did they tell you that they think it was my fault that he died? That they think I acted irresponsibly and put the whole village at risk? That they think I talk too freely with bad people and strangers? That they intended to have me whipped publicly for all this and only punished me in private because of public opinion? That they find me a problem?"

"Mari, for goodness' sake hold your tongue," shouted Clopas. "What are you trying to do? Are you trying to sabotage Eli's efforts to obtain a husband for you? Have you already decided that you are not prepared to marry Joseph?"

"No, Clopas, please, no. But how can Joseph decide if he wants to marry me if he does not know the truth? You do want the truth, don't you, Joseph?"

Joseph had looked aghast during this exchange. His whole planned edifice had rocked and shuddered.

"Why, Mariam, of course I want the truth. But surely it is for Eli and Clopas to tell me in their own good time. You seem a little headstrong."

"I don't know the best way to say things for my own good, Joseph, that's true. Our ways here in Nazareth are probably rough and ready compared with how you behave in Jerusalem. And certainly Uncle Eli thinks I am too impulsive and think too much for myself, although he had me educated to do so!"

"Is what the girl says true, Clopas?"

"Certainly the last remark about being impulsive."

"No, I meant the things she accused herself of."

"I'll put you in the picture on recent events here, Joseph, don't worry about that. Mariam, I think that is enough for the moment. Go back home and help your mother. If Joseph wishes, you may have a further meeting this afternoon."

"Yes, Clopas. I'm sorry if you think I was wrong to say what I did."

"I think a quiet talk between Joseph and myself now, without your interruptions, would be best. So run along, Mari. I'll let your mother know during the day when you should see Joseph next."

Mariam turned and, feeling her dismissal acutely, dragged her feet across the courtyard. She pushed open the door of her own home, found just her mother, and sat herself cross-legged on the floor.

"Well," inquired Anna cheerfully, "how are you getting on with Joseph then?"

"Oh Mother, I think I've just gone and upset everything!"

"Why, what do you mean?" replied Anna in alarm.

"I wanted Joseph to like me despite all the things Uncle Eli and the others say about me. And then I found out he hadn't told Joseph anything of what has happened and I just blurted it all out, and now I think I've put Joseph off and Clopas was angry with me and I've spoilt everything!"

"Mari, come on, it can't be that bad. What did you tell him?"

"About how I put Father and the whole town at risk and how I was punished and that Uncle Eli said I must be married."

"Did you, love? Just bluntly like that?"

"More or less, I'm afraid, Mother."

"Don't worry about it. I'll try to find out if you've upset him and apologise for you and ask for another chance. But try to be more cautious, child; respond to what you're asked, don't try to take control. You're barely thirteen. You haven't enough experience yet to use good judgement."

Mariam sighed and stood up.

"Now stop fretting about it, and give me a hand. Take Benjamin with you and go and milk the goats, will you, please."

In Joseph's lodging meanwhile, Clopas had, at Joseph's request, been putting him in the picture over recent events and Mariam's role within the dramas.

"Don't hold these things against Mariam, I beg of you," confided Clopas to Joseph. "The girl has been punished more than enough for what, frankly, Eli set in train, and I bear my part of the guilt. Any fault on Mariam's side was no more than childish naivety. And the girl behaved very well under stress. The community here respects her more rather than less because of it, although Mari herself seems unaware of this. I assure you it is true. Any resentment or criticism in the village is aimed at us, not at your bride-to-be."

"These things I can accept and I find your words reassuring. But other things I saw with my own eyes: her forwardness, her lack of respect for her elders. And I found her statement that Eli was seeking to negotiate a marriage for her, in consequence, disturbing."

"These characteristics are no more than childish enthusiasms, Joseph. She is an idealistic girl with a strong sense of fairness and justice – which, heaven knows, we test to its limit on occasions! Yes, I'll be frank with you. Eli feels she needs someone to control her, that if she is not curbed soon, she will grow to be unmanageable. But surely, someone of your age and experience of life could cope with a thirteen-year-old:

you could discipline the girl to accept and appreciate the conventions expected from a wife."

"You make your point, Clopas. But what about the other matter she mentions? Have there indeed been other marriage negotiations?"

Clopas was silent, then realised his silence or difficulty in answering was providing its own answer.

"Yes, Joseph, there have been. She was turned down by Isaac of Capernaum – a Zealot colleague of her father, who held her in part to blame for his colleagues' deaths and his own perilous situation. And other exploratory negotiations have come to nothing when the family's links to the Zealots have come to light, because of fears of retribution, or damage to business, should Herod wish to exert pressure. Negotiations have not foundered on Mariam's character, Joseph, of that I can give you full assurance."

"How real is the fear of political persecution?"

"No-one really knows, Joseph. I think the fear is much greater than the reality. If Herod or the Romans wished to ruin our family, it would have been enacted long ago. The whole area is seething with hatred for Herod and his Roman ways. Nearly everyone in this locality has had links at some time or another with hill outlaws, but the Romans have only supported Herod when the activity has been blatant, and then only to make an example of someone, before losing interest. If you are really worried on this score, why not marry the girl and take her to your home in Bethlehem – the connection will not be made there. But I shouldn't give the matter further credence if I were you – the local Zealot bands are dead or put to flight, and the state is too preoccupied with other matters to give any further thought to primitive raids on backwater Jewish villages!"

"I thank you for your frankness, Clopas. If your father extends his hospitality, I should like to stay a while longer yet to get to know Mariam better, before consenting to the betrothal."

"There will be no problem there, Joseph. If you want employment whilst you're here, I'm sure Eli could obtain work for you temporarily as a craftsman's assistant in the city yonder."

"That would be very convenient. I shall have a word with him accordingly."

"One last thing, Joseph. For the sake of the girl, keep from Eli the things of which she spoke to you. He will be suspicious that she is trying to undermine your betrothal, and his subsequent behaviour could put in jeopardy the very thing we all desire."

"What do you mean?"

"I fear he'll punish, or exert further pressure on the girl, and this could cause Mariam to react against you. She will not be forced and that fact infuriates Eli, who is only then all the more determined to have his own way. But, despite this, it is Mari who has had her own way so far – at some cost, of course, but the girl has guts, that I will say!"

CHAPTER 18

ANNUNCIATION ONE

I AM WATCHING THEM IN THE *vineyards harvesting the grapes. All that is, except Joseph. He has been contracted for a couple of months to a carpenter in Sepphoris, who is engaged in constructing villas for many of the new settlers who are moving there. He cannot leave without breaking his contract. All other members of the family, though, are needed. Eli has a considerable stake in his vineyards: they are the chief source of his wealth and support other members of the family, who now come to help.*

While the adults and older children pick the grapes and in the evenings, tread the fruit, the youngest children play on the terraced slopes without the need for supervision. As dusk falls, the women prepare provisions for the next day and the girls fetch water so that all can cleanse themselves from the dust of the fields and the crimson stains of the grape juice.

For two days the activity has been feverish and the harvest is sufficiently bountiful to indicate a further two days' work with everyone at full stretch. Then, in the last minute preparations for the field, Mari is despatched in haste to supplement the water supply, and in her dash, turns her ankle on a rock and falls. Feeling foolish, she picks herself up and brushes the dust off her old tunic, which has been retrieved specially for the harvest, but finds difficulty in putting any weight on her right foot. She massages the ankle and limps to the well to fill her water pot. On the return to her home, she has great difficulty in walking in a way that does not spill the precious liquid, but evolves a method of dragging her foot that keeps the jar in reasonable balance.

At first Mari is scolded for taking so long, but then her mother observes her swollen ankle and makes the girl lie down while she applies some soothing ointment. The flesh under her fingers is inflamed and puffy, hot to touch, and Anna sees the girl is obviously in pain. If she helps in the fields, not only will she be slow, she'll cause further damage to the ankle and be ineffective for the rest of the harvest. She is therefore left on her own, to take her time, putting the beds away and cleaning the rooms round the courtyard; and then to rest her ankle, while the others spend a further day in the vineyard.

Now is my opportunity.

After watching the others go, Mariam limps around the room, completing her chores, then forced by the pain in her ankle, she lies back on the mattress out of the heat of direct sunlight and eases her leg into a position where the ankle is supported and ceases to throb. She is on the point of dozing off, when I open the door of the house quietly – she hears nothing, but a shaft of sunlight suddenly floods the room. At first she presumes one of the others has returned for something, then she sees me. Mariam sits up in fear, crying out as she twists her ankle slightly in her involuntary movement, and gapes at the fair-haired stranger (am I still a stranger to her?) now bending at the foot of her mattress.

"What are you doing here? Please don't harm me! My mother and my uncle are not here. I'll tell you where you can find them!"

"Mariam, don't be afraid of me. It is you that I've come to see. I have a message for you."

"A message? What sort of message? Why do you bring it to me rather than to my uncle or my mother?"

"I have watched you, Mari. I have talked with you before under the fig tree. You are special, Mari. You have been tested and found worthy of a very important task."

"How do you know? Who are you? Are you a priest?"

"I am a messenger, Mariam. I serve God and do his bidding. I interpret his will, and at his inspiration, I go, I come, I act, I create."

"Sir, I am confused. I don't understand. What do you want me to do?"

"Don't upset yourself, Mari. God has chosen you to be the mother of the king, the Messiah. You have prayed to God and he has heard your prayer."

Mariam is speechless. She cannot believe her ears. She thinks she is daydreaming. She shakes her head as if it cannot be. She clutches at the side of her mattress as if to save herself from drowning, to hold fast to something solid.

"Sir, sir, I am overwhelmed. But why me? I am so small, so unworthy. There are many far wiser than I, richer, more powerful. No-one will believe me!"

"Mariam, God has chosen you; he has not preferred others, so accept his choice. Do not be afraid: he will be with you. He will protect you. Many will be angry with you, will criticise, but they will be ashamed and disgraced. God will be just like a shepherd: he will hold you in his arms like the lambs you care for yourself."

"Sir, if this is what God wants of me, then I must do what he asks. I have always tried to be his servant, so it must be as you have said. But what should I do?"

"Mariam, be patient. Wait. You'll find out in due time. Pray. Read the scriptures. Seek God's guidance in all that you do. Be careful that you listen to God and not to the advice of men. Above all, Mariam, remember that God has chosen you as you are; be confident that he accepts you now. Do not seek to change; be your natural self!"

"Will I see you again? Will you return to tell me what to do?"

"I don't know, Mariam. Maybe. I too must seek inspiration and dare to follow it, creating action out of dreams."

Maybe you think I'm deceiving her, that I do know, that I see the future. I assure you, reader, I don't. I have to wait for enlightenment too.

"Sir, sir – - ?"

"Enough, Mari. I have to go. Wait and think and be prepared. Let God take the initiative. Pray for insight and the courage to react, to seize the opportunity."

"Should I – - ?"

"Shush, Mari. Be still. Farewell, my child."

And I bend over the trembling girl and kiss her tenderly, then lay my hand upon her head and gently tilt her until I'm looking deep into her eyes.

"God be with you, Mariam."

And before she can frame another query, I'm gone, the door swinging softly behind me. I wait outside. I can sense the turmoil I have sown. I want to go back, comfort, reassure, even move her on to the next stage now, but I feel I am too impatient – that inner voice tells me to wait. She needs time to readjust her thoughts…

Immediately Mari springs up, nearly falls over as she tries to hobble on her forgotten leg, and hops to the window, peering after me with great urgency. But she cannot see me. The courtyard is bare. Swirls of dust eddy in the morning heat. I am hidden from her eyes.

She limps back to her couch. Her mind is racing. Her adrenalin is flowing. She is excited. She cannot sit still despite her impediment. What does this mean? Has she invented everything because she wanted it so? Has she misunderstood perfectly innocent remarks? Has she read more into it than was meant? How could she have misunderstood? But what did it mean, when, how? With a lurch of recognition, she remembers Joseph is of King David's ancestry, as she is herself. Is this the secret? Is this the sign that she will marry him? When will he next be back from Sepphoris? When will he ask again to see her? Will she confide all that has been told her to him, or will he think she's mad?

Mari stumbles across the room to the little cupboard where she keeps her meagre possessions. She extracts the scroll that Eli gave her on her twelfth birthday, sits on the floor and pores over it. Her eye fixes on the second text:

"My father and my mother may abandon me
But the Lord will take care of me."

Her eyes mist over with grief for her father. Will her mother one day leave her as well? What did that fair-haired stranger say?

"God will be your shepherd, he will gather you
Like a lamb in his arms."

Mari stands at the foot of her mattress, deep in thought.

"Let me trust you, Lord God. Lead me like a shepherd to the stream. I pray for the support of my mother and the rest of my family in all I have to do. But if I am alone, look after me like I look after my sheep. I will do whatever you want me to. But I will often need your help."

She walks across the room to the window and looks out at the streaming sunshine. She feels calmer. And she suddenly realises that she did not limp there. She tests her ankle; it holds her, she feels much better. The swelling is going down. I breathe a sigh of relief. I can safely leave her now.

CHAPTER 19

GETTING ACQUAINTED

OSEPH WAS HOME FOR THE Sabbath. Mariam saw him come in late the previous night, just before dusk, from her vantage point at the window overlooking the courtyard. She kept watch for him while she supervised the children during preparations for the ritual at the synagogue. However, she saw him only when they made their way down to the sanctuary, the men walking on ahead, deep in conversation, ignoring Anna, Miriam and the children following in their wake. She watched him in the middle of the congregation, with her uncle and Clopas, as she pressed her face to the slats which confined her to the Women's Court. Her heart leaped in secret thrill when Rabbi Joel was invited to give the exposition, and chose the words from Isaiah:

"Arise, shine, for your light has come
And the glory of the Lord rises upon you.
See, darkness covers the earth
And thick darkness is over the peoples
But the Lord rises upon you
And his Glory appears over you."

As he compared their times of enemy occupation with the darkness covering the earth, he spoke of their hope for salvation through the Messiah that God had promised, and as he intoned prayers on behalf of the congregation, Mariam bubbled inwardly as the promise kept coming to her: you are the living answer to this prayer and no-one but you knows it. She peered through her fingers and looked at the congregation, solemn, pious, dull; and thought: what if they knew? How would they react? Would they be as excited as I am?

And then, in the afternoon, Joseph was sitting in the shade, watching Mariam as she played with the children in the yard. He saw the instinctive way she handled them, perceived the confidence they had in her. When they were playing happily, with Mariam only holding herself ready to intervene if necessary, Joseph called to her, "Mariam, come and sit with me here in the shade and talk. The children will be fine on their own."

Mari's heart skipped a beat. She had been waiting and hoping for Joseph to say something; she had been conscious that he had been silently scrutinizing her now for over an hour and she had found great difficulty in behaving normally. She squatted on the ground at Joseph's feet and waited for him to say something. The man was shy, she realised. He did not seem to know what to say to her.

"Joseph, do you like children?"

Although he had been struggling for an opening gambit, Joseph was thrown by Mari's question.

"Well, of course, it's one's duty to build a family and have sons to carry on one's line."

"Yes, I know, Joseph, but I mean, do you actually like children?"

"I think so, Mariam, but it's a long time since I came into contact with any. I have watched you with James and Jude and the others and I can see you love them."

"I do, Joseph, I do. They always tell you what they think and they give you a good hug when they want to, and they like it when you just feel like cuddling them."

Even as she was talking she was making eyes at Mo, and the little girl trotted over without reserve, and plonked herself unceremoniously on Mari's lap, putting a thumb in her mouth, and fingering the end of the cord round Mari's waist.

"See what I mean? Would you like her on your lap?"

"No, Mari, she knows you. I expect she'd be afraid of a stranger like me."

"Not if I'm with you, she won't."

"Don't disturb her, Mariam, she's comfortable with you."

There was a silence. Mari lowered her head to hold her cheek against the little girl's.

"When I get married, I want lots of children. I'd like a boy first. Perhaps he'd be very special? What about you, Joseph, do you want a big family?"

"It would be in God's hands, Mariam, it is not ours to choose."

There was another long silence.

"Tell me about your home in Bethlehem!"

Gradually Joseph began to unwind with her, describing his room, his workshop, his neighbours and the people for whom he worked. She wanted to know about his family and childhood, but he seemed to clam up again, as though she was pushing on a painful wound. Mariam sensed this and sat alongside him, moving Mo carefully to one side so that she could touch him, slip her arm through his. Joseph started and began to pull his arm away, then accepted the contact even though he was clearly uneasy. Mariam took up the conversation and chattered on about the children, her mother, her work in the fields. Finally she asked him, "Do you think God has a plan for each one of us, Joseph?"

"For some people he has. He has a plan for our nation and that means that certain individuals must be obedient to his vision."

"I bet he has for everyone. I know he has for me!"

"Really, Mariam? Do you want to tell me about it?"

"I'm still trying to find out exactly what it is; but I'm sure there is a plan."

"Am I in that plan, do you think?"

"I don't know for sure, Joseph. But I think you are!"

"I'm glad about that."

She waited to see if he was going to give her any more clues to his thoughts. But she would have to be satisfied with that. She wondered if she ought to say anything about the Messiah. But she sensed not. He was not ready for that yet.

Over the evening meal with Eli Joseph was very reticent. He was polite, he responded to Eli's discourse, but volunteered nothing.

"Joseph," said Eli firmly as the meal was being concluded, "tell me how you are getting along with Mariam."

Joseph thought carefully before replying.

"She is a strange girl in many ways, Eli."

"Strange?"

"Don't misunderstand me, I can't help but like the girl. She is young, attractive, good about the house and accomplished in a wife's duties. But I've never met anyone quite like her before!"

"You don't have many dealings with children and young people in Bethlehem, do you?"

"Well, I suppose not; it must be partly me. But she seems so outspoken, so forward; she talks to me as if I was her friend instead of a future fiancé. She tells me all sorts of things without reserve, things which if I were in her shoes I wouldn't dream of saying."

"Does she offend you?"

"No, Eli, certainly not. In many ways I like it thus. She fascinates me. Her company excites me. I feel her enthusiasm spilling into me. But all the time I feel ill at ease. I never know what she is going to do or say next; she will ask me a direct question and sometimes I do not know what to say to her. It is very unsettling."

"You should not let her treat you in this way. Tell her to observe the proprieties and give you more respect. Tell her that if she displeases you I will chastise her over my knee in front of you. That should bring her to heel."

"In some ways, Eli, I like her as she is. To talk with her is an adventure. It's just that my upbringing has made me vulnerable to her approach: our Jerusalem ways are full of rules and etiquette."

"I know we are a crude people here in the north, Joseph, and you will need to make allowances for that. The children are not brought up with the strictness you and I knew, unfortunately. But I have my standards, and Mariam, despite her intelligence and personality, sometimes stretches them to the limit. It is part of my plan that she should conform more closely to become a good Jewish wife. If you will take on this role of moulding her thus, you will have my full support, you must know that!"

"Yes, I understand what you are saying, sir. Can I ask you a question? Is she a religious girl? I can't make up my mind about her."

"She has been taught the Torah as well as any child and has had a wider general education than any girl of her age, of that you may be sure. She has always been naturally interested – Rabbi Joel will tell you that she has frequently asked him for a loan of the scrolls to study in the synagogue. Yet sometimes she worries me that her obedience to the scriptures lags behind her understanding of it. Why do you ask?"

"She gives me the impression of someone who is well read, but seeks to impart her own interpretation instead of being satisfied with the traditions handed down. She says things which make me wonder if she values her own opinions and judgements more than the holy tenets of our law. She often talks about God as though she knew what he was thinking, even to the extent of recklessness with the scriptural word."

"You alarm me, Joseph. She is treading dangerous water. I pray that you will help me save her from herself before she goes too far. Some of the wildness of her father is in her, but it is being channelled in different ways. Ardent nationalism I can understand, even support – with due caution. But her lack of judgement will lead her to blasphemy if she is not careful; we must protect her. She has such great potential that to lose her in this way would be a dreadful waste."

Eli was pacing the room, thinking, agitated. He swung round on Joseph, and brought things to a head.

"Come, Joseph, let us beat about the bush no more. Are you willing to take her as your wife, with all the support I've promised you?"

"I've given it a lot of thought. I may regret my decision – it could cause me more pain and tribulation than the safer way – but really there is only one answer I can give. Yes, Eli, I'll take Mariam as my wife, provided she will consent."

"Good. Do you think there is any chance of her refusing you?"

"You will have to ask her yourself, Eli. I would have said she will accept me, but I cannot read her yet; she could well choose the unexpected."

"She'd better not do so. I've had enough of her independent will. It's time she appreciated what is being done for her. Assume that your engagement is accomplished and I'll fix the betrothal for three weeks' time, to coincide with her thirteenth birthday. I'll act as her father, of course, and in the interim period we can negotiate the bride price and your future living accommodation here. I'll honour all I promised. But tame her, Joseph; exert your influence over her; don't let her run so freely with the children; wean her off her mother's influence, which I sometimes feel is not always good for her."

"Are you going to tell her?"

"Would you like to?"

"Yes, I think I'd prefer to break it to her. I shall that way gauge her true reaction. If she consented to you, I would always wonder if she consented fully or felt some fear of you."

"Don't give her too much licence to refuse, Joseph. If she does try to delay her answer, or even try refusal, send her to me. You'll not get anywhere by being soft with her." Next morning Joseph was up at first light and as he was crossing the courtyard, spied the door of Anna's room swing open.

"Mariam, can I have a word with you please?"

Joseph was stopping Mari as she was on her way early to replenish the water supplies.

"Sir?"

"Mariam, I had a long talk with your uncle last night. I told him that I would agree to a betrothal between us. Will you give your consent to be my wife, Mari?"

Mariam put her water pot on the earth, and looked at him, her eyes distant, conveying nothing. She was making him nervous.

"Mariam, if you'd rather not give an answer this instant, think it over and let me know later in the day. Perhaps I've surprised you."

"Joseph, no, you've not surprised me. I've been giving a lot of thought to it, because of course I've always known why you're here. I'm ready, Joseph. Yes, I'll give my consent."

Both hesitated a moment. How should they react? Then, simultaneously they turned; Joseph walked back to Eli in relief. "Eli, she's consented. Let's think about the consequences."

Mariam left her water jar standing and rushed back into her home.

"Mum, Salome, Becca, Ben, guess what! Joseph has asked me to be his wife! And I've said yes!"

While the children crowded around, flinging questions at her, Mari, overcome with the magnitude of her decision, threw herself into Anna's arms and burst into spontaneous tears so that everyone was silenced, wondering what on earth had happened. Anna stroked her hair, calmed the girl until she raised a tear-streaked face and Mari smiled wanly at everyone.

"What a silly way to tell everyone you're going to be married! I just feel a little shaky, that's all. I'll be all right in a minute."

"When will the betrothal be, Mari?"

"Oh, I didn't think to ask, Mum!"

"I think you'd better let Salome go for the water, and you and I will sit down calmly and work out what we need to know and do."

CHAPTER 20

THE BETROTHAL

*T*HE FAMILY WAS GATHERED TOGETHER, squashed into Eli's largest room: his son, his daughters and their spouses, Anna's sisters from Judea, their husbands and all their children. Anna was there, of course, with her children. Elizabeth and Zechariah from Ein–Karem were the only absentees – they had sent a message to say that Elizabeth was unwell. And, amid the hushed and expectant circle, in the small space that was free of limbs and robes, stood Joseph and Mariam, while Eli adjusted his white robes and held up his hands unnecessarily to gain everyone's attention.

"Dear family, it is an honour to have you all present with us here to celebrate with Joseph and Mariam as they make their betrothal vows. We are especially pleased to see those of you who have come so far to grace us with your presence. I find myself in an unusual role here tonight for I am acting as father to both Mariam and Joseph. Mariam, of course, is known to me since birth, although it is only in the last few months that I have legal responsibility for her. Joseph, I welcome you into our family, for as I promised, I offer you a home and work here in Nazareth. From henceforth you shall be my adopted son."

The adults looked at Joseph and applauded Eli's generosity politely.

"I could say many more things about you both at this time…" He was acutely sensitive to the fidgeting of the many children present, "…but now is not the right moment. I ask you, therefore, Joseph, to perform 'Qiddu-shin', to sanctify Mariam as your future wife."

Joseph turned, and looked at Mariam standing beside him, adorned in her pale blue tunic and a decorated new girdle, her embroidered shawl around her shoulders, her dark hair glossy and flowing under its crimson band. Her eyes were bright and wide. Her face was flushed and animated. She stood erect to her future husband's shoulder and looked up at Eli towering over her. Anna stared at her daughter through blurring vision, sensing Mari's vulnerability, knowing that there was nothing further she could do now, only pray that she had made the right choice.

"Mariam," said Joseph, holding a tiny silver coin between his fingers, "be thou consecrated unto me by this, according to the Law of Moses and Israel."

Eli nodded to Mariam.

"Do you consent to be betrothed to this man?"

"I do so consent."

Mariam lifted her right arm and opened her palm to receive Joseph's symbol. They briefly touched, then she closed her hand round the tiny coin.

"By this vow and symbol," announced Eli, "you are both set aside for each other, the wedding to be completed between you as is our custom in a year's time from this day. You are now promised to each other; you may not be released from this vow, except by a bill of divorce. May God bless you and keep you pure and free from sin, that in the fullness of time he may reward you with prosperity and many sons."

Eli lowered his arms from the blessing and continued on a lower note, "And now it is fitting to mark Mariam's thirteenth birthday on this very day, so that the banquet prepared and now ready for us is a double celebration. Let us join the happy couple to drink a cup of the best wine from my own vineyard, before the ladies and children withdraw to Clopas' house, where their repast is awaiting them."

When the banquet was well underway and all had assuaged their initial hunger, Eli rose with Joseph from his table and sent for Mariam to join them. He took the newly betrothed pair into the room in which Joseph was currently lodging, and said, "This is your home now, Joseph. You may spend some time with Mariam here apart from the stress and noise which is around you. Before I leave you to yourselves a while, though, can I just remind you both of the customs which now accompany your status."

For a moment, Eli fixed his gaze on Joseph and said to him, "Whilst most of what I have to say is for Mariam's benefit, I am cognisant of the fact that many of our customs and traditions here in Galilee differ from your practices in Judea, and I would not wish you to cause offence by ignorance. To the contrary, it is my belief that we are not so rigid here in the formalities which apply in the south, and I would not wish you, Joseph, to be unnecessarily constrained, nor to be anxious if Mariam is behaving in a way you do not expect. On the other hand, when our rules are broken, justice and retribution can be a little summary here, and you would perhaps consider it to be harsh and brutal compared with the due legal processes that I know are practised in Jerusalem."

Eli paused for breath and then continued, "You are both of course consecrated, reserved for each other. It goes without saying, I trust, that flirting and dalliance with others is forbidden; indeed it is considered unseemly that you are at any time alone with a member of the opposite sex who is not of your immediate family. Other than that, there is no restriction on your movement, Joseph. As far as you are concerned, Mariam, you may not talk to any man, or boy who is of age, unless you are in company and then only when spoken to directly and it would be rude to be silent. This taboo excludes, of course, relations with Clopas or myself or any sons-in-law when they are visiting our house, or the priests and rabbis at the synagogue. You are to be modestly attired at all times so that you do not cause temptation in other men. During the coming months you will spend much time with your mother preparing your bridal outfit – and I will see that you are generously provided for, Mariam, as if you were my own daughter."

"Thank you, Uncle."

"You will, of course, continue with your womanly duties: helping your mother in the home, fetching water, looking after the children and my flocks as you have been doing for several years now. But I ask you, Mariam, to adopt a little more dignity; remember now who you are. Stop gallivanting about like the little children, careless of your modesty. Comport yourself always as if you were in adult company. Practise the ways of a wife so that you may find the role easier when you are wedded to Joseph."

Mariam said nothing; she was just looking Eli firmly in the eye and listening attentively. From time to time Eli paused, seeking her reaction, some reassurance, a signal that she would comply. This she denied him, not with insolence or rebellion. She contained her feelings and gave no hint or expression to her thoughts. Occasionally she glanced at Joseph, allowed a glimmer of a smile to flit across her face, then turned once more to her uncle, matching his solemnity with equal mien.

"And now, both of you, to your relations with each other. We do not deny you here, as I believe is the case in Judea, any private discourse with each other. In public it is best when you are together that you are chaperoned, but here in this home you may be alone. We trust you to refrain from sin and fornication – that is all we ask. Society here is unsophisticated – lax morals are not tolerated. Above all, virginity of the bride is all-important: inability to prove this on your wedding night would be a disgrace to all of us, which would cause much distress. And as you know, we are not slow to punish transgressors here in Galilee. We have our own Jewish law and priestly traditions; we pay little heed here to Roman law, which imposes some penalty restraints in more populous parts. So do not embarrass me. As a rabbi here in Nazareth I am expected to uphold our customs. Do not by your behaviour force me to have to subject you to the full weight of local retribution. Do you know what I am talking about, Mariam?"

"Yes, sir!"

"You have had some taste of this already in your young life. I do not wish to repeat this experience. I cannot, nor will not, ever make an exception because you are now in effect my daughter. On the contrary, you can expect exemplary discipline from me to demonstrate only that I impose the law without fear or favour!"

"Well," said Eli after a suitable pause to let all this sink in, "I trust I will not have to repeat any of this in the future. Let us now relax and enjoy the remainder of the banquet. You may remain here in each other's company for a while, but do not deny your guests too long."

Eli made as if to add something else, perhaps a word of encouragement, but if so, it froze on his lips, and he exited abruptly, leaving them awkwardly standing, isolated.

"Come and sit down, Mari. Let us rest a moment, or do you want to get back to the fun with the women and children?"

"No, Joseph, I'm happy here with you."

"Good. Can I ask you, Mariam, are you truly happy? I want you to be happy. You know that, don't you?"

"Yes, I know that. You are kind to consider my feelings. It is all a little overwhelming. I confess I feel a bit numb. But I am happy that we are to be married. It is our destiny I accept without reservation as ordained by God."

"You are truly a religious girl, Mari. You bring God into everything."

"I have been brought up to believe that this is true for all Jews, and I have found it so in reality. Is it not so for you?"

"I, too, have been taught the same. Perhaps I do not find it comes so naturally to express this belief as freely as you do in normal conversation."

"It does not seem strange to me. I talk about whatever I think or do without hindrance or reservation. I find it very hard to keep secrets."

Perhaps if Joseph had been a little more acute, sensitive to Mari's words and eager probing, he would have encouraged her to reveal the stranger's message to her. But, after a pregnant pause, he changed the subject.

"My contract in Sepphoris runs for a further four weeks, Mariam. I shall be home for the Sabbath and will have opportunities to see and talk to you as your uncle has described. After that I am likely to be on the far side of Lake Genneseret, working in the town of Capernaum for several weeks and I shall be away from home, except for festivals."

"Oh, I see."

"You will be all right here I know; life will be as before. I'm sure you've plenty of things now to prepare for our wedding."

"Yes, of course."

"Mariam?"

"Yes?"

"Mariam, I..." Joseph hesitated and stared at his bride to be. "Mariam, let me just look at you for a moment. You are a very lovely girl and I am a very fortunate man."

The girl blushed and offered him her hand. Joseph took it awkwardly, gave it a quick squeeze and let it drop into her lap.

"Perhaps we'd better go back to the feast now, Mariam!"

"If you think we ought to?"

Joseph swallowed and nodded, rose swiftly and offered Mariam his hand to assist her to her feet.

"I'll see you at sunrise if you're up to fetch the water; I'll be leaving early for Sepphoris."

"I'll be there, Joseph. Are you going now?"

"I think I'd better. Goodnight, Mari, and God bless you."

"Goodnight, Joseph. May God bless both of us!"

CHAPTER 21

THE STONING

ARI HAD BEEN WALKING TO the market with her friend, Bilpah, exchanging gossip about weddings plans, which for the older girl were to be celebrated shortly before the rainy winter period set in, some two months thence. Concentrating, as she was, on their discourse, Mari was not really watching the passing groups of people, though from time to time both girls were greeted by women from their part of the village, or mothers of their friends.

For some obscure reason, Mari suddenly looked up and, since she was facing the sun, distinguished shapes ahead of her with difficulty. Towering over other moving figures, though, was the bare head of a man through whose hair the sunlight was reflected, as though it were on fire. With a start Mari recognised the fair-headed stranger and before she could control herself, she realised she was trembling all over. As nonchalantly as she could, she remarked to her companion, "See that man ahead of us, that one that is so much taller than the others. Have you seen him before?"

"No, I don't recognise him, but he is very distinctive, isn't he! I bet he is the man I heard my father talking about last night."

"Oh? What did you hear?"

"He said that there was a tall stranger in town, staying with Althaeus the tax collector. He was appalled that a stranger could only get hospitality in that den of iniquity, but perhaps the man was up to no good."

"We once had a stranger very like that man, who asked for lodgings at our house. Uncle Eli wouldn't let him stay, because he was afraid of Herod's spies."

"Perhaps he's the same man. If he is a spy, only that collaborator would give him houseroom."

"Did your father say what his name was?"

"He did say. I can't remember; I wasn't really listening. I think it was Elijah or something like that!"

"What! The same name as the prophet?"

"Well, that's what I heard. Perhaps he said something else similar and I converted it to 'Elijah' because of the name's familiarity."

"He's not with anyone. I wonder where he's going?"

"I know, let's follow him. If it is to Althaeus' house, it will not be far out of our way."

The two girls, whispering conspiratorially behind their hands, kept other walking figures between their quarry and themselves, and sure enough, he turned down the narrow lane just before the market square.

"It is him!" confided Bilpah in jubilation as the man stopped outside Althaeus' gateway. The stranger, caught in mid-stride, glanced quickly behind him and saw the two girls hovering at the corner. Mariam froze as his gaze pinpointed her own, and she felt embarrassment creep up her backbone. She knew that he knew that she had been following him. When would he contact her again? It was both the man who called on Eli several months ago, and the messenger who talked to her under the fig tree. She knew that now for certain.

"Come on, Bilpah, let's finish our business in the market and get home!"

"What's the matter, Mari? I thought you had plenty of time."

"I've remembered something I promised Mum I'd do. Let's get on quickly."

"All right, if you must. I was looking forward to company and a good long natter!"

Over the evening meal, Mari tried to steer the conversation round to the stranger in the town, without displaying too much obvious curiosity. Her mother didn't react at first, but luckily Rebecca took up the theme and said that James and Jude were talking about him during the afternoon. In the end, Anna eventually conceded that she was aware of the man's presence, and that he had been seen in the town before.

"Uncle Eli knows it is the man who once asked for lodgings here. He still thinks he may be a spy. He's seen him hanging around near this part of the village, appearing to watch our house. Don't have anything to do with the man, any of you. He could be dangerous to know."

Two days later Anna asked her daughter to go down to the well to fetch water.

"You needn't hurry back. I don't require the water immediately. The children are playing down there somewhere. If you find them, you can stay with them a while, but bring them back with you."

They were there. As soon as they saw Mari coming they ran to her and mobbed her, all shouting at once. She tried to calm them down, laughing and joking with them. They were overjoyed to see her – she had not spent much time with them recently.

Rebecca said, "There was a man here. All on his own, fetching water himself. Just fancy that!"

"And he asked all about you," added Jude solemnly.

"What did you say?"

"He asked all about you," the boy repeated patiently. "What you were like, you know, whether you played with us, and whether we liked you, that sort of thing!"

"I told him you were the best sister any girl could have!" chortled Rebecca breathlessly. "We all did. Even the boys said you were great, for a girl!"

"Did he say why he was asking the questions about me?"

"No."

"Did he say who he was?"

"No."

"Did you ask him?"

"No."

"A fine lot you are. Weren't you curious why he was asking all those questions?"

"We didn't think at the time," said Salome, biting her lip and thinking hard. "He seemed so friendly and so interested. He seemed to like you and wanted to know if we did too! I'm sure he didn't mean you any harm, he was much too nice for that."

"Did he say anything else?" Mari looked at the circle of children in mock exasperation. Benjamin looked at Mari.

"He said he helps the poor and he was glad that you are mercy!"

"No, you silly," contradicted James, "he said Mari."

"No, he didn't."

"He must have meant merciful then."

The children began to lose interest in the topic of conversation and begged Mari to join them in a game.

"Provided you help me lift this water up in a minute. And come home without any argument!"

And so they played. They helped Mari draw the water, and came when she called them without loitering. But when they got home, Mari was still shaking.

Something was wrong. The streets of the village had seemed empty – just a few women hanging around at their doors, gossiping in little huddled groups.

"What's happened, Mother? Why are there so few people about?"

"All the men are down at the synagogue."

"Why?"

"That Samaritan girl living with Althaeus has been caught redhanded in adultery."

"You mean Rachel?"

"Yes, that's the girl."

Mariam was frightened. Her mind immediately flew to Althaeus' lodger. Not her stranger, he couldn't have done that, he was only with the children an hour or two ago!

"Who was she with, Mother?" She waited in trepidation for the answer.

"Joshua, the potter's eldest son. Shame on him, with a young wife and three tiny children. It's them I feel sorry for: they'll probably be driven from the village."

"What will they do to Rachel?"

"I don't know. That's why the men are meeting at the synagogue at the moment. They are questioning her and Joshua and passing judgement on them. I don't give much for Rachel's chances – she's pretty unpopular everywhere and no-one's got much sympathy for Althaeus. Most of the men have condemned her already just to spite that obsequious trickster, though he is probably as angry with her as everyone else. After all, she's all he had, and now she's humiliated him."

"What a mess. I don't think she's ever been very happy."

"Well, she won't be now, when they've finished with her. She'll be lucky to escape with her life."

"They won't really condemn her to death, will they?"

"I wouldn't discount it, my child. It's not that unusual, especially when a loose woman or prostitute is taken with a Jewish family man. She has violated the most sacred family ties – a sin abhorred above all others. Leave it at that, Mari: there are little ears listening and it's not necessary for them to know all the details at their age. Get the two girls to give me a hand with grinding the wheat."

Even as Mari turned to carry out her mother's command, she heard Eli calling in the yard, "Ah, Mariam, you are there. Come with me!"

"Why, where are we going?"

Anna had appeared at the door of her house, looking quizzically at Eli and Mariam.

"Down to the synagogue. The Samaritan girl, Althaeus' whore, has been condemned. I know she's pestered Mariam and the children. Come and see her retribution!"

Anna held up one hand as if in remonstration.

"Eli, it's not necessary to expose Mari to that brutality, surely?"

"It will do her good to see how we deal with immorality in this village: she's got to learn sometime and better now before she's tempted."

"Our Mari would never behave like that girl!"

"I'd rather not see, please," pleaded Mari, her face paling with shock.

"Nonsense," said Eli drumming his staff on the ground with impatience. " I've told you to come, so stop arguing, girl, and practise some obedience for once."

Mari looked hopefully towards her mother, perhaps anticipating further objection from that quarter, but Anna was just shaking her head ruefully. She had seen Eli's determination, and knew it was useless to try to dissuade him.

Mariam had to interject a couple of running steps to keep up with Eli, who was striding towards the synagogue, along with a number of other women and youths, who had heard the rumour and were hurrying to satiate their curiosity.

"What is going to happen? What are they going to do to Rachel?" asked Mariam breathlessly.

"You'll soon see, my girl. And let it be a lesson to you. Never, never be tempted. The Lord God abhors such immorality and roots it out for destruction. Do not have any pity for the girl; it is God's punishment that you will see inflicted."

As they neared the synagogue, Mariam could hear a noise, and she flinched from the unruly mob, which she saw as soon as they turned the last corner; for the crowd was everywhere, running, heaving, loosening rocks and stones from the hillside, from the rough track, even from the walls of the neighbouring houses. Men and youths were red and sweating, their outer garments stripped and thrown over walls or on the bare earth.

Eli propelled Mariam towards the kernel of the mob, past groups of women clustered at the periphery, to the front, where one or two of the other rabbis stood, seemingly impassive in their long white robes. In front of the semicircle of the crowd was the bare white wall of the western flank of the synagogue, the sunlight glaring back at the excited mass. Before them was a simple post, with an iron link fastened to the top: the place where summary justice had been meted out to generations of miscreants, by means of the lash.

A sudden shriek went round the crowd and the youths, still gathering rocks, came running. For round the side of the synagogue two men were dragging the struggling girl, who was trying wildly to free herself from them. She was barefoot and unveiled, her hair had been roughly shorn, and her tunic was hanging free, ungirdled. She herself was not crying out, because she was saving all her energy for her frantic efforts to escape – a vain effort, as she was bound to the men by both her wrists. They dragged her over the rough ground towards the stake, and she suddenly went limp and began to scream and curse them with verbal violence.

The men had got her to the post, and two more untied her and forced her wrists into a noose, which was secured to the ring so that Rachel was stretched, facing the crowd, almost on tiptoe. Her face was contorted. She was still shouting out in fear and anger.

Rabbi Jethro held his arms in the air to bring the crowd to order. The deafening noise subsided until only the girl's howls rent the air.

"Shut her up," commanded his voice, and one of the men at the whipping post delivered a stinging blow across her mouth, then seized the neckline of her tunic and ripped it in one movement to her waist. The shock of the slap and the violence of the tearing of her cloth had silenced the girl momentarily, and Jethro hurriedly addressed the crowd, "We have found Joshua ben Matthew and Rachel of Samaria guilty of adultery and condemn them according to the Law of Moses. Joshua has been banished with his family from our town and we are here to carry out the sentence to which this whore has been condemned. She shall be stoned to death!"

Mariam was tugging at her uncle's sleeve and seeking to bury her face in his robes.

"It's awful – she is so young," choked Mari, nearly in tears. "I want to go, I don't want to see this."

Eli pulled the girl brutally away.

"Don't be so soft. I insist you watch everything. It will teach you a lesson you'll not forget. Now pull yourself together and see what befalls a girl who disgraces this community."

Rachel had begun to scream and cry out again and amid her howls, Jethro gave the order for the stoning to commence. A rain of stones and rocks peppered the thrashing girl; one had caught her leg, drawing blood. A second wave of stones, then more haphazard missiles followed, as the assailants groped for more rocks, each in his own time. One or two of the larger rocks were beginning to find their mark with sickening thuds, causing immediate shrieks of pain torn involuntarily from the girl's lips. Her legs were smothered in blood. One arm was dangling from the stake at an awkward angle as if it had been broken. Her torn tunic was now gaping open to reveal stinging red and broken flesh. Her tunic was stained in an ever-widening circle of blood around her groin, where a large rock had smashed into her, now creating a scream of anguish which had overwhelmed everything that had gone before.

Until this moment Rachel had thrown her head around to defend herself from the missiles aimed at her face. The pain now besetting her body, and her exhaustion, the blinding sun beaming straight into her eyes, took their toll and she began to slump. She stopped trying to evade the stones. Two consecutive rocks caught her about the head – one above her eye, the second breaking her mouth and nose – causing blood to spurt.

Mariam clutched at Eli, who forced her head up and turned it so she had to look.

A further volley of rocks was now finishing the girl off. From her limp position, she would seem, mercifully, to have been unconscious. The rocks battering her body drew further blood at each direct hit, her tunic was soaked through and torn, her head was now gashed open, her legs were broken.

Mariam was now gasping for air, arms flailing, as Eli held her.

"Please, can we go? I'm feeling ill. Please, Uncle!"

Eli was wondering whether to take any notice of the girl, when she retched and was violently sick right at his feet. He waited until she seemed to have emptied her entrails, then hustled her from the front of the crowd to the rear, where he scolded her and wiped her face with a cloth.

Mariam was sobbing now, coughing up phlegm and vomit, wiping her face haphazardly with the cloth her uncle had thrust in her hands.

"For goodness sake, pull yourself together. Do not have any pity for the whore; consider the damage she has caused. Think of Joshua's wife and family; think of all the families she has violated over the years; think of the insults she hurled at you, even accusing your own father."

Mariam was so absorbed in herself that she did not react to her uncle's words.

"Be glad that such a viper has been removed from the earth and that men are free from her temptation."

Mariam rubbed her eyes with the soiled cloth, and looked up between her tears, to focus quite by chance on the solitary figure of Althaeus standing silently at the edge of the crowd. He was not shouting or crying or joining in with the mob. He was looking dazed, forlorn, confused.

"Please, God, be merciful to them," whispered Mariam in a tiny voice.

"What did you say, Mariam?"

"I said a prayer."

"Pray that you always remain pure and worthy of your husband."

Eli averted his eyes from Althaeus, whom he had now seen.

"Go home, Mariam. I have matters here I must attend to."

She was alone now. Others had stayed to the bitter end, to hurl useless stones in vengeful wrath, obliterating the last vestiges of humanity from the crumpled torso, and watched the cutting down and burial outside the consecrated area. As she stumbled over the rough track, not looking where she was going, she could still hear the baying of the crowd, the shouts of derision. She could smell the sickly odour of sweat and fear. Once more she staggered to the verge, and retched, but this time, although she felt her stomach heave, she could do little to assuage the nausea. She was now shaking from head to toe, feeling faint.

I can hold back no longer. She must be comforted.

She senses suddenly my strong arms round her shoulders.

"Mariam, calm yourself. Do not be afraid!"

At first she thinks it is her uncle, or perhaps Clopas, who must have been there somewhere in the crowd. But my voice is different; she knows instinctively who it is.

"Mariam, your pity speaks well of you. Trust your own judgement. You are right to be appalled. Do not let them harden your heart."

"Sir, it was awful."

"Go home, Mariam. Draw new strength. I'll come to you soon, to acquaint you with God's will for your young life. Go home now, and be comforted in the arms of your mother. She will understand."

Mari nearly choked as the bile rose in her throat and she expelled another stream of vomit over the rough stone guttering. She coughed and spat out the last foul remnants of her mouth, and wet her parched lips with her roughened tongue. She straightened up and again mopped her dripping brow, then looked round to see her comforter. He was gone, nowhere to be seen. Had she imagined his presence, his words to her? Surely not; they were not expected. Yet how could he disappear so quickly?

She half thought of searching for him; then she was overcome with unutterable tiredness, and it was as much as she could do to drag herself through the empty street back to her home. She leant against the door of her house and pushed through it, flinging herself face down across the mattress in the corner. She lay there, sobs shaking her body, while Salome, Rebecca and Benjamin stared at her, frightened and confused.

"Why is Mari crying, Mum?" shouted out Rebecca. "Has someone hurt her again?"

Anna came hurrying through from the yard at the side of her room, where she was baking bread.

"Oh Mari, love!" She looked at the others. "No, nothing has been done to Mari. She is upset because of what she's seen. Don't bother her now. Go and play with James and Jude, all of you." Anna chased the whining children out into the courtyard, then sat alongside Mari on the mattress, lifting and cradling her head in her lap.

"The first time is dreadful, I know. I was older than you when I saw my first stoning and it disturbed me greatly even though I knew it was deserved. You'll get used to it, Mari. It's a rough old world, I'm afraid."

Mari lifted her eyes to her mother. They were blazing, seemingly in anger, and Anna recoiled in shock.

"I do not want to get used to it. To treat anyone like that, whatever they have done, is evil."

"Mari, do not misplace your sympathy. The girl was evil too. And what about the family she has destroyed?"

"Has killing Rachel helped? Did Joshua's wife want her dead?"

"Perhaps she did, Mari. Who can tell? Things she has said and done have upset you mightily in the past; there have been times when I could imagine you joining in the condemnation."

"If that is the case, Mother, I pray for forgiveness. I too bear guilt for wanting such a thing to happen. Now that I know what it means, I cannot bear the knowledge."

"Mari, I did not mean to blame you. You must not think that. You could not hold yourself responsible in any way. For goodness sake, child, you are much too sensitive. Forget Rachel. She was not worth your pity. Think of yourself. Think of your future. Joseph will soon be home again for a few days. Don't be all miserable; he will not understand or tolerate your reasons."

"Leave me for a few minutes, Mother; I'll try to cope. Let me have a cup of water and when I feel a bit better, I'll go and fetch the children. They'll not let me dwell on things."

"Good girl, that's a sensible attitude."

Chapter 22

Annunciation Two

*N*ow. It has to be *now*. *No doubt about it. I cannot wait any longer.*

Joseph has come and gone. At the very time when Mari needs his company to talk things through and test her feelings, Eli has arranged a contract for him in Capernaum, which he was obliged to take up within two days of the completion of his work in Sepphoris. They didn't have much time to themselves. If they had had longer, perhaps Mari would have mentioned... In the event, she heeded her mother's advice. She was careful in what she said, objective, practical. Joseph sensed that she was behaving differently, but could not put his finger on it. And now he would not be home until after mid-winter day.

A week later Mari has dropped into her old natural rhythm. She is busier than ever; in addition to minding the animals during the day, fetching water, helping around the house, and cherishing the children, she has her wedding garment to make and embroider. She has already been up early on this baking autumn day to turn the flock loose on safe pastures just outside the village; perhaps later they will need leading to a source of water. The boys are at school. Salome and Rebecca have taken Mo and Benjamin down to the market. Mari is patiently stitching her wedding garment, sitting at the doorway of her home, whilst her mother is baking, indoors.

Her mother's voice reaches her. "Mari, we're running low on water. I think I shall need some before this evening. Perhaps you'd go and fetch some before it gets too hot. There's no particular hurry though – I don't need it this minute."

"Right, Mother, I'm just finishing this coloured thread. I'll fetch the water now."

At last. My cue.

She searches for the large water jar, pours the little remaining into a smaller pot and lifts the empty vessel easily onto her shoulder. Despite the lateness of the season, she is quite warm in just her tunic. She glances at the sky, sees clouds lazily forming and dispersing and thinks no more of it. By the time she has reached the well, she is quite hot so she lowers the vessel to the ground, and sits on the earth, leaning against the rim to rest before drawing water. For a few moments she allows her mind to wander. How much longer will she be able to maintain the pattern of her day, the freedom to achieve this liberty, this privacy? Will Joseph allow her to be alone, to watch the birds soar and the flowers waft in the breeze, or will he insist she stays veiled closely inside the tiny confines of his home?

She is daydreaming in the warm sunshine, when a lone figure appears on the track leading to the well. Am I in her dream? It is not the normal hour for the women to come, so Mari is surprised and just a little disappointed to be interrupted in her reverie, for she has intended to share once more the matters churning through her mind with her God. As I come closer, Mari is astonished, and not a little alarmed, to see it is the figure of a man, travelling light, with no baggage of any description. She lifts herself onto the wall of the well and smoothes her skirt, to restore her modesty, and waits to see what I will do. My head is covered so she does not recognise me at first, but my height is unusual and I appear very different to the local people, so she knows it is the stranger who is lodging with Althaeus. She becomes nervous and excited because she senses at once that this is no chance meeting; I have come searching for her. She glances round on all sides, fearful that she will be seen alone with me. What should she do? If she runs from me, I would catch her in no time; and she would display her fear. She cannot escape. She sits still and waits; she knows this is going to be important.

I stand in front of the beautiful dark-haired maiden, and lift the cloth from my golden sun-flecked curls. I smile down at her and after a long pause, after I have drunk in every aspect of her, I ask, "Please lower your water jar and let me have a drink!"

It is a strange, even significant request; but Mariam does not stop to question or demur. She leans over the parapet, lets her jar splash in the water below, and lifts it up, straining with all her might, her left leg wedged against the wall for leverage. She pours a little into the metal cup chained to the well and offers it to me.

"Drink, sir."

I lift the cup to my lips and drain it in one draught. Mari has sat down again and waits for my next move, her heart pounding within her. She reaches out to the water jar and bumps against it, knocking it over and spilling the water she has just drawn, watching it trickling in rivulets through the dusty ground, wasted.

"Mari, do not be afraid. I'm the same messenger as before. All that you do still pleases God."

I smile at her and look for her response. A flicker of doubt is traced across her face. She hesitates. I sit beside her on the well, assuming an intimacy which troubles her.

"What is the matter, Mari? I can see something is worrying you... Tell me; I shall not put any pressure on you."

I know Mari wants to explain that her family have given her the strictest instructions not to be with any man alone, except her betrothed, accompanied by the most fearsome threats, but she is embarrassed to tell me; she does not want, in some ways, to repel me, because she longs to hear my message. But it is creating turmoil within. So she tells me about Rachel and her confused emotions: her guilt, her pity, her pain at the girl's suffering contrasted with the judgment of her own family; her obstinacy in the wake of the others' views, who are more learned than she is in these matters.

"She hurt me when she said awful things about my father, but surely God does not destroy in such a vengeful way? After all God was her maker. He wouldn't rejoice to see her suffer, would he? And yet the priests said they were only carrying out God's law."

"Mari, the scripture says that when the Israelites fled from the Egyptians out of slavery, and Pharaoh's army was swept away in the flood, the angels round God's throne began to sing in praise; but God rebuked them, saying, 'It is my creations who are drowning. How dare you sing!'"

Mari turns her head to look at me with questions in her eyes. My answer is still rolling round her head.

"Mari, let me tell you a story from our history. Are you acquainted with your ancestor, Tamar?"

"No, sir, I've not been told about her."

"Jacob's son, Judah, married his eldest son to a girl from Canaan. Before long he died and, as was the custom in those days, the next son inherited his brother's widow. Before long he too was dead, and Judah feared to arrange a marriage between Tamar, the young widow, and his last remaining son, unless he should die also. When she saw that Judah did not intend to honour the tradition, but abandon her, childless, to her fate, she cast off her widow's weeds and adorned herself and waylaid Judah, masquerading as a prostitute. The man was snared and had his way with her, the outcome of which was that she became pregnant. In disgrace she was brought before her father-in-law, who condemned her to be burned. Then she produced the seal from his girdle, and his staff, given her in lieu of payment, and he recognised his guilt and had mercy on the girl. And God was pleased to have her bear two sons."

"Sir, I think I know what you are saying, but help me to interpret."

"Despite her sinful act, God did not condemn Tamar, for her guilt was instigated by another. Moreover, God used the act as part of his plan, as is seen by the blessing of twin sons, from whom, dear child, you are descended."

"How is this relevant to Rachel's death?"

"Despite her behaviour, was Rachel responsible for her upbringing? Might not God have brought good from evil? Is it God's will that Joshua's children will be destitute, abused and exploited in turn and thus exposed in due time to like temptation? Yet the pride and self-righteousness of human intervention constrains God's actions."

"Perhaps God will protect and call Joshua's children through their suffering, like Tamar?"

"Mari, I stand corrected! For you have wisdom beyond your years!"

"Sir, do not make fun of me. It is a serious and tragic business."

"I did not mean you to interpret my words this way. I accepted your rebuke as if from God's lips himself, for you were right – or at least, one must own the possibility."

"You astonish me, sir, for I am a mere girl and am lacking in experience and wisdom."

"On the contrary, my dear, you are honoured and chosen by God because the wisdom you have complements your natural gifts, enabling God to communicate with you, call you to his service knowing you will listen and obey."

"You talk to me of God's call. I am ready. That I have already indicated. When will I know what I have to do?"

"Very soon, Mari, very soon indeed."

"Sir, I am overcome with curiosity!"

"I admire your spirit, girl; but it is no wonder that you disturb the orthodox among your relatives. You know the Messianic texts from the prophets?"

"I believe so, sir. I have listened to my uncle and the rabbis. Eli and my mother are both from King David's line, which is a source of much pride to them; they have acquainted me with the prophecies. My father died in the hope that he could help fulfil them."

"Then you expect a King of Kings from David's lineage who will defeat the weapons of war itself and establish a kingdom of justice and peace? Mari, that time is coming now!"

"Sir!"

"But it will not be all joy, Mari; sometimes the way for those involved will be very painful. The scriptures say as much. Can you share that pain, Mari?"

There is a long pause. "This is a real question to me now, sir?"

"Yes, Mariam, I am asking you that question."

"I don't know what I can bear until I am tested, sir. I know this: if God needs me to suffer before his plan can work, then he will help me bear it. I have to trust that, so even if I don't know really what I'm saying, I tell you now that I am ready to share the pain, as well as the joy."

"You have wisdom, child. Love wisdom and she will make you great. Embrace her and she will bring you honour. Wisdom is better than jewels: nothing you can ever want will compare with her!"

"They are beautiful words, sir."

"You appreciate them because you too are a poet. Don't look so surprised, Mari. Salome, Rebecca and the other children have confided to me that you are a great teller of stories, and that you sometimes make up little rhymes to help them understand the mysteries of beauty."

"You take notice of what the children say?"

"Of course, Mari. They tell the truth without considering the consequences. They are not dissemblers! Children are the true poets, questioning everything except the love about them. A poet remains a child until he dies. God wants you as you are, Mari, a true child of his. Others will try to age you. Let your eyes remain those of a child: vulnerable, sensitive, idealistic, great pools of pain."

Mari turns slowly, draping herself across the rim of the well, and stares at the black still water, which contains her reflection. She locates her eyes, and in staring, begins to feel dizzy, endangered. She may fall.

"It is risky!"

"How well you strike intuitively to the heart of the matter! Yes, lovely child, it is risky. You are very vulnerable. But God cannot bring about his promise unless you dare to act. If you want a shield from life's dangers you will be sterile, deprived of power and inspiration. God calls you, of your own free will, to expose yourself to risk, to danger, so that you may be consort in his creation!"

"What you say, sir, fills me with fear. How can I be worthy of such honour? What if I should fail?"

"There are many Jewish girls, Mari, whose heads are full of dreams that they will be chosen to bear Israel's hope. They yearn to impress, they seek the right marriage contract, they seek priestly guidance. Let me tell you another story. In the beginning the letters of the alphabet vied with each other to be the first within God's holy word, the Torah. The letter 'B' made its claim with 'blessed' and 'beginning', but the letter 'A' was humble and did not press its claim, so God rewarded her by naming the first human 'Adam', just as he now chooses you to bear a second Adam."

"Sir, you seem to know so much. Who are you?"

"I am the messenger, Mariam."

"Yes, you said that before. But you must have a name?"

"I am the one of whom it was said: 'before the great and terrible day of the Lord comes, I will be sent'. I am the messenger of the presence. I am the voice that calls you, the one bidden to carry out the will of the Lord upon you. More you need not know."

"How do I know you are all the things you say? My uncle thinks you are an evil man come to spy on us."

"I cannot prove to you otherwise, Mariam. That is one of the risks you have to take. Listen to your own conscience. Ask yourself: 'If God is calling me, what are the risks of disobedience?'"

"You make it impossible to say no."

"For you, perhaps, Mari. Many would refuse."

"What is going to happen?"

"Give me your hands, Mariam."

The girl seems to draw in breath, and with great deliberation, as if this were the most momentous decision of her life, offers me her open palms. I take the proffered fingers, fold them and enclose them in my own.

"Listen carefully, Mariam, to what I tell you, and hear me through until the end."

Mari nods in submission, swallowing in her nervousness. The sun bursts from behind a cloud, bathing her in light. She had not realised that it had been obscured for a while, but she is conscious of its renewed presence as she screws up her eyes and sees my silhouette delineated in the golden glow.

"Innocent child, beloved of the Lord God Almighty, I greet you and bring you wonderful news."

Mari is bold. She senses my sudden formality and earnestness and looks me directly in the eye.

"Do not be afraid, Mari: God has chosen you."

I pause and smile at the girl.

"Mari, you will shortly be pregnant and give birth to a son. He will grow to greatness and will be the Messiah the whole nation has been expecting."

Despite her preparation, the moment when it comes is nigh too much for her. The certainty and confidence drains from her face. Bewilderment takes hold. She does not want to challenge. She has been told to wait, but she cannot contain her questions.

"Sir, when will this be? I am still a virgin and my betrothed is in Capernaum at least until mid-winter. And our marriage is not due to be celebrated until my fourteenth birthday, nearly nine months away. Are these arrangements to be changed?"

"Mari, God will cause the seed to be implanted in you. He does not need the human agency of your betrothed. God's power, his spirit, brought here by me, his messenger, will cover you. Your innocence, your purity, will not be defiled if you submit in meek obedience to God's will. Your consent is all that's required; before we part today the child shall be within you."

She hesitates a moment. Is she suspecting my intentions?

"But my family, sir. How shall I explain my condition? I shall be disgraced and condemned. I shall be shamed and die!"

"Listen, Mari, once more to the words of the scriptures that I'm sure the rabbis have taught you in the synagogue. Did they not show you all the prophecies about Israel's expected saviour?

'Do not be afraid; you will not suffer shame.
Do not fear disgrace; you will not be humiliated,
For your maker is your husband –
The Lord Almighty is his name –
The Holy One of Israel is your redeemer.'

Take these words to your heart. God means you to apply them to yourself; he will protect you."

I watch the battle raging inside Mariam's mind, her struggle to believe. She needs further encouragement.

"Your mother's cousin, Elizabeth, from Ein–Karem, has been visited by God's spirit also. You will know that she has been barren for many years and has borne the heartbreak of her childlessness. She too is now pregnant several months and is to bear a son, who will prepare the way for your own child. Did you not know this?"

"I knew my aunt could not travel to my betrothal celebration because she had been afflicted in some way, but I didn't know the true cause of her absence."

"You will find it as I say. The lady, who thought she was well beyond child-bearing age, is overjoyed, and your news will be confirmation of her own experience."

Mari sits on the well rim, pensively. Her hands are still enclosed in mine. She senses the implications and significance of the next few words. How can she choose? She cannot postpone the decision – hesitation is to deny. Now is the risk that must be taken.

"I am the Lord's servant. I accept what you have said. Let it happen!"

For a few moments the two of us remain seated, locked by our hands, warmed by the sun. Gradually the shadow of a cloud creeps across the hillside and, edging up on us, engulfs the well and claims the pathway towards the village. I relax my grip on the girl's hands and stand before her.

"What do I do now?" she whispers.

"Go before me, Mariam, down to the Tabor stream where you sometimes water your flocks, and you will know there what you have to do."

She too stands and turns toward the east and moves slowly, as if in a trance, directed by my voice. Her mind is so full that she sees nothing but her inner world. Grass and sky and earth and trees live on another plane.

A mile or so she walks, until she is adjacent to the hillside upon which the lonely fig tree stands where she so frequently shelters from the heat. Automatically, unthinkingly, her eyes sweep the bare stubble and brown vegetation; a movement focuses her eyes, and she walks, fascinated, as a tiny whirlwind swirls around a spot just a few yards from the tree. It does not seem to move, yet straw and dead grass and dust are spiralling upwards, nearly to the height of the tree before it disperses in the air.

She looks behind her to point it out to the stranger, then she turns right back in surprise. There is no sign of him. He has vanished into thin air! Is this all there is? Has he no more to tell her? How will she know what she has to perform when she reaches the stream? Has he taken the short cut over the hill and will she find him waiting to greet her when she arrives at the waterside?

The sun is still behind the cloud and she shivers a little, tightening the girdle of her flimsy tunic as if in nervous gesture. I can read her mind with clarity. In my absence, she is fighting blind panic to turn around and run home to her mother. Without my soothing words entangling her in arguments she cannot gainsay, the doubts and foolishness of her predicament crowd in upon her. She can read through others' eyes the accusations that will be made against her. Some will impugn deliberate wickedness; at best naivety to the point of foolhardiness, credulity strained beyond belief.

She has so many questions.

Could this man be cruelly tricking her, having established her night and day dreams? Despite his fair angelic face, is some evil lustful stark reality masked behind his open manner intended to seduce her trust? If he is an angel of darkness plotting to deprive her of her innocence, will she be protected by the Lord God, who sees and knows her motives? She would like to seek advice from her mother, even Joseph, yet she knows instinctively what they would say, whilst rejecting that implied counsel. She is presuming what is going to happen; assuming she still has the power to refuse the act itself. Yet perhaps it has already happened? Did he not say that she would conceive by the very act of her consent, which she has already given? It might be too late: the seed might be growing even now within her womb.

The image of Rachel's bleeding unconscious form imprints itself upon her imagination. Inevitably she identifies herself with the sin that brought her there, feels herself bound and stretched, exposed to ridicule and shame, waiting for the first mortal wound. Yet strangely her mind moves on from this centred image to the background of the girl; the tales she told of ritual couplings with the gods to bring fertility and new life to the earth, the myths of virgin births, temple acolytes who became mothers of gods. It is disturbing her – pagan excitement fills her with horror and fascination simultaneously. She sees herself as a sacrificial victim, laid out, exposed upon the altar awaiting the glinting dagger. Her mind somersaults to the oft-told story of the boy Isaac offered thus by Abraham and his last-moment rescue enabled by the ram caught in the thicket. Will she be spared at the last resort, once she has proved her obedience to God's call? Is it all a further test to check her loyalty and faith?

All the time her mind is racing onwards, her frail body is trudging reluctantly towards the appointed place. She sees the silver glint of the distant water, the green lushness of the vegetation despite the lateness of the season, the brooding barren hills encircling this oasis. She knows now, despite all her valid and logical misgivings, that she is going to obey, to take the risk. Why should the stranger fill her mind with such exotic messages, incredible claims, if all he wants is her seduction? She is only small: if he just raped her, she could not resist. Why the façade?

I feel her scrutiny and blanch at the intensity of her suspicions. Am I guiltless or am I tainted too with temptations tearing at the edges of my mission?

Her mind moves on. If she has discerned rightly, why the need for fear? If God has performed this miracle, will it not be easier for him to protect his child and his chosen vessel from the wrath of man? Logic then is to take the risk; obey. But the decision is not taken lightly; the emotional turmoil is not dulled.

"Take a deep breath," she says to herself. "Take your courage in both hands. Let me trust you, God; help me to banish disbelief."

She is standing at the water's edge, staring vacantly as if lost, as if the place were unfamiliar. She is just beginning to wonder if the stranger is spying on her here, whether or how she will be instructed.

Indeed, I am still watching.

Then suddenly she seems to know. She dips her hands into the cool stream and lays her clothes, folding them carefully, beside the frothing water. She wades into the centre of the stream, naked, and stands, ready to do what comes naturally, next...

Chapter 23

Who Am I?

*A*LTHOUGH THE SUN IS HIDDEN *for a moment behind a swiftly moving cloud, the quality of light is perfect. The late autumn day has a clarity of vision that permits those that would, to observe the distant horizons with precision. Perhaps it presages the winter rain that soon will fall. The time is noon; the sun is directly overhead even though at this moment we cannot see it. It is temperate. The landscape is empty.*

To the left, upstream, the water glints over rocks as it twists between the dun-coloured hills, smooth and bare, flanks rising to a plateau beyond which gorges lead down to Lake Genneseret. Opposite, a steeper bare escarpment hems in the little river, forcing it to curve round towards us through the green glade, before it flows away slowly, with more depth tugging at the long green fronds, which grow and luxuriate just beneath the surface toward the opening of the valley; to human settlements beyond the next obstacle of lower hills, self-contained and looking southwards.

In the foreground, at our feet, brown leaves drift onto the squelchy mossy bank. Just behind us young trees are stripped of the last few vestiges of autumn foliage, revealing the intricacy of their veins, exposing their true beauty.

Please, reader, understand my mission. I have to carry out God's will, enact it. That is my purpose and my role. Have I feelings? Do I share the human bonds and snares of lust and power? Can I love? Please see it through my eyes and judge me if you will!

But have I deceived myself and you, the reader? Am I really the Archangel or Elijah, or am I like the god Zeus, who transforms himself to human or beast-like disguise to have his way with some virgin of high beauty or modesty? Am I that spirit of God, that element of the Trinity that some say is that which produces action and reaction within the heart or mind of the believer? Am I that element of the book that is the will and archetypal intent of the author? Or the element which inspires and provokes within the reader the ability to create its own reality, and moves to pity, joy, worship or carnal degradation? Am I you, the reader?

Or am I just a man, a spy, taking advantage of a pure naïve young maiden, just as her uncle would have it?

The veil overhead, cast by the cloud, is suddenly torn away; the sunlight streaks between the vapour, dazzles on the water's surface, spotlights the naked figure standing knee-deep in the swirling stream.

But this is no beloved of our imagination. There is a real girl standing there, vulnerable and trembling, experiencing each second as if eternity. Look at her through my eyes. She is just old enough to bear a child; to understand and with consciousness, obey God's will. And she is just young enough to be a virgin; to retain childish perfection, a natural unspoilt openness untouched by adult wiles or deviousness.

Watch the water surge around her knees, eddying from the firmness of her calves. She does not seek to hide anything from us, because she does not realise we are here. Just be aware that at this moment she is perfect – there are no flaws, nothing to disfigure yet. Her smile is turned inwards. Her huge brown eyes laugh and cry and hurt and hope. Her raven hair spills from the one piece of clothing she has forgotten to remove: the crimson band that pulls it back from off her forehead, so that she can see, if she so desires, what will befall her.

She waits, anticipating our next move. At this moment she is water nymph, mythical naiad, Beatrice, Laura; Rachel, Rebecca, Zipporah, all women at the well; priestess, vestal virgin, sacrifice, wisdom personified. She is a vessel that is without blemish, intact, pure of line, full of inwardness, outwardly composed. She is accepting, soft, tender, feminine; beautiful and utterly passive. Stop dreaming and look!

She is Mariam, oft called Mari, thirteen-year-old daughter of Anna and the deceased Joachim; ward of Eli, Pharisee of Nazareth; betrothed of Joseph, who at this very moment is carving and fixing a lintel above a door in distant Capernaum. She has never known a man. She is scared, but loyal and obedient to her God.

I want to prolong this moment; take no action, but fall for what I see; I do not want to spoil her or mix her with my messy emotions. Can I cleanse and purify my, our, roles? When I act, what Pandora's box will I unlock? What consequences will I unleash? Have I also got to take a risk? I thought it was all one-sided, but I was wrong! I look and love. Completely, absolutely, totally, unprofessionally, for I have a task to accomplish. I thought I was immune. I understand now why God's messengers are called on to act but once. No more can I return undiminished to serve another role. Forgive me – I burn myself in what I do. My muse, my inspiration is the love of you, dear Mari. The purer, nobler love of the Almighty is an abstract goal that fades and thins into the background of your kaleidoscope hues!

"Mari, turn around and face the current of the stream. Lower yourself gently into the cooling waters; immerse your limbs; let the bubbling liquid wash over you, caressing your body. Lie back; just keep your shoulders above the surface, open and receive the surging flow. Do not resist. Close your eyes, Mari; let the hot sunlight print scarlet on the inside of your eyelids. Do not look now as the shadow passes over you!"

A Poem

*T*HE SHIP OF SUN-GOD RA climbs up his fiery path
   Sending shadows like pillars of ivory
   Made by giants of old or red kerm-king.
The rigid tower is bedecked with flowers of winter

To celebrate the ritual; lo, the dead will rise
Amidst the ring of burning bush and fleece
Where hides the ark, the sacred vessel, grail
By the well of virgin water, now laid bare.

Sacred glyph of rose and lily, seat of wisdom
Consent to catch and hold the lightning lance
Which pierces the blood-red silver chalice
On the sacrificial altar sheathed in velvet.

Stand against the wind, swallow stinging blades of grass
Wherein the snake will squirm; engorge the stone
In the wallowing grave, tangled in the weed
Which streams in fervent chaos round the slippery womb.

Feel the ice-cold flood sweep round and through the crevice,
Surge and retract, caressed by breeze and light,
Stroking the senses while the earth stands still
And time suspends its magic potion deep in space,

Till the fountain bursts in cascades of golden stars,
Explosive energy, raw word of life
Springs reborn with insight, muse inspiring,
Poetry imagined by a child; the bitter truth.

To fathom this precious seed of fertile legend
The virgin must submit as Hebron girls
Fling down the flowers. Within the maiden lass
I grow, white-winged butterfly in the chrysalis.

CHAPTER 24

I Am Mari

*D*EEP, DEEP WITHIN ME I know what is happening, but I shall not admit it lightly. I have kept my eyes shut as I was commanded. I know what I want to believe. Certainties have been diffused in the cold mountain water that has numbed my feeling, or confused it sufficiently to maintain a sort of innocence, or at least, its possibility.

I lie in the running water, feel it swirl about my limbs, exerting pressure on my thighs, my breasts. And despite the coldness, I relax, offer my body to the water, let the dappled sunlight flicker on my eyelids like reflections of the sparkling stream. The fronds of slimy weed flowing just beneath the surface brush against me, moving all the time. The water washes over me, bathing every particle of my skin, even inside my very being.

And in the coldness and from the hypnotising movements within my eyes, I grow dizzy, unreal, as if dreaming; I sense a burning flame within me that the flood cannot extinguish, a sense of calm wellbeing that the chaotic water cannot disturb. The flame scorches as if it is driving me asunder, then it draws my mind into an ecstasy I cannot describe. I want to cry out in pain and shock and joyful satisfaction all at once, but I cannot form the words – I don't know what sound leaves my lips. Then I feel relief flooding me; I have been accepted, been obedient. Whatever happens now, I cannot change my mind. It is accomplished. I am no longer alone.

I open my eyes. I look to the sky above; blue; the clouds have gone. I am cold; my teeth are chattering. I try to turn on one side so that I can look around behind me. I roll onto my hip and slip momentarily beneath the water as I coincide with a gurgling wave and emerge coughing and spluttering, blind until I have shaken the spray from my eyes. The stranger is not there. He has gone. I know. I am sure that this time it is for good. I cannot tell you why – I just sense it in my bones. He has given his message, accomplished his task. We will search for him in the future, that is quite possible, but we'll not find him. The funny thing is, I'm quite relaxed about it. Before the tryst he made me nervous, curious, excited. Now it is done; I cannot look to him for help.

I crawl out of the water onto the empty bank and shake myself like a dog that has been gambolling in the stream. Despite the warmth of the sun, I am still cold, and brush my skin vigorously with my bare hands to scatter the water droplets, massage the goose-pimples. I use my discarded loincloth as a towel to give the sun a chance to dry my body, then I pull my tunic over my head, leaving it loose so that the air can finish the drying process without leaving me clammy.

I stand beside the narrow river, staring at the rushes at the edge and I am Miriam, watching over her infant brother in the tiny reed basket. I have daydreamed this many times before; only this time I keep reminding myself that I am in the middle of an even greater story – if what the stranger said is true! A new Moses to lead Israel out of slavery, down within my belly. I cannot contemplate the awesome reality of this; I am going mad, I must be!

I bend and stare at my reflection in the clear waters, trying to judge if I look any different. It is hard to tell – because the river is flowing fast, my image shatters and shimmers and I cannot fix it long enough to study. My eyes trace the stream back towards its source, which is a subterranean spring under the massif where Mount Tabor is found. And it flows towards the lake near where my father lost his life. As I look I feel tears welling up in my eyes; I remember my father's words to me to bring him news of the Messiah if I could. Why could he not have lived to share my secret?

CHAPTER 25

THE WATER FILLED JAR

$\mathcal{J}$ AM AMBLING HOME ALONG THE track towards the well. I am feeling a little drier now, and I stop near the solitary fig tree to pull on my loincloth, which I have been holding in the sunlight. It feels a little damp between my legs but it is not too uncomfortable. My mind is numbed; I am not thinking clearly at all, but I am buoyed up by a sense of wellbeing. The well comes into view, and it is deserted. Good! I shall not have to explain my absence to anyone; I will fill my water jar and make for home.

The water jar is missing. Surely it cannot have been stolen? I'm convinced I left it there, leaning against the parapet. Panic begins to creep over me as reality prises open my defences. How long have I been gone? I look for the position of the sun and my stomach lurches with fear – for the globe is well past its southerly point and indicates that it is a couple of hours into the afternoon. I have an absence of at least two, possibly three, hours to explain. How can I start?

I rehearse what has happened in my mind and realise with horror that there is nothing that I can readily admit to. The meeting and the conversation with the stranger, the walk to the river, my bathing there – all inexplicable. Unless I tell them the truth. And who will believe it? The more I repeat it to myself, the less plausible it sounds.

I have broken into a run although it is much too late for that. All I have achieved is to arrive outside my house totally devoid of any conclusions on what to say. I push the gate open and go inside, totally unprepared.

"Please, God, help me now; protect your servant!"

The door to my home is suddenly flung open. My mother is there, looking absolutely distraught.

"Mari, thank the Lord God, you're safe! We all feared the worst when we found your water jar. Where on earth have you been?"

"I went down to the river."

"What for, child? How could you give us so much worry?"

"I'm sorry. I didn't realise you'd be worried. You told me there was no hurry, and I was hot so I thought I'd cool myself in the water."

"But three hours, child? How could you be so thoughtless? It's so unlike you."

"I looked everywhere for the water jar, but couldn't find it."

"When the children returned home and hadn't seen you, I sent Salome and Rebecca back to look for you. They found your jar, already filled, but no sign of you. They spent ages, calling and searching, then gave up, Salome carrying the water home."

"Did you say that the water jar was already filled?"

"Yes."

"Well, I didn't fill it. It fell over as I put it on the ground and all the water spilt. I left it until I returned from the river."

"Salome!"

My sister comes running; she has of course been listening to every word exchanged so far.

"It was filled, Mother, right to the brim. It was so full, I had to pour a little out to be able to balance it on my shoulder."

"Well, that's another mystery, child. What are you going to say for yourself? If I didn't know you better, I'd accuse you of meeting someone you didn't want us to know about!"

I don't want to answer, not in front of Salome, anyway. I try to busy myself silently with Mother's work, but only get in her way. Eventually the others go out to play in the courtyard.

My mother and I are left on our own. Rather than question me directly, she is waiting for me to speak; I can sense it. And I still don't know how to begin, what to say. Once I admit to her what I think has happened, the die is cast, and many things will be taken out of my hands. Nagging still at the back of my mind is the doubt that I have been tricked, that my experience by and in the river was a delusion brought about by a mixture of my own daydreaming and an opportunistic stranger with a roving eye. In which case, perhaps the message of my pregnancy is a myth: a story told to gain my co-operation, and the forecast baby boy will not materialise, I need not therefore admit anything to anybody until it is seen to be necessary.

My mother is still waiting. My thought processes are clogging under her gaze; I am being rushed. How can I think I can say nothing and no-one will ever know? If I am not pregnant, what will happen on my wedding night? Joseph will know I'm not a virgin, won't he? Will he disgrace me, divorce me, have me burned or stoned to death? But am I a virgin or not? It seems stupid to say this, even to myself, but I'm not absolutely sure I know the answer, technically at least. I saw no blood, but I was immersed in the fast-flowing stream. I felt no pain, but I was both numbed by the cold and burned by the sensation in my mind. I offered myself to God; if a mortal took me in disguise, am I guilty of my own seduction?

"Mother, I've got something to tell you," I hear myself saying, divorced from what I am thinking.

My mother looks at me sharply. Her eyes are so penetrating that I wish immediately that I had not opened my mouth. But I can't stop now.

"I did meet someone."

"Child, how could you after all the warnings you've been given."

"It was someone very special, Mummy. And it was not my fault: he came to search for me."

"Go on. Tell me the worst."

"You know the stranger who is staying in Althaeus' house? You know, the tall blond man?"

"Yes, Mari, I know who you mean only too well. You're confirming my very worst fears."

"He came to me at the well and asked me for a drink, then told me all sorts of strange prophecies about myself. He kept quoting the scriptures and told me that I had been chosen to give birth to the Messiah!"

I try to look at my mother to discern the effect this is having on her, but dare not.

"Then he told me to go and bathe in the river on the path to Mount Tabor, so I did. That is why I took so long." I suddenly have an inspiration. "He must have filled my water vessel whilst I had gone to obey his words!"

"Mari, you have never lied to me before. Why are you telling me this silly tale? You surely don't expect me to swallow it, do you?"

"I can't say anything else; it is the truth!"

"Then you're more naïve than I thought you were. All this study in the synagogue has gone to your head and you're starting to delude yourself. Mariam, it's dangerous nonsense. Stop going off alone, letting your mind fancy all sorts of wild thoughts; stay here with me and keep your concentration on reality. There's a lot to do. What on earth do you think Joseph would make of all this talk? Uncle Eli had to persuade him that you would be a good obedient wife as it was, because he saw evidence of your independent and rebellious nature. If he heard just one whisper of all this nonsense, he'd be off. And then how would we find you a husband?"

I want to tell her more; it's going to be harder later. But after what she's just said, how can I add anything? I can see in her eyes that she fears to ask what happened at the river; she does not want me to say.

"I'm sorry, Mother, I've done my best to tell you. You'll see the truth of what I say when I'm pregnant, as the stranger foretold!"

"I didn't hear that remark, Mari. I'll not react to that. I just pray it doesn't mean what I fear it means."

"Oh, by the way, Mother, the stranger said that cousin Elizabeth is having a baby too and that he's going to be a prophet who prepares Israel for the Messiah. You didn't tell me that that was the reason she and Uncle Zechariah never came to my betrothal banquet."

"How on earth did you know Elizabeth was pregnant? Who told you?" My mother is shaken by my words, then she seems to recover. "Oh, I'm sure some tittle-tattle is going the rounds. A pregnancy as late as Elizabeth's is news. Probably one of Eli's daughters picked up the story during the banquet, and I dare say it's now village gossip."

"But why didn't you tell me yourself?"

"Well, it seemed a bit odd at the time. Your aunt seemed to be hysterical, we thought. Zechariah was so ill, he couldn't communicate with anyone, and we wondered if Elizabeth was just going funny in the head. But we've since had news confirming that she is expecting a child shortly after next Passover. It is extraordinary after she has been barren all her life."

"Then you see, Mother, what the stranger told me was true. Why shouldn't what he said about me be true as well?" I add excitedly.

"Oh, Mariam, do not dream away your youth in idle speculation. I still tell you it is dangerous."

But she does not seem to me to be quite so convincing in what she has said. I think I've said enough now. The seed is sown. I must wait for it to grow.

Chapter 26

Morning Sickness

My mother won't let me go out of her sight. Ever since I told her of my meeting with the stranger, she has been protective of my honour. Salome takes the flocks to graze now. Sometimes Rebecca goes with her, especially now that Benjamin is at school, along with James and Jude. Mo spends quite a lot of time playing at our house or in the courtyard, particularly if Rebecca is with Salome. In fact, it is only when I'm playing with Mo that it seems like the old times again. Most of the time I'm bored. Don't get me wrong – there is a lot to do around the house, but I find it constricting and oppressive not to be allowed out of the courtyard gate. I'm not even asked to fetch the water now. I was looking forward to Joseph's return, but we have received word from Capernaum that his contract's been renewed for another four weeks. Perhaps it's as well. I don't think I could face telling him what I've told my mother and I'd feel a fraud if I said nothing! Perhaps the worst is that after all the fear and excitement of the stranger's visit and his message, despite the incipient dangers, nothing has happened.

I keep trying to feel if I am any different. But, try as I might, in all honesty, I can find no clue. It is an anticlimax. I even sometimes pray for another sign, despite the danger it will bring. It is a relief, I suppose, but a very boring one.

The routine was broken last week by Bilpah's wedding. We were all invited to the feast, which lasted for three whole days! Salome, Rebecca and I all lit our lamps for Bilpah and Jonas; they came into our courtyard while we sang to them. Then we joined them in procession to Jonas' house at the other end of the village. Bilpah and I had several private little chats together despite the noise and dancing. She seemed a bit let down, didn't think Jonas' lovemaking efforts had been worth waiting for! And she confirmed that the stranger that had lodged with Althaeus had left the village, some time ago, in fact. Suddenly he'd just left without a word to anyone. No-one really knew who he was, or where he'd gone. Even Althaeus was said to be mystified, although no-one was prepared to take the initiative to talk to him seriously on the subject. I tried to extract further information from her about the stranger, but I don't think she knew any more.

Anyway, when I woke up this morning I felt stiff and sore. I was cold at first. I could see and hear rain falling and I just pulled the bed cloth tighter round my body. As I did so, I reacted to the movement, conscious of an irritation and sensitivity around my breasts. I sat up and probed further. They didn't look any different, but when I pushed and squeezed them, they felt tender and bruised. When I could see no cause, I didn't give it a further thought until a few minutes ago. I was helping Mother divide up the food for the children's breakfast, when I suddenly came over faint and nauseous and had to sit down. The smell of the food was making me feel sick, and I yawned biliously and took a few deep breaths to get some fresh air into my lungs. I thought Mother looked a little old-fashioned at me, but I didn't think any more about it until now. Because, sitting outside despite the cold drizzle sweeping in from the east, I've suddenly begun to feel very sick again. I think I can get by without making a fuss, but it has set me off thinking.

You may think I'm daft, despite all I've said about the stranger and his message, but I have not been checking myself for symptoms of pregnancy. Despite my knowledge about sex and conception – difficult to avoid knowing from early years in the crowded conditions in which we live – no-one has said very much to me about pregnancy. After all, why should they? They don't expect me to need to know until I'm married; doubtless Mother is storing it up to tell me one evening when we're embroidering together, and the younger children are in bed. And the youngest child here, little Mariam, is nearly six so there has been no intimate talk of symptoms that I have been party to. I overheard Miriam telling my mother that she thinks she is pregnant again, but I heard no details. What I do know is gleaned from girl talk, mainly round the well, and I don't pay much score by a lot of that talk as I know by experience.

What I'm leading up to, is that I haven't had a period now for over two months. And the soreness of my breasts and my sickness has only just brought to mind the possible meaning of my period's absence. I didn't start to menstruate until about a year ago – Bilpah tells me she had her first when she was only eleven. And I've been very erratic: it has sometimes been exactly a month, sometimes longer, and once or twice the flow of blood has been so slight I have scarcely noticed.

The sudden realisation of what might be happening to me is enough to send me into another bout of nausea and fainting, and I am beginning to shiver in the dampness. A gulp of cool air, and I pull my tunic tightly around me and stagger indoors, to be met by my mother, who looks pityingly at me. I think she believes it is my time of the month and this must give her some relief. I guess that she has been counting the days, even if I have been oblivious of their meaning.

Released from housework for an hour or two, I lie upon my mattress, pondering. Should I say something of my suspicions to Mother, or should I wait until I am surer? Although I said I was getting bored because nothing had happened, I am now overcome with fear and apprehension, my stomach churning everything to liquid. I find myself praying under my breath, so that Mother cannot hear, "Please, Lord God, tell me what to do. Let me know for certain if my condition is caused by the baby growing within me that your messenger said would be the Messiah! Show me when to tell my mother. Protect me from the anger of all those who will not understand or believe me. So be it, Lord."

After a few minutes with my eyes closed, I find I am feeling a little better, so I get up and begin to move around. I play for a while with Mo and soon I have forgotten all about my symptoms. Is this an unexpected answer to my prayer? Whether it is or not, it certainly helps me to decide to say nothing yet to anyone.

Next morning I awake with a lurch. I get up instantaneously, still half asleep, and only just reach the courtyard before I am violently sick. I am still mopping the sweat from my forehead, when I feel my mother's arms across my shoulders.

"What's the matter, Mari? Did you feel sick yesterday? Are you having your period pains?"

I feel in no fit state to reply. Already I can sense a new wave of nausea waiting to erupt, then afterwards I am drained and exhausted. I cannot defend myself, hide my vulnerability; it is too much effort and I will just have to trust my mother by confiding in her, "No, Mum, I've not had a period now for over two months. It's just that I feel sick each morning."

I try to snuggle my shuddering body into her warmth, but even as I do so, I sense her alarm.

"What are you saying, Mari? Why didn't you tell me this before? Are you quite sure?"

"Sure about what?"

"Not having had your period."

"Yes, I am."

"Apart from your sickness, do you feel anything else?"

I tell her about my soreness. She draws me into the house and, opening my garment, gently examines me until I exclaim when she presses me where the swelling pulls under my armpits. She looks hard at me and even in the dim light she seems visibly to have paled.

"Mari, are you sure you've never been with any man? You're showing every sign of being pregnant."

"I told you back at the beginning of winter, Mother. I told you that God had sent a messenger to me to tell me that I would bear a boy child. But you wouldn't believe me."

"But Mari, did he go with you? I mean, did he have intercourse?"

"I don't know. He suggested I lay down in the water – I think he did, or I did anyway – and I shut my eyes. He said that I would conceive direct from God without knowing a human."

"Child, I don't know what to say. I am appalled. I thought you were daydreaming, trying to execute some indolent or headstrong whim of yours to take yourself off for a while. I never thought you were serious. You'd better sit down and tell me all about it before the others get up."

And so I sit alongside my mother, and I explain exactly what happened, as best as I am able from start to finish. She occasionally interrupts and asks a question, just to be sure she has understood what I am saying.

When I am finished, she cradles me in her arms; she is squeezing me so tightly that she is hurting. I have no idea what is going through her mind; what she is going to say next. I have abandoned any thought of trying to influence or direct her.

"Mari, we must say that you were raped. That is true, you know. The man tricked you, took you off to a place where you could neither protest, nor escape. Yes, that is what we'll say."

"But, Mum, that's not true at all!"

She ignores me entirely. I don't think she's even heard what I just said.

"We'll have to search for the man and make him marry you. Joseph will never have you now. Uncle Eli will be able to trace him: he has many contacts."

"No, Mother, you've got it all wrong. I don't want to marry that man; I'm meant to marry Joseph. That was the message I have to obey."

"What's the good of a message that is impossible to put into effect? Do you really think a good Jew like Joseph will swallow all his convictions to marry a girl who is having someone else's baby? I shall not even have the heart to try, Mari. And as for Eli, I know him a lot better than you. If you back me in accusing the stranger of rape, you've got a chance. He will be angry but the law is on your side; he'll come along with us, to hush up the scandal. But if you stand out for your version of the truth, he'll go berserk. You'll never convince him; there will be no way in which he can avoid condemning you. And my pleas for mercy will be like straw in the wind, for his sense of justice and duty is much stronger than his compassion. He will loathe the fact that you are jeopardising his position as rabbi and elder in the community. He will need to make you a public example, Mari, to maintain his credibility. For goodness sake, do not push him into that choice, for we will have no hope."

"I am frightened. But everything the messenger said has come true. Surely, Mother, if what the stranger said is God's will, I will be protected?"

"By whom, Mari, by whom? I will be honest with you, child. I don't care what you have done. I love you and I always will; in all the hardships we have endured you have been a constant support to me. I can't bear to think of being without you. Since Joachim's death, I've relied on you even more for someone to talk things over with, to confide in. If it were within my power, I'd defend you; I'd take you away until the child was born. We'd give it to the Temple. But Mari, I can't. I need Eli's support, and that I can get only if we operate according to his rules. I've never told you this, but I'm frightened of the man: he's so inflexible. I'm convinced that if his own right arm offended him, he'd cut it off! He's tolerated our presence because it was his duty. If you give him a good reason to repudiate that responsibility and keep his conscience clean, he'll seize it with both hands. Please, I beg you, don't give him that opportunity! Let us tell him my way!"

I don't know what to say. I can tell my mother is scared and this petrifies me – I have never seen her not in control of herself except when father's body was unrolled. I'm afraid to hold on to what I believe to be right because of her tears; but how can I go along with her? It will make a mockery of all I have done so far; it will surely jeopardise God's plan for me and my unborn son? I can't answer her, not now at any rate.

"Do we need to say anything for the moment, Mother? Let us pray for guidance, ask God for a miracle!"

"You still believe, don't you, my child! You just can't see the catastrophe that has befallen you. Leave it for a day or two if you must. But every day we cover up, it will become more difficult to defend yourself with the cry of rape. Already there will be suspicion – we will need to say why you failed to complain at the time of the act itself. A couple of days then, no more!"

When the children come in for breakfast, I go up to the roof.

"Please, Lord God, be merciful to me. Show me what to do." Over and over I repeat these phrases; I can't think what else to say. And when I pause for breath, all that I can think of are the words of the messenger quoting the prophet: "Do not be afraid; you will not suffer shame", and my own text: "My father and mother may abandon me but the Lord will take care of me".

Was it for this moment that they were consecrated to me? Is it the sign?

The answer comes very quickly, and so simply, that I know it must be God's will. As I clamber down the stone steps into the courtyard, Uncle Eli emerges into the wintry sunshine. Seeing me, he waits at the foot of the stairway. I cannot escape him.

"Mariam, for how long have you been sick?"

I did not know he knew. His question shakes me, I can think of no other answer.

"For several mornings now, sir. How did you know?"

"Miriam saw you this morning. You cannot hide the truth, child. Why are you so sick?"

His eyes are blazing, transfixing me as I stand on the bottom step of the staircase. He knows. Instinctively he knows the truth.

"Because I am pregnant, sir."

Will he rave and shout, be upset, lose control? Eli, as always, is master of himself. All he says, almost between clenched teeth, is, "I knew it would come to this. Despite all I tried to do to warn you, I knew you'd bring disgrace on us and yourself." He pauses dramatically. "Stay inside your home until I've talked further with your mother."

I've done it. I've said it. Another milestone is passed. I'm in your hands entirely now, God; in human terms I'm lost. I've put myself at total risk for your sake. Please don't let me down.

CHAPTER 27

Do Not Bring Me to the Trial

"**W**HY, OH WHY, DID YOU do it, Mari? After all our conversation, how could you? You must have been possessed!"

I scarcely hear what she is saying. Since mid-morning I have been consumed by nerves whilst Eli, Clopas and my mother have been closeted in Eli's room, discussing my confession.

"Are you listening? Thanks to your obstinacy I've just endured over an hour of arguing on your behalf. Eli wanted to wash his hands of you; he is bitter that you've repaid his interest and support with shame and disgrace that will reflect on his position in the community. He thought you'd be sensible enough to learn from your caning, not to mention your presence at Rachel's stoning."

Tears are blurring my eyes; what I can't bear is my mother's hurt. Uncle Eli's anger is much easier to ride. I can't answer. I stand mute before her painful accusations. Eventually I mumble, "What is to happen to me then?"

"After much dissension, your uncle has reluctantly agreed to seek a private examination of your case by the elders of the synagogue alone. He is risking his own position by asking this favour for you. A public hearing would be far more unpredictable, and, if it condemned you, almost impossible to countermand. I have only obtained this limited support for you, however, by pressing the culpability of the stranger and asking them to consider what happened implicitly as rape. That will be hard enough to defend since it has taken all this time for you to admit it."

"But, Mother, we've been through all this before. I cannot blame God's messenger. And having gone this far in accepting God's will for me, must I throw everything away by denying what's happened?"

"Mari, Mari, don't you understand the seriousness of the charges against you? Don't you understand you're fighting for your life?"

My mother then bursts into tears and sinks to the bed in front of me, leaving me standing, horrified. I am numbed, shaking like a leaf. She turns her tear-stained face to mine. "Are you so full of pride, Mariam? Would you kill yourself and fill my life and that of your sisters and brother with so much sorrow, because you cannot admit that you may be wrong? If ever I lay my hands on that man, I'll wring his neck that he should have so turned your head!"

"When, Mother, when have I to answer them?"

"I don't know, Mari. Eli is at the synagogue now, trying to fix things. You'll have to wait until word is sent back."

I feel despair now for the first time. I thought it would be easier than this. I had even convinced myself that at least some of the rabbis would be excited at my news – after all, it is what they've been praying for all their lives. When Salome, Rebecca and Benjamin went out, they knew something serious was wrong; I could see Rebecca had been crying. They had probably been told to say nothing to me. The pain of those I love is undermining all my resolve. I am tempted to give in. While I am thinking these desperate thoughts, I hear the door open and am vaguely aware that Clopas is talking quietly to my mother. Then he turns to me and says, "Put on your shawl, Mari. It is time to go. Eli has persuaded the elders to hear you in private. Pray that you answer them humbly, seeking their compassion!"

I am led into the Women's Court, and the door is shut and locked behind me. The school lessons have apparently been abandoned for the day and the boys sent home, for all the rabbis – Jethro, Joel, Simon and my uncle – are seated behind a table on which rest scrolls of the law. My mother is taken to one side by Clopas, within earshot and he stays with her, out of my direct line of vision. I am made to stand in front of the rabbis.

I have known all of them from my childhood. Joel in particular has been like a friend, encouraging my searching and learning of the scriptures. Yet as I look at them, seeking a softening, some response of friendship or goodwill, I see set cold faces, steeled to feel nothing. I cannot fathom their expressions. It is going to be very formal, very difficult to make them understand.

Rabbi Jethro is the spokesman. He coughs and clears his throat, and looking straight past my shoulder, declares, "Mariam, daughter of Joachim, ward of Eli, we are here to perform a very painful duty, following your confession this morning under Eli's questioning. As a measure of our respect for him, and your late father, we are agreed that you should be examined in private, to hear your explanation. Afterwards we are empowered to carry out the requirements of the law, according to our judgement. Do you understand what I am saying?"

"Yes, sir," I answer very nervously.

"This morning you confessed to Eli that you believed the cause of your sickness to be that you were pregnant. I ask you formally before all here present if you confirm this. Is it your belief, Mariam, that you are pregnant?"

I hang my head and reply very softly, "Yes, I do believe that."

"What causes you to think so?"

"My sickness and my soreness, sir, and the fact that I have not had my normal period for over two months. I have talked with my mother and she is sure that my symptoms are those of pregnancy."

"You are betrothed to Joseph of Bethlehem?"

"Yes, sir."

"Could he have made you pregnant?"

"No, that is not possible. He has not been with me in that way. Also, he has been away in Capernaum for nearly three months."

"I wish to make quite sure of that statement, child. I am not asking you to accuse your betrothed falsely, but do not deny any relationship out of modesty or loyalty. If he has made you pregnant, it is reprehensible and some punishment will be appropriate. But the matter could be solved by accelerating your marriage plans without accusation of adultery."

"No, sir, Joseph is innocent of any offence towards me."

"Your honesty on that point does you credit, even if it does not help your situation."

I begin to relax a little. Perhaps they will be sympathetic after all.

"I am advised that you hold the stranger that lodged at the house of Althaeus the tax collector responsible."

"He advised me that I would become pregnant, sir."

"He told you that you would have a baby?! Before he had intercourse with you?"

"He told me I would have a son."

"And despite this extraordinary statement, you allowed him to go ahead?"

"At first he did not say when I would have the son, sir."

"He forced you then, by tricking you in some way?"

This is the crucial question. Now is the time I have to bend, to compromise, to save my family and my honour. All I have to do is mutter 'yes', and they will search for him, and fail to find him. Surely I can make that small step?

Yet, try as I might, nothing comes out. It is as if I've been struck dumb, I cannot move my lips; my tongue is parched and cleaves to the back of my throat. I am sweating and blushing furiously. Helplessly I answer, "No, sir."

The silence is painful. Vaguely I hear my mother gasp, then she makes choking sounds into the folds of Clopas' cloak. I look fearfully towards Uncle Eli, and see that he can scarcely contain his fury at my answer. I suppose he has made some deal with the others that will salve their consciences and mitigate the disgrace to his own family, and my answers are not going according to plan. Even in my desperate situation I can't help feeling a glimmer of satisfaction at his discomfiture, as though what I was saying had nothing to do with my fate. Then, even as I say the words, my mother's cry of despair comes back to my ears: 'Don't you understand, you're fighting for your life!'.

"Where did you meet this stranger?"

"By the well."

"Did you have an arrangement with him?"

"No, sir. My mother sent me to fetch water. The man came while I was drawing and asked me for a drink."

"Did he assault you at the well?"

"No, sir, he quoted scripture to me and told me that I had been chosen for a special task."

"And you believed him?"

"I wasn't sure at first, sir. But he had seen me in Nazareth before and told me that I had been chosen by God for something special."

"What were these passages of scripture that he spoke to you about?"

I explain as best I can. The quotations are etched into my memory. When I say them aloud, the elders react in a most shocked manner and start arguing amongst themselves. When they have finished their private disputation, Jethro turns back to me, glares at me in a manner that I have never seen him adopt before and thunders,

"Mariam, daughter of Joachim, are you telling me in all seriousness that you claim to be carrying the long-promised Messiah?"

"That is what the stranger told me, sir, and I believed him."

There is total uproar. Uncle Eli stands up and tears his robe in anger and distress. Jethro stands over me as though he is going to hit me, then he turns abruptly and goes into a huddle with the others.

They hurl questions at me without restraint now, so fast and furious that I can scarce answer before the next question. I cannot think carefully any longer; I just abandon all attempts at weighing my words. I tell of our previous contacts, everything. When they have drained me of all the import of our conversations, they press me further for the intimate details of what happened in the Tabor stream. They will spare me nothing. I must tell them in explicit humiliating words how I felt the urge to strip and obeyed this without compulsion, how I closed my eyes, my feelings, everything.

I try to protect the mystery, plead that I didn't know the means by which I had conceived my son. I am dismissed in scorn; they tie me up in argument until I find I am admitting knowledge of a physical union because they give me no other option.

"And you still say that the outcome of this lewd coupling is to be our Messiah, the pure and royal king that must come from David's lineage and will lead this country to freedom?"

It is horrible. They are twisting my words, making them seem like filth when what happened was beautiful and full of meaning. I am crying. I can't answer their hateful questions; I can only fling myself on God's mercy. "Please, God, help me! Do not abandon me! Have pity on me and on your son!"

There is a sudden shocked silence. They all seem to shrink from me. Jethro eventually summons strength and says with menace, "What did you say then, girl?"

When I have recovered sufficiently to realise what I have said, I am shocked. The words just seemed to escape, naturally, without any conscious thought on my part. I cannot explain my cry for help. I cannot add anything. I do not answer.

"We have heard enough. Anna, take this girl into the robing room and keep her secure there while we pass judgement on her."

I am led into the tiny room off the synagogue court and the door is shut and barred behind us. What is my mother going to say to me now? I am more afraid of her angry words than the sentence that the elders will pass upon me. I know she is crying. I can feel her body shaking against mine. I feel strangely calm, unreal; I ought to be petrified, but it all seems to be happening to someone else, not me. My mother starts to say something, but breaks down in further floods of tears. In the end I can bear this no longer. I hear myself saying, "Mother, please. Do not cry for me. You are making me more upset."

"Mari, how can you be so calm? You condemned yourself from your own lips. Oh Mari, why, why? I thought we could save you. Don't you value your own life?"

"God will protect me."

"Child, I wish I had your faith. I pray that you will not be disillusioned, but I fear the worst."

"If the child within me is special, God will not let me die."

"Mari, if, when we return, they condemn you to death, as I fear they will, do not remain proud and arrogant to the end. Plead with them, beg for mercy, admit that you may have been mistaken. They will surely not kill you for being too naïve and credulous. And it is still private; they will not have to explain themselves to the men of the village."

"Mother, I do not know what I will do or say. I am trusting myself to God's will. He will decide."

"Mari, whatever happens, let me say this to you. I do not know if I believe your stranger's message: I think he tricked you. But I admire and respect your belief and your steadfastness to what you think is right. However, child, my mother's instinct wants you back in my arms, mistaken, cheated, abused maybe, but still my darling girl. Oh Mari, I love you, I cannot bear to see you like this."

We fall once more into each other's arms and cling tightly for mutual support. It seems an eternity.

At last we hear the latches being unfastened. We are being fetched. Suddenly all my strength seems to disappear. Doubts flood my mind. I am going to die. I cannot comprehend what I am thinking. I am made to stand in front of the elders. Their faces give nothing away.

"Mariam, daughter of Joachim, listen to our judgement."

Rabbi Jethro touches his forehead and then pauses while I fidget in my nervousness.

"From your own admission you have had intercourse with a man who is not your betrothed. At best you are guilty of fornication, but according to the consecration vows you made to your betrothed, you are technically guilty of adultery. On top of this, before us this morning, you have heaped further ignominy on your head, making fantastic and blasphemous claims to excuse your sin. By all the statutes of our law you must be condemned, and death by stoning is your just desert."

I hear the fateful words and begin to black out. Jethro is fading from my sight. My legs are crumbling. I vaguely hear voices, hurried, urgent, in the background, and find suddenly that I am being lifted. Clopas has clamped me round the waist. I am told to take deep breaths. Then to listen: Jethro still has more to say.

"Mariam, I have told you what the law demands. But it is within our power to temper justice with mercy. It would be a day of great sorrow and shame to us to have to condemn you to the same death as the whore Rachel, you, the daughter of the martyr Joachim and ward of our respected colleague. We are therefore minded on a compromise. Your execution shall be stayed for a while. A search will be made for the stranger and he will be questioned to corroborate your testimony. If he admits to misleading you as you describe, providing you concede your error, your sentence will be set aside. Your child, too, must be aborted and arrangements for your future renegotiated between your guardian and your betrothed, who may be expected to wish to divorce you. Rabbi Eli will discuss with your mother what arrangements he has in mind to save the reputation of your family. Therefore, instead of a public stoning as the law decrees, we are minded to have you whipped here in private before these witnesses alone. In that way no-one need know your disgrace and we shall not be accused of applying the law in a discriminatory way, because of Eli's relationship with you. Do you understand what I am saying?"

I am not to die. God has protected me: that is all I can think; the rest has not sunk in. I nod in silence.

"Your punishment, even so, is not a light one. You are of age; your sentence is the full adult chastisement of thirteen lashes of the three-tailed whip, thirty-nine stripes upon the bare flesh of your back and thighs. The shock of the pain itself is likely to cause your body to reject the foetus within you. If this is the case, it will save you further suffering, although you will be much weakened through loss of blood from your womb as well as from your stripes."

Jethro turns from me and has a whispered conversation with the other elders, then he adds, "There is insufficient time to inflict your punishment before the midday gathering here in the synagogue. You will therefore await your penalty until the hour of worship is over and all the people are dispersed. Your mother may remain with you if you wish and help you prepare yourself."

Jethro and Joel lead me across the Women's Court to a locked door in the far corner. Although of course I have taken my place here each Sabbath since my majority alongside Miriam and my mother, I have never really taken any notice of it before. Joel inserts a heavy key and releases the lock, so that the door creaks open to reveal a bare room, lit only by a narrow slit open to the air high above the eyeline and out of reach. The walls are whitewashed. The floor is stone. There is no furniture of any description.

We wait at the entrance until my mother has caught up with us. Then Joel slips into the room and re-emerges from behind the door, holding something in his hand. He shows a piece of cloth and a rope to my mother, then throws them across the floor, saying, "Get her ready immediately. Undress her and tie the triangle of cloth round her waist so that her genitals are covered, seeing that she does not offend the law. Then bind her wrists together with the rope in front of her body, leaving a length of cord on either side so that she can be secured during the whipping. We will come for you when we are ready."

Mother steps into the room and I am shoved after her by a push against my shoulder so that I am caught off balance and stumble against her. The door is slammed behind us and we hear the key turn gratingly in the lock. Neither of us says a word; we even avoid looking at one another. To break the tension, I whisper, "How soon will it be?"

"Perhaps an hour, Mari. I have lost track of time. We shall hear the chanting when the hour of worship begins, then perhaps half an hour until the synagogue is empty again."

I stare vacantly round the bare cell. Then in the shadows behind the wooden door, I see the whip hanging from the nail and next to it, cane rods of different lengths and thicknesses. I cannot take my eyes off the whip. There is a smooth wooden handle with a metal ring at its base, which is balanced on the nail. Trailing from this grip are three leather thongs of different lengths, the longest nearly reaching to the floor. I look in trepidation to my mother.

"Is this what they will use?"

Mother does not need to answer. Her eyes say it all, brimming with tears. She nods and bites her lip. I put out a hand tentatively and touch the leather. I begin to gasp for breath: it is so clammy and oppressive in here despite the winter season, which is drawing to its close.

"Leave me for a moment. I want to pray."

I shut my eyes and try to concentrate, but the words won't come. All I can see is that whip. My imagination is tearing me apart. I cannot think of God. I do not want Mother to see my difficulty, so I pretend, standing rigidly, sweating in the effort to make the words flow. Nothing; I am blocked with fear.

I am still straining when I hear the key squealing in the lock. Surely they have not come for me already: it can't be ten minutes since we were left. It is Joel again, standing silhouetted by the bright light of the court.

"I've come for your clothes."

My mother explains that we have not yet prepared ourselves: we thought we had more time.

"Give me your clothes now."

"Are you taking Mariam already? I did not think the midday service had even started."

"It will be some time yet before she is fetched. But I have come for her clothes. She should be prepared."

"I will bring them out to you when I have prepared her."

"Do not argue, woman. I want them now. You!" He turns abruptly to me. "Strip and hand me your clothes."

I try to shield myself behind my mother as I hand him my shawl and loincloth, then untie my girdle and pull the tunic over my head.

"Now bind her and cover her and be ready next time I come."

He is gone and we are again locked in. I am shocked that the person I always thought my friend seems so cold and angry. Mother has picked up the skimpy cloth apron from the stone floor and is untangling the twine. She places the cloth in front of my belly and pulls the twine taut until it cuts into my hips, and knots it securely. I pull it down so that the tapering material hangs loose in front of my groin.

"I'm sorry, Mari, in view of what has just been said, I think I ought to tie your wrists together now. I do not want to give them any excuse to increase your punishment."

I offer her both arms stretched forward together and hold them where she can bind them without difficulty. At first she pulls the cords too tightly, so that the rope cuts into my wrists. Then she tries again, leaving an inch or two of play.

It is done. I am prepared; trussed and offered, as if in sacrifice. For some strange reason, I feel liberated. I have ceased to sweat in fear; I accept what is to come is inevitable: the price I have to bear for the privilege of obeying God's will.

"Let me be in peace now, Mother. Before I found it hard to pray. Now my mind is full."

She leans forward and kisses me.

"Thanks," I murmur.

I am now totally vulnerable, Lord. This I think, in silence. I've done everything you've asked of me. I cannot even move my hands. I am bound and in your hands. I have dared everything; I have risked everything. Often I didn't want to; I have feared this moment, feared this consequence. And now it has happened, I find that I can accept it as your will. Your messenger asked if I could bear the pain. Is this what he meant, literally? He said that I would be protected from shame and disgrace. It would be shame and disgrace to have denied your call.

Aloud I pray, "Lord God, protect your servant now. Put your arms around your unborn child so that no harm comes to him. And help me to bear the agony as I accept your will for me. I am ready now. So be it."

The time is come. Of course I am afraid, but I am under control. I try not to think of my soft smooth skin; I concentrate on the tiny creature growing deep within me and pray with all my heart that he will be cushioned by my flesh and blood. I am afraid for him. My mother gives me a last squeeze and hug. "Be brave, my child. I shall pray for your prayers to be answered."

I am brought into the court where punishments are carried out when screened from the populace. The cold rough floor and the silent watchfulness of the rabbis bring back a certain reality to my circumstance that I had nearly banished. It is not going to be so easy after all. Rabbi Joel has laid his outer robe to one side and has picked up the whip that was hanging in my cell. So he is to be my chastiser: my tutor and my best friend's father. Will he let that influence him? Will he hold back from striking with his full strength? I guess not from his attitude so far and his expression, which is hard and devoid of contact with me.

My palms are placed flat against one of the pillars and the cords are tied round the column so that I am leaning forward, arms outstretched. My legs are positioned slightly apart so that I am balanced, offering my bare body to their will. My apron hangs loosely from my waist. It will cover the letter of the law, and nothing else. All this, as if in slow motion, sensitive to every movement, touch or implied command. Jethro stands immediately in front of me, so that I can see him if I lift my head.

"Mariam, when I give the word, your punishment will commence with stripes to your back and shoulders. Keep your head high, for the longest lash will wrap around your body, cutting into your breasts. If you drop your head, you could be caught by the lash across your face, causing severe and possibly permanent injury. Before the rabbi moves on to flog your buttocks you will be given time to recover and be offered a sip of water. Do you understand?"

"Yes, sir."

"Then hold still, and be ready. Let the punishment commence!"

There is a fearful silence. I push with all my might on my palms and try to keep my head high, my eyes tightly closed.

The shrieking wail of the lashes and the burning agony that encircles me are instantaneous. I find I am howling in pain, scarcely aware that the voice is mine, disembodied, echoing in the chamber. All I sense is the ring of excruciating throbbing flesh. My eyes open wide and my head hangs forward, searching for the weal.

"Hold your head up!"

I cannot continue in this wretched present tense. To relive this hour of agony cannot be justified. It would be repetition, and fake at that, for how could I think clearly enough to describe each vicious stripe. It is one long confused indescribable pain sensed tenuously by that part of my mind which somehow forced me to hang on, keep my head high.

Need I tell you of this whipping at all, you may ask? Should it not be my secret? Does it not seem like boasting in hindsight? On balance, I think, to understand me, you have to know the whole truth. It is easy to gloss over the implications of my decisions, choices. I have known the risk; I know the barbarous practices of my generation. You have to know how vulnerable I was. Perhaps the full trappings of a judicial flogging were unknown to me; but I had seen, for just this cause I suppose, poor Rachel's brutal death. And it is important that you are aware of this scarring when you struggle with me to weigh the consequences of possible future threats and behaviour. I am no longer an innocent child. I grew up during this awful hour and its immediate aftermath; you must convince yourself of that reality. And to believe, you must experience.

You will have plenty of time to piece together what happened. In days to come, you'll see my scars: there will be no hiding them.

In retrospect then, looking back from some further point in time, let me just admit to one further incident in the litany of pain. They had finished the first part of my punishment and had waited a while for me to rest and recover a little of my composure. I was particularly fearful of the next stage, perhaps erroneously, for I saw the assault of the lash upon my flanks and belly as a direct threat to the existence of my promised son. When, therefore, the long leather descended for the first time across my buttocks – before it could encircle me – I gave a superhuman burst of energy, which must have loosened the rope around the column, allowing me instantaneously to double up to protect my child. The whip wrapped itself around my forearms and I shrieked in pain. The sudden violent movement snapped the twine around my waist, and as I was dragged upright and re-secured to the pillar, tightly, the apron fell to the floor, leaving me totally exposed. My chastiser ignored this flouting of the law and repeated the stroke, to which I now had no defence at all. I learned one further vital lesson: my fate and that of my unborn son were left to God, and God alone. No human agency or endeavour would help us now.

I was carried afterwards to the cell, where my mother attempted to comfort me and ease my limbs into prone positions that would be bearable. During the flogging I had twice fainted from the pain, and I continued to drift in and out of consciousness whilst she applied balm, as tenderly as she could, to my weals and broken flesh. Not until nightfall could I be taken home. In order to maintain secrecy, I was carried by Eli or Clopas – I know not which – under the cloak of darkness back to my house and laid face down upon my mattress. All night my mother sat up with me, stroking my hair, sobbing quietly, holding my hand while I struggled to control the pain.

CHAPTER 28

OUT OF THE MOUTHS OF BABES...

A WEEK HAS PASSED SINCE THE events I've just described. I can just about bear to return to the present, although I'll have to be very careful. For the first time since then, I've been permitted into the fields to work without supervision.

All last week Miriam accompanied me, partly to make sure I did not collapse, but also, she confided to me, to report back to Eli whether I was undertaking sufficiently strenuous manual work to increase the possibility of a natural miscarriage. She did not push me hard. She did not criticise her father-in-law, but neither did she attempt to censure me. She let me take my time and rest when fatigue became too much. She nursed me each morning when I was sick and restrained me gently when the retching caused my aching limbs to spasm. She let me lay my shawl upon the stony ground and loosen my tunic to minimise the friction, giving me warning if there was any risk of observation.

Doubtless she reported back to Eli that my symptoms of pregnancy persisted. Perhaps this is why I'm allowed today to venture forth with only Salome, Rebecca and little Mariam as my accomplices.

We have been digging up stones and weeding now for nearly two hours and the sun is beginning to gain real springlike warmth. I am hot and aching, and tell the others to finish off the bottom strip of the field while I find our midday food and undo the waterskins. I lower myself gingerly onto my knees beside the bag which contains the victuals, and seeing the others still busily occupied, I take the opportunity offered by the privacy to make a quick examination of my weals and bruises. The swellings and ridges of my flesh are now replaced by bruises: black, yellow, ugly shadows round my thighs. If I pull my tunic down, I can just avoid displaying them, but as I kneel here, my shift lifts and exposes the weals to the light. If I puff up my shift and peek inside, I can see the purple furrows on my breasts as well as feel the aching soreness with each movement of my arms. I am going to be questioned in a minute, of that I'm sure. This is the first time I've been alone with my sisters since I confessed to my mother about my pregnancy. All the way here I could see that they were itching to find out what had happened to me. They could not take their eyes off the rough burn marks on my forearms, the glimpse of bruising under my tunic hem. What have they been told? And when they ask me, how much shall I tell them? They are shy with me; they are troubled, for inhibition is normally quite foreign to their characters. Even Mo daren't ask; Miriam must have warned her in some way.

When they are done, they scamper to me and squat upon the bare dry earth, eating ravenously. They take long swigs from the waterskins, then sit and stare. They want to ask me now. Someone has forbidden them to question me.

When I am putting the waterskins back into the bag, I deliberately turn and lean away from them, so that they can see the backs of my thighs right up to my loincloth. With my face away from them, I ask, "Well, have a good look. What have they told you?"

There is an uneasy silence and some fidgeting. I look back. "Please, girls, someone must have told you something!"

Salome, flustered, offers, "Mother said we're not to say anything."

"Just Mother?"

"And Uncle Eli."

Rebecca can stomach her curiosity no longer.

"Mama said you'd been punished because you'd been seeing a man, not Joseph."

"And?"

"Not much more, really. Uncle Eli was angry and you'd been whipped." She pauses and looks meaningfully at my arms. "How did you get those marks?"

"If I tell you, will you keep it to yourselves? Swear to tell no-one?"

All three chorus, "Yes!"

We make a pact; I trust them, and they will be in trouble too if they let on that they know. I wonder if Mo can be entrusted with the secret, but the little girl is all agog and the others nearly scare the living daylights out of her on what they will do if she betrays us. I have never had any secrets from these children. I can't bear to have them now; I need to find sympathetic ears, someone who will believe. Am I irresponsible? If they fail me, can I not take the blame? After all, no-one has sworn me to secrecy. Are they too young to know the truth? Or better able to discern it?

I tell them. I start with my punishment and then go back to the rabbis' examination. I do not, of course, say anything about the threat of stoning, nor that this sentence is suspended only for the moment. Apart from obvious murmurs of sympathy, they are eager to hear about the fair-haired man and his dealings with me, as I knew they would be. After all, they were implicated; they had been accosted at the well and pumped for information about me, which they had freely given. I do not have to watch my words with them – I tell it unadorned and unambiguously. They are not concerned with the method of conception, only the news of the baby's identity as Israel's Messiah catches their real interest. As soon as I repeat the prophecies and tell how the messenger linked them with my condition, they thrill without constraint.

After much chatter, laughter and wonderment, Mo sidles up to me and whispers in my ear, "Can I feel the baby?"

"Of course not, silly, he's still far too small; it will be weeks yet before he's big enough for you to feel."

She looks so disappointed that I add quickly, "But you can hold your hands where he is growing even if you can't feel him yet. Do you want to do that?"

Mo nods vigorously.

I beckon her towards me and lift my tunic so that she can slip her hand inside my loincloth, careful not to raise my shift too high lest she see the stripes still emblazoned round my ribs. I gently guide her podgy little hand inside my waistband and hold her against my warm belly. She can't feel a thing, of course, except me, but her eyes glisten in unadulterated excitement.

The other girls are watching carefully.

"Surely you two don't want a feel as well?"

Salome nods a little shamefacedly and Rebecca grins, "Yes, me too!"

"Go on then, you sentimental fools!" I exclaim amicably, and hold my waistband out so that their hot and grubby hands can press against my tummy. Rebecca pushes forward and yanks my loincloth down so that she can look as well as feel. She sees the weals, and recoils in horror.

"Mari, what have they done to you?"

I explain as superficially as I can; I try to emphasise the positive, how despite all the efforts to destroy my baby, he seems to be surviving still. It is a sobered Rebecca who brushes her hand so softly across my stomach that I can hardly feel her. Her fingers pause for a moment on the black and yellow bruises; she checks momentarily that the skin is smooth despite its appearance, then she steadies her palm and waits as if she were expecting the child within to kick.

"When there is something more to feel, Rebecca, I'll let you hold me, don't you worry."

She takes her hand away and looks at it with awe. She believes.

Salome now follows diffidently. Although she is less boisterous than the others, she is just as keen in her way, and takes her fill. I let my tunic drop, and, still on my knees, I open my arms and sweep them all in; we are all laughing and crying at the same time.

When their merriment has subsided, I add, "I'll be going away soon. Your Aunt Elizabeth, who lives near Jerusalem, is having a baby too, and they've sent for me to help her and learn from her." I daren't tell them the real reason.

"Aunt Elizabeth?" exclaims Rebecca with a mixture of amusement and disgust. "She's old; why's she having a baby?"

"That's a miracle too, Becca. She's had a messenger saying God has heard her prayers after all these childless years, and she will have a boy too, who will help prepare the message for my son."

"How do you know that, Mari?"

"The fair-haired man told me."

"Was he an angel, do you think?"

"I don't know about that," I laugh, "he seemed very much flesh and blood to me!"

"Aren't you lucky! I wish I could bear the Messiah!"

"I'm not so sure," interjects Salome. "It can't be very easy. Look at what's happened to Mari already. What does Joseph make of it all?"

"I don't know. In fact, he doesn't even know I'm pregnant yet."

"It doesn't seem very fair on him, does it?" says Salome reflectively. "I wouldn't like to come home and find my betrothed was having someone else's baby, even if it was a miracle."

"You're quite right. I'd like to tell him myself, but Uncle Eli's said that I must leave it all to him at the right time. That is one of the reasons you must promise me not to tell anyone else, not even Mama or your mother, Mo."

"I promise, really I do," says the small child. I just hope it doesn't escape one day in her excitement.

Each day I grow a little stronger and less stiff in my movements, although my bruises are still very sore to touch. My morning sickness persists, however, and the skin around my breasts and armpits seems stretched and irritated in a way quite unconnected with the stripes. I still have trouble in sitting comfortably and prefer to sprawl on my tummy or kneel. Gradually I forget. I make the most of the children's presence; I sense their suppressed excitement when I am present. They are hugging themselves with glee at the secret they contain within, that the grown-ups do not know! Despite the alleged purpose of my Jerusalem visit, I cannot really believe the baby will be aborted. The faith of my sisters strengthens my resolve and trust. And there again, I am convinced that if cousin Elizabeth has had a message from God about her baby, surely she'll believe my account as well?

We go tomorrow morning. Joseph has come home tonight, but although we greeted one another fulsomely enough, we were not left alone; Uncle Eli hung around in the room, ears pricked waiting for me to let slip any clue upon which he might pounce. Joseph knows that I am going to stay with Elizabeth and help at the birth of her baby.

"It will be good experience for you, Mariam."

Little does he realise how relevant, how soon! Later Uncle Eli comes to our house. The girls are sent to play on the roof, and when he thinks we are alone, he beckons my mother and grasps me by the waist, pulling me towards him.

"Listen to what I have arranged. We leave tomorrow morning at sunrise. All my sons-in-law are here now, except for Joshua, and he will join us at the crossroads near Mizra. We go direct to Jerusalem in three days, where one of Zechariah's servants will meet us and conduct Mariam to Ein–Karem. On the journey, Mariam, you will often be in contact with Joseph. You are to mention nothing that has befallen you, absolutely nothing. That is an order. Do you understand?"

"Yes, sir."

"What is more, you are to do nothing that will give away your secrets. If you feel sick in the mornings, you are to hang back with Clopas, who will keep his eye on you. Should Joseph notice and become concerned, you will feign weariness, being unused to such journeys, and I will depute Clopas to stay with you, whilst the rest make good speed. At all times you are to ensure that your remaining bruises and weals remain well hidden. You will only bare your arms and legs to wash, well away from the other members of the party. Should, by accident, Joseph catch you unawares, you must explain the marks on your arms as burns from a rope with which you were playing. If other weals are seen, then at most you must admit a caning administered by me, for speaking with a stranger without a chaperone being present. When you return we shall determine what he needs to be told; even then, you will leave it in my hands, child, as negotiations over your continuing marriage plans will need careful management."

Eli pauses for a moment, and drinks from the cup of wine that my mother has poured for him.

"Now for even more serious matters. I have entrusted a letter to Zechariah, which spells out the reason for your banishment. Rumour has it that he is finding difficulty with speech; all the better if so: your secret is more likely to be kept. I have asked him to get his wife to arrange an abortion for you. Elizabeth is well versed in such matters – she has consulted many doctors and magicians with claims to expertise in child conception, birth and pregnancy diseases, and Jerusalem is rich in such skills. For suitable cash down, all things can be arranged. I have enclosed a sufficient sum of money to procure the service you require. It grieves me that I shall have to use my hard-earned resources so. You will remain with Zechariah and Elizabeth until you are totally recovered, and then you may stay to help Elizabeth until after her child is born, and the immediate requirements of the law have been fulfilled. When you are ready to return, Zechariah will send word, and I will ask Clopas to bring you home."

Eli takes another draught of wine and wipes his lips on his sleeve. He fixes me with a penetrating look and adds with emphasis, "My enquiries to find your so-called messenger have been totally fruitless. I am convinced the man was a spy and mischief-maker, who saw the chance to exploit your naivety and use you to discredit me and cause dissension in the village. Technically the death sentence still hangs over you, until the stranger can be found to corroborate your story. In reality, I have an understanding with the other rabbis that they will let the matter rest, as long as you return home in due season without child and Joseph does not make a fuss. However, and let me stress this to you, child, it all depends on your obedience in this matter. The pregnancy must be terminated. I'll have none of this obscene saga about bearing the Messiah, as if such an event could come from the coupling of a foreign trickster and a wayward credulous disobedient girl. I'll brook no argument. If for any reason you dare to return home still with child, I'll have you publicly pilloried and stoned to death, unless the crowd condemn your blasphemy as witchcraft and have you burned. I'll not have any pity: I shall disown you and look on with nothing but anger, sharing in the righteousness of the Lord cleansing his temple by means of blood-sacrifice. I'm giving you every chance to obey, for your mother's and Joachim's sakes. Do not let them down, even if your own life seems worthless to you: a heinous crime in itself. Mariam, I'm not asking now for your obedience; I am demanding it. I'm asking if you understand what I am saying. Do you believe I mean it?"

Throughout this petrifying speech I have been quite dumb. I have felt anger boiling up within me. I have wanted to protest, to shriek out, "no!" Then I realise that I must play for time. Perhaps Elizabeth will refuse to co-operate; perhaps in Jerusalem there will be another sign; perhaps the messenger will return and speak to Eli or Clopas, or even Joseph, so that they are convinced. Perhaps I shall run away. I must leave it to God and contain my revulsion at Eli's attitude and speech.

I swallow my pride and nod my head. To say the words of betrayal out loud is expecting too much.

My mother hastens to put my gesture into words.

"Of course she understands, Eli. You could hardly have made yourself plainer."

CHAPTER 29

PILGRIMAGE

VERYONE IS UP AND GETTING in each other's way. My mother has been packing sufficient food for the journey. Salome and Rebecca have been attempting to help. Benjamin makes no such pretence. I am being attacked by a last minute bout of nerves, or morning sickness – or both – as I realise that this will be the first time in my life that I shall be away from home. It could be a couple of months before I return, and my imagination even now runs riot over what reception I shall receive then. Perhaps this is the last time that I shall play here with Benji. He chases me around the room until he is stopped by Mother for fear of him breaking something.

The others are gathering in the yard. Clopas is saying farewell to Miriam and the children. I have my pack. My shawl is round my shoulders. Mother turns me to face her, adjusts the shawl so that it covers my arms as well, kisses me on both cheeks, then embraces me, tears in her eyes.

"Be obedient, my child. Please come home to me with all this behind you. Every day I will pray for the Lord God's protection for you. Send me word how you are getting on, and give my love to my cousin Elizabeth and her husband."

She gives me a final hug, and then draws something out of her garment and slips it into my hand.

"Take this, Mari; let it be a reminder and keepsake of us. But don't let the others see it. Farewell, my love."

I grasp the little stone or brooch and slip it quickly into my pack, and give each of the children in turn a kiss and a hug. They are calling for me now. We must be gone: the sun is showing in the east beyond Mount Tabor.

We make our way purposefully out of the village. There are fourteen of us in the party: seven of our family so far. That includes three of Eli's sons-in-law, as well as Clopas, Joseph, Eli and myself. Rabbi Joel and his wife are coming. My friend Hannah has been left in charge of the younger children for the Passover period. Then there is Matthias the scribe and his three sons, the eldest bringing his young wife, Ramah, who is only a couple of years older than I am. At least there is some company for me on this journey. I had thought I'd be the odd one out and very conspicuous.

When we have cleared the village, I hang back and retrieve Mother's gift so that I can examine it. It is a pretty little amulet on a chain to hang around my neck. On it is carved a tiny bunch of grapes on one side, and the head of a beautiful young woman on the other. I am minded to put it on, except for my mother's words not to let the others see. I wonder why she said that.

I am so absorbed in studying the amulet that I don't notice Ramah joining me until she speaks.

"What have you got there, Mariam? Let me see."

Instinctively I try to hide the gift, then realising she has already seen it, I show her, saying that my mother gave it to me.

"What a funny present to give you!"

"Why?"

"Don't you know what it is?"

"She said it was a keepsake to remind me of her."

"It's an amulet that the gentiles use to ward off bad luck during pregnancy. Jewish women aren't meant to need them, but I know many are superstitious and keep the tradition going 'just in case'. Fancy giving one to an unmarried girl like you!"

"I'm betrothed to Joseph."

"Yes, I know. I guess I shall need to use the amulet before you do."

"Why, are you pregnant?"

"No, not yet. At least, I don't think so. I hope to be soon, though. Jacob wants a son very badly. We've been married nearly a year now and he's quite disappointed that I'm not pregnant yet. I say, can I borrow your amulet to wear?"

I don't want to let her have it now I know what it is. I read it as a secret message from my mother; does she really want me to keep the child despite all she has said to me? Perhaps I'm assuming too much from it. Nevertheless, I want it close to me. I don't want to arouse Ramah's suspicion, however, so I say to her, "Yes, if you like. Let us make a deal. You wear it during the day and I'll have it at night, to remind me of my family at home."

"Thanks, Mariam. I'll see if it brings me any luck when Jacob comes to me tonight."

"Don't tell anyone what it is, or that it's mine, will you? My mother said to tell no-one."

"Ah, so she knew what it was! No, Mari, I shan't tell anyone. I don't want even my husband to know that I'm putting faith in a heathen amulet. He's a very strict Jew and he'd be angry with me."

Ramah takes the amulet from my hands and drapes it over her head, the long chain allowing the image itself to nestle between her breasts hidden in her shift.

"Thanks, kid."

"You'll let me have it back tonight?"

"All right, when I've done with it. I'll sneak out of my tent when Jacob is asleep and return it to you."

By this time we have dropped some way behind the others, and Ramah suggests we run to catch up. She sets off at speed and I try to follow, but I am still feeling nausea, and running brings stabs of pain to my back and bottom. I move as smoothly as I can manage and eventually catch the group up, though I must unconsciously have been grimacing.

"My, you're out of condition," teases the girl. "I thought you'd outrun me with all the outdoor work you do for your uncle."

After a further hour or two's walk, as the sun nears its zenith, we come to the village of Nain and we all spill into Joshua's little house to refresh ourselves and rest a short while in the shade, before moving on with Joshua and Susannah, who now join our party. As we get underway again, Susannah seeks me out and falls into my rhythm. I like Susannah. She is always cheerful and good fun. I like her husband, Joshua, as well; he is the nicest of Eli's four sons-in-law – not so formal or pompous as the others.

"Well, Mari, how's you then? I gather you're off to help Elizabeth during her confinement and act as midwife's assistant. Get some practice in and I'll let you help when my time comes!"

"Why, Susannah, are you having a baby too?"

Susannah laughs.

"I ought to be." She digs me in the ribs with a knowing smile on her face. "But I don't think I am yet. If I have to wait much longer, I'll tell Joshua he'll have to redouble his efforts!"

I look at her a bit shocked.

"Get on with you, I'm only teasing. I've a feeling it won't be long before we have children running around our home. I was sorry you didn't come and live with us. It could have been fun."

I make as if to reply, but she holds up her hand to stop me.

"Yes, I know, Mari. I don't blame you for not wanting to marry that Zealot. I only met him once and I found him a bit uncouth, not to mention dangerous to know and house."

We walk on a bit further in contented silence. Suddenly I notice she is squinting at my arm. I look down and find that my shawl has slipped, exposing the burn marks across both forearms. I cover them again quickly. She makes to grab the shawl to prevent me hiding the weals.

"Mari, what on earth have you got there? What have you done?"

Caught in surprise, I blink as I try to think of my excuse. I'm sure she must have noticed my hesitation and reluctance, but she says nothing when I say, "Oh, it was an accident at the well. I had the ropes wound around my arms and I let the full weight of the laden jar slip back into the water."

As we make our way towards the Jordan at the end of this first long day, I begin to limp and lag behind. It is Susannah who first notices, and drops back to chivvy me on with her banter and good humour.

"Have a quick rest, Mari, then we'll catch up with them."

As I sink gratefully to the grassy bank beside the track, she notices.

"Mari, you've been whipped quite badly. Don't deny it; I can see the marks plainly. When?"

I tell her as much as I dare and implore her to keep my secret. She seems to sense there is more, but the rest are in danger of disappearing over the horizon.

"Come on, girl, we'd better hurry to catch up the others. And come to me for help; I'll not tell."

That night, in the women's tent, Susannah puts her bedding next to mine, as if to screen me from the others. Ramah is outside somewhere in the darkness, with Jacob I guess, and Joel's wife is already fast asleep. I have been resisting Susannah's probing curiosity, when Ramah sneaks in, leans across Susannah, whom she thinks is asleep also, and whispers hoarsely, "Thanks, Mari. With a bit of luck, perhaps that will do the trick."

Then unfortunately she drops my amulet in the darkness somewhere between Susannah's form and my bedroll. She leans over to search the floor, as I do, and Susannah sits up and joins in, merrily chortling, "What are you two up to? What big secret have we here?"

And, of course, she finds the amulet. I can't see her face in the darkness, but as she hands it to me, she whispers, "We must have a further chat tomorrow, Mari. Go to sleep now: you'll need all your strength, because it's a hard trek on the rough paths beside the Jordan."

But for a couple of hours I cannot get to sleep. Susannah is going to quiz me further in the morning, I know she is, and she suspects more than I'm meant to reveal.

When we set off in the early morning, I try at first to miss Susannah by joining the men in the main party. I fall in beside Joseph and say to him, "I thought you were trying to avoid me."

"Whatever made you think that, Mariam? I thought you were happy in the company of the women."

"I was. But that doesn't mean I don't want to talk to you as well."

"That's good. What do you want to talk to me about?"

"Nothing in particular. I just want to chat."

And so, for a few minutes, we fence with one another, making polite conversation, talking about his work in Sepphoris and Capernaum, and the preparation and making of my wedding dress. I'm in a peculiar frame of mind. I keep flirting with danger as I talk mysteriously. I think, of excitements at home, but he will not take the bait. I daren't tell him what has happened to me; I have been forbidden. Yet I want him to be curious, to challenge me so that he forces me to tell. It seems so obvious, but he does not seem to notice. I even let my shawl slip a little, so that my bruises are visible. He does not look. Clopas sees though, and coming alongside, he whispers in my ear, "Mariam, watch your shawl!"

Joseph carries on talking, not even being aware of this rebuke to me.

By the early afternoon we've waded through the shallow Jordan about which I've heard so much. It is certainly lush and green, but the river is much smaller than I had imagined; I think I've dreamed so much about it, read so many references in the scriptures, that the muddy stream is a bit of a disappointment. The shelter given by the trees and bushes along its banks is welcome, though, and the flow does narrow and deepen from time to time to look more like a proper river.

After we have rested and eaten a midday meal in the shade of another grove of trees, we continue on a narrow path with the river on one side, and rocky outcrops on the other. It is difficult to walk more than two abreast here, and I find that Susannah has sought me out. I know what this means. Much as I like her, I fear her incisive humour. I am vulnerable to her approach; how can I keep secrets from such a natural companion who wants to be my friend?

We drop back out of earshot of the rest of the party; Susannah is manoeuvring this. She makes no preliminary probing, but comes straight to the point.

"What's the matter, Mari? I can see that something's wrong. Surely you can trust me with your secret, whatever it is?"

I hesitate. I say that I've been sworn to silence. She looks at me in pity, then says, "Well, if that's the case, girl, I'll not make you break your vow. But I think you need a friend; I think you want to share whatever burden it is you are carrying alone. I am here; trust me. However shocking your secret is, I'll not condemn. I'll be on your side."

For a long time we continue our walk in silence. I shift my load from time to time to ease my sore shoulder being rubbed raw by the straps of my bag. She has offered friendship and trust. I need both. But again, dare I take the risk?

We stumble along the path into a rocky sunlit clearing. Back from the riverbanks, the rolling barren hills come to an abrupt halt in small jagged cliffs, eroded, with landslides of sand and scree.

"Susannah, I've got much to tell you, but I must ask you to keep my secret, even from your husband."

"I give you my word."

And I unburden myself as we walk all afternoon along the banks of the Jordan. It is a great relief. When I am near the end of my telling, I find I am crying. She puts her arms around my shoulders.

"Mari, your story is extraordinary. So much so that I do not believe you could have made it up. I believe you. If you ever need a friend, come to me."

"What do you think I should do, Susannah? Should I let them kill my child?"

"Shush, Mari, don't distress yourself so. Put yourself in God's hands. He's looked after you so far, protected you from the worst. He'll watch over you in the future, just you see!"

I slip my hand into hers and we walk for a while alongside the lush pasture and glass-like river, which at this point is flowing very still and deep.

"Thanks, I feel much better now. It's been awful having no-one believe you."

"Who knows, Mari? I need to be aware so that I don't betray you by mistake."

"I thought you said you'd tell no-one?"

"Don't worry; it's just if I know, I may glean something from what the others say. Does Joseph know anything?"

"No, nothing at all!"

"Is that really wise, Mari? He seems a good and sensible man to me."

"I'd like to confess everything to him, but Uncle Eli and Mother have forbidden me. Eli says that he will tell Joseph when the time is right, when I've got rid of the baby. Then he'll try to stop him divorcing me if he can."

"I suppose you'd better play it their way, but it seems a shame to me."

We walk slowly for a few minutes in silence while we catch up with the meandering column, which by this time has been joined with other groups of pilgrims all heading towards Jerusalem.

"You'd better take your bag back, Mari; otherwise someone will wonder why I'm helping you." She'd taken my bedroll and food as soon as she knew why my back was so sore. Then, as an afterthought, she adds, "You didn't tell me who else knows."

"Uncle Eli of course, Clopas, Rabbi Joel, Mother and Miriam at home and the other rabbis. And I told my sisters."

"That's a risk, isn't it?"

"I don't think so, Susannah. I just had to tell them. You see, they are the only other ones who believe me!"

"Poor old you! Come on, we'd better look cheerful, or they'll be suspicious about our conversation."

The sun is beginning to drop low in the sky now and we are approaching – so I'm told – the town of Bet Shean, where the Jezreel Valley crosses our path. There has been some discussion on whether we should enter the town to seek lodgings for the night, or at least set up our tents under the protection of the townsfolk, but the men now believe that the caravan is sufficiently large to form its own protection. While some are busy erecting the tents, and others discuss the camp site's defence and lookout duties, Joel's wife Leah, Ramah, Susannah and myself, with a couple of women from the other parties, are sent to the town's well to draw water for the night. All the other women are joining their menfolk for the Passover. For Susannah and Ramah, it is their first trip to Jerusalem and they listen with eagerness to the stories and experiences with which the other women regale us.

Then they turn to me, obviously curious as to my justification on the pilgrimage – an unmarried girl without her parents. I explain I am en route to my cousins in Ein–Karem, to be present at the birth of their first-born. They quiz me idly for a moment, but when Susannah throws in the news that the mother-to-be is in her late forties and all had assumed she was past the age of childbearing, the conversation rekindles and all kinds of speculation are bandied about.

"You'll have your work cut out, child," opines one of the women I do not know. "It's a well-known fact that a first-born that comes late in life is often handicapped or sick in the head. Such a shame when the little one has been awaited with such longing!"

"It goes rough with the mother too," adds the other. "Often a difficult confinement, often too much for an older, weaker woman."

"Don't frighten the girl," says Leah gently. She does not normally say much to any of us. "Many are successfully carried, despite what you say."

I don't know what to make of Leah. Does she know my secret? Surely Joel would have told her of my trial and whipping, yet she shows no hint of either pity or hostility. I have known her for many years – after all she is my friend's mother – yet she is polite, non-committal, as if she is not interested. Perhaps she has been kept in the dark by her husband. Then, though, I would have expected more friendliness. It is most puzzling.

In the morning Susannah and Ramah want me to go with them to the town; it's a Roman town, they tell me, with wide streets and columns and big gateways. I'd like to go with them – I'm curious too: I've never been out of Nazareth before, except to Nain. But it's no good. Although I wasn't too bad yesterday, I feel awful this morning. I pretend I want to wash something down by the river, and go off on my own while the men are packing the tents up. I just about make it and am violently sick at the edge of the water. I am mopping my brow and trying to rid my throat of the last bitter dregs, when I look up and see three curious, not to say petrified, children gaping at me. I try to smile at them and open my mouth to say something, but they flee from me, scuttling through the undergrowth. I feel hurt. In all my days I think this is the first time I can honestly say that children have run away from me, except in jest.

By the time I get back, the tents are all rolled up and the men are ready to go. Susannah and Ramah reappear, full of their account of the sights, and saying that many more pilgrims seem to be joining us from overnight lodgings in the Jewish quarter of the town. The three of us are scolded by the older women for neglecting our share of the work and we are sent to fetch water quickly for the day's travels, while the men complain at having to wait.

As we go south, the character of the river seems to be changing. Instead of the narrow river meandering between grassy banks, the watercourse is becoming wider and untidier, with mounds of sand and shingle separating out strands of trickling water. In some places the thick vegetation conceals the water altogether. The path keeps splitting and reforming, like the river, and several times, as Ramah, Susannah and I are now near the front of our caravan, we make a false trail and have to turn back as our path peters out at the river itself, or into the undergrowth. Back from the valley, catching the morning sun in pink-orange glow, is the escarpment of the Samaritan hills, jagged, but flat topped, with the gash of the Jezreel Valley clearly visible. To the left, we are squinting into the sun streaking shafts of light over the barren canyon edge, high and brooding. I want to pause, let them carry on and stay here beside the glinting water to watch the insects hover, to sing and rejoice in the morning dew. As we trudge our way south and the day wears on, the heat becomes stifling, humid. I long to throw off my shawl, loosen my girdle and lift my skirts, but I dare not. I must suffer in silence, letting the beads of sweat roll down my neck, feeling the clammy moistness of my arms and waist and back. I look at Ramah enviously as she frees her clothing. I must pretend to be at ease; I cannot show my discomfort.

In the afternoon we see the Judean desert to our left. The barren crevices which this morning were swathed in wispy white mist now shimmer in the haze. The vegetation becomes more sparse, and even though it's spring, greenness gives way to mottled browns and yellows. For our last night in the open, the pilgrims camp on the river just before the ford that is the main route through Jericho to Jerusalem. As the sun sets, the heat loses its strength rapidly. The air becomes cool, then cold as I pull my few clothes tightly around me, glad now of my shawl. Although we are now many, the noises of the camp are hushed and I lie awake, listening to the strange sounds of the desert. The insects hum and chirrup, deafeningly, punctuated by weird howls from the distant hills. I thought at first that they were stray dogs yowling in the night, but Clopas tells me there are jackals and hyenas out there somewhere. The men are building a fire that is sending up a cascade of sparks, and even when we close the flaps of our tent, we can still see the flickering shadows.

I am homesick tonight. It is eerie and I suddenly long for Mother, Salome, Becca and Ben. I feel very vulnerable here, as though I am cast off in the middle of a lake with no-one in sight, no breath of wind. I shudder and clasp my amulet, which Ramah did not bother to beg from me today. I draw my knees up and tuck my hands into my tunic and gently massage my smooth stomach. Somewhere inside there is my child. He needs me more than I need anyone. I pray, moving my lips, forming words that no-one but God will hear.

"Be with us, Almighty God. We are far from home and feel frightened." And I remember the words of my text and repeat them comfortingly to myself, "My father and mother may abandon me but the Lord will take care of me."

The last day of the journey. The wind is blowing lightly into our faces from the west, as, one by one, we ford the river. We have to lift our tunics as the water swirls round our thighs, but I wait until I'm near the back of our procession, and deliberately let my hem drag through the water. It will soon dry. It is a long uphill pull now, the widening track climbing into the ravine with nothing but barren rock on either side. I wouldn't like to be making this journey alone – the men say there are many bandits here waiting to attack unwary travellers. We pass soldiers marching in the opposite direction; they are said to be patrolling to protect the pilgrims, but it seems a little unnecessary for there are now straggling bands of people in front of and behind us, as far as the naked eye can see.

We are through the city of Jericho before morning is over and I stare in amazement at its wide streets and pavements, all the drains and sewers, and marble and grand stone buildings. Clopas answers my incessant questions.

"Just wait until you see Jerusalem's palaces and the Temple, Mariam!"

That must indeed be something! Everywhere there are avenues of palm trees growing from the dusty soil. And then, on the edge of the residential area, many stone buildings only half finished, which will swell the size of the city enormously.

By early afternoon we have Jerusalem in sight. It is a huge place, with great walls and palaces, and Clopas points out the shining building, which he says is the Temple. I was feeling tired, but, like the rest, have quickened my feet as our goal draws near. To our right, as we near the city, two canyons cut into the vast plateau. The city itself climbs up two hillsides and we make our way round to the left, past slopes that are filled with acre upon acre of olive groves. We reach the edge of the city wall at last and I stand in awe as I look up to the sentries way above us. I am quite overwhelmed. We trundle in through a huge gateway – Clopas says it's called the 'Sheep Gate' – and the caravan breaks up as pilgrims find their way to their lodgings. I have never seen so many people: there are crowds thronging the street; the noise is indescribable. The dust and heat and clamour – and perhaps the excitement – seem suddenly all too much for me and I feel faint, and have to sit down on some stone steps, while Susannah holds my head between my knees and I draw deep breaths.

Joseph comes over to me, concerned that I look so exhausted. I tell him of my stupor at the crowds, but he says it will get much busier still; there are two days yet to Passover and many more pilgrims still to be absorbed.

"Where will you all stay?" I ask, but of course Joseph has his own small home in Bethlehem only three or four miles away, and I gather that Joshua and Susannah are joining him, while the others are staying with friends and distant cousins in Bethany, whom they meet each year at festival time. As I am standing, bewildered, below the Great Courtyard of the new Temple, Uncle Eli, for the first time in four days, comes over to speak to me.

"Mariam, you must come with me to find your kinsman, Zechariah, who is expecting you. He will take you to his house tonight, so we must waste no time, for you have some distance still to travel."

I had not thought that I would have to make my farewells so quickly. Almost before I realise it, I am bidding a swift goodbye to Ramah and the other women. Susannah gives me a hug, whispering as she does, "Remember, Mari, do what God tells you, not men. And count me as your friend. If you're in trouble, get word to me and I'll come to you. 'Bye, love. Peace be with you."

Clopas gives me a long hard stare.

"Farewell, Mariam. I hope next time we meet will be happier than this. Be guided by Eli and Zechariah: they are men of God. If you obey them, all will come right, you'll see."

And he gives me an awkward squeeze of the wrist. Then they are gone and I am clambering up a flight of stone steps, trying to keep up with Uncle Eli, who is a dark silhouette flapping in the breeze ahead of me. I am now very nervous and afraid; my biggest fear at the moment is that if I falter, I will be lost in this sea of alien humanity.

We reach a vast open courtyard, which manages to absorb a seething crowd yet still seems spacious. Flocks of pigeons wheel around the court, then descend, strutting around the paved surface while sparrows are darting everywhere, pecking at debris dropped by the many pilgrims. But my eyes are drawn inexorably to the Temple itself; I have never seen such a magnificent or gigantic building. I want to ply my uncle with all sorts of questions, but I daren't. He is rushing on ahead of me, impatient and curt. He clearly knows exactly where he is going and I trail after him, a few paces behind, trying to keep up.

We reach the outer columns of the building itself, and Eli turns, telling me to wait – I can go no further without defiling the Temple precincts in my present state. I am worried that he is going to disappear and I shall be entirely alone, engulfed in this multitude. Then, just as he is slipping from my sight, another man dressed in rabbinical white robes steps from the shadows and greets him. I know instinctively that this is Zechariah, although it is many years since I met him at the wedding celebrations of one of Eli's daughters. I expected, I don't know why, an old man, bearded and gnarled, but he is in the prime of life – in his early fifties I would guess –

and is vigorous in his body movements. He is gesticulating with his hands as he nears us, and I assume they are in conversation.

Eli points to me.

"Zechariah, this is my niece, Mariam. She is ready to accompany you home and give your wife a hand in preparation for your child. Keep her until after the birth and as long as she is useful. Send me word when she is to be fetched and I will send Clopas or one of my sons-in-law to bring her home."

Then Eli turns to me.

"Mariam, we have a problem. For some reason your uncle is unable to explain, he seems incapable of speech. I had no idea he was afflicted in this way, nor whether this is a temporary or permanent disability."

Zechariah smiles at me, holds out a hand and places it in blessing on my head. He seems to be trying to welcome me. I don't know if I should say anything or not. Before I can make up my mind to greet him, however, my Uncle Eli continues talking to Zechariah as if I wasn't here; perhaps he intends me to hear all he says.

"Zechariah, I sent you word that you could assist me in a matter of grave embarrassment by housing Mariam for a month or two. I did not trust the confidentiality of the messenger, so I did not disclose the full import of my request to you. I know that Elizabeth is very close in spirit to this girl's mother, Anna, and would wish to help her in her hour of distress. Mariam is causing us great offence and bringing disgrace on the whole family in Nazareth. May I plead with you to help us find a way through all this mess, as I have requested in this letter."

Zechariah takes the scroll from him and reads silently, intently, while I wish the earth could swallow me up. I can guess what the letter says. How will Zechariah's attitude change? Will he refuse to take me into his household? The letter is long. Zechariah peruses it for an age and finally rolls it up and tucks it in his robes. He is expressionless; he gives no clue to what he thinks. Eli hesitates a moment, clearly wondering whether to seek for response, agreement, but is nonplussed by the other's determined silence. Quick courtesies are exchanged. Zechariah beckons me to his side to indicate I am to stay with him and Eli is gone, without a word to me.

It is strange, walking with a dumb man. I don't know whether to be silent too, or to chatter away to make up for him. Normally I would only talk in response to conversation initiated by the older man. I don't know, although I can guess, what the letter says. Is he expecting me to defend myself, explain and justify?

We walk out of the city in silence, as I gaze in stupefaction at the city's buildings. At this stage there is much to occupy the mind and my eyes dart in all directions, devouring all they see. We cross right through the city, leaving it at a gate to the north-west, and find a twisting road descending along the tortuous hillsides to a plain, with hazy brown and blue hills on the skyline, vibrating in the late afternoon heat haze. When we are on the open road, Zechariah places his right hand on my shoulder and leaves it there. It is a bond between us replacing speech and at first I am happy that he seeks this physical contact. After a couple of miles of walking though, with my load slung across my right shoulder, I am beginning to feel excessively sore from the constant friction on my bruises, which, though they are healing rapidly now, still ache under pressure.

I break my silence.

"Sir, I am tired and aching. Can I put down my load and rest awhile?"

In response, Zechariah merely points into the distance and keeps walking. I am discouraged at first and am having to make a real effort with every step. But now I know what his gesture meant. Ahead of us, beside the roadway, is a well, a few travellers lounging round its rim. I drop my load to the ground and take my turn in the queue to draw water to give him a drink; then I sit and drink myself, having refilled my waterskin. I begin to try to talk to him.

"How is my Aunt Elizabeth?"

He nods and smiles. Apparently all is well.

"I thank you for receiving me. I will help you in any way I can while I am here."

Again he nods and accepts my statement. I try again.

"I do not know for certain what my Uncle Eli has said to you about my circumstance, or what request he has made of you. I would wish to tell you of my experience before you act on his letter."

Zechariah raises both hands and gestures insistently in a way that I take as a rebuke. He does not want me to say anything. He puts his finger to his lips and then to mine, as though he is seeking them closed. Is he refusing my request, or merely telling me to hold my peace at this moment? Whatever his meaning, it has restored my anxiety. I am plunged once more into uncertainty when I thought he was beginning to show friendliness. Now the barrier has been re-erected, and his face is discouraging any further discourse between us.

I make no further attempt at conversation as we trudge across the plain and the road begins slowly to climb again towards the hills, which are now clearer in outline. But I am not paying much attention to the scenery. I am preoccupied with my inner turmoil, sick with fear at my possible reception. Will I be in disgrace here too? Will they let me try to explain, or will I have no say? Shall I be forced to undergo the abortion straight away without my consent? How will my aunt react to Eli's letter, or will Zechariah keep it to himself, conferring only with other rabbis and elders?

As the sun begins to sink beyond the hills to the west, the detail that was becoming apparent is lost once more within the bland opaque shadow. I cannot see my destination.

CHAPTER 30

MAGNIFICAT

HEN I REACHED EIN–KAREM LAST night I was dog-tired. Each step had become a major effort. I ceased to interest myself in either my journey or my destination. I suppose I noticed that Zechariah's home, which opened straight onto the street rather than into a yard, was larger than my own, although nothing like the size of Eli's total property. It was dusk when we arrived. I had been on the road for over twelve hours and travelled nearly twenty-five miles. I was, as I said, on the verge of collapse. My aunt met me at the door, took one look at me and ushered me under her wing, scolding Zechariah for driving me so hard. The poor man could not answer back and it was hardly his fault that we had journeyed from the other side of the Jordan within the day. Short of staying in Jerusalem – and where would we have found lodgings? – there seemed to me no alternative. It was nearly dark anyway by our arrival.

Aunt Elizabeth made no attempt to greet me with any flourish; she saw that I was fed with the minimum necessary to stave off hunger pangs and carried my scanty belongings into a small side room where a couple of goats were tethered. We laid out my bedroll and I lay down as I was, unwashed, and within minutes, was fast asleep.

I wake just before dawn and hear movement in the room next to mine. I detect muttered voices, but cannot decipher specific words. Then, just when my anxieties are surfacing to prevent further sleep, I doze away and next time I open my eyes the sun is streaming through a little side window. I lie for a while in silence, listening to the movement around the house, then prop myself on one elbow and yawn. As soon as I do that, I feel the surge of nausea welling under my breasts and stagger out of bed before realising that I can probably recover by taking a few deep breaths.

I pull myself together and venture into the other room, where I know I will find my aunt. I am not sure whether Zechariah will be there; I have no idea what he does, whether he goes each day to the Temple or has business in the village here.

"Mari, come here into the light, my girl. Let me have a look at you. Goodness me, you've grown since I last saw you. That must have been all of four years ago now."

She is alone in the room and, despite her copious dark blue outer garment, I notice first her bulging stomach, which she does not seek to hide, as she stands there. Indeed, she is proud of it. I force my gaze upwards to look into her face, and see her weather-beaten skin creased in smiles, as she stares with open curiosity at my still slim form.

As I step closer, she strides the gap between us and falls on my neck, embracing me so tightly that I find I am leaning forwards, almost unbalanced, over her protruding baby, so that I am forced to trust myself completely to her hug.

"Welcome to my house, cousin. I pray that you will be happy with us, staying as long as you wish. I shall find your company very comforting as I near my time." She pats her bulge and grins conspiratorially at me. Does she not know why I am here? Is this cheerfulness in spite of, or because of her knowledge?

"Come and sit down and have something to eat. We can talk then for as long as you wish without interruption. My husband has gone back into Jerusalem to assist with preparations for the Passover celebration." That statement answers one of the questions forming in my mind.

I must know if she is fully in the picture about my presence here. I cannot keep up my end of the conversation all day without that knowledge. Every moment I put it off will make it harder to ask the vital question.

"Aunt Elizabeth, can I ask you something?"

"Of course, Mari, anything you wish."

"Have you read the letter Uncle Eli gave your husband?"

Elizabeth stops in mid-movement and replaces her instant smile by an intense look at my face, holding my gaze without flinching.

"Yes, I have, love. Do you know what it says?"

"No, not exactly."

Elizabeth goes to the corner of the room, where a heavy wooden chest lies on the floor, lifts the lid and pulls out the scroll I recognise. She hands it to me.

I recoil, surprised by her action, incredulous that she is inviting me to read it.

"You can read, can't you, Mari? I'm sure they told me when I was last in Nazareth that you were a very bright girl and you'd been kept at school longer than usual."

"Yes. I was just surprised you want me to read it. Uncle Eli wouldn't show me anything, although he told me what he expected before I left my home."

"It is just as well you see it, girl. I don't want any secrets from you: we both need to know where we stand. You will not make any better decision for being ignorant."

"You've read it, and are still being friendly towards me? Is it really not so bad, or are you on my side?"

"Read it yourself first, Mari. There's plenty of time for us to talk about it, get to know one another better. Don't race to any judgements, and I'll not do the same! We've both got lots to talk about, but I understand you need to face this issue first. Look, I'll not crowd you. Take the scroll into your room, and read it alone; take your time. Then we'll talk."

I take my piece of bread and cup of goat's milk and sit down on my mattress. In trepidation I unroll the parchment, and slowly read, while the blood races madly around my arteries:

Zechariah, greetings!

This is a painful letter to write and I beg your mercy and that of your gracious wife, Elizabeth. May the Lord protect her at her time of joy!

To you, the impending birth of a child brings the fulfilment of long-awaited prayers. In contrast, similar news brings nothing but shame and disgrace on our household. Your cousin, Mariam, after so much charity has been lavished on her, has repaid us by confessing that she is pregnant, and that not even by her betrothed, Joseph of Bethlehem. When I sought to protect her before the elders of the synagogue, she compounded her sin with that of blasphemy by claiming wildly that she had been visited by a messenger from God, who made her pregnant and told her that she would bear the Messiah, if you please! It was all that I could do to prevent her condemnation and stoning on the spot. I managed to get her remission to a whipping, on condition that she was excluded from Nazareth until her child had been aborted.

I am placing our fate, and hers, in your hands. For the love of your wife's dear sister's child, Anna, I implore your assistance. Should the girl return from you still pregnant, she will be put to death. She knows this, yet still seems obstinate. You are wise in the ways of the world, and I know your wife, because of her long-standing fertility problems, has the contacts who can arrange the necessary termination without endangering the girl's life.

After the girl has recovered from what I am asking of you, please retain her services to assist your wife during the final days of her labour. I will send my son or one of my sons-in-law to bring the girl home in due course, when you are ready. I will of course repay all your expenses incurred by the girl's abortion and upkeep.

Eli of Nazareth.

I lay the letter down and think. There are no surprises at all. Zechariah and Elizabeth know the worst; I am relieved that I have not got to make further revelations to them. Despite this, they are treating me with courtesy and care. Seeing in the written word confirmation of the consequences of holding out against Uncle Eli's will brings a chill and dread to my heart, but somehow I cannot sense any judgement here. If they are lenient with me, though, and I manage to persuade them not to kill the child within me, I put off the time of sorrow till my return, when my ordeal will be magnified beyond measure.

I finish my frugal breakfast in solitude, then rejoin Elizabeth, who is waiting for me.

"Come and sit beside me, Mari, and tell me in your own words what has happened to you. Is it true that you are pregnant?"

"Yes, Aunt. I have been carrying the child about three months."

"You see what your uncle says he wishes us to arrange for you, and the consequences of disobedience. Is it your will, too, that we act for you in this way?"

"No."

"Then tell me why, Mari. Help me to understand."

This is the third time within the last two weeks that I have told my story to a sympathetic audience: my sisters, Susannah, and now Elizabeth. Each time I have grown in confidence; I have had more time and opportunity to elaborate. Elizabeth has the time and inclination to listen to everything. When I hesitate, or gloss over some little detail, she picks me up, until she knows it all. She wants to know the exact words of the messenger, his appearance, the texts he quoted. She will not let me slide over my ordeal – she makes me bare my soul, my prayers; she explores with me my certainty that God was and is sustaining, protecting and ordering my life.

And at the end, and it must be nearly two hours since I first sat with her, she looks at me and her eyes seek mine. We throb with understanding, the two of us. Words seem almost superfluous. She is just about to speak, when she starts suddenly and clutches her stomach. I look at her, raising my eyebrows in alarm. She shakes her head slowly.

She is still smiling. She stretches out her hand, places it comfortingly on my knee, then holds it on my head as if to bless me.

"Mari, I believe you. I know all that you have said is true."

My heart skips a beat at her words. After all the suspicion, worry, doubt and tension, it seems too good to be true. Even my whispered conversations with Susannah and the children were secret hidden episodes that could not surface, that could not be shared.

"You need no further argument? You accept all I say, without further challenge? You don't think Uncle Eli's right?"

"Mari, I tell you again. I know what you say is true. I too have met the stranger you describe. My child, too, Mari, is an answer to prayer, and God has prepared him to be prophet to the Messiah. All this I know and Zechariah also. The message was too great for him to bear; he's lost the power of speech ever since he knew. All that you said has fallen into place. God has chosen you, sweet child, above all others to bear the king of kings. We are privileged beyond measure, blessed beyond our capacity to understand it. My pregnancy has been a joy throughout. Many have shared with me, even Zechariah, despite his handicap, our great contentment. But your arrival here and the story that you bring confirms and transforms everything. I marvel and thrill to all you tell. I want to smother you with kisses. I cannot express my elation and excitement. And Mari, at this very moment, when just now we looked at one another, I felt the baby stir within me. It was his first movement, Mari. He is alive! It is the first time in all my life that I have felt such a sensation! Mari, Mari, what has God done for us? How can we express our joy? Oh, Mari, words absolutely fail me!"

And she literally dances round me, her eyes so bright that for a moment I think she has gone mad. I am stunned. Her reaction is totally unexpected. I had not conceived that this is what she'd do. I feel the tears welling in my eyes, the force of shock, relief. Deep, deep emotion that I have stifled for the last few months comes brimming to the surface and boils over. I am in floods of tears, being rocked in Elizabeth's arms. She is singing to me. I cannot hear the words for I am not capable now of listening. I am being drowned in the emotional tidal wave let loose in my soul. Together we are praising God. Words come choking from our lips. We both sing and clap our hands and throw time to the winds. It's a wonder all the neighbours have not come storming round out of curiosity to see what's going on.

When we calm down a little, thoughts come flooding to my mind: new insights which I want to share with her.

"It's unbelievable; it's a miracle that the Lord God has chosen me, me, just a simple peasant girl. I have absolutely nothing to offer him. Just think of it, Auntie, in days to come everyone will look back and call me special because of what God's doing in me. I know now that God loves and honours those who trust him, and he ignores the proud and famous and men of power, even mighty kings. He loves the humble, those of us who have no airs or graces and come before him just as we are. He accepts us and ignores those who think they've earned his blessings! Oh, Auntie, we are seeing God fulfil the promises made to our nation since time began. The prophecies are all coming true!"

My aunt is standing transfixed at my outburst.

"Child, you are wise beyond your years. God is wreaking a miracle in me – he is permitting an old body to forget its age, revitalise its youth in new creation. And you, he has taken your young untrammelled mind and simplicity of faith and filled you with his ageless wisdom. God is indeed speaking to you, Mari, and through you."

We both sit upon the mattress, our emotions ebbing, drained and exhausted in our happiness.

"Let us rest a while, Mari: we cannot take any more at the moment. There are days enough spreading ahead of us to share and explore all things together."

I lie on my bed. I cannot sleep – my brain is far too active, forming and reforming the words and experiences we have just been sharing. It is a long time since I made a little rhyme up for the children. But I find words of poetry rolling round my head, and I seize each phrase and savour it until I know I shall remember and one day write this down for my children to recite. I resolve to remember things to tell this child growing in my womb. Will I be honest enough to tell him everything, my good and bad times? How will it affect him? Will knowledge of my suffering as well as joy bring him unnecessary guilt, or will it let him know how special he is, confirming his destiny?

For days we live off the energy generated by this hour of shared revelation. We consolidate the details; remember further incidents, whose relevance we grasp anew; acquire new insights, which we rush to share, one with the other, wherever we are, whatever we are doing, as if there is no time to lose. Zechariah returns sometimes from the city, on the periphery of our joy, as if he were deaf as well as dumb. Elizabeth has told him of our destinies, I know she has. And he has not shown that he disbelieves; he feels his loss of speech is already punishment enough. It has been a strange Passover. We shared the meal, of course we did. Yet this festival, this highlight of the year, was so overshadowed by our other joy that it too became a diversion from the path we were treading. With hindsight, perhaps we should have seen the festival's relevance to our situation, and gained new insight to glory through it, rather than dim its lustre. Be patient with us, though. You don't see the pattern when you're living in the middle of it.

At other times we just relax and catch up on family gossip. My aunt is eager to hear news of my sisters and of Ben. She loves my mother, and as we talk, she embroiders an intricate pattern on a garment that I am to take back as her gift to her favourite niece. She has a little weep when I describe in detail how my father was killed and delivered to our home, and reminisces with affection about the times when my grandmother sought refuge in Ein–Karem and about the childhood of my mother. You see, when my mother was born, my aunt had already been married five years and still no baby had been granted, so that the newborn girl was like a substitute for her own child. As Hannah had two other girls to bring up, Elizabeth found herself more and more helping with the care of the children, just as I did myself in Nazareth.

She tells me about her family here, whom I have not seen for many years. The old man, Eleazar, her father, who had long been a widower, died last year. She shows me keepsakes of him with affection, though at other times, from the things she says, I suspect he was not easy to live with in his later years. She tells me many things I never knew about my other grandmother, her own sister Hannah, who died only a year after my mother left home as Joachim's young bride. My mother rarely says much about her; I suspect the shock of losing her so soon after she had moved away caused great distress, which she tried to blot from her mind. Apparently she died very suddenly from a fever. One day she was drawing water from the spring, baking and caring for her other daughters' children. The next, she was tossing on her bed with great sickness and did not survive to nightfall. The first hint of alarm that reached my mother was days after her mother's burial. My grandfather on that side of the family also died many years before, whilst my mother was still a girl of tender years.

Elizabeth is more expansive about Ruth and Mariam, Hannah's other daughters. Ruth married a Galilean who'd come to the community at Bethphage on the outskirts of Jerusalem – a skilled craftsman who has done well, and has a string of daughters aged between thirteen and seventeen and boys of ten and twelve. The eldest girls themselves are married and living away from the family home.

"It would be a good opportunity for you to see them, Mari, but I don't think at the moment either of us can contemplate the return journey, even if Zechariah accompanies us on one of the days he is due at the Temple.

"I can't, anyway," she says, patting her round stomach.

Elizabeth's other niece, Mariam, was divorced by her husband several years before and left to bring up her two daughters, now about my age, whilst the boy stayed with his father and new wife; they had a tiny house on the edge of the village of Emmaus, a further seven or eight miles to the west. I would have liked to have met these girls, but I understood from my aunt that they had a hard life which left them little time for visiting and it seemed unlikely that we would meet, not at least before the birth of Elizabeth's child and the ensuing celebrations.

Each day, when I am recovered from my morning sickness, I help my aunt around the home. The village is built around a spring, which provides our water, so I go there morning and evening to draw, sometimes taking an assortment of garments with me to wash in the bubbling stream and dry on the boulders that line the flattish bank. I get to know the other women and girls, some trailing younger children, several with babies suckling at the breast. At first they are consumed with curiosity, but it is aimed at Elizabeth's astounding news, and rumours of the reason for Zechariah's dumbness; they do not guess my plight, for my presence to assist Elizabeth seems quite natural to them. A question or two about my living in the north when Ruth's and Mariam's daughters are nearer at hand, then disinterest on my account. I have settled into a rhythm, useful around the house, especially as Elizabeth rests during her final month. There is plenty of time for us to talk and each day we explore God's work in us. I find Zechariah's scrolls of scripture, in which we search for further meaning in the prophets; we pray together; we sing psalms and holy songs. Elizabeth lets me borrow parchment and writing implements so that I can transcribe the poems in my head, and she proudly shows them to her husband, who nods good-naturedly, or else is humouring me, I know not which!

One morning, just as I have returned from the spring, water jar on my shoulder, singing softly under my breath, Elizabeth tells me to put the jar down and sit with her to discuss something. I expect our usual casual chat, relaxed and cheerful, but she looks serious and strained today.

"Mariam, we can't avoid it. It's time the two of us had a further serious talk. You've been here over three weeks now and since the first day we've not said one word about your uncle's letter."

"Do we have to, Aunt? Is there anything to say? Surely all that has happened between us shows how wrong Uncle Eli is?"

"But, child, what about his threat? If you go home with the child still inside you, he says he'll have you stoned. He says so in plain and brutal words. Do you think it is possible he is bluffing, just to scare you into obeying him, or is he even testing you to see how sincere you are in your belief?"

"I'm sure he means it. He is not the sort of man not to carry out what he threatens; he does his duty to the letter of the law, irrespective of inconvenience to himself. I believe he means it. But then, God has protected me so far. Won't he look after me this final time?"

"I knew you'd say that, Mari. Your faith is admirably strong and there is no way I wish to put doubts into your mind. But we have to face the facts. It is easy when you and I are alone here, without pressure; but when you return to Nazareth and face your uncle's anger, your mother's sorrow and shame, your sisters' crying, the rabbis' condemnation, what then? Will you still be so strong?"

The creeping hand of dread catches round my heart, the slight hesitation, the re-entry of uncertainty.

"I'd like to think I'll not change my decision; to go all this way, then falter at the last hurdle would be an awful shame and disappointment."

"I know, child, I know. But I must put to you these thoughts. You can't go back to your threatened fate in Nazareth without thinking them through to the ultimate conclusion."

I am silent, absorbed.

"Let me try again. Zechariah brought me a note home last night from a midwife in the city who is associated with one of the Canaanite temples where they practise all sorts of magic. Apparently they often cleanse the temple acolytes and priestesses from unwanted pregnancies and would be prepared to do the same for you, in accordance with your uncle's wishes, for a suitable offering of cash and sacrifices. I do not approve, of course, of their practices or heathen thinking, but I know no believing Jewish midwife who would help you in this way."

"Auntie, you're not in earnest with me, are you? I can't believe you would suggest such a dreadful thing."

"Child, don't be so vehement with me. You think life is so simple, black and white; you've never had to compromise. I am making the offer because I love you, no more. You are the one who says your uncle is not bluffing."

"I'm sorry, I did not mean to be angry with you. I was just surprised that you would even let me contemplate such action, let alone suggest it yourself."

"Well, I have my answer. I admire you, Mariam. I wonder at your faith, which far surpasses mine, despite all God has done for me. Were I in your place, would that I could make so momentous a decision with so much trust."

"You would, I'm sure you would."

Elizabeth reaches round me and kisses me.

"You sweet child, you believe the best of everyone, don't you. I pray your faith in human nature is not disillusioned."

I am about to correct her, when I think better of myself. It will sound priggish and act as further rebuke and I have hurt her enough already. I truly did not mean to, but her suggestion caught me off guard.

"I knew a girl once who said she was a dancing girl at one of those heathen temples. I didn't really think there were any in Israel itself."

"I'm afraid so, Mari. Jerusalem is full of them and so are the surrounding towns. There are so many races here and each has its own religion. We are lucky that our king has seen fit to rebuild our own Temple, so that it dominates the others."

"My uncle says that King Herod is a wicked man who desecrates the Jews and all that they believe in."

"Well, Herod has a funny way of showing it, if your uncle is right. He has fought for us Jews here, and obtained the dominant role for us with the Romans, despite the fact that he is an Idumean. How can that be evil?"

I find this conversation interesting. Uncle Eli had led me to think that pious Jews thought the same way as he did. I have learned during the weeks that I have been here in Ein–Karem that even an orthodox Jew like Zechariah, as far as I can communicate with him, has many different views. I have learned too that Zechariah and Elizabeth consider the Galilean ways of village justice to be crude and barbaric, although they experience the results of the political turmoil in the capital city. But, as they say, only the ambitious and the powerful suffer, and they choose to get involved. For the ordinary citizen, life is much more liberal; at least alleged crimes are judged impartially and sins are dealt with as private matters in which the state has little interest. There is little behaviour that cannot be settled by divorce or financial compensation.

I am still curious about Rachel and try to find out more about her life at one of the temples, but Elizabeth seems reluctant to say too much. Perhaps she doesn't know. What she hints at, however, confirms the story Rachel told me. I tell her of the girl's sin and condemnation and my horror at the manner of her death.

"Mariam," says Elizabeth, placing her hand on my knee, "Mariam, my child, this is the death they are threatening to impose on you if you return home in this condition. Do you really understand the danger you are in? Has it registered with you?"

"Yes, Aunt."

I think it has. I think I can truthfully say that. I have thought about it much, but recently, here, so far from home, it has seemed curiously disconnected from me.

"I'm not sure it has. You know, we could help you escape here in Jerusalem if necessary until your child is born and have it adopted so that no-one in Nazareth would know that it still lived. Then your child could still be the Messiah. He could be brought up by someone else, just as Moses was."

I haven't thought of that. And what comes over me is a surge of disappointment, of anticlimax. Does God just want me to bring his Messiah into the world and then abandon him to another and never be part of his grand plan? Am I being selfish to want to be his mother and stay in the centre of this huge miraculous event?

Chapter 31
The Precursor

$\mathcal{E}$LIZABETH IS IN THE BACK room being examined by the midwife. I have done everything I can for her, have fed her, bathed her, run for assistance when the waters broke. Zechariah is in the synagogue, praying for his wife; he is worried, I know, for her safety and also prays for a healthy son. For over a week now I have watched over my aunt as she has neared her time, and now it is happening.

I have been sent from the room during the examination. I wait, alone, listening to the murmured conversation, punctuated by low groans and sudden silences. I kneel upon the floor and pull my shift up to my neck to stare at my own belly. I put my right hand on my tummy and grope gently down to my abdomen. I know. I am beginning to show now. I feel my rounded flesh, which I can still hide under my loose tunic, but soon I shall have to leave off my girdle. I am full all the time, as though I had just eaten, yet I constantly experience hunger pangs, and am always coaxing Elizabeth for another titbit. It is over four months now, not far off five. My sickness is gone, and I feel fit, even if a little heavy.

We have talked more about my return to Nazareth in these past few weeks. After what she said earlier about having the child spirited away and adopted, she has offered me a home here; she has invited me to stay on until my time is due, has said she'll take my son and bring him up as her own, if I must return to my betrothed. In this way she thinks we'll all be saved. Perhaps she is right: this is God's solution to the impasse. But I am reluctant to commit myself to her suggestions; I feel I must wait and see what comes, still trusting God to show me the way. What she proposes somehow does not feel right; it doesn't seem God's way to me. Am I being too proud?

One evening, Zechariah, through Elizabeth's interpretation, asked me if I wanted to submit myself to the water ordeal in the Temple. Apparently there is a ritual in which a woman accused of adultery drinks a potion of infected water. If she survives she is considered innocent. But if the infection takes hold, it may cause inflammation of the intestines or acute cystitis and eventual impotence or even death. If I undertook this without infection, I would be given a certificate of innocence by the Temple authorities to show to the elders of the Nazareth synagogue. Elizabeth was sure I would pass the test with God's full protection. But before I could make my mind up, Elizabeth started her labour and I cannot now be spared from the house.

My arm is still resting on my naked stomach, as I let my mind run on, when suddenly I am returned to reality by a cry of anguish from the neighbouring room.

"Mariam, come in here!"

The midwife's call brings me running into the room.

"Don't be so alarmed, child! It's perfectly natural. Run and tell Zechariah that the birth has begun. Then come back, as fast as you can, and give me a hand."

I am gone and find Zechariah standing, face to a pillar, in the sanctum of the synagogue. I cannot get to him, so I go as near as I can and whisper through the trellis of the Women's Court, "Zechariah, come quickly. The baby's being born."

He does not hear me. I am embarrassed to raise my voice louder as there are others in prayer, and for a girl to shout in the synagogue would be considered sacrilege. I raise my voice slightly, and another man turns from his prayers to look at me, with frowning countenance.

"Sir, I beg you, ask Zechariah to listen to me. I have an urgent message for him."

To my relief the man understands and taps Zechariah lightly on the shoulder, pointing to me. He comes over, looking alarmed.

"Come quickly, Zechariah, Elizabeth's in labour."

The next twelve hours pass amid much worry and anguish. I am with my aunt all the time, trying to soothe and help, but she frightens me with her pain and wild shouts. The midwife leaves from time to time, but checks each hour or so before leaving me in charge once more. Zechariah stares silently from the doorway, minutes at a time, in mental anguish, with contorted face. I am so tired that it is as much as I can do to keep my eyes open. I feel the lids closing, then another shriek of pain makes me alert once more as she endures another contraction while I grip her wrist and mop her brow.

On one of her checks the midwife suddenly becomes businesslike. "The baby comes," she cries to Elizabeth. "Tell her husband it will not be long. And fetch some water and put it beside me."

"Watch me," she says, "it will be a good education for you." Does she know or guess about my pregnancy? Surely not!

Then I am totally absorbed by the activity – a participant, fascinated and enthralled, straining and grunting subconsciously with my aunt; so much so, that in one of the brief pauses between the next onslaught of pushing, I notice sweat is dripping from my brow and my soaked shift is stuck to my body. I have been told all about childbirth, of course, but this is the first time I have been present and fully aware of the total experience. When Ben was born, I was but seven years old, and I suspect I was kept away from the room during the critical moments of labour and the birth itself. I am glad I am involved. I know the worst; it may spare me some of the fear and anxiety when my time comes. At the same time, my eyes are opened to the pain and blood and general mess; I had not envisaged it thus.

I am by Elizabeth's head when the midwife finally frees the blood-streaked baby from the mother and see her lift it, the purple umbilical cord twisted and coiled. I cannot see the most important fact and await the midwife's next words with trepidation. Will they kill our dreams? Defy our confidence and throw all our assumptions back in our faces?

"You have a son, my dear," says the beaming woman, holding the crying infant aloft, "and he seems perfect in all respects."

I breathe a sigh of relief and look at Elizabeth, who smiles weakly at me, an exhausted, pained but knowing smile which I am meant to share with her. I hurry to fetch Zechariah while the midwife washes the boy and cuts the cord. The man's look of thankfulness when I impart the news to him is enormous. In one surprising gesture, he nearly lifts me from the ground as he flings his arms around me and hugs me so vehemently that I feel crushed. Then I'm trailing in his wake as he dashes to his wife's side. I have never seen him move so fast.

CHAPTER 32

DECISION TIME

HE LITTLE HOUSE IS CHOKED with people and the noise is deafening and confusing. As well as all our neighbours, my Aunts Ruth and Mariam, with all their children are here; and a couple of grandchildren, babes in arms. Their cries are joining those of the new baby, who is currently bawling his head off, the poor mite just having been circumcised, as it is the eighth day since his birth. Clopas is representing the family in Nazareth, and whilst the gifts are being presented to Zechariah and Elizabeth, I am spared further confrontation with him. Several people have brought animals to contribute to the feast, which we are now trying to prepare in the inadequate space available. One of the men will kill the fowls and beasts tomorrow, leaving the carcases for roasting and presentation by those of us who will remain at home, while Zechariah, Elizabeth and the men go to the Temple to consecrate the baby and name him.

I am relieved to have plenty to do, and be surrounded by the guests and other visitors. Yesterday, when Clopas arrived, after courtesies had been exchanged with Zechariah and he had viewed his son, he sought me out and saw at once my condition. I have always, I thought, got on quite well with Clopas, but I was dismayed at his treatment of me. He dealt with me like a delinquent child, caught redhanded in some nefarious act. Any attempt to explain or reason with him was dismissed with scorn; he had expected me to obey Eli and found the continuing existence of my baby offensive and insulting. He expressed disappointment that Zechariah and Elizabeth had not enforced Eli's wishes, but said he would refrain from criticism for a day or two, to avoid spoiling their celebration. Then we had been interrupted, there had been no further privacy afforded for any further conversation of this nature, and for decency's sake Clopas had desisted from making public comment.

The next morning Zechariah, Elizabeth, Clopas, Ruth's husband, sons and a number of male neighbours set off early for Jerusalem, leaving Ruth to organise the celebratory meal in preparation for their return in the evening. Two of her daughters have their own young children to look after, but there are five of us – Ruth's daughters Rhoda and Leila; Mariam's Rebecca and Zilpah; and myself – who are squatting outside the house, plucking the chickens ready for the pot. As we work, we chatter, of course, like any group of girls. Rhoda boasts about her recent betrothal to the favoured son of a prosperous merchant in Bethphage, and Leila talks about her father's current efforts to select a husband for her too. Rebecca and Zilpah are envious. They, as daughters of a divorcee, will find it much harder to get suitable husbands and will have to settle for less favourable matches. As yet, nothing is in prospect, even though they are the same age as their cousins. I am naturally asked all sorts of questions about Joseph, when I am being married, where we will live and so on.

In the middle of this light-hearted banter and further speculation about our future lives, Rhoda suddenly turns to me, winks mischievously, and says, probably in all innocence, to the others, "Look at Mari squatting there telling us all about her Joseph, and dreaming about her future family. If you ask me, I don't think she's waited for the wedding. I think she's got a secret hidden under her bulging tunic."

All eyes turn to look at me. Instinctively I try to pull in my shift and draw in my breath, but I can't help blushing as I do so.

"Look, she's going all pink," says Leila gleefully. "I think you've hit the nail right on the head."

"No," I try to protest, "it's just the way I'm sitting," but before I can do anything further, all four girls swoop on me, so that I drop the carcase in a flurry of feathers, and try to grab my tunic and hold it tight against me. For a few moments we are all engaged in a tussle, then I find my arms pinioned behind my back and they are lifting my shift to get a good look at me. I cannot hide anything now. It is too obvious when they see my naked flesh. The laughter and teasing subsides into scandalised gasps of self-righteous horror as they gawp at me and prod my defenceless swollen belly. I cannot deny their accusations. They assume Joseph could not wait and has had his way with me. I want to protest, defend Joseph, justify myself, but this does not seem the time or place.

I try to ask them to keep my secret, but already Leila has rushed off to her older sisters, who are suckling their babies inside the house, and she is blurting out the scandal to them. In no time at all, I am surrounded by a gaggle of inquisitive and inquisitorial women: my aunts and cousins, criticising, judging, comparing my situation unfavourably with their own circumstances, commiserating with my distant mother. I try one tentative defence to claim a special birth – a miracle linked to that of my aunt, now on her way to the Temple. It is a disaster. The mood turns from curiosity and scandalised gossip to one of disgust and ostracism.

I am found jobs to do that are the dirtiest, and most menial. I am isolated from the others by being sent to fetch water and to do the washing. I am not good enough now to join in the general merriment. I am unclean.

The day drags on and I feel sick at heart. I had so looked forward to meeting and talking to my cousins, and it's all in ruins. It seems so difficult to explain and I feel depressed. If I find this situation oppressive and intolerable, how will I cope with Uncle Eli and the elders back in Nazareth? How will I deal with scorn and ridicule? My resolve is being sorely tested; I long for Elizabeth to return; I need her help to restore my hope and purpose. Perhaps it is the suddenness of it all – one moment we are all laughing together, the next, for no apparent reason, I am uncovered and exposed; I have not prepared for this.

When I return from one of my errands – I have been dawdling to avoid the pressure of enforced solitude inside the house – I see that the Jerusalem party has reappeared and animated conversation is taking place, with Zechariah in the centre of the huddle. There is an unnatural excitement in the air, an edgy hysteria that is reflected in the shrill voices, the overloud asides, and I sidle up to those on the periphery of the conversation to find out what is going on.

"Ah, Mari, there you are!" My Aunt Elizabeth pounces on me, hurrying through from the room where the food is being prepared and laid out. "A most wonderful thing has happened! Your uncle's voice has returned. It's a miracle! It happened during the naming. I had just told the priest that the boy was to be named 'John', as we had been instructed. Everyone queried this – we've never had a 'John' in the family – and they wouldn't take my word for it. They turned to Zechariah to seek his confirmation and he wrote for them, 'His name is John.' Then to my amazement, he suddenly started saying the name out loud. 'John, John,' he said twice, as if he didn't believe it himself, then he began to shout and laugh, and we were all overjoyed and made such a noise that another priest had to come over and ask us to keep our voices down – we were giving offence to the worshippers. Oh, Mari, you can't believe how relieved I am. We think it is a miraculous answer to our prayers, granted to us when we carried out the instructions given by the young man who spoke of God's will for us."

I am very pleased for Elizabeth. It makes her joy complete. She is beaming at everyone, savouring her hour of triumph; undoubtedly in the past she has been sensitive to the implied criticisms and barbed remarks from these same relatives and neighbours. Now she has a child to confound them: one who is marked out by his belated birth, and the mystery imparted to it by Zechariah's vision and temporary speech impediment. I have been longing for her company in order to confide my own problems with the others, but I am loath to spoil her joy: it doesn't seem fair to burden her with my little complaints.

I return to preparation of the meal, glad that Elizabeth has sought me out, as though she is aware of my isolation. As I move around, fetching and carrying, I catch snatches of conversation and check myself when I overhear Ruth telling Clopas about my pregnancy. I can't hear every word, and I try to melt away so that they do not know that I am listening. Clopas appears to be indicating that he is well aware of what she is whispering to him, and from his gestures, telling her not to spread the gossip more widely. Then they seem to sense my presence, without looking at me, and abruptly change the subject.

When I next bring food through to the table, Clopas draws me on one side.

"Come outside a moment. I want to talk to you further and I'm sure you can be spared – there are enough other women about."

We walk in silence down the street, which at this hour of dusk is virtually deserted. All the way to the spring I keep expecting him to say something, but there is just a tense expectancy between us. I dare not start the conversation. There is no-one drawing water now: it is too late. We sit on the rock beside the trickling water.

"Well, I understand everyone knows your secret now."

"Yes, the other girls guessed."

"You did not tell them?"

"No, Clopas, I tried to hide it from them, but they forced me to reveal it."

"I thought from something said that you had volunteered the information. I'm glad to hear it's otherwise, although common knowledge of your condition makes it harder for all of us to treat you with any mercy."

Clopas thinks for a moment, then looks me full in the face.

"Why, Mari, why have you not obeyed my father's instructions? He's been fair to you in covering up your situation, he's sought time to resolve your difficulty, he's put his own position with the other elders in jeopardy, he's even talked Joseph into not revoking your betrothal."

Clopas' last words quicken my heart and I say hurriedly, "Is Joseph still really prepared to marry me?"

"He is, Mari. My father told him you'd return from Ein–Karem an obedient and chastened girl, ready to obey him. He has been promised even more generous help to set up business in return for a swift marriage and his suppression of the fact that you are no longer a virgin."

"Is he prepared only to marry me to receive Uncle Eli's extra favours?"

"You are a peculiar girl, Mari. No, I think he was only too relieved to be given an excuse not to have to repudiate you. I think he genuinely likes you. But news of your pregnancy upset him dreadfully. He could not understand it at all."

"I really am very sorry about that. I have never wanted to hurt him."

"Well, you've gone a funny way about things if that was your sincere wish. And now look at you! He can't possibly marry you now. If he took you in this condition, he'd be ridiculed. The fact that all your relatives here seem to have discovered your pregnancy means that we cannot keep it secret in the family, even if we wanted to. Anyway, you're already showing; your frame is too slight to be able to hide the child any longer."

"So what can I do?"

"You haven't answered my question yet. Why did you not obey your uncle, and allow Zechariah to arrange the termination of your pregnancy?"

"Have you asked Zechariah and Elizabeth that question?"

"No, Mariam, I have not. The responsibility is yours, not theirs. You are not a child now, you are an adult in the eyes of the law, accountable yourself."

"Yes, Clopas, I am accountable. Accountable to God. I am surer than ever before that this baby inside me is God's chosen Messiah. How can I break that trust?"

"Mariam, you are not still full of that nonsense, are you? These sorts of things do not happen to ordinary people like you and me. They are fancies come from too much reading of the scriptures; we should never have encouraged you so much. I'm afraid a ruthless stranger has taken advantage of your credulity and fed you a story just so that he could slake his lust. Although it beats me why he picked on you, or how he knew you'd fall for it!"

"Elizabeth and Zechariah believe me."

"What?!"

"I said, Elizabeth and Zechariah believe me."

"I know you did. What web of lies have you woven to trap them into supporting you?"

"I haven't told them any lies. Aunt Elizabeth asked me to tell her everything. She found my experience tallied with her own. She knew I was right."

"And Zechariah? Surely he does not believe?"

"I think so. It is difficult to tell, since he has been dumb. I have had no chance to talk to him since his voice returned. But my aunt has told me that he believes."

"I will talk to him myself. I can't believe it of him. He is such a sensible, down to earth man."

"Will I be allowed home, Clopas?"

"You know the penalty as well as I do, Mariam. Your sentence was only put aside provisionally; it was not cancelled. And you have not fulfilled that condition. How can the elders ignore your deliberate disobedience?"

"So, if I come home I will be put to death?"

"If you put it so baldly, yes."

"And there is no possibility of mercy; no consideration that God's message to me might be genuine?"

"Mari, if you insist on that defence, you will rile them further. If you confess your sin, if you humiliate yourself and beg for forgiveness, perhaps... although I do not see how they can ignore your blatant rejection of their command to you. But if you claim to be following God's will, you are accusing them by implication of standing in God's way, and you will be accused of blasphemy, if nothing worse. You could finish by being burned if you are not careful."

He lays his hand on my arm.

"I'm sorry, Mari, to be so blunt, but you must wake up to the risks you are running. Sometimes I think it is not real to you; your imagination just takes over and persuades you that you are telling one of your inimitable stories to the children."

"I have no option now. I have to go on."

"I must admit that by your past decisions, you've severely limited the options now open to you. For a start, an abortion at nearly five months is much more dangerous to you than it would have been when you first came here."

"I cannot do that. I have told Zechariah and Elizabeth that I do not want that arranged and they would not fix it now even if I changed my mind, because they are convinced the baby is God's will."

"If they will not risk it, then I will court their wrath if necessary by taking you myself to have it done."

"You?! You would take me to a heathen temple and sacrifice to a Canaanite goddess just to obey Uncle Eli's will?"

"Not just to obey my father's will, Mari. I want to save you. Whatever you may think, I care what happens to you. Your mother is my friend. You have cared for, and loved, my children. How can I be indifferent to your fate? But surely there are other ways of terminating your pregnancy than at the hands of heathen sorcerers?"

"Ask Aunt Elizabeth if you wish; I don't believe she knows of any. But you are wasting your time. I will not have this baby torn from me."

"Don't talk to me like that, Mariam. That is not going to solve our problem."

"I will stay with my aunt then. She has told me I can if I wish."

"And drive a wedge of enmity right through our family like a sword, so that Father and Zechariah are permanently at odds, and your mother is cut off from her sisters here as well as her cousin? If you do that, you'll never be permitted back to Nazareth again; you will become a stranger to your mother, brother and sisters. Is that what you want?"

"What other alternative are you giving me apart from caving in to Uncle's will?"

"Is that such a terrible thing for a young girl? Are you really so proud that you hold your views more important than those of a pious and experienced Pharisee? If you, mistakenly, believe that you would be disobeying God, then let your uncle take that responsibility from you. If you obey your duty here, there can be no divine retribution on your head."

He is beginning to wear me down. I am heavy and oppressed. My mind is struggling to meet his arguments, but instinctively I know I must hold on for all I'm worth, even if I run out of logic to counter his pressure.

"Clopas, I'm just a weak, confused girl. But this I know: God will protect me and my child if his message to me is genuine. I'll fling myself on his mercy. If I'm wrong, I'm lost anyway. What have I got to lose?"

"Mari, you've got everything to lose: your husband, your family, your reputation, and that of all of us. Don't talk like this."

I am too weary to resist much longer. His constant reference to my mother and Ben, Rebecca and Salome is tearing me apart. I cannot find words now, but tears are coming to my rescue. I cannot stop them. Great wracking sobs are convulsing my body. I do not try to control them, but just give up and let them flow. I feel suddenly his arms about my shoulders; he is trying to comfort me. When at length I am drained of my emotional charge, he says, in a totally different voice, "Mari, my child, my heart bleeds for you. I wish I could offer you some respite, some escape. I may think you mistaken. I cannot fault your courage. Come home now, Mari, you've had enough. I'll not push you further at the moment. You're too exhausted to think clearly enough to take a logical decision. Come, we'll talk further with Zechariah and your aunt."

That night, after I had endured renewed name-calling and insults from my cousins, and they had eventually given up in boredom, we lay on the roof of the little house. The others were soon asleep, but I tossed and turned, my limbs aching and sore, my heart pounding with dread and worry. I could hear the sound of voices emanating from the room below and I guessed that Clopas, Zechariah, Ruth's husband Simon, and the women were discussing me. Occasionally I could hear raised voices, the odd snatched word, but not enough to make any sense. Eventually I drifted into a restless sleep.

I am awake long before the others, my eyelids heavy, and my mind muddled, half dreaming still. I do not know what has woken me – I assume it is just that I was in a light sleep, the noise of livestock stirring perhaps. As I open my eyes, I realise that someone is kneeling beside me.

"It's alright, Mari, it's only me, Elizabeth. I could not sleep and I wondered how you were doing."

I open my eyes wide and stare at her from my prone position, but before I can say anything, she adds, "The others are still fast asleep; we'll not disturb them."

"How long have you been there kneeling by my bed?"

"A long time, Mariam, watching you toss in your sleep. You've been dreaming, child. Your features have been agitated."

"I haven't slept very well."

"No, I don't expect you have. Did you overhear us talking last night?"

"I heard something, but couldn't hear what you said."

"Clopas talked to us at length about your situation. He has to go home today and is expected to take you with him. You guessed that, didn't you?"

"I suppose I did."

"You needn't go, you know. Zechariah and I will let you make your home here."

"Did you tell Clopas that you believed me?"

"Yes, Mari, of course I did and Zechariah gave his support too."

"Did it make any difference?"

"I think we've confused Clopas, who is torn between his concern for you and loyalty to his father."

"What about the others? Do they believe?"

She looks sadly at me, trying to find some word. Her hesitation betrays her.

"No, Mari, I'm afraid they don't. They think I'm hysterical, that my head's been turned by my own late pregnancy, and they think you're bad and are just using us."

"Oh."

Elizabeth squeezes my hand and, to my distress, I find she is crying.

"Auntie, if I stay here, will your friends and neighbours accept me? Will they shun you because you've taken me in?"

"Mari, I've told you, you're welcome to stay here. What matter about the rest? God will look after us."

I make my mind up.

"Auntie, thank you for your offer, but I will not impose upon you. My place is at home. I will go with Clopas today, and place my life in God's hands."

"Mari, Mari, don't," she wails, and I look around to see if any of the others are awake, disturbed by our raised voices.

"I must," I say with faltering resolve. "What does Zechariah think?"

"He will allow you to stay."

"But he doesn't want me to."

"He is in a difficult position, Mari. He does not want to fall out with Eli and your family. Nor does he want complaints to be made to the Temple authorities that he is condoning adultery. But he has already learned the consequences of disobeying God's will and he knows that if he has to make a choice, he will support you."

"I will go."

I pack my meagre belongings like a ghost, ignoring and ignored by the others, except for little touches by Elizabeth, who is trying to hide both her distress and her relief at my decision. Zechariah has given Clopas a letter to deliver to Eli and the elders, seeking clemency on my behalf, asking them to consider the consequences of countermanding God's will, giving evidence of his own experience. I know, because Elizabeth has told me exactly what he has written. All morning I am being whispered about, but no-one says anything to my face. When the time comes for our departure, Zechariah presses me firmly to his chest and prays over me, blessing me and calling down God's protection over me. Elizabeth enfolds me in her bosom, kisses me over and over and sobs unrestrainedly. She lifts the baby, John, into my arms and lets me have a long last cuddle. The rest studiously ignore me, until I can take it no longer.

I stand on the raised floor and clap my hands. Several heads turn towards me in astonishment.

"Listen to me, everyone! I am going now so you needn't worry about being ashamed of me any more. You probably won't see me again, because I'm going home to Nazareth, where I'm under sentence of death. I want to say goodbye. I want to thank you, Uncle Zechariah and Aunt Elizabeth, for believing me and letting me stay with you. I want you all to know that baby John is very special: he will be a great prophet. And I believe the baby growing inside me is going to be the Messiah, the saviour of our country. I believe – "

"Shut up, girl," Simon yells at me. "For goodness sake, Zechariah, tell her to stop this madness. Clopas, get her out of here."

"No, Simon," says Zechariah softly, "let her speak. It is my house, and she has my permission."

There is murmuring and whispering. I can feel the antagonism. All of a sudden I cannot think of the right words.

"You will see; God will look after me," I finish lamely, and bury myself weeping in Elizabeth's skirts.

I feel my head being lifted up and Zechariah's hand resting lightly on my scalp.

"May the Lord keep you and protect you; and lift up his countenance upon you and give you peace. May he bless the fruit of your womb and preserve you to be the hope of his people Israel. Shalom.

"Clopas, I entrust this girl to your care, to see her safely back to her home in Nazareth. In so far as you are able, I charge you to protect her against false accusations and judgements, and I ask you to convey this letter to whoever would condemn her for nothing more than listening to and obeying God's voice. Will you do this for me?"

"I will, Zechariah."

"Then go in peace, both of you, and may the Lord be with you."

CHAPTER 33

THE ESCAPE OPTION

FOR THE FIRST MILE CLOPAS is in deep thought. I follow him northwards; we are making for the highway that takes the plains through central Samaria rather than the way we came in the Passover caravan. When we reach the brow of the hill, he turns back to look at the roofs of Ein–Karem. At last he speaks. "That village used to be called 'Ain–Rimmon', dedicated to the pomegranate god. Each spring, at the budding of the scarlet blossom, he would hold festival court with the queen of flowers, whilst wild drinking and dancing took place in the village. The heathen worship has been stamped out for many years now, although I can't help but feel that the atmosphere still pervades the place."

What does he mean? Why does he say that? Is he accusing me of heathen practice; or is it mute criticism of Zechariah? Surely not: he is priest in the High Temple itself. He gives me no more clue. He turns his back and we trudge onwards in the dust towards a new horizon. When we take our first stop, and sit beside the track, quenching our thirst from the waterskins, Clopas looks at me for the first time, as though shaking himself out from self-absorption.

"You're a brave child. And I know this now. You believe what you are telling us. I cannot and will not accuse you of deliberate lying and deceit."

My spirits lift. I smile at him and look to see if his countenance softens.

"I'm confused, Mariam. I can't see how your claim can be true, but your faith is impressive, and clearly you have won Elizabeth's and Zechariah's trust and support. Whatever else is said, you do not deserve to die."

I go to fling my arms around him in thankfulness but he stays me with his hand.

"Do not rejoice too soon, Mari. It will not be easy to persuade others to change their judgement. They have not seen Elizabeth, have not heard Zechariah's testimony. A letter does not bear the same stamp of authority. I shall speak for you, Mari, if I am permitted, but without the conviction I have seen in others."

He falls silent again. I am wondering if I ought to say more; is he offering me an opportunity to test my own persuasive skills? I look again. I think not – he is withdrawn, reaching deep inside himself.

"We are less than ten miles from Jerusalem, Mari. Do you want to run away, forage for yourself and your baby? Someone in the city might take you in. You could beg, you could throw yourself at the mercy of one of the heathen temples, sacrifice your own honour for the survival of your prince. I can't force you to come with me. I shall not try to chase after you if you were to go."

He has shocked me. Does he really think this is my best chance? Has he been brooding all this way, to offer me this way out?

"No, Clopas. I will see it through. I will come home."

"I thought you would."

As we walk onwards, his offer turns over in my mind. Have I been a coward, fearing to put myself totally in God's hands? Am I resigning myself to the inevitable that I know, fearing the complete dependence on the unknown? Am I preferring my own way to that which is being prepared for my son? Each step northwards confirms the impossibility of changing my mind, and I still wrestle with myself. I am too preoccupied to notice how much ground we are making, to fear the dangers of the open road, and to experience the new and open landscape. My highway lies through the inner eye.

We pitch our tent and go quietly about the practicalities, each aware of what has to be done without asking the other. Still we are preoccupied, and do not talk much. I do not sleep much either. It is not the physical condition, for late spring brings the balmy nights, when it is pleasant to be out in the open. I am not afraid of Clopas, even though we are alone together. It is an irony, I muse, that I, accused of adultery, am permitted to spend the night here with a married man without a separate tent; indeed, I feel his warmth and after we have been restless for an hour, he puts out his hand to me, and we join in mutual comfortable contact.

I sleep. And in that sleep the horrors of the dark run wild, untrammelled by any control I or he can wield. Sea monsters, the great Leviathan, surge to the surface, sucking in giant tsunamis which drag me to the ocean floor, then leave me floundering as the sea floods back in a towering tidal wave above my head. My limbs are torn asunder, I see an arm floating in the debris, a leg is washed ashore, I try to swim but I cannot respond for I am just a torso rolling and being tossed in the surf. They say you cannot dream in colour, but they are wrong. The cold green sea is red, stinging my eyes with its sticky mess, oozing, oily, so that I am a gull whose wings are broken, fouled by black tar, terrorised by bully boys throwing stones at my limping, squawking form.

I am being shaken awake, but it is pitch black; I can see nothing. I hear a weird keening noise and realise with terror that it is coming from my own throat.

"Wake up, Mari, stop that noise, please wake and don't be scared. It is only me, Clopas."

I have stopped howling and try to sit up, in confusion. Clopas' arms are around my shoulders, trying to restrain the awful shuddering that has gripped my body and which I cannot control.

"Mari, do not be so frightened. It is only your imagination. You must have been having a nightmare. It's all right now."

I cannot stop my reaction, for I have burst into tears; I cannot explain it.

"Mari, you are young still and you are scared. I am truly sorry to see you like this. My job is to protect you; do you want to change your mind about going home?"

This for some reason forces me to take a grip on myself. I cease my sobbing and rub my eyes and fill my lungs with the fresh night air.

"No, Clopas, no. We must go on. Just help me to be brave."

He eases me back to a lying position and throws his arms protectively around me. I feel quite safe now.

"Go back to sleep, love. I'll ask God to send you dreams of succour and of life. Shut your eyes and trust me. I'll watch over you until you've got some inner peace."

CHAPTER 34

CONDEMNATION

*W*E HAVE ARRIVED SAFELY AT Nazareth. I ought to be relieved in view of the stories you hear of the dangers of travelling in small groups through Samaria. But, of course, I'm not. As we walk through the narrow streets at the bottom of the village, I'm half hiding behind Clopas, for fear of being seen by the villagers. If they see me, they will want to stop me and ask about Aunt Elizabeth and my stay in the south – it is only natural after over two months' absence. And I'm sure that if they really look at me, my pregnancy will be obvious. I have taken off my girdle so that my shift hangs more loosely in the hope that it will disguise my shape, but I have to lean slightly forward when I'm standing even so, to avoid showing. A couple of men greet Clopas but ignore me, and a group of small children recognise me and wave, but they are too young to be embarrassing. My real worry though is the imminent meeting with my family again. I want the first shock and fear and disappointment over quickly: that moment will be worse than the tearful recriminations that will follow.

We enter the courtyard. Even outside I can hear the whoops and shrieks of the children playing, and as soon as the gate is opened, they come running in excitement. I am mobbed by Mo and Benji and Rebecca. Salome and the boys crowd round as well, all laughing and talking at once. In the midst of all the chatter, Jude's voice suddenly cuts piercingly through the cacophony of noise, "Mari, why are you so fat?"

There is an awkward hushed pause as they sense I am confused by the direct, almost insolent question. Salome looks at me knowingly, then glares at poor Mo and Ben, willing them not to give the answer they're not meant to be aware of. Clopas tries to make a joke of it.

"It's all that rich food they've given her in the south, and a life of luxury, being waited on by servants. Now get back to your home, boys, and let Mari go to her mother!"

He hustles me away from the children and whispers as we go, "I don't think you'll find your mother surprised at your condition; she may be a bit tearful, but I'm sure she'll support you."

He is right. I look straight at my mother's familiar face and see the pain in her eyes, masked by the smile of welcome with which she greets me. She has appraised me at a glance, and as we embrace, she holds me against her own body, feeling confirmation of her fears with her own belly where I was carried fourteen years ago. Some of the children burst in through the door behind me, but Mother sends them packing.

"Leave us alone for a while. You'll have your time with Mari soon."

Then all she says is, "Tell me."

I do, as simply as I can. She does not interrupt. I include the birth of John and Zechariah's experience. I relate Aunt Elizabeth's belief. I say that Clopas has a letter from Zechariah as my advocate, which he will give to Eli. I finish.

"Has Uncle Eli softened? Will he show me mercy? What will Joseph think?"

I had not realised how old my mother looks although she is but twice my age. Her face seems more deeply lined than I remember, her skin more coarsened, her voice more worn. She adjusts her veil and puts her hand on my shoulder, uncovering as she does the amulet she gave me hanging round my neck.

"I think Joseph loves you, Mari, and is capable of persuasion. But I fear your uncle. You will have a hard time with him. He feels genuinely outraged at your condition and even more so at your defence of it. He is acutely embarrassed at the shame to his position, and is committed to judging you impartially for fear of accusation of family bias. I'm afraid that means that in fact he will deal with you more harshly; that notions of pity and mercy will not be entertained by him to demonstrate those virtues, which admittedly, lie fairly deeply hidden within him."

"What will happen, Mother?"

Her eyes well with tears, and, after a struggle to rein in her emotion, she gives way and clutches me in seeming desperation, sobbing loudly as she hangs around my neck. This answer grips my entrails like ice and the cold sweat of fear envelops me. I start to tremble, cold in the stifling room.

"Mari, try not to let the others see that we've been crying."

"Have you told them anything?"

"No, I dread now what I'll be forced to say."

"They know that I'm pregnant and why."

"When did you tell them that?"

"In the fields before I left for Ein–Karem."

"They've not said a thing. I'd never have guessed that they had the remotest idea."

"They believe me. The only thing that they do not know is that I am still under threat of death. They saw my stripes."

"I hardly know what to say."

"Do you believe me, Mother?"

There is a telltale pause, a hesitation, before she dares reply. It betrays her; whatever she says now, I know that doubt will remain.

"Don't say what you think I want to hear. I am big enough to take the truth."

"I want to believe you, Mariam. At times, I think I can; then I am assailed by doubts. It seems so extraordinary, I cannot comprehend it."

"Do you believe I would have come back here, still with the baby inside me, if I did not trust God's promises?"

"I think you believe it, Mari. I am now sure of that. At first I thought it was an extreme example of your obstinacy, your forwardness, pushed to the limit by Eli's equal strength of character. I thought how like him you were, both digging in to repulse the other."

A little face peers inside the door.

"Can we come in yet?"

"Alright, Benjamin. You and the girls."

At this, the door is flung wide and all three charge in and swarm all over me. When they settle, Ben on my knee, the other two leaning either side of me, our mother says to them, "I gather Mari told you her news before she went away. You need not keep it secret from me any longer." She smiles at them. "You're a very loyal lot, but you could have trusted me, you know."

We all talk now of babies and the signs. They ask lots of questions about John and his parents, and then want to know how much my son is growing. I don't mind their avid curiosity – it is natural – but I do dread their reaction when they realise the consequences of this event whose shadows they cannot contemplate.

Eventually Mother sees the danger and decides that she must quell the excitement.

"Children, you know already that Mari has been punished because having a baby before she is married is against the law. It will still be difficult for her: people might be angry."

"What will happen then? Will anyone hurt her?" Salome asks thoughtfully in a subdued voice.

"I don't know, really, I don't. Will you pray for her, as you have each day she's been away?"

"If anyone tries to hurt her, I'll stop them!" exclaims Benjamin belligerently and everyone bursts out laughing. He has pricked the tension and the future fears are banished in a rough-and-tumble that reaches near the edge of hysteria.

Suddenly there is a knocking at the door. Mother and I look at one another in alarm, and Rebecca and Ben cease their antics. It is Clopas, looking grim and flustered.

"I'm sorry, Anna. Eli wants Mariam at once. I've pleaded with him to give her time with you, to eat and rest, but he will not have it."

"We'd better come, then."

"Not you, Anna; he stressed just Mariam."

"But I can't leave her alone with him, especially if he intends her harm."

"He told me I was to forbid you to come."

"Let me go, Mother; it won't make any difference in the end. If he is angry over a little thing, it will not help my cause."

Mother clings to me as though she is bidding me farewell. I am alerted and alarmed by this, and give her a lingering glance, before accompanying Clopas across the yard.

"I'm sorry, Mari, he won't even let me stay with you. I've done my best; he's had Zechariah's letter."

I knock timidly on Eli's door and enter.

He is standing on the raised floor of his living room, pacing agitatedly up and down, and scarcely looks at me, where I stand, trembling, in front of him. I am really scared now. He turns to look at me and I see that he is angry – so much so that he is choking over his first words.

"You, you... malevolent fornicating whore, you Jezebel, you insolent heathen prostitute; you've brought down shame and disgrace upon your whole household! I've done everything I can to bring you up as a credit to your faith and us, and look how you repay me!"

I am stunned and speechless. I am groping in panic. Am I meant to reply to this? No, he is merely gasping for breath amid his diatribe.

"Explicit instructions I gave you! I warned you! I warned you before witnesses! You cannot plead ignorance. I spent hours talking the other elders out of instant retribution when you were found to be pregnant, and then blasphemed instead of accepting the way out I offered you. They agreed reluctantly when I made promises on your behalf. And now look at you! You've not even tried to put my orders into effect! You're even proud of disobeying me, so much so that you've persuaded Elizabeth and Zechariah of all people to excuse you, instead of carrying out my wishes."

He waves what I recognise as Zechariah's letter in front of me in fury, only inches from my nose. I flinch and cower, fearing that he is going to strike me.

"Aren't you going to say anything in your defence, girl? Are you struck dumb too, like Zechariah professes to have been?"

"What can I say?"

"Well may you ask! Isn't it a bit late to think of that now?"

"Would you listen if I tried to defend myself?"

Before I can react, I receive a vicious stinging blow to the side of my face and am knocked off balance. I stumble up again, hand clasped against my burning cheek, only peering to see if another blow is coming. He has said something, but I've no idea what. My eyes are blinded with salty tears and I grope in darkness to recover my thread. I am not given the chance.

"Enough of this tomfoolery! Why should I show you mercy, or your wretched family? You've done nothing but sponge off me since you sought refuge in my household. Your father put all of us at risk, your mother hasn't a bean to support her multiplying brood, and now you overtop the lot!"

"Sir, what will you do to us?"

"We'll release poor Joseph from his bonds to you for a start. That is the least we can do for him. And you can face your accusers now at public trial; I'll not stop it. And if you're condemned, I'll be there, casting the first stone. Afterwards your family can be gone from my house and from this town, and good riddance to them!"

"Sir, please, no, it's not my mother's or my sisters' fault."

"You should have thought of that earlier. What's more, I know your mother; I've no doubt she's encouraged you in these airy-fairy notions. As far as I am concerned, she can sell your sisters in bondage to the Romans or to a heathen temple – I couldn't care less – then go on the streets and beg, as long as she doesn't do it here."

"Oh, my God, have mercy on us, have mercy on us," I beg in tears, falling to my knees in front of Eli's pulsating form.

An iron grip seizes me by the shoulder and yanks me to my feet, propelling me at the same time towards the door of the house. I can feel the seething rage pent up in his fist, blindly forcing me to go in front of him. I am rammed against the wooden door, so that I hurt my arm and shoulder as it swings open under my weight, and I stumble into the dazzling sunlight. I am half pushed, half dragged into the street, and feel the stares of startled passers-by and cringe at my public humiliation. I stagger awkwardly in front of him, unsure which way to go, until he hisses in my ear, "The synagogue, you trollop, and if you dare blaspheme again in your defence…"

He says no more, but what he has said is not disguised in tone, so everyone around must have heard it. I avert my eyes, looking only at my stumbling feet, and try to will myself into invisibility. The nightmare spectacle through the busy street ends abruptly when we reach the synagogue and I am pushed into the sudden calm, where the noise of our movement is magnified. Across the Women's Court my bare feet slap the coolness of the flagstones. I sense the building is deserted. I think he is going to put me inside the little cell where I was held before the whipping, but he unbolts the adjacent door, which leads to the room where the animals and birds for sacrifice are kept until the time for killing comes. Inside I see movement in the straw, and a couple of pigeons flutter at the glimpse of daylight. Before I can assimilate this sight properly, I feel myself hurled into the room and I stagger forward, falling on my face amid the straw, the squawking birds and larger beasts, which panic at my sudden intrusion. Whilst I am still trying to recover and regain my balance, my uncle, still in foul mood, shouts at me, "You can stay there where you belong until we've decided what to do with you. You're unclean; give me your clothes or you'll contaminate the very beasts about you!"

I don't grasp his meaning at first, then, when his words sink in, I understand he means to have me locked in here, naked, and left among the animals. There is really no way I can disobey him. If I resist, he'll seize me and rip my clothes off, such is his present temper. Ashamed, I try to hide from him as I pull off my shift and loincloth, and turn my back to shield my naked belly from his eyes. I hold out my garments tentatively, and they are snatched from my hand with a violence that almost rips them before I can let go. In the next movement the door is slammed in my face and the bolts drive home, as I adjust to the dim light which percolates through the tiny slit high on one wall, and nearly choke on the overpowering odour of animal dung and droppings which impregnates the filthy straw.

I find, to my surprise, that my overwhelming emotion is one of relief. He is gone; I am left in peace; I can gather my confused senses, which are still shocked by the rapidity of developments within the last few minutes. The movement of the animals around me is comforting: I am not frightened by their presence. I am aware now of the bleating of a lamb, and a couple of kids, as well as the strutting and fluttering of at least half a dozen doves, and I try to make soothing noises to calm them. I squat, talk softly and hold out my open palm to one of the cowering goats, and my patience is eventually rewarded, as both larger animals lose their fear and start to investigate by sniffing inquisitively at my outstretched arm. In the end, they let me stroke their noses and nuzzle against me, searching me for food, in vain, alas.

I find a clean patch of straw in the centre of the little room, and kneel, sinking back to rest upon my calves. I contemplate my nakedness and think that Eli meant to humiliate me in the way most shocking to his imagination. He and the other rabbis detest nakedness in any form except when they are intentionally stripping all dignity from their victim. It is associated with idolatry and heathen practices; the hated Roman games, which flagrantly offend my compatriots' prudishness. It is synonymous with impurity and lewdness; ritual uncleanness; the ultimate in contempt.

Yet strangely, I find their attitude rather silly and certainly unnecessarily causative of such virulent offence. No-one worries when little children run around with nothing on, the sun streaming on their bronzed bodies. No-one bats an eyelid when a child of ten or eleven bathes naked in the river or goes over his father's knee for a sound spanking. Yet but a year later, modesty is affronted when too much bare limb is glimpsed beneath the flowing veils and shifts when you try to raise water from the well. I actually like the feel of no restricting cloth pulling at my limbs; I sense a freedom that infects my mind, that symbolises a closeness that I feel with God's world around me. Don't tell anyone, certainly not my uncle, that I have always felt it easiest to pray with nothing on – he would be horribly shocked and think it most impious of me.

Does he think that God would be so easily embarrassed? That I would tempt him by my nakedness? Can't God see right through me to my very soul – surely that I should be so transparent is far more shocking?

Perhaps you're thinking now that at this moment the last thing I can put my mind to is prayer. Funnily enough, my head is filled with clarity. Everything is gone: the confusion, the humiliation, the fear, the obstinacy; replaced by a pervading sense of calm, precision, a need to be articulate. Should I share my prayers with you? They are very personal. I have always been taught to be private. They are for God's ears alone, not to impress others, not even my own mother. Perhaps just a clue; I am nothing now, totally vulnerable, totally in God's hands. I pray for Mother, for Benjamin, for Rebecca, for Salome. I pray for Joseph and Clopas; Miriam, Mo and the boys. I pray for Aunt Elizabeth, John and Uncle Zechariah; for Rachel; for my father. I pray for my sheep and goats, who will be missing me; for the animals here around me awaiting the sacrificial knife. I even pray for Uncle Eli, though it is hard. Above all I pray for my child, nestling within my bloated body; I press him, encircle him with my loving arms. He is why I'm here. He is the one I must protect. He is the one I expect God to shelter and sustain, or else his promises are impotent, and that cannot be.

I do not know how long I take. When I surface to myself again, the light has faded, so that I can hardly make out any more than the outline of the beasts around me. It is not cold and I am quite comfortable although the straw scratches and irritates when I shift position to ease my aching thighs and arching back. I begin to wonder what my family is doing now. Do they know where Eli has taken me? Would they have been watching through the shuttered windows, have seen my undignified departure? Does Mum know of Eli's threat to throw us out? What has she told the children? The more I think about them, the more I feel guilty; I have no right to condemn them for my vision. I have the right to accept the consequences of my own behaviour, but not the right to impose on them. A few minutes ago, it seemed so beautifully simple; and prayer, I thought, would calm me even further, not sow seeds of doubt and guilt.

When will Mother come to see me? Will they let her? What if Joseph comes – will he condemn me too? Will he be angry, not let me explain, or will he allow me at least to furnish justification to my claim? It is dark now. The stable is a dank stinking blackness; I cannot even see my hands groping before my face. My legs are stiff and I stand and stretch, then try to move to exercise a little. In my blindness I stand in excreta from one of the animals, and slip, causing my thighs to stretch taut, tearing the muscles. A streak of pain shoots through my back and stomach nerves and I scrabble about on all fours, kneeling, oblivious to the filth whilst I panic that I have harmed my baby. I roll over and lie on my back, clutching my stomach, and gradually the ache drifts away into the darkness. I realise with thankfulness that I have not done any lasting damage, just scared myself a little. I feel dirt adhering to my body and grasp a handful of straw and try to clean myself without really knowing if I have smeared it further. All my anxiety and fear have returned. No-one is going to come tonight: it is too late. My mother is lying in her bed, crying; I'm sure of it. Perhaps they'll never give me a chance. I shall be dragged out of here, naked and filthy, in the morning, to be laughed at by the mob and stoned to death, without ever seeing anyone I love again.

My fear courses through my body. My palms sweat, my tongue is dry, my bowels are gurgling with nervous diarrhoea, which I can keep back no longer. I try, ashamed, to find a black corner and squat, apologising to the sleeping animals. And now I suffer my own stench as well as theirs. I crawl as far as possible away from my miserable territory, and bury myself beside the dormant goats, feeling their rough warmth on the smoothness of my back. The earthy contact restores some of my former lassitude; perhaps I have no option but to resign myself here to share the animals' fate. I slumber, waking numerous times; I do not know, there is no way of telling, how long since I last stirred. At length a tinge of the dullest light allows ghostly shadows to be seen. The day is breaking.

Once I can see properly, I try to clean myself as best I can with the only handful of fresh straw that I can find. I am about to give up, when I hear footsteps outside, then the harsh sound of the bolts being drawn back on my door. I kneel in a ball, protecting my shame as the stable floods with brilliant sunlight, and notice only that it is one of the rabbis silhouetted in the doorway. The figure stands rooted to the spot, then a voice, not unkindly, says, "Goodness me, girl, is that you, Mariam? Why are you naked? Where are your clothes?"

"Uncle Eli took them away, sir."

It is Joel, Hannah's father.

"I will bring you water and a cloth so that you can wash yourself. When you are ready I'll bring you some bread and water while I fetch your mother with a change of clothes. You cannot remain naked in this place: it is indecent and against the law."

That makes me feel a little better.

They bring my mother to me two hours later. Just before she came, I was led into the cell where I had been kept prisoner once before. We embrace and she gives me a fresh loincloth and a tunic to put on. Eli had not given back my own clothes. The tunic is an old one of mine – too small, especially tight around the waist. I have to leave the girdle off. Even so, it exposes the fact that I am pregnant to anyone who sees me.

My mother has been crying. Her eyes are bloodshot and puffy; I doubt if she has had much sleep. I feel guilty that I have not been so distressed or disturbed.

"What about the children? Do they know?"

"Yes, Mari. I left them now sobbing their hearts out. I have been up all night with one or other of them. They saw Eli drag you off and I had to tell them something. I think Salome has a fair idea of what might happen to you. She is very withdrawn this morning, won't talk to anyone."

Her words affect me so much that, for the first time since my imprisonment here in the synagogue, tears come to my eyes and I cannot stop them. I can't forget that I am doing this to them.

I look up at the whip and rods hanging on the wall.

"What are they going to do to me? Am I going to be beaten again, or will it be worse this time?" I can't make myself actually spell out the ultimate punishment to her.

"Eli has summoned the men of the village to a judgement here at noon. They will hear you briefly, then condemn you."

"Are their minds already made up? Can't I say anything to persuade them?"

"As far as Eli is concerned, you are already judged. Your sentence was only suspended at your previous hearing because of his pleas for you – at least, that's what he says. He promised his colleagues that you would take certain actions that would enable them to show mercy. His attitude now is simple. You did not carry out your side of the bargain, nor did you intend to. He has no way now of seeking special treatment for you without exercising favour just because you are of his family. He will not do that; you know his overriding sense of duty, to a fault. I am sorry to be so bleak, my love, but to let you have any hope would be to mislead you totally."

"When will they carry out the sentence?"

My mother looks at me in great anguish.

"Immediately."

"Today? In just three or four hours' time?"

"I'm sorry, Mari, I'm truly sorry, yes."

I can't take it in. I cannot believe it has really come to this. Our conversation seems remote, as though it has absolutely nothing to do with this flesh and blood beneath my flimsy garment. All the exhilaration, the relief as my friends and relatives have begun to believe, is to be dashed to nothing, just because Eli will not change his mind, will not even listen. A great wave of despair pours over me, crushes me, makes me want to give up and let them do whatever they want, without challenge.

"Can I see Salome, Rebecca and Benji first?"

"Mari, what would you say to them? Think. Is it really fair? They are already very upset. Is it not easiest to let them be? Let them remember you in happier moments."

"Mum, you talk as though I'm already gone."

This sentence breaks her up. She wails and flings her arms around me and we rock each other until we are exhausted.

"Can I see Joseph, then?"

"I'll try, Mari. Even at this moment he is trying to talk Eli into showing mercy to you. If he gets nowhere with him, he's vowed to come down here to tackle Joel and Jethro also. He is doing his best, Mari."

At that moment there is a clattering at the door and Joel is there, beckoning Mother to follow him.

"Joseph has come. I'd like you present in our discussions."

"Mum, will you come back?"

"I don't know, Mari; if I can, I will."

"Don't go, please. I don't want to say goodbye."

"Don't panic, Mariam. If you are condemned, your mother will be permitted to bid you farewell, if she wants to, before you are led out to execution."

The door closes. I am alone. I prostrate myself upon the floor.

"You promised, Lord, you promised. 'My father and mother may abandon me, but the Lord will take care of me' – that's what the scripture says. Please, Lord, please fulfil your promise."

I say it again and again as I beat my fists against the hard floor. But my mind keeps drifting to my other text: 'My devoted servant, with whom I am pleased, will bear the punishment of many'. What does this mean? Does it refer to now? If I am to be sacrificed, what good will come of it? Will not my son, my Messiah, die also?

CHAPTER 35

LAST CHANCE

I DO NOT KNOW HOW LONG I have been lying on the floor, beseeching God to rescue me. Perhaps it is a few minutes only. It seems an eternity. I am aware of Joseph's presence only when I hear the words, "Get up, Mariam, I want to talk with you."

Light is flooding the little cell; the door is wide open. Then it is closed. We are together in this airless little space. I look at him. He is staring at me. I realise this is the first time he's seen me since our journey to the Passover; the first time he's seen my pregnancy. I wish I knew what emotions are filling him right now. Is he with me?

"Mari, you are still my betrothed. I loved you. Why have you done this to me?"

"Sir, I did not want to hurt you. I really did not understand at first what was involved in obeying the command that I was given. I believed, and still do, that I was carrying out God's will."

"It is hard for me to accept this, Mariam. I am of David's lineage. If God wanted you to have a son that would fulfil the prophecies, would he not use me as the instrument?"

"When we were betrothed, I was sure that was God's will, so I was equally surprised when the stranger told me to be ready then."

"Mari, look at me. Tell me honestly, did the stranger have intercourse with you? Did you do it willingly, or did he force you?"

I pause, trying hard to sift my memory, to be as open with Joseph as I can. I owe him that at least. But I find my memory muddled with the meaning.

"It is a very hard question. It seems so dreamlike now. I was told to obey, without understanding what I did. I accepted that God's will was being done to me. I let the water of the river flow into me, and in that swirling flood it was difficult to distinguish exactly what was happening. Perhaps he did take me there in the water. Perhaps it was symbolic only. I did not feel defiled. It did not seem that my virginity had been violated. No-one has ever sought to examine me. Should I ask for such a test? Do you think it possible that I am still intact?"

"Mari, I do not see how that could be. In any case, the issue is not just a physical one. You are bearing a child. The fundamental question is the identity of the baby within you. Are we to believe you or do we pity that you have been misled?"

"I know what I believe. I will not renounce it."

"Even though they condemn you to death?"

"What is the difference now in any case? I have, I'm told, long passed the time when I can expect mercy by giving up my claims and forfeiting the baby's right to live. Not that I would, even if I could."

"I can't help admiring you when you're angry! I like your spirit, girl, even when they've done their best to break you."

"Can I ask something of you, Joseph?"

"If you want me to save you, I'm already trying, but I cannot perform miracles."

"No, Joseph, I wasn't going to ask you that. It was about Mother and my brother and sisters. Uncle Eli has threatened to throw them out of their home because of what I've done. I feel awful about that. You have a small home in Bethlehem. If Eli carries out his threat, could you look after them? Or at least help them temporarily to see that they come to no harm? Perhaps Elizabeth and Zechariah would help too – they believe in my mission, and would have pity on my family."

"You ask a difficult thing, Mari. It is you I love, not them. Are you thinking that I should marry your mother, or your sister Salome?"

"I haven't really thought it through at all. I don't mean marriage: I'm just afraid of their homelessness and the threats that my sisters would have to be sold for them all to survive. I can't bear to think of that."

"Who said that to you, Mari?"

"Uncle Eli."

"Don't believe that. He would never wilfully shirk his duties in such a callous manner. I'm sure he was only trying to seek your submission by frightening you and making you feel guilty. I promise you, Mariam, if it comes to that – and I don't believe it will – I will ensure that they come to no harm."

"Thank you, Joseph. I'm glad I asked you that."

"You fill me with shame. In the very hour when you are in crisis, when I expected to find you collapsed in terror and self-pity, all I see is your concern for others. No-one whose attitude reflects this concern can be an adulteress and blasphemer and all the other things they say you are."

"I was afraid you'd be angry with me too. If I know that you respect me, it will help me to be brave when the time comes. Will you be there when they stone me, Joseph? Will you stand where I can see you until the end? I shall fix my eyes on you and ignore the rest."

"Mari, don't say these things: I cannot bear it. How can you be so calm? If all else fails, I'll be there. I give you my solemn promise, although I'd rather be anywhere else on earth."

"Thank you, Joseph."

We leave a long pause. Both of us are struggling to think of what to say next.

"Joseph?"

"Yes, Mari?"

"Joseph, will you hug me and my child?"

He is awkward and confused, but tender. He lets himself soften a little and puts a tentative arm round my shoulder, then as I snuggle towards him, the other arm slips round my waist and pulls me against his robes. He can feel my belly now against his own; I move deliberately against him. I want him to make my baby his, by being part of it. As we stand there, clasped together, he whispers in my ear, "Mari, I did not want to tell you this, in case it gives you false hope. Last night I had a dream. I'm sure it is a sign. I've told Joel of my belief and he is even now consulting Eli and Jethro as to its meaning."

"Tell me, Joseph, please, what was your dream?"

"I dreamt that you were bound outside the synagogue, alone, and opposite you was a mob of Baal's priests, all screaming for your blood. Then Elijah came and called down fire. From the clear blue sky a bolt of lightning came and struck your naked flesh and all rushed forward to jeer at a cindered corpse; but you were unharmed, your flesh as pale and unblemished as a pure young maiden. Then I saw that the fire was devouring your accusers. The flames raged around you, and there in the middle you bathed your flesh in clear spring water. The droplets, as they ran from your body, sprinkled with the sand, leaving a text etched upon the barren earth:

May he be pleased with my song
For my gladness comes from him.

And after that, Elijah was taken in a whirlwind and disappeared from view."

"What do you think it means, Joseph?"

"I think God's wrath will fall on those who condemn you. They will die in torment, perhaps in the everlasting flames of Gehenna. And you will be exalted, for that which you create comes directly from God."

"Joseph?"

"Yes, Mari?"

"Has anyone ever told you of the texts that Uncle Eli gave me in a personal scroll for my twelfth birthday?"

"No. I have no idea."

"That text you saw in your dream was one of them – the only one of three he gave me of which, until now, I had not seen the direct relevance."

"Is that really so? You mean... Eli himself gave you that text?"

"Yes."

"Let me go and tell Eli and the others straight away. It cannot be coincidence."

Dare I hope? Has God intervened? Or is there some innocent and natural explanation? And even if there is, how will Eli and the other rabbis interpret it?

After a few more tense minutes, the door opens to the daylight once again. This time it is my mother.

"Come quickly, Mari! They want to talk to you before the village men assemble. Perhaps there is some hope – Joseph has told them something which has put doubt in their minds."

I am led into the rabbis' chambers behind the worship area. As well as the three elders, Clopas and Joseph are there, standing with my mother. Jethro calls me to him, and begins the questioning., "Do you have a scroll of personal texts?"

"Yes, my uncle gave them to me."

"Can you quote them to us?"

I do so, without hesitation.

"Who knew of these, beside yourself?"

"Uncle Eli, my mother… perhaps Clopas – he was present at my birthday feast when I was given them."

"Have you ever told them to anyone else?"

"No, sir."

"Could your mother have told Joseph?"

"She could have done, but I don't know when or why."

Perhaps Mother has told Joseph and they have invented the dream to rescue me. I'm sure that thought has crossed their minds.

"Tell us about the stranger who, you claim, announced to you that you would bear the Messiah."

"I saw him several times before he told me that directly, although he told me often that I had been chosen by God for something very special. He always surprised me – he seemed to come and go so suddenly. I felt mesmerised by him; he looked right into me, as though he knew my every thought and feeling. It was uncanny."

"Did he ever say who he was? Did you ask him?"

"Yes, I asked him. He usually said he was a messenger, sometimes a messenger from God. Once he said he was the prophet come to prepare for God's special mission."

"Many believe that Elijah will come again before the Messiah reigns. Did he ever refer or allude to Elijah?"

"No, I don't think so, sir."

Eli turns to Jethro and I hear him mutter something, shaking his head. In return, I catch a few of Jethro's words, "…I find that all the more convincing. She could have lied to tie in with Joseph's dream." They turn back to me.

"Did the stranger ever discuss scripture with you?"

"Yes, sir."

"What passages did he expound?"

"Sometimes he quoted from the psalms, or about God's love of Israel from the 'Song of Songs'. But usually he showed me how the prophet Isaiah had foretold Israel's saviour, and how he would suffer the scorn and cruelty of men. He asked me if I was strong enough to bear pain."

"I didn't ask you that, Mariam. Just answer my questions, please." His voice was gentle though, not angry.

"Mariam, if we were to give you one final chance to renounce your claim and promise to let you live, even let you have your baby as long as it did not happen in this village, would you do that for us?"

"Sir, you are making it very hard for me. I am frightened. I do not want to die. I do not want to hurt my family or bring shame to them. But you are asking me to deny the very experience which has sustained me through all my trials. I want to live. I want my future son to live. But I do not want it to be because I have denied God's will, or refused his call to me. Are you asking me to make that choice?"

"No, Mariam; it was a theoretical question. If your extraordinary tale is true, then it cannot be foresworn. If however, as seems more likely in this treacherous world, it is a tissue of lies, either deliberate or naïve, born of the wickedness of the stranger, or yourself, or both of you, then you are already beyond redemption and should suffer the penalty of the law in all its severity, despite the pain this would bring through our close association with you and your family."

"Sir, God has given me the answer to the doubts I had. He will surely enable you to discern what is right for you to do."

"Mariam, daughter of Anna, ward of Eli, consider carefully before you answer this next question. Did you commit adultery with the stranger? Do you admit it? Did Rabbi Eli warn you before other witnesses of the consequences of such a sin?"

"I received a call to bear a child: the Messiah. I accepted and obeyed. I did what I was told to do. I bathed in the river Tabor and there the stranger visited me."

"Did you not suspect him?"

"I trusted him because of what he told me."

"Did he tell you anything else apart from your duty there?"

"He told me about my cousin Elizabeth's pregnancy after so many barren years. That she would bear a son who would announce the Messiah to the world."

"So you knew this before you were sent to Ein–Karem?"

"Yes."

"Did you tell your cousins immediately of your own condition and its cause?"

"Yes, sir."

"And they believed you?"

"Yes, as Zechariah writes to you in his letter."

"What letter?"

"The one that was entrusted to Clopas to give to Uncle Eli."

This statement causes some consternation. Jethro looks to Eli and Clopas; the latter is nodding vigorously in confirmation of my words. My uncle is clearly embarrassed and has a quick word with Jethro, who ceases his questioning of me. After their consultation, Jethro tells Joel to take me back to my cell, and I am hurried out of their presence as if they do not wish me to witness their disarray.

In the solitude of my little prison I dare to hope. Jethro's words seemed fair; he did not rant or argue. Perhaps I am raising my sights too soon, allowing the glimmer of optimism to colour my sense of judgement. I look round my tiny room and focus on the instruments of torture hanging before my eyes. If they spare my life, perhaps once more they'll submit me to the ordeal by whip. A wave of panic and shuddering overtakes me before I steel myself with the thought that such a punishment can be borne; I have done so before. I reach inside my shift and clasp my unborn child within my flesh.

"My son, let us be brave. Let us trust God to bring us through these next few hours; claim his protection once more, as he has sheltered us already. Let us be strong and suffer his will if need be. I doubt this will be the last time either of us is tested."

I do not find it strange to talk thus to my baby – indeed, it seems the most natural thing in the world. Then, even as I kneel there in stillness and silence, I think I feel a movement. I hold my breath; perhaps I am mistaken. Then I am sure. Another tiny quiver in my womb: a strange tickling feeling that fills me with unspeakable joy! The whole room explodes with light! I rock myself, I sing, I praise my God. How could one tiny flutter swing my mood so violently?

My door is being unlatched once again. I look up in anticipation. It is my mother. I fling myself into her arms, in great excitement.

"Mum, I have felt the baby moving; he's alive. I can't express the joy I feel. Please tell me this is a sign of hope! They can't kill us now, surely…?"

I look up into my mother's eyes, and behind their tears, I see she is smiling. One hand is ruffling my hair, then she is kissing me on my brow and on my cheeks.

"Oh, Mari, Mari, you are saved!"

At first I do not comprehend the meaning of her words. I am still thinking of my new experience, even as I feel the child lurch once more within my womb.

"Did you hear me, Mari? You're free; you're safe. They will not seek your trial or condemnation."

"How? You mean... they believe me?" Her words are beginning to sink in.

"They do not disbelieve you any longer. Joseph refuses to divorce you. Clopas gave you support as well, told them of Elizabeth and Zechariah and all that he had seen. When Eli realised that his fellow rabbis were loath to condemn you, he switched his tack completely. He had feared criticism from his colleagues, felt that his reputation as an incorruptible judge was on the line and would not grant you any favours."

"And they are going to let me go? Without any further punishment? Will they let me keep my baby?"

A big hug and another kiss.

"Yes, my love. You are not a sinner and lawbreaker any longer. You are the Lord's Chosen One!"

CHAPTER 36

I AM ELI

I'VE GOT TO GET A grip of things. How I handle the next hour or so is going to be crucial to my standing and reputation. For weeks I've been working with the problems posed by my niece and her far-reaching and extravagant claims. Since her return from Ein–Karem she has created a crisis which has been totally outside my control. Throughout, I have assumed that I would be forced to balance the emotional outpourings of my own family with the lucid and uncompromising standards of the law, as advocated by my rabbinical colleagues. I have been girding myself to bring down the wrath and resentment not only of Anna, but of my own son and his wife, not to mention the frantic outcry of all their children. But such sacrifices of popularity, I persuaded myself, were necessary to uphold justice: if I refused to condemn the sinful, then my right to administer impartial judgement would be undermined.

And now, of all things, I find myself forced onto the defensive by my own colleagues, who've reminded me that a death judgement would be the second by this rabbinical court inside a year and lead to recriminations that we hold a barbarous court. They have also completely lost their nerve in the face of the girl's steadfast defence of her claims, the endorsement by Zechariah and now Joseph's traumatic musings. Do not misunderstand me – I do not wish the girl dead. Over the years I have invested heavily in her upbringing, and her waste would be prodigious. On the other hand, I find the outright vindication of her position hard to stomach; I'd be much more relaxed if we had struck a compromise.

I accept that there is now sufficient ambiguity in the interpretation of recent events to justify suspension of our judgement. Whilst it is possible that Joseph and Mariam's mother have conspired to invent evidence to back the girl's claims – and both have considerable motive – I trust the young man's apparent lack of guile. I do not believe he could practise deceit without some indication of his guilt. I also lean on Clopas' views, normally a source of much commonsense; and he, of course, was alone with Mariam throughout the journey from Judea.

I find myself asking: does it matter what I believe? If the political implications of yet another Messianic claimant are sufficiently distant in time to ignore in the short term, should I not be thankful for a way out of a most embarrassing situation? If I was still certain that the girl was deceiving us deliberately, despite the beckoning call of expediency, I'd like to think I'd maintain my integrity. However, I have to admit she has me rattled. Despite the precociousness and audacity of her explanations, I give her a grudging respect. I have to be decisive. If I am to acknowledge that she may be right, it would be better to throw one's whole self behind her claim, and glean at second-hand the authority reflected from her newly acquired status. Heaven help us all if her child turns out to be a girl!

In a few minutes' time, the men of the village will be crowded into the synagogue, summoned to try and to condemn the girl.

"I think you should outline our findings," says Jethro, passing the responsibility back to me. "You alone know the full story." My reproof that his testimony might bear more weight because of its impartiality is dismissed by all the others. I sense a taste of 'you forced us into this position by your advice – now get us out of it'.

Already knots of men are drifting through the outer courtyards and gathering in the main hall of the synagogue. I deliberate with Jethro, and when the majority have assembled, I call Anna to bring Mariam into the Women's Court, where she can be seen. At least the child looks angelic and vulnerable, without a trace of the elaborate artifice which so antagonised this village to Althaeus' whore. I watch as the men look intently at her through the partition, then, having satisfied their curiosity, turn to await my words. I take a deep breath and commit myself. There is no turning back.

"Greetings, brothers. Peace to each of you. I make no apology for summoning you to this hearing, although since my call much new information has come to hand which alters the complexion of the matter of which we are to speak. I also declare my interest and involvement, for the matter to hand affects my own niece and ward, Mariam, daughter of Anna and of the late patriot, our kinsman, Joachim. I offered to cede the advocacy of the case to my colleague, Jethro, as he would claim greater impartiality, but my fellow rabbis wish me to present the case to you, as I am best acquainted with the relevant details. Brothers, I have to tell you of signs and answers to our prayers which bring much honour to our community, though should the heathen gentile or one of Herod's treacherous informers betray us, we have much to fear."

A low murmuring of resentment growls around the chamber. Good. I can build on this.

"Our daughter, Mariam, has been found with child. Her condition, as you see, is obvious to all."

I hold up my arm to quell any surge of spontaneous expression of disgust.

"My initial reaction, like yours perhaps, was to blame her and her betrothed, Joseph of Bethlehem. But I soon established that Joseph was innocent of the deed. We sought to establish whether the girl had been assaulted, but she claimed an extraordinary tale. Although initially sceptical, my colleagues and I have tried to test or disprove her claims before bringing her to judgement before you. The girl has sought to convince us of a miraculous conception, beyond her understanding, accepted by her in abject deference to the will of the Almighty as made known to her. Brothers, she was visited by a stranger, who came and went at will, much like the blessed prophet Elijah, as foretold in our Holy Writ. This angel, as I will deem him, unveiled God's plan that she should conceive a son through the power of the Spirit of the Lord, though yet a virgin. We sought to test the Spirit by ordeal – the girl was flogged to the adult limit – yet the fragile lives of mother and child were spared. Despatched to Judea, to wait upon her cousin, she found that she too had been visited, and late in life was bearing a son, whom also had been foretold in the scriptures. Attested by a priest of the High Temple in Jerusalem, Mariam returned to us, and promptly her betrothed, Joseph, was warned in a dream that he should not reject her – by many signs and indications that give proof that this can only be a part of God's mysterious plan for us." I pause briefly to let this sink in.

"Brothers, do not condemn this girl, but support her and her family, in her time of honour. I propose that Joseph of Bethlehem, descended, like Mariam herself, from our glorious ancestor David, should wed the girl in due season but not be brought to her bed until her son is born, so that the words of our prophet Isaiah may be fulfilled: 'And a virgin shall conceive and bring forth a son'. For, brothers, our daughter here has been promised, no less, that she will be mother of David's royal son: our king and deliverer from the hated foreigners, our long-awaited Messiah."

A gasp and buzz of conversation fills the court. Before incredulity can grip the community, I turn for confirmation from those standing round me,:

"Joseph of Bethlehem, do you so witness here before God and men?"

"Rabbi Eli, Jethro, Joel, brothers, I am so convinced. God has spoken to me in several ways, climaxing in a dream of clear intent."

"And Clopas, have you not evidence also?"

"I witnessed conversations with Zechariah of Ein–Karem that confirm your every word, and I was bringer of a letter to you affirming his belief that Mariam had been blessed by God himself."

"Jethro, have you not tested the evidence put before us impartially, to ensure I was not favouring my own household?"

"Rabbi Eli, I confirm your statements and strongly support your proposal that Mariam be wed to Joseph as soon as the child is born."

We have presented a united front. The murmuring is of excitement, drama, astonishment. There is no voice of discontent. No-one seeks Mariam's condemnation. She has no enemies. We have enabled them to clear her name. Assent by acclamation!

"Well handled, Eli, a masterly presentation!" My colleagues surround me and offer their congratulations. "Take the child yourself and indoctrinate her in all the prophecies so that she may do us credit in the eyes of God. You are well qualified to complete the task you have begun."

Mariam has been released back to her mother's home. Joseph is in residence with me, having completed his contract in Capernaum. I have not suggested any further work in that quarter, but have recommended his services in the immediate locality to the extent that he may remain under my roof until his marriage is consummated. I need now to consolidate this successful outcome through private discussions with all concerned. Joseph is my first responsibility.

I invite him to join my evening meal, which Miriam has prepared for me and set out ready. I watch him, as he eats silently, waiting for me to speak. He is a strange young man in many ways – mature in self-containedness with his ability to cope with adversity; yet strangely shy in company, deferential, unsure in his own estimation. I feel naturally protective of him, as though he needs saving from himself. Despite his age, he seems still childlike in many ways.

"Joseph, are you pleased at the way things have turned out?"

"I am very grateful for your intervention, Eli, and the lead you gave today. Your opinion was vital, and the way you presented Mariam's case to the assembly undoubtedly saved my betrothed's life."

"Thank you for your compliments, Joseph. I am relieved for both of you that we could produce such evidence to bolster Mariam's claim. Do you agree with my suggestion that the wedding should follow immediately on the birth of Mariam's son?"

"Yes, if you think that is the right and appropriate time."

"Good. That is settled then. The child is due in a couple of months, near the girl's fourteenth birthday. You will of course take her into your house here. We will help you educate the child, and should you be away on business at any time, you will have full support from your family here."

"I am grateful, Eli."

"I shall settle some property of mine on the child. No-one shall say the Messiah lacked provision from his family; we shall give him the best start that any Jewish boy could envy."

"You are most generous."

"There is one other matter of which I wish to speak. There is a rumour reaching us from Tiberius that the Romans are proposing new taxation laws and will conduct a census where property and family must be registered. If this is the case, you will need to register your property in Bethlehem."

"When is this likely to be?"

"I do not know for certain. Within the next few months for sure. I am reminded though of the Messianic prophecy of Micah that the expected one shall be born in Bethlehem, the town of your birth. Why don't you take Mariam when she nears her time, stay for a while in your own property, let her fulfil the prophecy by giving birth there, and register at the same time? It makes much sense and could help in later years if there are arguments about her son's authenticity."

"But, Eli, should she not be with her mother when her time comes? She will need the help and reassurance of her family, especially for a first child."

"In an ideal situation I would agree with you. But what an opportunity to fulfil the scriptural prophecy – think how this will strengthen his claim when the time is ripe! Surely you have neighbours in Bethlehem who could help you with the girl? And look how God has protected her so far; he will not desert her at the last stage of fulfilling her destiny. Think about it. Do as I say, my son, and you'll see God's will enacted."

"It is an idea. I'll discuss it with Mari and her mother."

"Joseph, take your own decisions. Mariam is already too strong-willed. Exert your authority. The Messiah needs your hand to guide him – a strong male influence. Do not pander to the women. Do as I say, Joseph – tell Mari that this is your decision. Then, when you return, we'll celebrate. We'll fete your son and prepare the wedding feast. A further idea, Joseph: if your son is born in Bethlehem, you can take him to the Temple to be circumcised and named – that would be fitting for the royal child. We'll write to Zechariah: he'll arrange things gladly."

The next day I had a long talk with Anna and appraised her of my conversation and agreement with Joseph as I did not trust him to put his foot down with his mother-in-law-to-be! Then I sent the children out to play, so that I could talk to Mariam alone. I have to admit she looks a little wary of me.

"Mariam, are you grateful for your salvation?"

"Of course, sir. And I thank God that he answered my prayers."

"He spoke to me too, Mariam, through your betrothed's dream; I recognised God's voice in what he described, and saw my duty plainly. He showed me that it is my duty to act as head of the household here, to offer the surroundings of substance in which your son can be nurtured as a Jewish first-born should, of whom we should all be proud."

I think for a moment I see a warning flashing of her eyes, that she would contradict me, or put an opposing plan, but she thinks better of it and murmurs appreciation. I tell her of the wedding plans and of my suggestion that she gives birth to the child in Bethlehem. To my surprise she makes no protest, none at all.

"And Mariam, I've decided to make time available every day to prepare you in the reading of the scriptures. We shall study all the passages that have any possible references to the Messiah, so that as the boy grows he too can be prepared for his destiny."

"But, Uncle, what about my duties in the fields?"

"Forget those, Mariam. Your sisters are of an age when they can take them on; indeed in recent times, in your absence, they've already done so. You've too much to do, preparing for your wedding and the birth of your child. Come in each day and clean Joseph's room; prepare his food. Act towards him as a wife should, except save yourself for his bed until after your son is born."

"Yes, Uncle, I will do as you wish."

"And one final thing, Mariam. Try to grow up a little. Be more dignified. You are to be the mother of the Messiah. This requires you to have a certain presence, a seriousness of purpose, to be an example to Jewish womanhood. Cease your prancing about, frolicking with the children – no, Mari, don't protest – I'm not asking you to refrain from being with them. Just act with more authority. You are now their superior. Show it. Don't act at their level all the time."

She doesn't say anything to this. I fear this is an area where my advice will not be heeded. She forgets herself when she is with the children. Perhaps as I teach her the awesomeness of her calling, perhaps then she'll adopt the regality of her position. If God has chosen her, then he must also have chosen me to influence and mould her in the way she should disport herself.

I watch her go. I cannot tell how much she's listened. Is she really grateful to me or does she blame me for doubting her in the first instance? I have the nagging fear that even now her supposed submission to my plans is but a mask. And what do I do if her 'Messiah' turns out to be a girl? Do I denounce her and accuse her of witchcraft, deceiving all of us? Perhaps it would be better to leave her quietly in Bethlehem, and let Joseph take responsibility for what to do. He can divorce her if he wishes, anything, as long as he keeps her away from here. I'll have to speak further to him, to cover ourselves should the worst happen.

INTERLUDE 4

*R*EADER, WATCH WITH ME ONCE more.

Mari goes straight to the children. There is an explosion of mirth, combined of sheer relief, delight and excitement in equal measure overtopped by mutual love. Anna lets them be. Three months of tension pours out and drains away.

Yes, they all want to feel the baby. They can feel it move now. But they have Mari back, their Mari. Is she different? Not to them, she isn't.

Two months pass. For the children, it is as if she had never gone away.

CHAPTER 37

I AM JOSEPH

I LIE IN MY LONELY BED, wide awake, reflecting for the thousandth time on all that is happening to us. Last night Eli gave us a banquet, prior to our departure for Bethlehem. When we return, he'll throw an even more generous repast for our wedding, leaving me forever in his debt. As for me, I feel a sense of profound relief that we shall soon be on the open road, free to be ourselves, unconstrained by those around us. I think Mari feels the same as I do. I catch the look in her eyes sometimes – perhaps it is just weariness from carrying the child, perhaps the other children still pester her too much.

Much of the feast seemed so false. The neighbours were polite, but did not know what to say. How do you celebrate a wedding which will not happen until you return with a babe in arms? When the young bride is so obviously and hugely pregnant? When the whole village knows that she is said to be carrying the promised Messiah? That little Mari everyone has known for years is to be mother of Israel's salvation? I overheard some gossip in the corner. 'You'll see it end in disaster…' was all I caught; I did not want to hear the rest.

I look back with relish only at the picture I bring away of Mari curled up in the corner with the two sleeping little ones snuggled on her lap. She had tried all evening to conform to the wishes of her host and play the part of lady, in whose honour the feast was given. But when the food was put aside, and the necessary pleasantries exchanged, the children had grown bored and Mari had, to Eli's obvious displeasure, absented herself to amuse them in the antechamber. And my last vision of her, before retiring myself, was of her propping up her sisters, singing softly to her bonny niece, whose large eyes, beamed upon her heroine, were slowly drooping closed.

I cannot stay in bed much longer even though there's little needing doing. I am on edge, impatient to be off. I slip out into the early morning chill to check the beast that Eli's kindly loaned me. The pack is ready, but I will leave this to the last moment. Another figure is flitting in the shadows, equally agitated. Mariam's mother is as nervous as I am.

"Joseph, you gave me a start. You're up early. Surely everything is prepared?"

"I could say the same to you. I couldn't sleep: there is too much to occupy my mind. Is Mari still asleep?"

"Yes, she's huddled in the corner with all the children. Mo asked if she could stay with us last night, so there's four of them all wrapped around each other! I think she probably took some time to get to sleep herself; we chatted for a while, then I told her to save her strength for the journey."

"Anna, are you worried about her?"

"Of course I am, Joseph. What mother wouldn't be? I'd much rather her here with me for the birth. But I understand Eli's reasons and yours as well."

"Is Mari anxious? Does she want to stay at home?"

"That's difficult to answer. I think she has mixed feelings. She will miss the children, and I suppose I flatter myself enough to think that she'd like me present during her labour. But she's confidence in you, Joseph, and I can detect an urge to be free, to venture forth on the great adventure. I think she feels hemmed in by all of us; by Eli in particular. Since his conversion to her cause, he's gone from one extreme to the other. She cannot sneeze without him checking up on her. Every word must have some deep theological significance. She finds it too much."

"I know. I feel it too. I wonder if I ought to accept Eli's generosity in providing us with home and work – I can see conflict ahead, unless we concede mastery to him in everything we do. Mari will find that even more frustrating than I shall. But on the other hand, here she will be among family and friends. She is so young to be settling in a strange town with a tiny child. She needs people around her who will reassure and help her, not strangers judging her every move."

"There is one problem you will not have in Bethlehem. At least you'll have no need to broadcast the baby's foretold destiny – here the child would be the subject of continual curiosity. One angry glance, a momentary naughtiness, and the tale will spread round the whole village."

"You will give us your blessing, won't you? I do not wish to have her leave you feeling that her departure is resented."

"Joseph, of course I will. I love her much too dearly to let her see any hint of regret, except the natural sorrow of parting. Let me ask you this though, since we are not overheard. Are you really marrying her because you want to, Joseph, and not just out of kindness or of duty? Do you love her?"

"I answer gladly. I have come to love her beyond all measure. At first, I was intrigued by her, but disturbed by her forwardness and lack of inhibition. Then I was fascinated; she ensnared me in her web, as she charms the children, even the animals themselves.

In these latter days I have seen her strength of character, and respect and admiration have joined my feelings for her. She is a rare girl, Anna, and I am privileged to have her."

"Thank you, Joseph. You reassure me. She likes and respects you too. She is still young to know the depth of love, but the seeds are there. Tend them well and she will make a loyal and loving wife. When she is a little more mature, you will find an able and discerning partner too."

We both fiddle about, checking a few more unnecessary details, before Anna again turns to me, and lays her hand upon my wrist.

"Joseph, tell me truthfully. Does it hurt that she is bearing the child of another, even if it is from God? Can you really treat her and the baby as fully yours?"

"Of course it does a bit. I look at her often and a little voice within me says, 'why could not God have used me to seed the child?' I feel a bit frustrated that I cannot take her in my arms and demonstrate my love for her in a physical way. Then I reflect that I must accept God's will, and be thankful that he has allowed me this much in his grand design."

"You are a good man, Joseph. Be kind to her. Love her and her son. Your time will come; you'll take her in your arms, she will be yours. There'll be other children that are truly your own."

"Thank you, Anna. Your words are a source of strength for me."

"God bless you both. May he give you peace and joy." She embraces me for a moment in the darkness, then turns and slips away.

My memory of our actual departure is a medley of confusion and muddled images. Despite the early hour, the courtyard is awash with friends and neighbours wishing us godspeed, with Mari's brother, sisters and cousins getting in everybody's way. The donkey has been harnessed and loaded; the first round of farewells are said; and Mari is standing beside the beast, waiting for the final cue to let me assist her onto its broad back.

At that moment Anna reappears from her home, holding an ornate embroidered veil in front of her. It is her labour of love – Mariam's wedding headdress – and all are surprised to see that Anna is intending to give it to her daughter now, rather than waiting for her return and the wedding feast itself.

"Mari, my beloved daughter, take this veil of womanhood with you. Wear it on your journey: it is right that you are treated as a married couple. It will give you some protection from wagging tongues, and from some who would molest you."

She goes up to her daughter and places the veil over Mariam's head and shoulders. Even as she does so, Eli turns to protest, and makes as if to push it from her.

"No, Anna, do not break tradition. Keep it until the wedding night – only her husband can take it from her head."

He tries again to remove it, but Mari steps backwards, and the two youngest children, who have been chasing each other around her in circles, clutch instinctively at the long veil as if they wish to ensure that it is not taken from their idol. One child trips and there is a horrifying ripping sound as two childish hands pull the veil not only from Mari's shoulders, but veer towards different directions in their falling. Anna cries out in alarm, and both children realise that something awful has happened, breaking into piercing shrieks immediately.

Mari stoops to pick up the torn piece of cloth. Her eyes are moist, but she checks her voice and tries to soothe the children. She looks at her mother, whose face is betraying anguish at the spoiling of her gift.

"Don't scold them, anyone. It was an accident. Don't mar my farewell with recriminations. It will repair. It'll be a challenge to my skills that you have taught me, Mother! See, it's not torn through. I shall be dainty. The scar will not notice. When I wear it at my wedding, no-one but you will notice the blemish."

She stoops to the two children, who are just whimpering now, and slips an arm round each of them.

"You know what that means, don't you! As you've taken off my veil, it means you must take responsibility for me, just like I've looked after you all these years. See, Joseph, you've got some helpers. When I lead you a song and dance, you've got the authority of these two here to take me in hand!"

She hugs both of them and kisses them roundly on the lips.

"Be good, all of you. I'll bring you back a new baby: a special son like you've never seen before, and you shall help me look after him."

Mariam, with great deliberation, adjusts the damaged cloth over her loose dark hair and draws it down over her shoulders, so that the rip cannot easily be seen. Then she kisses both her sisters and says a tender farewell to her mother. We move off slowly, waving as we go; the children run behind along the street and right to the outskirts of the village. We wave and move on. The children stay there, little figures growing ever smaller, arms flailing in the air. Mari turns every few seconds, acknowledging their frantic signals. Only when the track curves round below the hill and we lose the village from our sight, does she settle down in comfort on the donkey. Her eyes are filled with tears. What should I say or do? I am filled with anxiety, for she is my responsibility now. How should I comfort her?

"Mari, don't cry, my love. We'll soon be home again. They'll be the first to greet you with your child."

"Oh, Joseph, I had this awful premonition. Suppose I was leaving Nazareth for good and didn't see them again? It was silly of me, I know. Be patient with me; I'll soon be myself again."

We plod on beside the track. There are few on the road and I am anxious. I have chosen the Samaritan route south, for I am fearful of bandits, particularly on the Jordan route to Jerusalem. I know Eli advised me against this route, for it means we shall be dependent on gentiles and Samaritans until we near Jerusalem itself, but I'd rather seek their hospitality overnight, and meet their traffic by day, than take the lonely path beside the river, especially in the desert region to the south. Mari is trustful of me; I don't think she realises the danger we are running as lone travellers. We have little of which we can be robbed, however, and I hope that we will not be easily mistaken for more wealthy voyagers.

For our first overnight stop we choose a village on the border of Samaria, and are welcomed with a small room at the back of a dirty courtyard, where many toddlers stare at us with curiosity. Mari is soon in her element, conversing with the tiny children, while I unload and tether the beast, and lay our beds out on the dusty floor. We are going to be together overnight for the first time. Has Mari given any thought to this? Will she be embarrassed? Should I have sought separate rooms, and exposed her condition to the speculation of our hosts? I mutter tentatively about the arrangement. I see from her expression that she hasn't even thought about our premature cohabitation.

"It doesn't matter, Joseph – I have no secrets from you now. We are all but man and wife. Shortly I shall be needing your help when I give birth. There will be no time for either of us to be shy then!"

When we settle for the night, I find I am searching her features with longing in my heart. Despite her strength she looks so fragile, her thin tanned arms and legs, bare to my gaze. Her frank brown eyes seem to me to bore into my innermost being; she must, I think with embarrassment, recognise the desire which I feel for her despite my attempt to stifle it. Perhaps it is the similarity of our situation with the wedding night. It is the first time in my adult life that I have had the sole company of a girl beside my bed.

I am resisting such thoughts and feeling guilty that I have them. Suddenly I sense her arms around my neck. The soft warm skin of her cheek is brushing against my brow. I feel a gentle fluttering kiss, moist and tentative, and as I turn towards her, before I can collect my wits, she is whispering, "Just hold me, Joseph. No more for the moment. I trust you. When the baby's come and I've been purified, then I shall be yours entirely."

She bends over me and kisses me again. I turn and take her in my arms, feeling the warmth exuding from her body.

"I love you, Mari, truly I do. I will care for you all my life; it is my one desire."

"Oh, Joseph, I feel safe with you. All my fears and worries disappear when you are here."

She snuggles in my arms, and within moments, it seems, she is fast asleep. I stare at her, inches from my face, and marvel at such trust. It truly frightens me, this awesome responsibility. It is enough to take on the cares of another human being, but one so precious, so innocent, so trustful; and the nature of the child within her, scares me uncontrollably. I cannot comprehend why she has not seen through me, lost her confidence, which is so ill-placed. As I hold her, counting it now a privilege to be awake and receive her trust like this, I pray to the Almighty for the strength I need.

"Give me faith like hers, Lord God; lead us in your protective arms." And cocooned thus, I fall asleep.

When I awake, my first sight is her face poised over mine: a great golden grin spreading from cheek to cheek.

"Joseph," she says excitedly, "Joseph, are you awake?"

I nod as best I can.

"Feel, quick, feel." At first I do not grasp what she is saying. Then she takes my hand and guides it to the bare flesh of her belly. "Can you feel him? He is kicking me for all he's worth!"

And indeed he is. Her smooth skin is pulsating under my hand, rippling and jerking in a most peculiar manner. As my hand rests on that sacred flesh, I feel a tiny lump pressing from her body. Perhaps it is the baby's elbow or even a tiny fist.

"See, you can feel him, can't you! Isn't it wonderful," she breathes at me in an awe-inspired voice. I move to withdraw my hand, but she holds me there.

"Stay for a moment; I want to share this time with you."

We kiss gently, and I am totally in her power as we lie together, enthralled by the tiny movements of the vulnerable limbs.

"He usually wakes me up. I think he just likes to play with me before the others claim me. He's certainly going to be an early riser!"

Two more nights we've spent upon the road. I cannot comprehend how much I've grown to love her. What I thought I felt at first is nothing to the real obsession she has now engendered in me. Every moment of the day is filled with her. No longer do I feel anxious that I cannot cope. Nor do I worry what she is thinking of my actions. I just lay all I am before her. She has everything I've got; more I cannot give. This is how I feel, and yet there will be more, when she is ready. But the present is enough. I live within her rules and am blessed in every smile, in every sparkle from those gorgeous huge eyes of hers.

We are moving through the centre of Jerusalem. I thought she'd like to see the city again – last time was so brief. I am just pointing out the different aspects of the Temple, when suddenly her face tenses, and she seems oblivious to all that I am saying.

"What is the matter, Mari? What has happened?"

She stares at me a moment, as if in horror, then her face relaxes, her hands fly to her lap.

"My waters," she whispers loudly to me. "They've broken. The baby's coming!"

I look and see the trickle of fluid running down the donkey's back, glistening on the coarse hair. I am alarmed and begin to panic. Should we look for an inn here where she can have the child? She notices my reaction, and grins at me.

"Don't worry, we've still got time. We've got hours yet. But let's be on our way; I want to be in your house by nightfall."

I make her comfortable on the donkey and lead them both back out of the Gennath Gate, this time on the Bethlehem road, past Herod's palace. We have scarcely gone more than half a mile, when suddenly Mari cries out again – a shout of part surprise, part pain.

"What is it, Mari?"

"My contractions have started. Wait a moment until this spasm is over. Our son is in a hurry to greet the world."

Despite my anxiety I cannot help but notice what she said: 'our son'. I clasp her round the waist and support her as she tenses while the spasms last. Her fingers tighten round my wrist and I notice her knuckles white with stress; then she relaxes her grip, smiling weakly at my worried look.

"Keep going, Joseph. I'm all right now."

I quicken the donkey's pace, but watch the beast carefully to see that the different rhythm is not jolting her. We are dropping away from the city now, through the valley of Hinnom – all brown earth, crumbling and dun, with little vegetation. The city is still well in sight, when Mari tenses a second time and tightens the reins around her palms. I stop the beast, and hold her once again. I look at her questioningly.

"Yes, Joseph, already."

When she is sufficiently recovered I note the spot, and drive the donkey onwards. We must have covered nigh on another half-mile, when the same grimace of pain grips my beloved's features, and I stop to take her in my arms. I do a quick calculation. At the present rate of progress, with these interruptions, we could take another couple of hours to reach my home. Then I have to obtain help, fetch water, make her comfortable; and that assumes the contractions will not dramatically increase in frequency. I am getting bothered – I'm not sure we are going to make it. I don't tell Mari this, of course, but urge her onwards.

We make another league or two, then her pattern changes rapidly. Very suddenly she is panting strenuously every few yards, scarcely recovered from one bout of contractions before the next pains hit her. I cannot stop to hold and comfort her each time she shouts in anguish. She goes rigid on the donkey's back, while I urge the beast forward, fearful, lest in her trauma she lose her hold on the animal and slip to the stony ground. Our progress now is dreadfully slow. The jagged skyline of Bethlehem is in our view, but it seems to get no nearer, and the sun is sinking fast. What is more, my little home is on the far side of the town, at the very outskirts, another half an hour's journey, even if we have no hindrance.

She is all in. She is trying not to frighten me, or articulate her fears, but I can see it in her eyes. One matter reassures me: if her labour is progressing so quickly, there is less likelihood of danger at the birth, or of complications caused by her comparative immaturity. As she tries to cope with yet another spasm that wracks her body, I hold her tight, and promise, "We'll not try to reach my house, Mari; we'll stop at the first house on this road and seek lodging until the child is born."

She can hardly speak to me now, but signals assent and relief with her eyes. Somehow we stagger into a little courtyard and I rush, panicking, into the house, seeking the owner, making a pandemonium.

A bustling woman of ample proportions turns, startled at my noisy intrusion, and at first deals brusquely with my wild demands. Then, slowly, my real panic dawns on her, and she dashes out to find my frightened Mari, on whom she has immediate compassion.

"Goodness me, girl, how far has this man driven you this day? Come with me; I'll find somewhere for you. We're overflowing in the house – many strangers are in town for the coming census – but we'll make room for you at the back, where we keep the livestock."

She puts an arm around Mari's shoulders and helps her forward. At once she recognises the advanced stages of her labour.

"Quick, man, take your wife in there. I'll run and get some cloth and water, and I'll be back soon. You're going to need some help."

I feel useless now, but do as I'm told.

Chapter 38

Labour of Love

*I*T'S ALL HAPPENING TOO QUICKLY. All the plans and foresight seem so remote now, vain and totally irrelevant. I'm dizzy with pain, pulled this way and that, everything blurred, unfocused. Rules and practices, traditions and good advice – what use are they in such a muddle?

Ah! I snatch my breath as yet another searing pain shoots through my abdomen. I grab the crumbling earth of the cave wall excavated from the hillside, and hold my breath, tensing, trying not to push, which my body is screaming at me to allow. At the entrance to the darkness, I clutch at God's hand in my desperation, "Please Lord God, be with us!"

That is all there is time for. We stumble into the dank smelly blackness, lurching over obstructions, voices mingling in my ears, but I cannot discern what they are saying. I don't even recognise Joseph any more. Perhaps the woman's back again. I cease to care.

They are lowering me to the floor and somewhere overhead a lamplight flickers, throwing shadows darting around the jagged walls.

"Lie flat. Raise your knees. Let your hips rest on this bale of straw. Roll this way. A bit more. No, not so much. Careful. Watch that light. Put the water here." The phrases splash around my brain, cascading over each other like a mountain waterfall.

I am stripped to raw essentials now. Joseph, the woman helper, my baby pushing, some bits of straw: that is all life is for me, no more is necessary. Sorry, Lord God, I forgot you; don't forget me! Nothing is articulated, but the thoughts are there. All my mother told me, I can't think straight, I hope I've absorbed it somewhere. It's just my intuition and the vague disembodied commands floating over my head. A voice nearby – is it Joseph? – says, "It's all right, Mari, you can let go now. Don't hold back any more. Push when you want to!"

I hear a voice say, "Let me do it, man. Don't be so tentative and shy. Uncover her. Pull the shift right back. Let's see what we are doing."

Hands scrabble at my side, and I am hoisted again. I feel the prickle of the straw. That's funny: all this pain and all I can think of is this stupid itch, which I want to scratch and can't because I don't know where my arms are!

Then I am feeling very light-headed. Weird thoughts rush through my head. I'm trying to form a perfect circle in my brain but each time I'm nearly there, it squelches out of shape. Another lacerating pain rips through my nerves, brings sudden clarity round about, and I see shadowy faces all watching me as if they're teetering over a pit with me deep below. They are animals, I realise with a start: donkeys and mules, sheep and goats. I relax and even at this moment smile to myself. My friends. I grin again, before another shriek is torn from my lips and my mind races back to full consciousness once more.

"Keep going, Mari, keep on; you're doing fine."

Am I doing anything, I wonder? It all seems out of control: so messy, so chaotic. Is this always the way when miracles are born?

"The head is coming. Not long now, Mari. Push. Keep going. Soon, soon, soon."

Someone's got my wrist and is squeezing so hard that they are hurting.

My thoughts are jolted. Any moment now the baby will be revealed. All this long time I've made just one assumption. A boy, the stranger said – a king, God's son, the Messiah. What if I've got it all wrong? Supposing, just supposing, in a moment's time, we know it is a girl? Will all be in vain? Will I be a fraud? Can the Messiah be female, with girlish wisdom and intuition to trick the priests of their prophecies and visions? Rachel said her temple was to a goddess: she prayed to Mother Earth. "Teach them, kid," she said. "Show them what impostors they are!" I know in this moment, with all my powers of intuition, that it is a girl. What will Joseph say? Can we ever go back to Nazareth; or will we be forced to flee, stay here in poverty and loneliness and try to snatch at hints and far-fetched novelties, keep the flame alive, or abandon ambitions? I know it is a girl. She is slipping fast. I feel her drawing out. My time is done. Hands are pulling at my legs. My power is gone. They know now.

"Mari," whispers Joseph in my ear in rapt excitement, "you have a lovely healthy boy."

CHAPTER 39
FINALE OR A BEGINNING?

I LOOK INTO YOUR EYES. THE smile, the depth, the love is there. We communicate. I have chosen you.

I have chosen well.

From the mouths of babes and sucklings, they shall know the truth. Mari, you are a child and you have seen the truth and acted on it. You may be vulnerable, but you are inviolate as well.

In this moment you are perfect.

Can this perfection survive the growing process? Will you always communicate thus with me, or will you hide some secrets from my gaze?

What will you tell me when I'm old enough to ask? Will you share your doubts and fears, your pain, the lash of whip and dread of brutal death? Will you strengthen me with this, or leave me to discover everything anew, in isolation, for myself – not wanting to hurt me or trigger my doubts, when such intimate sharing would have the opposite effect?

Will you let me be controlled by God, or seek to mould me round your own ideas of him? You defied your mentor, Eli; will you give me the same freedom?

Give me true love, daughter of Zion, virgin, mother, prophetess, Queen of Heaven. Let me find my Father; don't hide him from me. Let me share your tragedy and guilt, weep over Rachel's children with you. Talk to me, Mother, sing to me. Touch me. Let me see the flicker of pain behind your smiling eyes.

For the moment I can only gurgle and seek your tender nipple with my relentless tiny mouth. Treasure this moment shared together, Mother, Child Madonna.

Soon, the world outside will demand its say.

Madonna and Child.

AD2000

DURING THE SHELLING OF SARAJEVO, a young woman and her husband got trapped in the crossfire as they were trying to leave the battered city. As others ran on ahead, the girl faltered because she was pregnant. The youth dragged his young wife to the partial shelter of a church doorway. There, in the noise of guns – prematurely because of the shock – she gave birth to her baby.

> The young Hutu couple fled from Kigale to the Burundi border, where they found a makeshift camp with thousands of starving children and their desperate parents. The journey had taken its toll on the pregnant wife in particular, and the young husband pleaded with the few overwhelmed aid workers for some food. In the end he got a precious bag and sprinted through the milling crowds back to the barren stretch of earth where his emaciated young wife was struggling to give birth to her first child.

The young couple wandered up the dingy corridor, peering into each cot. The tired nurse from the Romanian orphanage gestured helplessly at each tiny suffering body. How to choose? Then the couple saw him. The baby lay twisted and dirty on the soiled mattress. "He's handicapped," the nurse explained dismissively. "We want him," the couple said in unison.

> The girl had followed her older brothers out of the favela on the outskirts of Rio when her father had got drunk and had beaten their mother up. She was ten. She lived in a concrete watercourse near the vegetable market with a group of other street children. By the time she was fourteen she sold herself to buy enough food for several of the younger children. Then she became pregnant. She was found crying one night by a nun, who brought her into the hostel, where she gave birth to a baby girl.

The prostitute put her twelve-year-old daughter on the streets of the Philippine Olongopo City, near where the American service base had been, in order to survive. Her own looks were fading and the young servicemen had no longer wanted her. Then the military base closed and the Americans went home. The girl found that she was having a baby and had nothing. Another girl told her about a hostel in the city where kind people would look after her. She allowed herself to be taken there, frightened and ashamed. There she gave birth to her pale-skinned son.

> The refugees fled from the Iraqi army, high into the barren mountains between Turkey and the Iraqi border, and existed in a few tents erected in the windswept valley, four thousand feet above sea level. One bitter winter night a young wife gave birth. Her husband wrapped the newborn baby in the sweater that the relief agency had given him.

The doctor from the aid agency picked his way through the dirt and stench of the muddy alleyway between the tarpaulins and corrugated iron shacks of Daravi, the largest slum in Asia. Half-naked toddlers were leaping from the crumbling concrete bases of the ugly pylons that carried electricity to the gaunt factories of Bombay, but not to the shanty town. Eight-year-olds pestered him for rupees. He took one look at the groaning woman in the dim light, checked the lack of running water and knew he must get her to hospital. But it was too late: the baby was coming. Somehow mother and child would survive.

> The teenage girl ran away from the children's home. An older girl had been bullying her, and she was afraid to tell anyone. She went to London. New so-called 'friends' introduced her to drugs and a cardboard home under Charing Cross bridge. Someone seemed to take pity on her, found her a room, then took advantage. She became pregnant and was thrown out. A Salvation Army captain assisted at the birth and handed the tiny bundle to the exhausted girl. At last she smiled.

BC7

𝕿HE SMELLY CAVE WAS IN the rocky hillside, two thousand feet up, lashed by a cold and bitter wind. The young girl had had a rough time in her village – few would have believed her story – she must have had guts to go through with it. She was very tired: three or four days on a lumbering donkey, the last few miles travelled with increasing panic as the birth pangs gripped her. The couple could find no lodgings. There she gave birth to her son and then, because of a threatened genocide, became, with her husband and young baby, a refugee in Egypt.

Appendix 1: Family Tree of the Characters in this Novel

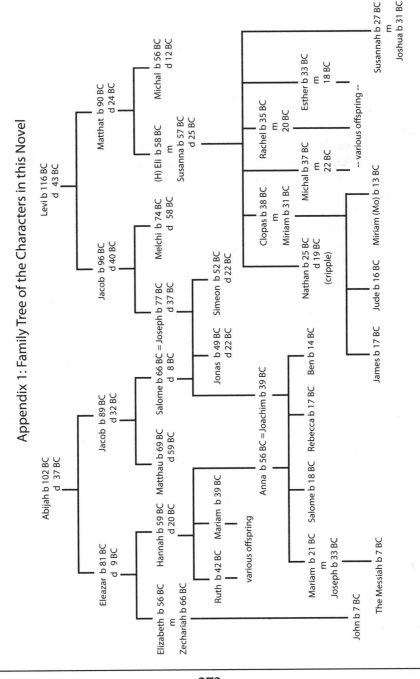

Appendix II
Historical Background Dates

63 BC	Roman conquest of Judea
54 BC	Caesar/Pompey Quarrel
49 BC	Roman Civil War
48 BC	Defeat of Pompey
44 BC	Murder of Julius Caesar
43 BC	King Herod appointed by Romans to the throne of the satellite, Judea and Israel
37 BC	Massacre of the Sanhedrin
31 BC	Alexandra and Mariamne executed
19 BC	Rebuilding of the Temple begins
14 BC	Political unrest flares
7 BC	Roman census ordered in Judea and Israel
4 BC	Death of Herod the Great

Postscript

S TATUES OF THE VIRGIN MARY depict a European woman in her late twenties or thirties, aloof, so pure that some claim she always remained a virgin; some that not only she, but also her mother, were untouched by human procreation. Painted masterpieces down through the ages depict the Madonna as a mature mother, haloed, looking at us in serene satisfaction. To me this is a puzzle. How could such a person have produced one of the greatest revolutionaries of civilisation: someone who rethought and challenged the traditions and perceptions of his culture, and founded another?

Why should God have chosen such a woman? Her son was accused of befriending drunks, outcasts and fallen women. He was executed by the Romans as a rebel and criminal in the most humiliating circumstances. Why could not God have used a soiled vessel as mother, whose soul was honest, unprejudiced, open to his will? Surely the founder of Christianity would have inherited some of the genes and character of his biological mother, so where is that gutsy free-thinking life-enhancing energy to be sourced? Is it all one-sided from divine intervention? Surely some must be in the mother's character as well.

Mary would have been young. Jewish girls in the first century came of age and were marriageable at puberty, set at twelve- and- a half years. The raw conservative culture of an obscure Galilean village – as opposed to the sophistication of the capital city, or even of Romanised cities in northern Israel: Sepphoris, Tiberius and Caesarea – would have ostracised and made an example of a girl suspected of breaking the taboos of her society by becoming pregnant outside of wedlock. She would have had a rough time.

Violence was not just prevalent in ancient Jewish society (as it was in most other societies and still is in some) but was a matter of course in the discipline of children. There are many biblical and talmudic references of the need to discipline a child through corporal punishment, lest the child not learn from his or her mistakes and wrongdoing; and this led later to capital penalties such as stoning, burning, decapitation or strangling, which were all permitted in ancient Jewish law for such crimes as idolatry, adultery, incest and murder. There are clear references to the situations in which fathers may beat their sons (and by implication, daughters) severely to avoid the disgrace of the child incurring the death penalty later, or even rules about when a father shall not be punished if he actually kills his son in the course of discipline. Mary was a child of this society and culture.

This book then, is my vision of the Madonna. It is my painting, my Madonna and Child. It is as valid as all those statues, old masters. You may not like it, but I am entitled to offer my interpretation too. It may not be true: this is after all presented as a novel, as fiction, but perhaps it holds within it a grain of truth. As her son famously said at his trial by the Roman Governor, "What is truth?"

Today, in the twenty-first century, there are still girls and young women suffering as I depict Mary did. It is still lawful in a few countries, mainly in the Middle East, to condemn children to death; and even the United States only banned the use of the death penalty for under-eighteen-year-olds a couple of years ago by a 5 – 4 margin at the Supreme Court, after years of campaigning by many both in and outside the USA. Still, girls are murdered by their brothers, uncles, fathers even, because of some chauvinist tribal tradition that holds a girl in shame and disgrace because she has been raped or tried to escape from some forced or abusive marriage. There are still girls like Rachel in this story, trafficked and sold into the sex trade and then treated as criminals instead of victims. There are still girls and young women condemned to be executed because of the sin of sex outside marriage. If you do not believe me, look at the files held by various human rights organisations.

For example, on 15th August 2004, Atefeh Rajabi was publicly hanged in Neka, in the northern province of Mazandaran, Iran, for 'acts incompatible with chastity' following allegations of a sexual relationship outside marriage. Her identity card gave her age as 16, but the Mazandaran judiciary claimed she was 22. According to press reports, she was mentally ill at the time of the offence and the trial, and she had no access to legal representation. The Observer newspaper on 16th October 2005 interviewed Maryam Namazie, an Iranian woman campaigning for the rights of Iranian women, including the case above. The article quoted her as saying about the obsessiveness of the theocracy there:

> "The law in Iran not only allows women to be stoned, but it specifies the size of the stones to be used; they mustn't be too small in case it takes too long to kill her and the mob gets bored; but mustn't be too big either, in case she is despatched immediately and the mob is denied the sado-sexual pleasure of seeing her suffer..."[1]

Such abuse is not only prevalent in the Middle East and in countries of the area with common traditions and religion. Abuse of women and girls takes place widely in Central and South America, with the authorities frequently being unwilling to arrest or prosecute the perpetrators of violence against women, or often even to admit that violence is a crime, especially if the abuse is by a member of the victim's family or the police or military. Widespread abuse of women and girls has taken place in parts of Africa, especially in times of civil unrest and conflict. And the so-called developed

---

1   One woman's war: Maryam Namazie personifies the gulf between liberal apologists and those who really want equality,
Nick Cohen, 16 October 2005. Copyright Guardian News & Media Ltd 2005.

countries in the West are all too often scarred by extreme domestic violence and neglect suffered by some of their children.

Some of you may find the level of violence perpetrated against Mary in this story intolerable or unacceptable; but I assure you it is no less than much abuse, for similar reasons, still abounding in the world today. If you feel angry at the treatment of the heroine of this fictional story, then try to change today's wrongs, remembering the words of Mary's son, Jesus, quoted in Matthew 25: verse 40, following his description of the last judgement when addressing those who had fed the hungry, housed the homeless, clothed the naked, or visited the sick and those in prison:

"I tell you, whenever you did this for one of the least important of these members of my family, you did it for me!"

For me, that challenge was in the eyes of the small streetgirl on Bombay Churchgate Station, to whom this book is dedicated. I do not know what became of her. Perhaps she too had the potential to fulfil God's will – but the evils of this world stifled that opportunity before it could ever flourish.

David Maidment
May 2008

BIBLIOGRAPHY

Linda Machin: *The Ancient Jews*

E Mary Smallwood: *The Jews under Roman Rule BC 160—AD 300*

H L Ellison: *From Babylon to Bethlehem BC 538—BC 4*

Abraham Bloch: *Biblical & Historical Background of Jewish Customs and Ceremonies*

John Marshall: *A Review of Corporal Punishment in Ancient Times*

Alfred Rubens: *A History of Jewish Costume*

Ora Hamelsdorf: *Jewish Women & Jewish Law*

Salo Baron: *A Social & Religious History of the Jews, Vol 1 — Ancient Times to the Beginning of the Christian Era*

Ronald Clements: *The World of Ancient Israel, Sociological, Anthropological and Political Perspectives*

Malka Drucker: *Celebrating Life, Jewish Rites of Passage*

Hans Jochem Boecker: *Law and the Administration of Justice in the Old Testament and Ancient East*

Livia Bitton-Jackson: *Madonna or Courtesan? The Jewish Woman in Christian Literature*

Nick Cohen: *One Woman's War: Maryam Namazie Personifies the Gulf Between Liberal Apologists and Those Who Really Want Equality*

BIBLIOGRAPHY

MELROSE BOOKS

If you enjoyed this book you may also like:

Fairland
Peter Prince

Elizabeth, a poor and frail little woman living on the streets of London, is given another chance at life.

Duchess Evelyn Ward invites Elizabeth to a beautiful house in Surrey - Fairland. She meets many other inhabitants, all with different backgrounds and stories of deprivation, but all with the same path. One by one the residents share their stories with Elizabeth, stories of hardship, pain and loss. She learns of the history of the house, and in her innocence asks many questions that teach her more and more about the Christian way of life. She learns the love of God and accepts Jesus Christ as her saviour. Eventually, Elizabeth is able to tell her own story and reveal a terrible secret from her childhood, but ultimately feels she has been able to experience healing and inner peace, away from the pain and the agony that has tormented her. *"I know that Jesus forgives me. He washed me clean. He forgave me all the evil things I did and he took them on the cross for me and now I'm free."*

Size: Royal Octavo 234 mm x 156 mm	Pages: 256
Binding: Hardback	ISBN: 978-1-905226-23-8

£13.99

Holy Orders and Completeness of the Church
H. J. M. Turner

In *Holy Orders and Completeness of the Church* the author seeks to describe the pattern of Holy Orders. He also uses sound ecclesiology to ask how bishops, priests and deacons ought to be related to one another and to the order of 'unordained' Christians.

Sources from diverse backgrounds are used throughout, often accompanied by translations from their original languages. In Holy Orders and Completeness of the Church the author does not examine in detail texts from the New Testament. Instead he concentrates on texts written roughly between the end of the first century and the end of the fourth - the formative period of development for early Christianity.

In this excellently researched work, the author's expert opinion is presented in a well-constructed and extremely clear manner, making the text accessible to both academics of theology and those with less knowledge in the subject.

Size: Royal Octavo 234 mm x 156 mm	Pages: 160
Binding: Hardback	ISBN: 978-1-905226-00-9

£14.99

Christology with Lonergan and Balthasar
Kevin Tortorelli O.F.M.

Christology with Lonergan and Balthasar by Fr Kevin Tortorelli is a fascinating exploration of Christology with special reference to the work of Bernard Lonergan and Hans Urs Von Balthasar. However, the book is not simply a study of the Christology of either Lonergan or of Balthasar. Rather, the author presents a series of lucid, concise essays covering and examining a range of relevant subjects in the spirit of these two theologians, all building ideas with the aim of answering, or at least forming a basis for the answer to the question that Jesus asked "Who do you say I am?"

The author explains research and analysis techniques with particular emphasis on the difficulties between historical-critical methodology and faith. He then discusses Jesus and Judaism, the humanity of Christ against the teachings of the rabbinic majority and the Hakamim boundary, and the conversion of Paul and the Church and Israel.

Size: Royal Octavo 234 mm x 156 mm	Pages: 128
Binding: Hardback	ISBN: 978-1-905226-13-9

£11.99

St Thomas' Place, Ely, Cambridgeshire CB7 4GG, UK

www.melrosebooks.com   sales@melrosebooks.com